Armageddon's Song

Volume 3

'Fight Through'

Map Illustrated

Andy Farman

CREDITS

Cover design – Andy Farman
Map Illustrations – Andy Farman

Contains depictions of violence and some sexual content.
Not Suitable For Children or Young Adults

Mr Andy Farman
PO BOX 891
Cebu Central Post Office
Cebu City
Philippines
6000

ISBN 978-1-326-18420-9

DEDICATION

There are two very special people who turned
my life around and are keeping it on the right track;
therefore it is only fitting that the third volume, which was
begun after our son was born, is dedicated to my
wife Jessica and Edward Eric.

CONTENTS

MAPS

ACKNOWLEDGMENTS

I have had a lot of help and encouragement in writing this series, in particular with this, the third part of the series. Retired bomber pilots, snipers, SFX experts, current helicopter pilots, a glamour model, serving and retired coppers, ex-servicemen and a former company commander turned banker.

Oddly, suggestions for a fifth and sixth book have been trickling in, and you do not even know how the story ends. I may be reluctant to write out the appearance of last minute characters such as moody teenage daylight walking vampires, and good looking vegetarian High School zombies. You know how trendy I am!

My thanks go to my Father Ted Farman and Andy Croy for editing. Andy and I both served in the Wessex Regiment in the 1980's, but we never met. To my niece Helena Brackley for research on Guiana and the European Space Agency. To Bill Rowlinson, Nick Gill, Tracey Elvik, Tobi Shear-Smith, Maxine Shear-Smith, Ray Tester, Steve Enever, Stuart Galloway and Chris Cullen for test reading; proof reading, advice on how to shoot, stab, blow stuff up and still show a well turned ankle. To my cousin David Farman, currently the only practicing Biggles with a current instrument rating in the family. I hope he settles into his new role of 'Gentleman Pilot' with ease, and a little élan. Thank you for the technical advice of the CH47 Chinook. Finally, but by no means least, to Haydee Velasco Flores for generously offering to lower her professional fee in order to translate the books into Spanish. It is on my wish list Haydee.

Foreword

Well I am in a decidedly different place now to the one I was in back in 2002 when I first put pen to paper to scribble down the opening lines of 'Stand To' on the back of a blank antecedents form.

I was sat in the Police Room in the basement of the ILCC, Inner London Crown Court. It was bitterly cold outside, the cold and damp were having an adverse effect on my knees which had taken a beating when I was an infantryman, running up Welsh mountains carrying my own weight on my back. They ached eight months out of twelve, they were certainly aching that day and I had a cold. Hell, everybody had a cold, it was January in England.

Eleven years on and I'm not a copper any more, I did my thirty but I'm still working on the same book, just a different volume and four hundred and fifty thousand words further along with it.

It is 92° outside and my knees are fine these days as it is always summer here.

The first two books were something of a learning curve and I learned a few things about who likes what, and who does not.

Teachers concentrate on paragraph structure and syntax whereas their former pupils are happy just to read an entertaining story.

You may recall the foreword in volumes one and two about my reasons for writing this yarn? Well I did not know how the story would be greeted across the water in America. It is a global story and the USA shares the stage rather than being a one man band as she is in so many military fiction tales.

Helpful suggestions have been sent my way that I carry out a re-write for the American market with the Coldstream Guards becoming a US infantry regiment and HMS Hood as the US ___ have also included a wish that I would cease misspelling so many words.

Well if I did re-write the book somewhere down the line then I certainly would not keep the title in fact it would be an entirely different book.

I have made some good friends in America over the years and they come from various and diverse backgrounds, just like everyone else. They tend to come from law enforcement, the military and the film industry. They are capable, professional and heroic as are their opposite numbers in other countries and they have the same motivations and drives as their opposite numbers. This series however, Armageddon's Song, is not about America saving the world it is a team effort that also shows the other guys viewpoints on occasion, and it is not full of misspellings either, it is written in English, not American, and it is staying that way.

When I started writing this tale I had an idea of what should happen, where it should happen and how it should end. I did not aim to write a standard 80,000 word novel I aimed to write a detailed story which people would enjoy. I just hoped it would reach 80,000 words.

My style of writing is to imagine a course of events and rough it out. For example, the cruise missile attack on London started off as less than one page, 321 words, simply that of Janet in her office receiving a summons to meet the of battalion wives who are on the death message rota, accompanying the Padre to break the bad news to wives who have become widows overnight. I added detail and conversation. What came next was the 'how' of the missiles arriving, which included the Spetznaz member carrying out 'CTR', a close target reconnaissance of Canary Wharf. Janet's commute to work came next along with the collision with the spy, and finally the missiles effects on Canvey Island, the result of their arrival at Canary Wharf and what effect this had on Janet. That was 14,011 words.

It is the detail which takes time to add and the description which fills the pages.

Volume 1 was not 80,000 words, it was 150,000 words.

By the time I was a further 50,000 words along into volume 2 I was fairly certain I could bring in the story in three volumes but after six months writing it was clear the European war was only going to be done and dusted inside of at least four books, and there was still China to address in full.

The physical realities of how many pages and maps can actually be fitted in a 4'x6" paperback book became apparent. The answer is, less than volume 1. I had to set my paper size up to 6" x 9", although the Easy Reader editions required 7" x 10" for the larger print.

At least four volumes, and not three will be required to finish this tale of war, without scrimping on the detail. It is no longer a trilogy.

I will begin the final volume, 'Crossing the Rubicon' the day after I publish this volume, but the family, including the lively two year son, need a holiday as much as I do. All work and no play makes for dull prose.

For those posting grumbles about not realising volume 1 was not the whole story, I apologise, but you should go back and read the Product Description again, the bit that says 'Stand-*To' is the first book* ….. The 'Volume 1' in gold lettering on the front cover is also a bit of a giveaway.

Volume 3 is a deal busier than the other volumes, indeed for some 200+ pages it felt a little as if I was writing '24' as there is so much that is going on simultaneously in different international time zones on different parts of the planet as various threads throughout the previous two volumes come together.

Writing the operation orders for policing Europe's largest Latin American Carnival was easy in comparison, and markedly less than the 490,000 words, 1360 pages this tale has so far taken to tell.

I hope I cannot be accused of short-changing anyone.

Andy Farman.

South America

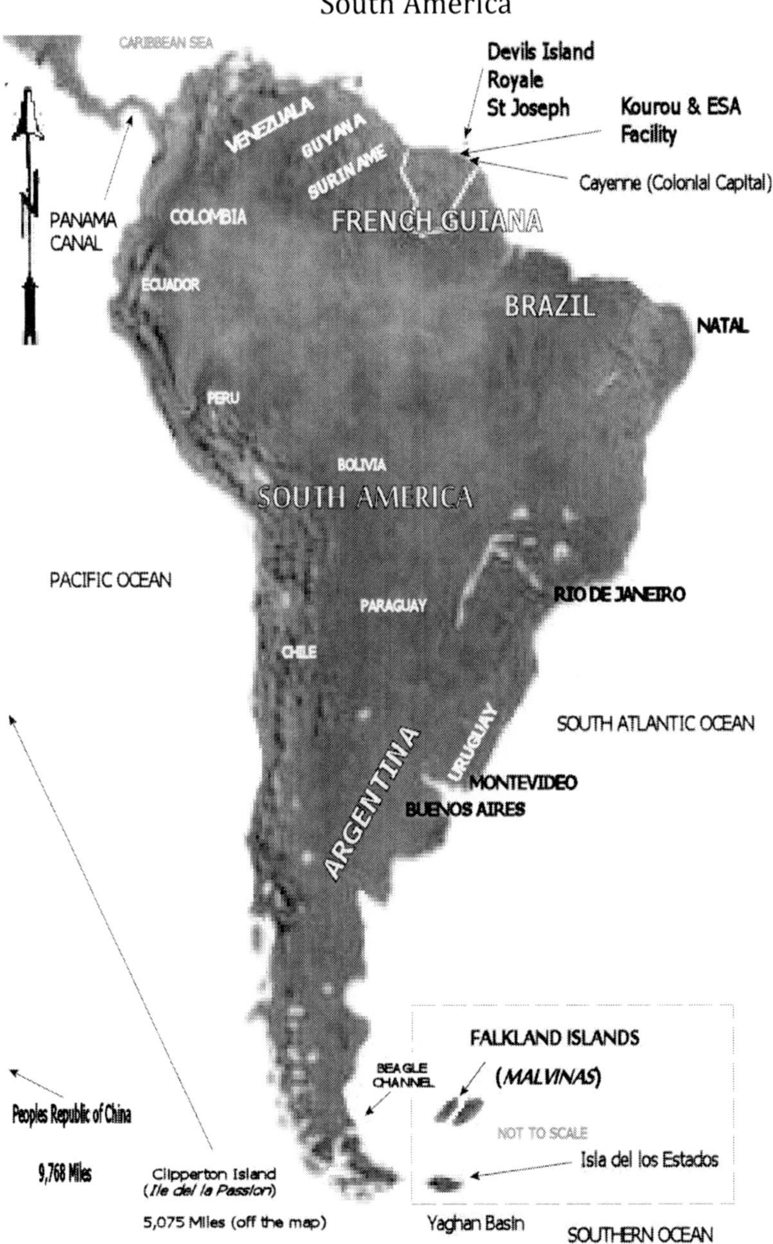

Prologue

Kourou River

"Aircraft action, *forward*!" a lookout screamed.

The second aircraft also came in from the direction of the ocean, but a scant hundred feet above the trees, its wings tilting as it followed the lie of the river, the bomb bay doors gaping open. The sound of the Rolls Royce engines passing above them and the roar of *Bao*'s and *Dai's* 23mm automatic cannon made Li flinch but his eyes did not leave the two falling objects, blunt nosed depth charges, not tumbling but semi stabilised, oscillating at the finned tails as they fell at an angle towards their target.

Tracer chased the Atlantique, spent 23mm shell cases rattled and rang against the metal deck.

Arkansas Valley, Nebraska, USA: 2057hrs, same day.

"What, may I ask, does General Allain intend to do about that?" The President followed on before Henry could answer.

"There is just a cobbled together, infantry heavy division sat in the way of god knows how many tanks so does he honestly believe that will hold them until our new Corps arrives on the scene?" with that he sat upright and raised a coffee mug to his lips while he waited for the answer.

Henry responded with four words.

With a snort that sent coffee splashing across the papers in front of him, the President choked in mid swallow.

"What?"

"He's going to attack." Henry repeated.

'FIGHT THROUGH'

CHAPTER 1

Argentina: Atlantic coast.

Rio Gallegos was the home port for the 350 ton ocean going trawler *'Maria III'* which had been enjoying a lean time of things in the Atlantic since the big battles between the Soviet submarines and the Americans, the Canadians and the British.

They had found fish, thousands of them, but all were dead and stinking on the surface. Silt stirred up by nuclear depth charges had not only ruined fishing around the Azores, *'Maria IIIs'* normal fishing grounds at this time of year, but had spread south to Cape Verde, spoiling the waters there also.

With the East and West at war and the normal military presence in those sea lanes absent, piracy off the African coast was on the rise and her skipper, Carlo Duellos, had wisely steered clear of that side of the Atlantic.

No one would be feeding his and the crews' families if they were being held for ransom in the African bush somewhere.

The British on the Malvinas had itchy trigger fingers as they half expected his country to take advantage of the war, by trying to retake the islands again. So an exclusion zone once more sat in place barring all but the foolish from those waters. No one was going to be feeding their families if the bastard British accused them of spying and locked them up.

Most of the local boats had gone west through the Straits of Magellan to fish off the Pacific coast, but Carlos figured that a lot of boats from Panama on down would be doing the same.

They had returned from the Azores with an empty hold and empty tanks, and Carlos was forced to go cap in hand to the local bank.

The bank manager was a reasonable man and he was a local too, but Carlos was not the only one having an unexpectedly bad season, the whole planet was, and that was likely to last at least as long as the war, he had pointed out.

Carlos went from the bank with only the manager's best wishes and had arrived at the bar the fishermen used as a kind of base when in port. Getting the crew together he had laid it out for them, they had no line of credit and no gas so he, Carlos, was willing to sell his truck if the rest of them were also going to contribute something towards the expenses.

Their engineer quit, either unable or unwilling to take a gamble on them finding any live fish, and a gamble it was. Worldwide food prices had hit the roof, so a full hold would set them all up for the rest of the year, but another disastrous voyage such as their last one would be ruinous.

The remainder had borrowed from relatives or sold heirlooms for them to fuel the '*Maria III*'.

They had just enough diesel and supplies for about a week's normal fishing, and so it was that they had set out once more, but with Carlos doing what he could to get the crew's next most mechanically minded member familiar with the trawler's elderly seven cylinder diesels.

They went from previously productive fishing grounds nearer home to those more and more distant, seeking the fish that had left without trace.

It took time and patience, going further and further south east with the crew sat about idle, becoming more and more despondent

On the fourth day, with the light fading and dark clouds threatening their sonar fish detector finally picked up a large shoal of whiting and the crew put '*Maria III*'s gear in the water for the first time that voyage.

The change in mood was palpable throughout the small vessel, from borderline desperation to one of desperate hope. It was food on the table for their families, but they had to fill the hold first and they were short-handed, so with rain setting in for the night they set to with a will.

The net came up full and the winch strained as it lifted the catch inboard to whistles and shouts of joy and relief. The gamble was paying off.

Again the nets went back over the side as Carlos stayed with the twisting and turning shoal.

By 3am the seas were picking up and the rain was gusting in horizontally but the hold was still only three quarters full.

Another full net with its flashing silver bounty was tantalisingly just below the surface when the winch jammed, and despite promises and threats it remained uncooperative.

Carlos called down to the make-do engineer to come up and take the wheel so he himself could try and fix the winch.

When the proper engineer had quit he had taken his tools with him, and he had also taken his ear defenders too, so Carlos was relieved on the wheel by a partly deafened novice ship's engineer.

Carlos removed the housing from about the winch mechanism and cursed the rain and the rusty and frayed cable which had bunched and snagged. At least, he told himself, at least they could invest in a new one once they got back to port and sold this catch.

The radar proximity warnings strident tone registered only as a faint beeping to the only occupant of the wheelhouse and the large return which drew closer with every sweep of the radar repeater meant nothing to him, but similar warnings should have raised the alarm with the watch keepers aboard the bulk carrier *'Istial Starwalk'* which was running without lights for fear of the submarine threat to shipping.

'Maria III' was reported overdue by Carlos's wife when the fuel they had taken on board was obviously exhausted and neither she nor any of the other wives had received word from their husbands as they would have done had the their boat called into another port for some reason such as a medical emergency or a mechanical failure of some description.

The Argentine Naval Prefecture, as the Argentinian coast guard is known, called the harbour masters on the Atlantic coast as far away as *'Maria III's* partially full tanks could have taken her and even lodged a request for information or sightings with the Anglos on the Malvinas, but the boat had not put into any port since leaving Rio Gallegos the week before.

Had the *'Istial Starwalk'* immediately reported a collision which had been felt throughout the vessel, and which was subsequently found to have left her bow damaged and scraped then the search and rescue operation could have begun immediately, and with a precise location. However, her master did not heave-to and did not report any collision until the ship docked at Auckland a month later and even then the insurance claim merely stated 'Colliding with unknown object' at a position some twelve hundred miles further north than it actually had, closer to the recent fighting and therefore easier to justify his reluctance to stop and investigate.

Gansu Province, Peoples Republic of China.

Nothing could muffle the sound a piton being hammered into rock, and on the few occasions that it had been absolutely unavoidable Richard Dewar gritted his teeth in the expectation of their discovery.

With the latest piton securely in place Richard attached through its eye, one end of a quickdraw, two carabiners with spring loaded gates and attached together by a webbing strap, before clipping his line into the free end.

The ropes they were using were a far cry from the stiff half inch hemp ropes Richard had first used as a Boy Scout, cliff climbing at Black Rock Sands in Wales, these were 10.5 cm ropes made from semi translucent man-made fibres which though not invisible by any means, did allow them to blend more easily with the background.

Gripping the rope he leant outwards, allowing the piton to take the strain as he peered upwards at the eighteen foot overhang he had reached. About an arms width away a crack in the rock bisected the overhang, and he knew from a recce through binoculars whilst choosing this route that this led upwards, widening all the time to become a chimney. Richard felt around his harness for another quickdraw, but one with a locking gate to attach to his harness. The movements of a climber can inadvertently cause something to press against the outside of a carabiners gate, a jutting rock or another item of equipment can open a spring loaded carabiner causing the rope or harness it was holding to be released, so he always used locking carabiners next to his body.

Clipping the new quickdraw to the one attached to the piton, he spread his feet and braced them against the rock before leaning outwards, reaching up and back for the crack to explore it with his fingers. Ideally he hoped to find a suitable seat for monolithic protection, a solid tapered wedge or a hex to jam inside where a runner could support his weight, but its sides were too smooth and parallel. He wasn't as fond of SLCDs, the mechanical, spring-loaded camming devices, or a 'camm' for short, which were the alternative to monoliths as they had a tendency to 'walk' when not under tension and work themselves free. He had no choice in this instance and at least the camm would be hanging vertically, a position from which it was least likely for it to work its way loose. Richard made his selection from the collection of various sizes clipped to his harness, and holding the device by its stem he pushed it up inside the crack as far as he could before releasing the four camm's at the top end of the single SLCDs stem which sprung outwards, the teeth biting at the rock. Major Dewar clipped another quickdraw to the eye at the stem and tested it by applying increasing weight. It held, allowing him to attach yet another locking quickdraw to his harness and clip it to the free end of the one he held. Richard was now supported in place at two points and still had both hands free, his feet were only keeping him steady whilst he worked so should the piton and camm come loose then only the man belayed-on at the last pitch, seventy feet below could arrest his fall.

The wind was only blowing at about 10 mph, a pleasant change from the 80 mph winds of the previous two days, but its wind chill factor lowered the sub-zero temperatures even further. The snow had not abated until about an hour ago, reducing visibility but covering their tracks whilst it had fallen.

Working in the shadow of the overhang he had removed his tinted goggles in order to better see what he was doing, but the cold and wind made his eyes water, causing his lashes to freeze into brittle whiteness. The only weapon he carried was an M4, the shortened version of the M16, hanging vertically down his back by the butt strapped between his shoulder blades, the weapons harness crossed over his shoulders and added to the weight he already carried and restricted his movements, but it was a necessity of the job.

Pulling on the piton's quickdraw with one hand he drew himself closer to the overhang, giving himself enough slack at that end to unclip himself from it with his free hand. It was that moment of truth which always made life interesting whilst climbing, discovering if the single SLCD was up to the task of supporting him above the abyss. Letting go of the piton's quickdraw he swung away from the vertical face to hang suspended below the overhang, 400 feet above the valley floor.

Lt Garfield Brooks and six of the soldiers were still far below on the valley floor, forming a perimeter and guarding the kit that would be hauled up, pitch by pitch. They were the only ones still wearing white camouflage clothing; the remainder had stuffed them inside camouflage jackets that more easily blended with the buff tones of the rock face until the snow line five hundred feet above.

Garfield lay on his back peering up at Richard Dewar through his binoculars, admiring the almost effortless ease with which the Royal Marine repeated the high trapeze act a further six times to reach the lip of the overhang. No records existed of any climbs here and in all probability no one had ever scaled the rock face before them. It seemed to Garfield however, that Dewar had climbed it a dozen times, so confident and assured were his moves. The climber's term for such a skilful climb up a virgin face is 'A Vue', a clean ascent first try, with no prior knowledge of the route.

The American lieutenant from Florida had never climbed anything more challenging than the trees in the family's backyard, before joining the service. Like every one of the Americans he had since gone through the courses run by the

US Army Northern Warfare Training Centre at Fort Wainwright, Alaska. He'd frozen his butt off on the Black Rapids training area completing his CWLC, the Cold Weather Leaders Course, but it was nowhere close to the – 40° he was currently working in. He had performed assault climbs in Alaska on the Gulkana Glacier, in Vermont and the Rockies, but Dewar on the other hand had hiked to both the north and south poles, climbed Everest three times, once without oxygen, and had two tries at K2, amongst other less well known expeditions to his credit. Any doubts Garfield felt about a Brit leading this operation had been dispelled within hours of their landing in China, the Royal Marine Commando wasn't just competent, he was quite expert at working in sub-zero climes and on rock faces.

Garfield remembered the first time he had come up against an overhang of similar proportions; he had shaken his head in a very negative manner as his brain took in the near impossibility of negotiating it. His instructor, a Ranger of many years' experience had climbed up beside him.

"Mr Brooks, sir...you ever hear of a guy called Winston Spencer Churchill?" and Garfield had frowned at the strange question.

"Do you mean the old wartime British PM?"

"Yessir that's him, he was a good soldier before he was a politician, and he had a saying that the three hardest things to do in life are to climb a wall leaning towards you, kiss a girl leaning away from you, and to make an after dinner speech...now I know you got a girlfriend and as an officer you know how to make speeches, which just leaves the leaning wall thing for you to do...now git your butt in gear and get it done before I kick your pansy ass off my mountain, sir!"

The advice had been absolutely useless in helping him conquer the problem, but it served to remind him that defeatism was not acceptable in the eyes of the army.

He now shifted his gaze upwards, looking at the eighty or so feet of chimney that ended abruptly where snow and ice capped it sixty feet from the top. They had been socked in for two days by the storm that had blown straight across the valley, coating the rock face, which they had descended that morning with snow that had been wind blasted into ice. Rappelling, or abseiling as the Brits called it, down from the top of the ridge in four pitches had seen them all safely down on the canyon floor, before crossing the exposed area in groups, one group moving whilst the remainder covered them

The route the major had chosen, initially went straight up for about a hundred feet of un-technical climbing, that is to say without the need for pitons and artificial aids. From there came a traverse, up and to the left for another hundred and fifty, rounding a corner two thirds of the way along. From the traverse it once more went vertical until reaching a narrow ledge, which varied in depth from a foot and a half to mere inches. Above the ledge, the rock was as smooth and seamless as if a team of giant plasterers had prepared it for painting, and below it to the top of the traverse was as equally unhelpful. The major had used pitons to secure runners to the face from the traverse to the ledge, and then along the ledge to below the overhang. Theoretically they could simply have gone straight up, in a technical climb all the way to the top, but they did not have the time to spare to hammer in pitons every few feet, even if they had that many with them, which they did not. They had lost time due to the storm and could not afford to hang about any longer.

Garfield lifted his over-white top and undid his 'yukes' jacket or extreme cold weather clothing system, in storeman speak, and replaced the binoculars before rolling back onto his front. In the entire time they had been on the ground in China they had seen no trace of another human being, it was as if they were on another planet. He checked that his small mix of troops from two countries and three different units, were still alert and on the ball, covering their assigned arcs. It was odd, he thought, that whereas his guys mixed well with the Brits of both units, there was coolness between the M&AW Cadre, Royal Marines and the SAS Mountain Troop guys. 'The Cadre' didn't consider themselves to be 'special forces' but they definitely looked down on the mountain troop soldiers.

To Garfield's mind this frosty attitude was entirely due to the media's love affair with the SAS. The Cadre were all instructors, in their peacetime role they taught the members of 3 Commando Brigade how to fight and survive in arctic conditions, how to climb, and how to operate far above the snow line where the air is thin. The Cadre did not wear any insignia or embellishments on their working or ceremonial dress, and even the Royal Marines own Special Forces, the little known Special Boat Service who received much of their training from the Cadre only wore a quaint little 'Swimmer Canoeist' badge, the letters SC and laurel leaves in gold on the right arm of their dress uniforms to set them apart. The American had seen nothing to make him doubt the Mountain Troop soldiers abilities, they were all very professional and good climbers, but the Cadre were very, *very* good. The levels of fitness were impressive in terms of stamina. He could beat the M&AWC's 'granddad', the forty-something Glaswegian, Sergeant McCormack, by several minutes on a five mile dash but he struggled to stay up with the man when they each carried their own weight in kit on route marches.

The parting of the ways would occur once the force reached an east/west running ridge above them, at that point Mountain Troop would go east seven miles to place remote laser designators, targeted on the vehicle assembly buildings, launch towers and satellite communications dishes of the space centre.

The Cadre and Garfield's men would turn west for the ICBM field where their designators would be sighted on the hardened silos. If all went to plan the troops would RV back at this spot before beginning the long hike to a disused mining strip, for a night extraction by the C-130 Hercules of 47 Squadron, Royal Air Force.

The extraction was totally dependent on the success of the F117As and B1-B Lancers accompanying the B2 bombers. Their job was to clear away enemy air defence radar from the target, and all the way back to the borders of India and Nepal.

Richard placed another camm into the crack running through the overhang, reaching across and upwards to position it six inches from the overhangs lip and attached his harness to it with a pair of linked quickdraw's. When he released the quickdraw to the previous camm though, there was a screech like fingernails being drawn down a slate blackboard, as the camm near the lip shifted several inches downwards and outwards. Corporal Alladay was belayed on to a large boulder at the last pitch and immediately took up the slack, feeding rope back around his body and bracing, locking his arms in toward his torso.

The tight rope stopped the pendulum movement of the major's body, and Richard held his breath, staring at the camm which had half emerged from the crack but had now taken a firm hold against a protruding nub. As satisfied as he could be that the camm was now secure he singled up on the quickdraw's securing him to the camm before reaching up beyond the lip of the overhang, his fingers feeling for a hold. Below him Corporal Alladay let out some rope, again allowing the major some freedom of movement.

Richard first found a finger hold, and then discarded it for a fracture coming off the crack, which afforded a better grip. To the left of the crack an angle of rock would afford him some purchase for his left foot. With his right hand in the fracture Richard wedged the fingers of his left into the crack and heaved, bringing up his left foot and planting the sole of the boot firmly before transferring his right hand to the crack. Bracing himself there he let go with his left hand and unscrewed himself from the remaining quickdraw, allowing it to fall way to hang from the stem. He was now out of sight of Alladay and tugged on the rope, signalling for more slack before working his body higher, hand over hand up the crack until he was able to jam the toe of his right boot into the fracture hold. With feet splayed and the fingers of one hand wedged into the crack and the other gripping the underside of an inverse lip.

Richard craned his neck to look for the next hold. Having got himself to this spot Richard now found that the next possible hand hold was a good seven or eight inches beyond his grasp, but after that the face promised easier going. It's not a problem, he thought, I'll use a camm in the crack to pull myself up. Reaching around to the back of his harness though he found that he had none left that would fit. His largest monolith was too narrow and he had used his last piton below the overhang, all he had left were ice screws, the hollow, rifled tubes for affixing runners once they reached the snowline. It was time to consider alternatives, and he unclipped his ice axe from his harness.

Through the eye on the helve's butt end he threaded a length of line, tying it off on his harness with six feet of line connecting the two. As if about to try and lever off the inverse lip of rock Richard jabbed the picks business end upwards into the space previously occupied by his fingers. Without weight being applied to the picks helve the ice pick would simply fall away, so holding the pick in place with his left hand he brought up his left foot onto the moulded handgrip before shifting his weight to rest upon it. It was a variation on the Stein Pull and gave the commando a somewhat perilous perch on which he now placed his other foot also, and twisted his body at the waist to face the rock with the palms of his hands flat against the rock face. There wasn't any way he could warn Alladay about what he was about to attempt, so if he screwed it up he would fall until the runner on the last camm caught him, and his momentum would then swing him into the rock face below the overhang with bone breaking force. Bending at the knees Richard steadied him before leaping, his arms outstretched and fingers already half hooked. As soon as his weight left the ice pick it came loose, tumbling way to dangle from the line tied to his harness. The fingers of both hands found the same lip of rock, but it was only deep enough for the tips. With his hands side by side Richard gritted his teeth and pulled, doing a chin-up until his eyes came level with his fingertips. He groaned with the effort and then let go his left hand, shooting it up into a narrow horizontal fracture. Gritting his teeth and with his biceps trembling the Royal Marine worked himself up hand by hand until eventually he could find purchase for his feet.

Garfield heard the beat of rotor blades first, echoing off the canyon walls in a way that made it impossible to judge the direction of the source of the sound. He had two men take up position with Stingers, finding spots where they could engage in either direction along the wide canyon, and where they would avoid causing friendly injuries with the weapons back-blast.

The FIM-96A had a maximum range of eight kilometres and a minimum range of one, the distance the missile would travel before it had armed itself. That minimum range could be a real hamper in the confined depths of the mountain canyon if they did have to engage, but that would be a very last resort, as it would announce their presence here.

Over four hundred feet up, Major Dewar felt the vibrations through the rock before he actually heard the sound of a helicopter, and breathed a savage

"Oh *shit*!" The only cover around was that of the chimney above him.

Up and down the rock face the troops pulled themselves into the cover of shadows and undulations in the rock before going very still, their camouflage clothing assisting in the deception. The men anchored to belay points tied off the ropes, before releasing themselves from their restraints and getting themselves concealed

Corporal Alladay however was stuck out on a protruding shelf in plain view until Major Dewar could signal he was safe to untie himself from his anchor point. Richard hauled his axe back up and clipped it to his harness before climbing as fast as he safely could toward the crack where it suddenly yawned to become a chimney.

Back on the ground Lt Brooks used his binoculars to check that everyone on the face was as near invisible as possible, but the major and Alladay were still in clear view.

The sound of the helicopter was growing louder and his Stinger men were looking over their shoulders at him for permission to activate the weapons infrared seekers. If the aircraft happened to be equipped with a sensor suite the super-cooled 'eyes' could register upon it, giving away their presence as surely as actually loosing off a missile at them, so he shook his head emphatically before again raising his binos. Richard had gained the lower reaches of the chimney and was squeezing himself inside, hollering down the face

"OFF BELAY...FREESTYLE IT, ALLADAY!" informing the NCO that he was safe to release himself but that he himself was not belayed-on, so putting weight on the rope that connected them would result in Richard being pulled bodily from the rock face. Alladay untied himself and went up the face, moving as quickly and surely as had his officer.

Appearing at first as a small dot, the Chinese helicopter gradually grew in size as it flew toward them between towering rock walls. Garfield looked desperately up at the Royal Marine Commando, willing him to climb even faster than he presently was.

Garfield had to make a decision, the aircraft was fast approaching minimum engagement range and the Stingers needed a few moments to acquire their target. He could stand down the Stingers and trust that Alladay would be able to get into cover by the time it arrived. Otherwise Garfield would probably blow the entire operation by ordering the men holding the weapons to engage and destroy.

"Sir?" one of the men asked, wanting to know what they were to do.

Now I know why they pay me more than a trooper, Garfield thought.

"Stand down and get into cover."

The approaching light helicopter looked remarkably similar to a French Aerospatiale AS355 Twin Ecureuil, the military version of the 'Squirrel', but was in fact a Chinese copy, the Z-11.

Until a couple of weeks before, the main natural hazard of operating helicopters in the region had been the dust and heat. The aircraft were all equipped for those conditions, with dust filters for the intakes and hot weather lubricants for the engines. The snow and plummeting temperatures had brought to a halt the increased patrolling that had become the norm since the start of the war. The sub-zero temperatures turned the lightweight lubricants into heavy treacle and the dust filters iced over, starving the engines of oxygen.

The Z-11s pilot was not ecstatic about being a guinea pig, flying the first sortie since the arrival of arctic standard lubricants. The dust filters had been replaced and a crew chosen to carry out a test flight, which proved to be the ones least in favour with their commander.

Two hundred feet up the face the commander of the SAS Mountain Troop detachment pressed himself as close to the rock as he could. Lt Shippey-Romhead could not see the Z-11; he had left the traverse to climb into shadow around a corner of rock, away from the approaching helicopter. The only holds here were widely spaced and his rope, tied off at the belay point below did not allow him sufficient slack to accomplish it easily, it was pulling him sideways. The young officer was spread eagled across the rock, uncomfortably overstretched and silently urging the PLA aircraft to hurry up and bugger off. The involuntary tremors began in his right leg, a phenomenon known to climbers as 'Elvis leg', where tired or over-stressed leg muscles display disquiet at the treatment demanded of them. The SAS officer cursed the rope that was contributing to his discomfort and concentrated on stilling the tremors in his limb, willing it to behave but his left leg came out in sympathy, trembling in unison to the right limb. Removing his right hand from its hold he eased it between his body and the rock, his fingers unscrewing the locking carabiner at his waist and releasing the rope. Breathing a sigh of relief he replaced his hand back into the fracture it had left, and noted with satisfaction that the tremors were already abating.

Corporal Alladay reached the shadow beneath the overhang and clipped himself onto a runner before assuming an attitude of absolute stillness. The helicopter was almost upon them, the beating of its rotors a physical thing that buffeted the senses. The British and American troops held their breath lest the fog of their breathing catch the eye of an alert crewman, but on board an aircraft never equipped with heating the door gunners sat behind closed side doors, peering disinterestedly through Perspex windows as they shivered in the cold and drafts of freezing air that streamed through the joints of the side door.

A clod of snow struck Richard on the shoulder, loosened by the vibration of the helicopters passing it fell down the chimney from the mass of wind-blown snow and ice that overhung the face, a fore runner of the tons that were to follow. He had just enough time to brace his arms and legs against the side of the chimney, pressing his back against the opposite side with all his strength before he was engulfed.

Garfield was following the helicopter with his eyes, the beat of the blades drowned out all other sound but a white, fast moving mass caught the corner of his eye. A falling wall of ice and snow blotted out the rock face and he shouted an alarm to the men closest to the base of the canyon wall where the bergens were stashed, but they were watching the PLA machine and his shout was drowned out by the beating blades. Two men disappeared before his very eyes, one moment they were there and the next they were buried under tons of snow and ice.

During an avalanche or rock fall down a vertical face the safest place to be is as tight against the rock face as possible. The falling mass has achieved a degree of forward motion, which will carry *most* of it outwards, not in towards the face.

Lt Shippey-Romhead had no warning at all until a whiteout replaced the view he had had of the rock face across the canyon they had descended earlier. Sucking in his stomach and expending the air in his lungs he made himself as flat as possible but could still feel the wind of the avalanche against his back. Just millimetres separated him from the down rush of snow and he clung with desperation to his hand and toeholds. A lump of ice about the size of a coconut struck the back of his helmet a glancing blow and his head rebounded off the rock and into the downfall, which dragged his body from its tentative perch.

Lambeth: London SE5

Situated as it is between Peckham and Brixton, two of the more violent suburbs of the British capital, the hospital that lay three quarters of the way up Denmark Hill have a staff with vast experience and expertise in dealing with gunshot wounds and stabbings. Those skills made Kings College Hospital an obvious choice for dealing with many of the more serious cases arriving back in the UK from the fighting in Europe. One such patient arrived under guard; the military policemen of his escort being exceedingly closed mouthed about their charge.

That he was a soldier seemed obvious from the remnants of camouflage cream that still adhered to his skin, clearly missed by the medical staff in Germany. However, the RMPs would not reveal his identity or the circumstances of his receiving his injuries.

A doctor in triage was beginning to get extremely frustrated with the lack of forthcoming information, such as the date of the injury, the dimensions of the blade and was it possible that any of the knife or bayonet's blade could have been broken off? Whether morphine had been administered, and if so then how much and when? She couldn't even get them to admit that the casualty was a serviceman. A Warrant Officer was in command of the escort but the doctor was being blanked in her attempts to do an accurate assessment.

"Listen mister, you people only police the armed forces so you must know something about this man...right?"

The military policeman answered with a half-truth, because he had been deliberately given the very minimum of information, and then warned that severe repercussions would follow immediately should even that small amount of knowledge be divulged.

"No doctor that is not right, we actually police the armed forces *and* their dependants, but we are here only to provide a guard for this prisoner until relieved by the civil authorities."

The doctor resisted the urge to grind her teeth, and tried one last time to stick with the logical approach.

"So where is his paperwork, you must have something to hand over to whoever is relieving you?"

The Redcap shook his head.

"No doctor, perhaps our relief will know more."

The doctor's eyes hardened and she squared her shoulders, but before she could launch into a verbal assault a slightly flustered senior manager for the Hospital Trust arrived and thrust a scrap of paper with hastily written details upon it. The length and width of the type of bayonet that had inflicted the wound, the casualty's blood group, and the details of his medication up to present time were all included. The doctor noted however that although his date of birth was shown, there was no mention of a name or next of kin for this man before her.

"Where did you get this?"

The manager was not about to reveal the identity of the very important person from whom the information had apparently originated. The patient, if he survived, was to be charged and prosecuted with a variety of serious crimes including cowardice, mutiny and war crimes. The media must be kept completely in the dark and as such the manager had been threatened with prosecution himself for breaching the Official Secrets Act if word got out. Such a prosecution, if successful, would of course void his pension rights he was reminded.

"That information is confidential and of a need to know nature. So, as you have all the details you need I suggest you get busy, doctor?"

As she had worked with less she put the annoyance and dislike of the National Health Services 'Yes men' behind her, and got on with the job.

The military policemen accompanied the unnamed casualty up to theatre, and waited away the hours as patients came and went from other OR's. The afternoon became evening, and eventually their relief arrived in the uniform of Her Majesty's Prison Service, but the surgical procedure dragged on.

The Yaghan Basin: 2122hrs.

There is a song about men joining navies to see the sea and getting their wish, seeing an unromantic Atlantic and a less than terrific Pacific but no mention is made of the wildest and stormiest of seas, those of the great Southern Ocean.

There are no land masses to buffer nature's energies and the stormy seas percolate north to make life interesting at times for sailor men in the southern Pacific and Atlantic.

On the edge of the Southern Ocean, at the Falklands Islands in 1982, the Royal Navy Task Force had an unpleasant time of it in ships built for the less aggressive Mediterranean and north Atlantic.

Currently, there were ninety eight seamen who could not see the third ocean but who were of a similar opinion as the songsters about the water above their heads at that time.

At 55°47'26.48"S - 64°24'51.40"W the *Admiral Potemkin's* coxswains fought to keep their charge on an even keel at a depth of one hundred feet as a floating antennae was streamed out behind them, dragged behind on the surface as they checked for any messages left them in the previous twenty four hours.

At 33,800 tons submerged the *Admiral Potemkin* was something of a lumbering behemoth in fact as well as looks. She had been laid down at the Rubin Design Bureau works at Arkhangelsk Oblast in 1993 designated as a *raketnyy podvodnyy strategicheskogo nazhacheniya,* a strategic missile cruiser, a *'Boomer'* in western naval parlance and NATO called her a Typhoon, but when the Berlin Wall came down because the arms race had bankrupted the Soviet Union she was abandoned before her reactor or VLTs, Vertical Launch Tubes, for her twenty ICBMs could be installed.

Her rescue had come during the long years of planning, of placing human and materiel assets into the West and waiting for the espionage to produce fruit. The blinding of the West's satellites without them realising had been an intelligence coup to cap them all, and also the signal to proceed with the many and varied parts of the next stage.

Neither Russia nor the People's Republic of China had the infrastructure and resources to operate diesel submarines at sea over a protracted period of time or indefinitely over great distances. The German Kriegsmarine in the last world war had perfected the refuelling and victualling of submarines at sea and even undersea refuelling was possible, given the right circumstances. However, there exists no method for victualing another vessel beneath the waves, which therefore renders the covert refuelling of another submerged submarine an operation of questionable worth. A fully fuelled submarine crewed by a collection of starving individuals is of no use to anybody.

When a submarine leaves for a long voyage every inch of space is used for storage. Floor gratings are lifted and boxes packed alongside one another before the gratings are replaced on top to prevent trips and falls, whilst making life hazardous for the taller members of the crew. Walking hunched over may not look particularly martial but it saved on painful meetings between cranium, steam pipes and the like until the fresh food was used up and the tinned goods at floor level thinned out.

So the *Admiral Potemkin* became a *Milchkühe,* a milk cow which could carry out FAS and RAS, 'Fassing' and 'Rassing', fuelling at sea and replenishing at sea, resupplying and rearming with conventional weapons any submarine requiring such and any diesel electric boat in need of refuelling.

Five of her six 21" torpedo tubes were removed and all available space was incorporated into storage. The vast void of her launch tube chamber was split into three fuel bunkers for diesel fuel with each connected by valves and it was these fuel bunkers which were the cause of the crews unhappy state.

The original builders, the excellent Rubin Design Bureau, had not been involved in her conversion and were only consulted on limited matters such as the replacement of equipment either rendered defunct due to the role change or due to corrosion as she sat on the slips for years, her hull incomplete and exposed to the elements.

Had her bunkers been multi-layered cells and linked via high pressure pumps whereby trim could be easily maintained there would have been less of a problem, but the three bunkers were mounted lengthways, pointing fore and aft and they could not discharge independently. For practicality the bunkers were filled and discharged from the portside, either by tankers or pumps on the quayside, or at sea from an oiler.

Much juggling of valves was required to prevent a list developing as the portside bunker filled and its contents gradually shared with the centreline and starboard bunkers via a main transfer valve and a secondary, neither of which were as fast as they could have been.

When the bunkers were filled she sat low in the water but her handling characteristics were little different to those originally intended.

As soon as she began servicing the small flotilla engaged on what was named as Operation *'Early Dawn'* those characteristics altered.

Once the Typhoon was no longer on an even keel it adversely effected the steering, making the tasking of holding a course difficult, and if the equilibrium within the tanks was not restored swiftly then over steering would follow until the bulky vessel began a noticeable zigzag course much to the annoyance of her captain and Lt Wei Wuhan of the Chinese navy.

They had taken the Chinese officer onboard soon after the modified Typhoon had been launched, and that was before the Chinese People's Republic's Politburo had even heard the sales pitch by Peridenko and Alontov.

Lieutenant Wuhan was the ship's interpreter and dedicated OCE, Officer Conducting Exercise, for Underway Replenishment.

Quite apart from adversely affecting the steering it also caused problems with the equilibrium of the vessel when dived.

Even a vessel the size of *Admiral Potemkin* can be effected by violent seas when submerged, unless at great depth.

The best cure for sea sickness is to step outside and look at the horizon but that was not an option, so with no fixed horizon to stabilise the brain the inner ear slipped in and out of synchronisation. In particular for those crew members navigating a passage from fore and aft, or vice versa, it could be an uncomfortable experience when the Typhoon was running relatively shallow.

Admiral Potemkin was 577.7 feet in length so the boat was 4702.3 feet short of the title, but when under the influence of the waves above that journey still became known as *Zhelchi Milyu*, 'The Bile Mile'.

Her primary role was originally to be that of supporting the inshore raiding flotilla in hit and run attacks on the Hawaiian Islands, before eventually heading to Australia for the fuelling and resupplying of forces seizing Port Kembla, west of Sydney, in the hours before China's invasion of Australia.

The industrial port had deep water for the troopships and freighters to unload, and ferry docks for the Ro-Ro transports to land two armoured and two mechanised divisions of the 1st Corps of the PLAN's 3rd Army. Its 2nd Corps was already loading back in Shanghai, whilst the 3rd Corps, largely reservists with second class equipment, was scheduled to use the shipping that was currently carrying 1st Corps with the Sino Russian fleet.

However, the planned raids on Hawaii had been shelved as impractical once major units of the US 2nd Army had moved into defend likely targets.

The 2nd Army's presence was not something that had been foreseen in the planning, but then there is one law of planning which never changes and that is 'No plan survives first contact with the enemy'.

Only in B movies are the other people completely predictable.

Various factors had altered the original plan. Ninety nine cities and military bases around the world that were supposed to have been destroyed were in fact untouched. The destruction of Pusan and the 2nd Army headquarters were expected to leave the US Forces in South Korea stranded and disorganised, left to wither on the vine and be easy pickings for later in the war.

The Hawaiian Islands and key points in Australia and New Zealand were now effectively hardened and no longer practical targets for small scale commando raids, which left *Admiral Potemkin* and the inshore raiders twiddling their thumbs in the wings awaiting a suitable specialist role to play in the war once the original missions were scrubbed or put on hold.

The French had also not behaved as predicted. Historically the greater good had only been a factor when the going was good, i.e., a benefit to the national good. Russia's Premier confidently expected the French to declare neutrality and withdraw completely from NATO once the new Red Army began rolling westwards. Indeed they had in 1966 separated themselves from the command structure, if not the organisation, following differences arising during the Cuban Crisis. But after the opening battles the French had not scurried off home, they had dug in a fought as fiercely as the other armies in the alliance.

The French had proven themselves to be unpredictable in the Premier's eyes and they also had a nuclear arsenal completely independent of NATO control along with the means to deliver those weapons, despite retiring and deactivating her land based tactical nuclear weapons. The army's battlefield *Pluton* and *Hadès* mobile missile systems, and three IRBMs, Intermediate Range Ballistic Missiles, in silos at the airbase at Saint-Christol were scrapped and their warheads recycled into nuclear fuel rods.

President Charles de Gaulle himself had been speaking directly, for he was always very direct, at the Russian people when he had famously said, with a Gallic shrug of the shoulders of course

"Within ten years, we shall have the means to kill eighty million Russians. I truly believe that one does not light-heartedly attack people who are able to kill eighty million Russians, even if one can kill eight hundred million French, that is if there were eight hundred million French."

The French navy's *Force Océanique Stratégique* comprising the SSBNs *Le Terrible, Le Triomphant* and *Le Téméraire* were all at sea and *Le Vigilant,* which had been undergoing a lengthy refit within the covered dry dock at Brest, had with much ceremony for the worlds press, been re-floated and towed to the old reinforced concrete U Boat pens to be moored in the open where her sixteen M45 ballistic missiles could be launched at both Russia and China if necessary.

The Premier believed that whereas the US President and the British would baulk at 'going ballistic' until the last moment, the French were an unknown quantity.

What was known though was her current ability to put up military satellites to replace those that Russia and China were destroying on an almost daily basis from their South American facility on the equator at French Guiana.

Both the *Ariane*, Italian *Vega* and now also, to add insult, the neighbouring *Soyuz* built launch facilities were being used solely for the launching of military payloads.

The French legionnaires guarding all three at the outbreak of the war had not only seized the *Soyuz* site and personnel not yet evacuated, but had also mounted an ad hoc resource denial operation. Augmenting their own tiny helicopter force of a Gazelle and Puma with a logging company's Chinook they had boarded the freighter *Fliterland* on the open sea as she attempted to carry ten *Soyuz-ST* rockets and boosters back to St Petersburg, denying Russia the use of ten valuable launch vehicles whilst themselves benefiting .

The *Vega*'s carried smaller communications satellites aloft and the *Soyuz*, while they lasted, and *Ariane* rockets hoisted the RORSATs up into the desired orbits.

Taking down the launch facility would leave the West with only Canaveral, Kennedy and Vandenberg, as fear of China's lack of inhibition in using nuclear weapons would deny them Asia's launch sites.

All the Premier had to do was advise his partners to exercise restraint when dealing with French Guiana, at least until NATO was broken in Europe.

So Operation *Early Dawn* was devised.

The Russian *Admiral Potemkin* and the Chinese diesel boats of the Inshore Raiding Flotilla were off the south China coast near Zhuhai practicing replenishment and fuelling at sea, along with other more warlike drills as they awaited deployment.

They exercised initially by day in the full knowledge that the NSA had been penetrated and for a time the Americans could not trust what their satellites saw.

The drilling in daylight progressed on to working at night, at first under illumination until they had built up skills and confidence.

Finally the lights had been switched off and from then on refuelling and resupply was carried out under operational conditions.

Crewmen on the blacked out casing wearing passive night goggles and safety lines attached king posts to the fore and aft ends of the conning towers to hold STREAM rigs, or the 'Standard Tensioned Replenishment Alongside Method' because the navy loves an acronym that sounds cool until first explained. This complex mechanism was assembled to supply food using pulleys and loadbearing cables under tension for the transfers, and also to feed across the fuelling hose, clear of the waves, to the receiving submarine's female receptor attached to her own conning tower.

Both vessels would have to exercise superb seamanship with expert hands on the helms as they ran parallel at thirty yards distant. Only the best coxswains' hands will be steering each boat because at 12 knots a 1 degree variation in heading produces a lateral speed of 20 feet per minute initially, and that is before hydrodynamics is factored in, the suction caused by two masses in close proximity, particularly if at least one of them or the ocean is in motion. The suction increases exponentially and a collision may be unavoidable if that happens, as the captain of a luxury cruise ship recently found to his cost sailing too close to a small Mediterranean island.

Ram Tensioners and a series of saddle winches kept the cable taut and also allowed some leeway before the cable parted due to an error of diverging courses, but seamanship of a high standard made it work. Senior Lieutenant Wuhan of the

People's Liberation Army Navy would have the fate of the entire mission riding on his cool head and language skills on each occasion. No radios could be used without compromising the mission and so all instructions would have to be passed by voice, via megaphone until a shot line was fired over to the receiving vessel, and that is attached to a cable for a sound powered telephone. The telephone cable is itself attached to a heavier 'Span Wire' which is heaved over and clamped onto the receiving kingpost, and with that secure the 'saddles' bearing stores and the fuelling hose are strung beneath it and pulled over.

With Strela surface to air missiles at the ready they simulated coming under attack whilst coupled and joined by the fuelling hose, they simulated man-overboard drills whilst coupled and joined together and even buddy-buddy fire fighting drills whilst coupled together because there is really no such thing as an 'Emergency breakaway', instead the 'Rasser's' and 'Fasser's', the replenishment and fuelling parties, just have to get a hustle on to de-rig the complex apparatus that much faster than they normally would.

That the issue with steering and trim was one that only a refit would solve was quickly realised. Earlier on they also discovered that the spanwire visibly vibrated when taut, but it ceased vibrating completely when the helmsmen got it wrong and the courses began to diverge. When that happened you knew the 2500 lb. breaking strain was all but upon you! It became the job of one of the leading hands to do nothing except watch the spanwire and shout a warning when that vibration could no longer be seen.

They were relearning old lessons and they learned well. Some procedures they simply made up as they went along, and if it worked then that became the SOP, the standard operating procedure for fuelling and resupplying submarines from another submarine, something not practiced in over sixty years.

The technically much trickier replenishment at sea of torpedoes and torpedo tube launched anti-shipping missiles was practiced at anchor in a sheltered bay, and with oil being pumped out into the sea by both vessels for the purpose of water calming. Bow to bow and separated by heavy duty inflated bladders the submarines were made fast to each other as torpedoes were manually fed tail-first from the Typhoon's torpedo tube and into the Chinese boat's torpedo tubes. Finding such a handy spot to carry out the task would not be an easy matter and both vessels would be open to attack, so quite aside from the back breaking toil involved it was an unpopular undertaking, made more unpleasant by the cleaning of the bladders, which was a filthy but necessary job as the oil would eat into them and perish the material within days otherwise.

Once their orders arrived the *Admiral Potemkin* slipped away south and avoided the main shipping lanes.

The Chinese boats continued their own role specific tasks for four more days of rehearsals near the uninhabited, sub-tropical Damang Island before topping off their tanks and following on initially diverse courses.

The converted Typhoon was waiting for them at the first refuelling spot, some six hundred miles south west of a tiny coral atoll.

That atoll was a circular ring of rock and sand that enclosed a freshwater lagoon, and a stagnant freshwater lagoon at that. Populated as it was by a quarter million bad tempered sea birds and one million inedible crabs only the most optimistic romantic, or a Frenchman, could have named it *Ile de la Passion.*

The trio of Chinese diesel submarines had almost dry tanks and the giant of a Russian must have been a welcome sight for each of them but they were barely one third of the way to their ultimate destination.

Again the quartet parted with the Typhoon running deep through the empty vastness of the Pacific to arrive ahead of them at the next scheduled rendevous.

The crew of the converted Typhoon arrived at their next assigned position 65 miles south of Isla del los Estados near the very southernmost tip of South America and settled down for a long and uncomfortable wait.

Bao was the first vessel to arrive, its bona fides established by Senior Lieutenant Wuhan on a dark night with a thankfully moderate sea. The transfer of rations as well as fuel went without hitch, but how they enjoyed the Russian rations was questionable. Tinned pork, tinned sausage and tinned fish were going to be pretty monotonous and peacetime rules in the Russian navy forbade continuous use of its tinned rations without added fresh produce in meals beyond eighteen days. The Russian tinned rations lacked the added protein edition of the western armies' variety.

The second customer arriving two days later was the curio of the Chinese flotilla, a type paid off from the Russian fleet decades before but her Chinese owners had maintained her well and added upgrades not available in her classes' heyday such as western acoustic dampening tiles and the propellers of an Improved Kilo, the quietest and most efficient that technology could build.

Dai was an elderly Juliett, a diesel electric cruise missile boat built to be quiet enough to get in close to carrier combat groups and sink those carriers, but she was built small as well as quiet in a time when missile defence left something to be desired. She only carried a maximum of four cruise missiles in VTLs, vertical launch tubes, forward of the conning tower.

That operation had been far more difficult as the weather had been back to its usual wild self. They had eventually relocated a hundred miles north with the rocky expanses of the Isla del los Estados acting as a windbreak.

With nuclear detonations up north evaporating vast quantities of sea water to condense in the cold upper atmosphere, blinding photo reconnaissance satellites and reducing visibility it had become a more manageable risk remaining in the lee of the island for the third and final northbound customer of 'Grigory's Gas & Drive-Thru Mart' as the crew referred to themselves.

The third submarine in the flotilla, *Tuan,* was early, only a day and a half behind the *Dai* and she had been in the area several hours before the *Admiral Potemkin* had risen up from the depths to check her messages.

The weather was far from placid and becoming progressively worse. The sun was an hour below the horizon before the submarines made contact and the complex ballet of matching course and speed could begin. No transfer of food and fuel were possible until Lt Wuhan was satisfied the helmsmen were 'in sync'.

Tuan was one of the original Kilo's, an elderly boat as were all of the submarines in the flotilla, but they were very well maintained. The life expectancy of a submarine working inshore and delivering the special forces to their targets was rather less than that of their conventionally employed sisters. China was not about to use more modern and less replaceable hulls whilst she still had a goodly number of the other variety on the lists.

Tuan she carried a small submersible piggyback upon her casing, as did the flotilla's other two vessels, and anchor points on the submersibles casings were for the special forces troops of China's army navy to be towed along clinging to the outer hull.

Both Typhoon and Kilo had their ECM, the electronic counter measure masts, and communications masts fully extended but EMCON was in force, no electronic emissions were permitted, all systems were set to passive/standby mode with the sensor arrays sniffing at the electronic airwaves.

The vessel's towed sonar arrays were reeled in and housed for the duration of this surface activity as a precaution against being damaged, or even lost by becoming entangled, 'run over' or sucked in to the other boats screws. Only those sonar sensors incorporated into the hull design were deployed but all they were hearing was the thrashing of the other boats propeller and the racket of localised surface noise.

Admiral Potemkin and *Tuan* had ploughed into heavy seas at 12 knots holding station on one another despite twice almost losing the fuelling hose to giant rollers. The RAS and FAS procedures were taking longer than they had for either the *Bao* or the *Dai.* The weather gods were most definitely not with them this night.

In the Typhoon's radio shack a blinking red light announced incoming flash traffic and the captain was immediately informed, but what could he do at that particular moment whilst dealing with the fuelling, break off until the transmission was complete? As per SOP's the radar was switched from *'Standby'* to *'Off'* lest it interfere with the incoming signal which would also of course register on the ECM for ten seconds or ten minutes, however long the message may be.

In the warmth and dry of the Admiral *Potemkin* the engineers were juggling the flow between the three long bunkers of diesel fuel in order to stay as near to an even keel as possible, as the rolling of the vessel was having undue influence on their efforts to fuel the Chinese Kilo.

Up top, the rain was hammering in almost horizontally with each icy gust of wind onto the lookouts, Strela operator, captain and Lieutenant Wuhan, who was still directing the FAS and RAS parties of both vessels by megaphone until they had ship to ship telephone communication.

On the submarines' casings the FAS and RAS parties looked like 'Dr Who' poor man's aliens in their passive night goggles and Day-Glo orange immersion suits, but each man was securely tethered to safety lines.

Forward of the conning towers the RAS parties had it the worst as they were unprotected from the elements. Freak waves tried to snatch them away and only the safety lines saved them but their task was completed well before the fuelling, and their rig unbolted and stored below in under twenty minutes, such was their competence even on such an evil night.

Of the three PLAN diesels only *Tuan* had expended any munitions, sinking the New Zealand flagged bulk grain carrier *Christchurch IV* that had been unwisely relying on speed rather than an escorted, but slower, convoy. However the replacement of those two torpedoes was neither requested nor suggested on a night like they were then experiencing.

Wind, spray and the rain were reducing visibility to zero for those without passive night goggles. They were also being deafened by the combined harsh roaring of the Kilo's diesel exhausts, the crashing of the waves and the impact of a million raindrops on the boats casings and the surface of the ocean.

But someone still noticed the dark winged shape that emerged from the rain heavy cloud before it actually overflew them.

"Preduprezhdeniye...vrazheskiy samolet!"

Lieutenant Wei Wuhan repeated the warning to *Tuan* over the loudhailer but no sooner had he shouted "Enemy aircraft!" when their cloak of darkness was stripped away.

The P3 Orion of the Argentinian Navy had been performing a grid square search for the missing *'Maria III'* when they had picked up a radar return and had naturally dropped flares to identify the vessel.

Had the Typhoon not been receiving flash traffic that was interfering with both submarine's ECM threat detectors then the Orion's crew would have found only an empty ocean illuminated by the flares.

The PNGs were now an unexpected hindrance and upon removing them the crewmen shouldering the Strela missiles took long moments to blink in the glare of the flare's white light before acquiring the Orion.

Alarms screeched aboard the aircraft which went a fair way to dispelling the shock the Argentinian crew had experienced.

"*Conqueror*....it's that murdering bastard Anglo, *Conqueror*!" a crew member shouted as the automated counter measure pods discharged more flares. The 1982 sinking of the cruiser Belgrano, though justified, was burned into the Argentine naval psyche, if not the nation's.

The mis-identification of the submarines was not challenged by the pilots who relied upon the recognition skills of the observers in the rear, but the co-pilot reached for the intercom switch to ask that the identification be checked by replaying the images being recorded by the Orion's video cameras in the belly and tail. But any thoughts of double checking and confirming the observers I.D of the surfaced submarines was forgotten by what happened next.

"Missile launch!" the observer at the rear shouted on seeing a flash as a Strela's rocket motor ignited followed by a bright and fiery tail light.

"The Anglo's are shooting at us!"

The missile, loosed by the *Tuan*, chased a flare and detonated harmlessly but on the *Admiral Potemkin* the Russian air sentry was still calmly awaiting a solid lock-on tone.

The cloud base beckoned just two hundred feet above but the pilot banked left, coming around and sending his contact report.

"Chato, Chato...Albatross Three... contact, contact, contact...53°44'22.97"south... 64°26'33.81"west... two British submarines on the surface...we are under attack by surface to air missiles....engaging with Harpoon and MK50!"

Argentina had declared neutrality at the start of hostilities but all the maritime patrol aircraft carried war shots as standard operating procedure on the underwing pylons in the form of a pair of AGM 84 Harpoons and MK50 torpedoes in the bomb bay.

"*Cease pumping*...close and secure master fuel pump valve!" Lieutenant Wuhan saw that the *Tuan*'s FAS party had jumped the gun, ejecting the fuelling probe before the flow had halted so that it was violently spewing greasy diesel onto an already slick and slippery casing as it left the receiver at their end.

"Haul back on the messenger return line...lively there; get that hose back aboa......" The firing of the Strela from *Tuan*'s conning tower drowned out his words and caused him to duck momentarily. He straightened up and leant over the conning tower's coaming.

"Standby to haul in the master messenger once they strike free the spanwire or it'll foul the screws." he kept his voice level as he called down to their own men but then noticed the leading seaman whose job it was to watch the spanwire was instead lending a hand hauling in the fuelling hose, obviously as desperate as any of them to get below the surface and away from danger. Wei looked in alarm at the spanwire to see it was rock steady.

With a report like a gunshot the cable parted where it was clamped into the *Tuan*'s kingpost, whiplashing across the gap between the vessels, cutting in two the Strela operator as he was about to fire and decapitating Lieutenant Wuhan who was still leaning over the side.

With the supporting spanwire gone the hose and probe dropped into the churning water between both vessels where the wake swept it back into the Typhoons port propeller which tore the hose and messenger lines away. The fuelling hose was shredded and dispersing harmlessly in their wake but the messenger line was sucked in and wrapped itself around the spinning screw, a later job for the Typhoons diver, *if* they survived.

With nothing left to impede the two submarines they steered sharply diverging courses. FAS parties on both submarines casings hung desperately onto safety lines and clawed their way towards the hatches as the boats heeled over and diving alarms sounded.

The bodies of both Wei Wuhan and the Strela operator were abandoned as the bridge of the *Admiral Potemkin* was cleared. Both men were obviously very dead, no physician was required to tell the bridge party that.

The Strela launcher carried an armed and primed missile and was dumped over the side out of expediency and safety by the captain.

He slipped after he threw it, losing his footing in the blood to land heavily with an oath but gaining the hatch and pulling himself through despite a dislocated elbow, adrenaline providing the necessary anaesthetic.

The Orion lost height dangerously during its turn but as the wings came level the warbling tone in their headsets told them that despite being in relatively close proximity to their targets the Harpoons seeker head had acquired a radar lock-on to the largest vessel.

Both pilots closed one eye as the missile left its pylon to preserve their night vision.

They were now closing fast on the submarines and inside the minimum engagement range for the second Harpoon so two MK50s dropped from the Orion's bomb bay with small drogue chutes deploying to give them controlled entry into the water. They were designed to destroy fast, deep diving submarines using a small shaped charge normally associated with anti-armour rounds, the sea water entering small apertures in the casings turned to fast expanding steam by a chemical reaction that produced a 40 knot speed which no conventionally powered torpedo could match at great depth.

The two submarines were less than a football field apart and still on the surface when the Harpoon released by Albatross Three penetrated the f casing of *Admiral Potemkin* and exploded in the diesel fuel bunkers. The Typhoon still carried 150,000 litres of diesel plus her entire inventory of reloads of 21 inch torpedoes and YJ-8 anti-shipping missiles.

Admiral Potemkin detonated like a grenade.

Titanium and steel burst apart, shards flying in all directions to pierce the *Tuan*'s pressure hull, starboard ballast tank and also the special forces submersible sat on the after casing. Her conning tower was peppered with shrapnel, seriously wounding the captain who was still half in and half out of the hatch being the last one to clear the bridge.

Roiling, angry reds and oranges of the fireball rose over three hundred feet, dumping blazing fuel over an equal area of the ocean surrounding it, engulfing the *Tuan* in fire.

Even had her hatches been shut, which they were not, she was mortally wounded and the arrival of both high speed MK 50 torpedoes merely accelerated her demise.

At only two hundred feet above the surface of the Atlantic Albatross Three bucked as it was lifted and buffeted violently by the blast of the *Admiral Potemkin's* violent end. A heartbeat later both pilots ducked instinctively as the airframe was struck hard by more than one piece of shrapnel.

The port wing rose as the aircraft commander banked right as much as he judged it safe to do, avoiding the fireball but the airframe was now trembling, a harsh vibration shaking it spastically.

The master fire alarm sounded as the fire warning light for the port outer engine glowed an urgent crimson.

That engines misfires were clearly audible to all the crew, the loud reports sounding like random spaced gunshots, and it was coughing like a sixty a day nicotine slave.

There first appeared black, oily smoke, a precursor to the flickering tongues of flame which seconds later escaped from joints between inspection panels in the engine housing of a clearly damaged Allison turbo prop.

The pilots and flight engineer engaged the engines fire extinguisher, dumping a flame retardant compound onto the engine, shutting off the fuel supply and following the engine feathering procedure.

It was standard fuel management to patrol with one engine feathered anyway so the aircraft was not in danger of falling from the sky with the other three engines operating normally.

Just a single pass for damage assessment took place but no more flares were required as the burning fuel provided ample illumination.

With footage of the destruction for analysis Albatross Three reported both submarines sunk with no trace of survivors and turned west for Tierra del Fuego, trailing smoke as it headed home.

操作'黎明' 'Cāozuò'límíng'
(Operation Early Dawn)

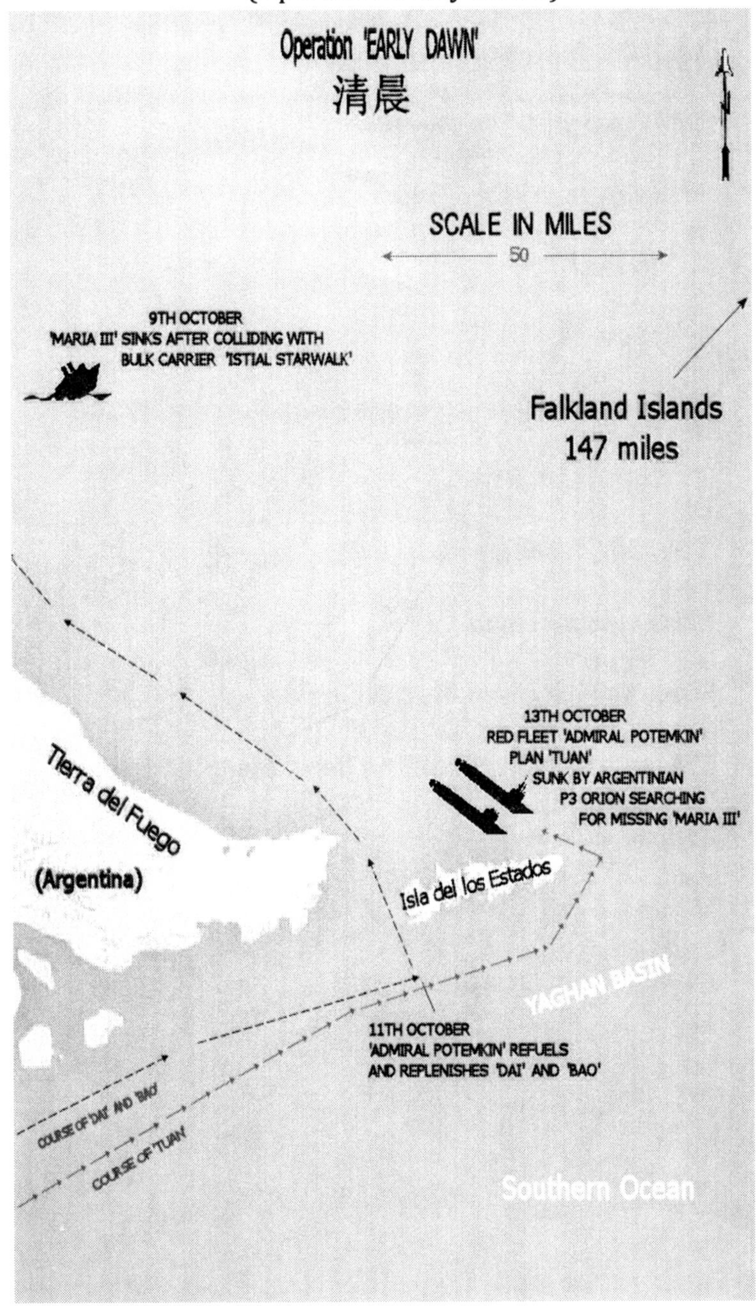

European Space Agency Map Key

A **'BAO's' submersible objective.**

B **'DAI's' submersible objective.**

C **Ile du Diable (Devil's Island).**

D **Ile Royale.**

E **Ile St Joseph.**

1 **ESA launch facility Northern perimeter blockhouse.**

2 **' SOYUZ ' launch pad.**

3 **' ARIANE ' launch pad.**

4 **' VEGA ' launch pad.**

5 **Space vehicle assembly building.**

6 **ESA launch facility Southern perimeter blockhouse.**

7 **Kourou airfield.**

8 **ESA Jetty.**

9 **Kourou River road bridge goal.**

European Space Agency Facility, Kourou.

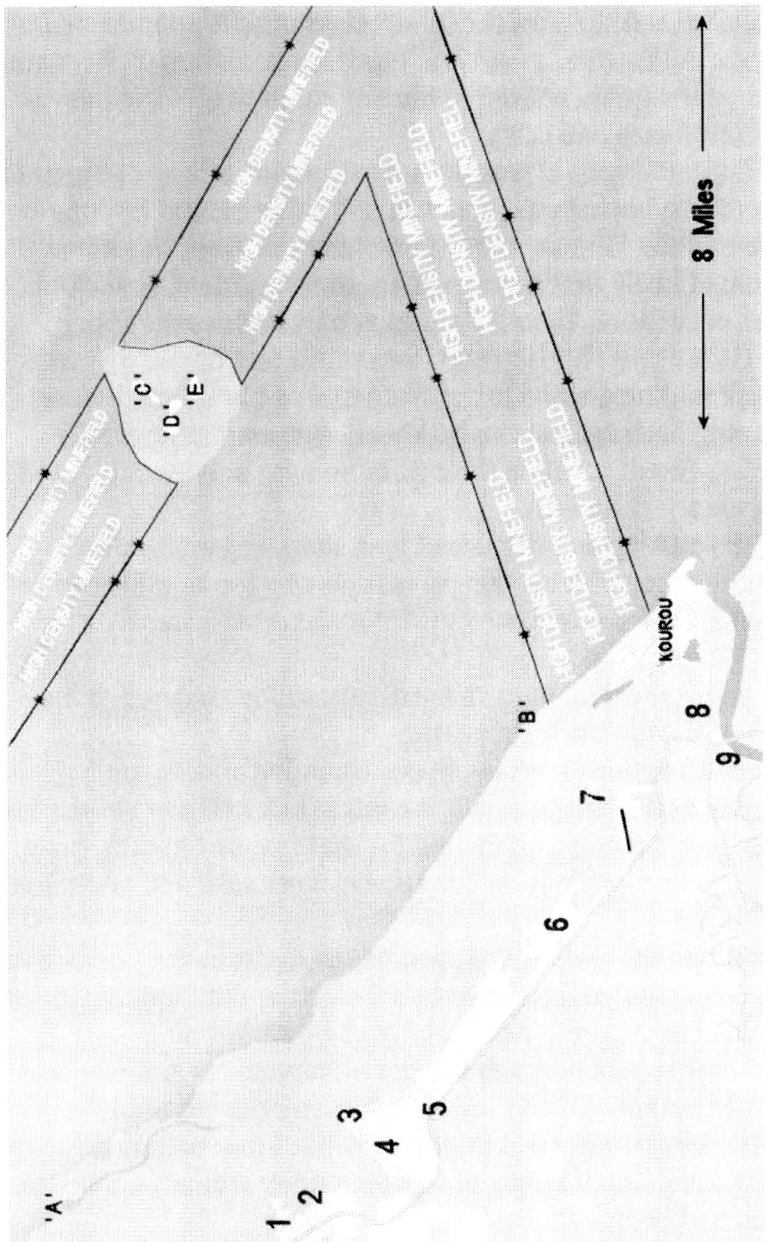

30.86 miles due north of Cayenne, South America

After three days awaiting the arrival of the *Tuan,* to rejoin with *Dai* and the *Bao,* the Juliett class missile submarine *Dai* sent a millisecond's worth of burst transmission to Fleet and then her captain retired to his tiny cabin to give the impression of confidence and calm.

Captain Aiguo Li was the second senior officer of the small flotilla, commissioned a month and a day behind his long-term friend Chen Xinhua who commanded the *Tuan,* but it now seemed likely that some mishap, some accident, or incident was preventing *Tuan* from taking part in this operation.

He sat upon his bunk and raised his feet to rest up on the small folding writing table that acted as his 'office', before leaning back against the bulkhead, contemplating on the difficulties of fulfilling their mission with only two thirds of the necessary resources.

His musing was disturbed by a sharp rap on his door.

Lounging with his feet up was no way for an officer to be seen and he straightened up before barking a stern.

"Come!"

It was the *Shui Bing*, the ordinary sailor assigned as his steward, announcing a visitor.

"With respect Captain, Major Huaiqing awaits you."

The 'Major' was actually a captain but a ship or submarine can have but one captain and for that reason Captain Huaiqing was given a 'promotion' for appearances sake and addressed as Major.

No salutes were exchanged below decks as the vessel was far too cramped for such martial niceties and Captain Li merely nodded an assent for the soldier to be admitted.

Their supercargo slept in tiered hammocks in the forward torpedo room where they managed to keep out of the way of his sailors going about their duties but those men represented eighteen pairs of lung and eighteen more stomachs than the boat had been built for.

A workable number in ideal situations, as the cooks just had an extra few mouths to feed, one hundred instead of eighty two.

However, the air scrubbers had to work harder and that was just running close to the surface with the snorkel extended to run the diesels and keep the batteries fully charged.

Going deep and running on batteries and internal air supply was another matter entirely.

The week before, they had been pinged by an unknown maritime patrol aircraft when they were off Natal, Brazil, where it was a bit far off for the French Navy Atlantique IIs out of Cayenne. But it hardly mattered who they were, it had been the first brush with the enemy.

They had been snorkeling as they ran just under the surface with the ECM mast extended of course.

Now there are two dangers in that situation, the first time under fire, and only one is the enemy aircraft. The other is a panicked dive with the diesels still engaged because a torpedo may miss but a diesel will suck every breath of air out of the boat before the Diving Officer realises his error. It had happened to the *'The Great Wall'* on a simple training exercise with students from the academy a few years before. She had been a Ming class, an ex-Soviet Romeo and someone probably ordered crash surface when they realised what was happening but a fishing boat found it drifting ten days later with all 70 students and crew dead from asphyxia.

Back to the *Dai's* first time under fire, and the aircraft had been doing a MAD sweep, its magnetic anomaly detector had picked up the distortion in the earth's magnetic field caused by the shallow running Dai's metal hull

The executive officer had the watch and he had done it by the numbers as if it were a drill, shutting down the diesels and engaging the electric motor before diving.

Whichever nation's aircraft it was, it had been known that either there was no friendly boat was in the area or they just did not care because they had immediately attacked with depth charges.

Luck had not deserted them entirely and the aircraft had departed, either low on fuel or suffering some fault but it obviously called for surface support because a half hour later a frigate, identified by the sonar as either the Brazilian *Liberal* or the *Constitucao,* had lobbed depth charges at them from its 375mm ASW mortar.

Sonar had first heard it thundering in at full speed from ten miles away and Captain Li had the two obvious choices, fight or flight. The first option was one he was confident he would win, but it would alert all the navies in the region that a submarine was in the area and that would hazard their mission. To run was not an attractive bet as more surface vessels and aircraft would join the hunt

A good look at the chart though had given him a third choice.

Captain Li settled the *Dai* into the mud close by the wreck of the *U598*, sunk seventy years before by US Liberator bombers, and there they waited out the depth charging.

There was doubtless an interesting exchange between aircraft commander and the ASW officer aboard the frigate as to the certainty of the aircraft's contact, but they endured two hours' worth of attention and twenty-three depth charges before the frigate departed. Fortunately, the aircraft did not return.

Quite apart from the terrifying experience everyone had endured, those extras bodies, the special forces troopers, had had a noticeably disagreeable effect on air quality. The carbon dioxide levels had been bordering the red line.

Today Captain Jie Huaiqing, second in command of the *Zhōngguó tèzhǒng bùduì*, the Special Forces Company, squeezed inside and once the steward had departed he sat upon the folding table's stool. Both table and stool were spring loaded to fold up against the bulkhead. A functional design but the stool could be challenging as it would do so when not actually being sat on. It was another good reason why alcohol was not allowed on board.

In the full knowledge that the ordinary sailor was in reality a Lieutenant Commander in the *Guójiā Ānquánbù*, the Ministry of State Security's naval division, the two officers exchanged formal pleasantries. On the captain asking him how he was filling his time the army officer produced a small book he had been reading from a map pocket. It was all about the life cycle of the genus *Dermochelys coriacea,* the Leatherback Sea Turtle, and he continued with the enthusiasm normally associated with train spotters rather than an officer in the Peoples Republics elite forces.

Outside the cabin the state appointed spy moved away back to his post in the small galley, satisfied that a regime toppling coup was not in the process of being hatched.

Indeed no insurrection was being planned, but nobody likes an eavesdropper so this game was played frequently.

"What news of the *Tuan*, Captain?"

The naval officer shook his head.

"None at all sadly, and I have sent a refueling query to our friends the *Admiral Potemkin* but they have not responded." He picked up a pencil and tapped it idly against his knee.

"I had hoped that on answering I would be able to learn from them when... *if*... they had fuelled *Tuan* near the cape."

After a few moments contemplation he shrugged to himself and then stood, retrieving a key from a chain about his neck with which he opened his small safe to extract his copy of the mission planning pack.

"I await instructions from Fleet but I think it sensible to work on a new plan that will also keep the Russians happy by not raising the target to the ground."

The Russians were fairly certain that had the launch facility been on UK or US soil no tit for tat nuclear response would follow as they were holding back from escalating the use of nuclear weapons beyond that of depth charges, a situation China and Russia were capitalising on, but the French were the atomic wild card in NATO's pack.

The original plan called for thirty eight SF operatives to sink the freighter *Fliterland* beside the purpose built dock at Kourou where the *Ariane* and *Vega* components were delivered by sea, thus severely delaying further launches as the satellites arrived by sea from France and Germany. They were also to drop the nearby bridge into the Kourou River to prevent the components being brought overland from more distant port near Cayenne.

At the launch pads, the approach ramps were to be wrecked with cratering charges because the rockets were transported erect from the final assembly building on roads that could not be more than 10° out of true.

Any rockets already on the pad could not be damaged without the risk of a catastrophic explosion but the same was not true of the sensitive payload sat on top and costing tens of millions of Euros. These could be rendered useless with a hundred Yuan's worth of machine gun rounds.

The key to the operation was that of speed and surprise as the opposition were jungle warfare specialist units, the 3rd Marine Regiment and the Foreign Legions *3e Régiment étranger d'infanterie.* The Legion guarded the space centre and ran France's jungle warfare school at Regina, 80 miles from the space centre and close to the border with Brazil. The marines themselves were all based along the borders with Brazil and Suriname.

The simplest of deception plans had ensured that the French regiments were being kept busy in the interior and along the border with Brazil two hundred miles from the Space Centre.

In time of war the price of gold goes up and an article planted in the popular Portuguese tabloid newspaper *Correio da Manhã* that told of a massive gold strike in French Guiana had been picked up by the Brazilian media and ensured that the always troublesome *Garimpeiros*, the illegal Brazilian miners, were considerably more numerous and more blatant in their trespassing than normal. This led to the Guiana Gendarmeries calling on the Legion and Marines for support as the miners were aggressive and often better armed than the policemen.

3e REI was effectively split in two by the Kourou River with its regimental headquarters near Cayenne airport and one of its two infantry companies at Regina, a few miles inland and in easy reach of the Brazilian border. These retained the regiment's small air detachment of a Puma troop carrying helicopter and a small Gazelle for reconnaissance and communications (the Colonel's taxi).

North of the Kourou, the legionnaires' assault engineers and anti-aircraft detachments guarded the space centre with the remaining infantry company, although a militia-like reserve company made up of former Legionnaires had a platoon in Kourou and two more in Cayenne.

The marines were even more divided, working out of company and sometimes just platoon locations that were dotted along the border. They were completely independent and self-contained sub units though; they walked into the jungle and survived on what they carried on their backs and caches dropped by their own river patrol's rigid raiders.

However, despite their abilities as jungle fighters, they were severely limited in their mobility having no air support and also a rivalry with the Legion that precluded their ever asking for assistance or support from that quarter.

The marines numbered five infantry companies, a Riverine Squadron and a heavy weapons company but they were not set up to quickly react to situations occurring outside their individual companies immediate areas of operations.

Between the small Chinese force and the shore were of course at least one suspected minefield and four surface threats in the form of a pair of *D'Estienne D'Orves* class ASW corvettes and two *L'audacieuse* offshore patrol boats which could make life interesting.

A flight of two Breguet Atlantique IIs had been stationed at Cayenne airport which would likewise serve to keep boredom at bay.

"My task of getting you close enough to launch your submersibles has changed little in real terms, but you are now light one third of the manpower and equipment required to complete your mission." He looked at the soldier and smoothed out the map.

"You are the resident expert on anything that causes blistered feet Captain and I am but a humble squid, as the Americans say." He tapped the map. "As I see it we have more targets than troops now, and for your information we have precisely three hundred miles worth of diesel fuel remaining so I am open to any suggestions you have on our completing the mission as well as a safe withdrawal that precludes walking as a means of escape and evasion." He ended with a grin.

Captain Huaiqing smiled a little smugly.

"We foot sloggers think on our feet even when we are sitting on our arses...it is already done." he removed from inside his shirts breast pocket a sheet of A4 sized paper with the brief outline of an alternative plan.

"It will, I promise you, require only that your delicate navy feet carry you up to your conning tower, and should you choose to stretch your legs on shore then that is up to you."

Li's eyebrows rose, intrigued, but he let the soldier continue.

"You will still endeavor to penetrate the minefields between the old French penal colony islands?"

Li nodded. "The ironically named Islands of Salvation; Royale, St Joseph and of course Devils Island...yes, it is impossible to mine the waters there. The tidal race would unseat mere weighted anchors even if it were deep enough to mine. But at high tide your submersibles have an hour's window to get on the landward side of the islands where it is also unfriendly waters for mining operations."

Li paused, glancing at the SF commander-by-default.

"Can you split your remaining forces and still complete all three primary goals?"

Jie Huaiqing shook his head.

"That would be highly unlikely, if not impossible." He said emphatically.

"*But,* if *Bao*'s detachment attacks the *Soyuz* pad as planned and I take ten men to attack the *Ariane* and *Vega* pads and that leaves eight soldiers that the navy can carry into the mouth of the Kourou to the dock. They blow the bridge as planned and you torpedo the *Fliterland* and burgle the Paris Fire Brigade so we can all go home."

Li coughed in surprise. "Paris?...*what*?"

"Health and Safety laws in the EEC decree that certain facilities be served by firefighting equipment and personnel of a very exacting standard. Those facilities are Class A international airports, fuel storage sites holding more than a quarter million cubic square feet of storage space for flammable gases and liquids, and...space ports."

Li still had a blank expression on his face, clearly not getting the connection and wondering what in the hell Jie was jabbering about EEC regulations for?

"The Paris Fire Brigade was geographically the closest French firefighting unit to meet the strict requirements so they have a fire station at Kourou Space Port *and* a storage tank of high grade diesel fuel for their appliances at the docks because the local stuff cannot be relied upon." He looked very smug as he continued.

"You really can't have rockets blowing up because the fire engine broke down on the way because of dodgy diesel."

Li shook his head. "I bet you were bullied at school for being a swat, weren't you?"

"It was in the intelligence briefing we had back in April." said Huaiqing waving a well-thumbed notebook.

"That doesn't mean you had to write it down."

"I had to...the snoring from all the naval officers was making it too hard to memorise."

All armies have to have a structured method of passing on orders in a way that gets the information across in a logical fashion. Everyone has to know the 'What', 'When', 'Where' and 'How', and who does what, and when, and how.

'Why' does feature, but far less than a career civilian would expect.

Jie had written headings in his notebook, the Chinese military's equivalent of 'Ground', 'Situation', 'Mission', 'Execution', 'Service Support' and 'Command & Signals' with sub-headings to those headings along with sub-headings to the sub-headings. The British call this 'a set of orders' and the process of briefing troops from them is known as an 'O' Group. China trains its leaders to brief troops along fairly similar lines.

'Execution' is all about who does what, and when, and this is a fairly comprehensive section. It includes a sub heading entitled 'Actions on:-' which is meant to cover all eventualities, all possible scenarios that may occur and endanger the successful execution of the mission.

A further hour put finer detail onto the plan and they both agreed that fueling the two submarines before withdrawing to a safe distance and putting a pair of shallow set torpedoes into the *Fliterland* was a long shot, but *Dai* had a good chance of getting the bridge demolition team ashore and sinking the freighter at its moorings.

Li pursed his lips, frowning and looking at the map, folded to show the coastline from Kourou to the border with Suriname. It had been far easier being second-in-command, he decided as he tried to think of alternatives.

Jie reached across and unfolded the map fully.
"I find that looking at the big picture helps me put the little picture into focus, and the only truly accurate way to do that is for you to put yourself in the enemy commander's shoes." A big green mass with few roads once you got ten miles from the coast was what the map represented.

"As the French commander I have nearly one thousand two hundred kilometers of border to guard, including four hundred and fifty kilometers of beaches that are nearly all suitable for amphibious operations of one form or another, and I have *two* regiments, who don't play well together, with which to do it... *aussi facile que la peinture sur l'eau...*'easy as painting on water', as the French say." Jie explained. "The beach will be the easier part of my mission. I won't have to deal with mines, wire and a whole regiment shooting at me...," he grinned broadly and added, "...unless I'm really, really unlucky!"

He would of course proceed with caution as it would be a great shame to have come all this way just to be rumbled at the last by an OP, a sentry or a roving foot patrol.

There was of course the element of the bizarre which had a way of throwing spanners in the works too.

He knew all about the Israeli arrest operation of an Arab militant that had been compromised by five hundred novices and nuns at a convent's beach barbecue.

Some things just aren't catered for in the 'Actions on:-' section of an 'O' Group.

There was another knock on the door of the captain's cabin and this time it was a signaler handing over a slip of message pad.

It was the response to his query to fleet headquarters.

Li read it twice and then with a regretful shake of the head he dismissed the signaler and handed the slip to Captain Huaiqing.

Al Jazeera News report: Argentina claims to have attacked two surfaced submarines south of Falkland Islands. Both vessels allegedly sunk. Salvaged items of wreckage displayed to media appear to be of Russian manufacture along with items of Chinese and Russian uniforms.

Proceed on assumption *Tuan* and *Admiral Potemkin* lost.

On conclusion, scuttle vessels and evade.

"*Bao* needs to be informed of the changes immediately." Jie Huaiqing said

Li nodded in agreement.

"High tide shortly after dusk tonight if memory serves, and I trust that coming ashore high up the beach isn't going to put you in a minefield buried in the sand is it?"

"We will not be bothered by mines on the beach." Huaiqing replied with certainty.

Li looked at him quizzically. Triggering a land mine on the beach would strip away the vital element of surprise that the operation relied upon.

"Another part of the briefing I slept through?"

"A little reptilian told me we will only have bored and sleepy sentries to contend with."

Captain Li shook his head slowly. This soldier was an odd one, always with his nose in a book when not working out in the limited space of the torpedo room, absorbing the most random information like a sponge. Nevertheless, he was intelligent, resourceful, and well respected by his troops.

As this new plan was their only viable option at completing the mission with the remaining resources, he had to trust Jie's abilities.

"Well I hope your reptile informant is correct or we are all screwed." He gathered up the maps and documents and returned them to the safe.

"Tonight would seem to be the night then, Major."

Chapter 2

Lambeth, London

It was curiously quiet in the forest, although Colin could hear the drone of outgoing shells passing far overhead and impacting in the distance.

Looking up through a gap in the foliage he could see the base of the clouds toward the horizon briefly illuminated by the flashes of the shells exploding but it was several seconds before the crump of their detonation reached his ears.

The flashes of light also served to illuminate the shapes of Russian paratroopers silently emerging from the trees across the fire break, the light flashing off the long bayonets attached to their assault rifles. AKs have their own folding bayonet but these were at least two feet in length with serrated edges.

None of his men were opening fire though!

"Enemy to the front...fifty metres...rapid... *FIRE!*"

No one fired a single round despite the Russians being all out of the trees now and clearly visible in the firebreak, and then he saw all his men were Corporal Bethers and their lower jaws were missing.

Their shoulders shook with mirth as they turned to stare at him, the only one of the fighting patrol not dead, the only one not disfigured.

He rose to meet the Russian's bayonet charge and gripped his own rifle firmly, but he felt it crack and then crumble to dust in his grasp.

His men were still shaking in silent laughter and not attempting to help.

"Give me a rifle someone!"

If anything they found his predicament even more hilarious and some were rolling on the ground.

"Here sir, come and get mine!" the voice sounded from behind him.

Robertson stood there holding out his own rifle, his face missing.

"But you are dead, you died yesterday!"

Colin turned back and froze at the sight of a Russian paratrooper charging directly at him, an impossibly long bayonet pointing unwaveringly at his midsection.

Colin tried to move, to dodge out of the way but his legs moved in slow motion.

He screamed aloud as the sharp steel transfixed him, driving through to pin him against the tree behind.

"Nikoli...help me mate!" he called out to his friend who had appeared in front of him.

But Fanny M glared with hatred at the British soldier.

"You killed me Colin, and I was just doing my duty. I saved you and you killed me..."

A nurse leaned over the mumbling, sweating patient, feeling for a pulse on the wrist handcuffed to the metal bedframe in the ICU at King's College Hospital in Lambeth.

Outside the sterile unit, two prison officers sat staring through a large glass window at the nurses' ministrations to their charge.

She took his temperature, noting and updating his progress chart before she moved on, and the prison officers attention returned to the paperback book and Angry Birds that were helping to pass the time.

RAAF Pearce, nr Perth: Western Australia.

The Australian continent was not yet under threat of immediate air attack but blackouts were in force across the country so as not to assist the enemy photo-reconnaissance satellites when they passed overhead.

The F-14 Tomcat entered the circuit with its crew spending a moment to peer down at an earth that was darker than the sky.

A vehicle with hooded headlamps on what had to be the Great Northern Highway on the right and a long and dimly lit train on the left satisfied the pilot that runway '36 Right' of Royal Australian Air Force Base Pearce was down there between them and the controller was not lying.

They were on finals and thirty seconds from the outer marker before the landing lights came on, and then they dimmed perceptibly the moment their wheels had touched the tarmac.

At the end of the aircraft's rollout the runway lights were extinguished, leaving the Tomcat with its engines idling. It sat there in the darkness at the end of the runway until a vehicle drove in front and a 'Follow Me' sign illuminated. The vehicle led the aircraft off the runway and along taxiways at a rate of knots greater than that demanded by the speed limits posted at intervals along the route. To the sides they could vaguely make out the dark outlines of war planes of various nations occupying No.2 Flying Training School's flight lines and dispersals that were meant for the PC-9 trainers. Those trainers were now off on one of the many Australian Air Force airfields that were otherwise occupied just by caretakers, who maintained the runways and limited facilities for times such as these.

Eventually the marshalling truck led the US Navy aircraft toward a track of temporary roadway panels to the open rear of a camouflaged netting hangar that faced back towards the runway.

Nikki Pelham shut down the engines prior to reaching the threshold before the 'hangars' interior, coasting inside and braking to a halt between blast walls created by old shipping containers filled with earth.

Filtered torchlight was the only illumination to assist her down from the cockpit, and she stretched and groaned at almost eight thousand miles worth of stiffness in her back and joints.

"So where's the welcoming committee of hunky Aussie surfers?"

Nikki turned to smile at her RIO.

Lt (jg) Candice LaRue hailed from Alabama and this was her first time outside the States, having only graduated as a Radar Intercept Officer four days earlier.

Nikki and Candice had been paired off at Nellis AFB where the Boneyard airframes were being delivered following refurbishment and upgrades to weapons, navigation and avionics systems. The parking ramps at Nellis had been crammed with early model F-14, 15 and 16s, rubbing wingtips with dozens of previously retired A-10 Thunderbolts, A-6 Intruders, AV-8B Harriers and venerable B-17s, the 'Buffs', known affectionately to the crews as the Big Ugly Fuckers.

Here at RAAF Pearce, some nine thousand five hundred miles from Nellis, a dark shape with an Australian accent bid them collect their gear and step aside as other dark shapes with American accents closed in on their aircraft and began the business of preparing it for flight once more. The external fuel tanks were removed, leaving the aircraft 'clean' until the armourers arrived but the internal fuel tanks were refilled.

All they had carried had been three hundred rounds of 20mm cannon ammunition for their rotary barrelled Vulcan.

Being curious, they had a little wander around and found a bunch of other USN F-14s, which had already been armed up. None of those aircraft were Ds; four were model Bs, including Nikki's, whilst the remainder were even older 'A' models with Pratt & Whitney turbo fans that produced less thrust than their own General Electric power plants. Beyond the F-14s they found the first Australian airframes, in the form of an RAAF Hawk with war shots on its hardpoint's, and a pair of venerable Aussie F111C bombers that were fully bombed up for anti-shipping strikes.

The F111Cs were forty or so years old but upgraded and certainly not looking their years. Australia had supposedly phased them out and replaced them with F/A-18s, but this pair certainly had somehow avoided being buried ignominiously in landfill sites with the rest of Australia's F111 fleet.

"Wow, 'Varks...I thought these were all scrapped?" said Nikki.

A voice from the shadows made them jump.

"A consortium wanted them for air displays; one to fly and one for spares...but the end user certificates were a problem so we kept them mothballed while they sort it out in the courts."

Beneath the port wing they made out two shapes on camp beds. One was snoring softly whilst the other arose.

"Gerry Rich." He said, and right on queue the runway flights came on, illuminating rugged and tanned features along with a broad, raffish smile.

"Flight Lieutenant Gerry Rich, and twenty five percent of the newly reformed 15 Squadron, Royal Australian Air Force at your service...oh, and we call them 'Pigs', not Aardvarks'." He jerked a thumb back over his shoulder at the snoring form. "That's Macca, he's me 'Wizzo', and he's from over your way originally."

"Oh really, where's that then?" asked Nikki.

"Alberta."

"That's Canada, not the USA." laughed Candice.

"Can you drive to the US from Alberta in a single day and without getting yer feet wet?" he queried.

"Sure, but..."

"Around here we'd class that as being next door neighbours."

Candice laughed in a way that told Nikki she was batting her eyelids furiously.

"Does that Mick Dundee style ever get you anywhere?" Nikki asked.

He smiled at Candice but he positively beamed at her pilot.

"Shaving with a Bowie knife right about now would have been hazardous."

Behind them a squeal of tyres and the roar of four Allison turboprops changing pitch to reverse signalled the flare path dimming to barely visible and then extinguishing as the Hercules finished its roll out.

"Lieutenant Commander Pelham, VFA 154, USS *Nimitz*." Nikki said by way of introduction, very formally and not leaving an opening for him to be otherwise.

"Lieutenant Candice La Rue, but you can call me Candy if you want." another voice wishfully added.

"Have you got a first name to go with that, Lieutenant Commander?"

"She'll tell you that it's *Ma'am,* but she'll answer to Nikki." said Candice.

The taxiing aircraft, a Royal New Zealand Air Force C130 drowned out what Nikki said to her RIO as it past and she firmly steered her away by the arm and back toward their Tomcat.

"You got to admit he's cute?"

"Nah." Said Nikki "Too much twisted steel and sex appeal." But she looked back anyway.

When the ground crew were done they all crowded into the back of a truck for the journey to the base cookhouse, and this was open for business 24/7 according to the ground crews.

Australian steak and eggs tastes pretty much the same as American steak and eggs but the fries were called 'chips', not that it mattered as neither aviator had eaten since somewhere over the mid Pacific and then the sandwiches had been curling up at the edges in the hot sun that shone through the Perspex.

It wasn't until the plates were empty that Nikki found her eyes drooping.

There were no comfortable barracks for the two tired aviators, and they were shown through a side door and along a short pathway to a small building, guided through the darkness by an armed RAAF corporal with a small torch. They were the only female crew there and as such shared a room which held nothing more than two canvas camp beds, plus pillows and blankets.

"Keep your flight gear handy, if you hear a siren it's an air raid warning and also the order to scramble...reveille is at 0600 and breakfast is at 0630 at the building two down from here. The Dunny's at the end of the hall...g'night."

Once the door had been closed they had looked at one another and shrugged. Candice rolled into the blankets upon one of the camp beds and fell asleep almost immediately, but Nikki lay staring at the ceiling for a while.

When Nikki had arrived at Nellis she had been feeling pretty low, and not without cause. A weeks' worth of tears and utter disbelief at losing her family in such a shocking manner was not nearly enough time to mourn and come to terms with it.

She had other commitments too and these kept her from wallowing in self-pity at the bottom of a bottle.

Arlington National Cemetery was too close to the Washington fall-out zone and had been closed until some future intensive clean up could be undertaken, so Chubby's funeral had taken place at his hometown near Detroit.

Someone had tipped off the press that she would be present, so she had spared his family, and herself, the embarrassment by telling the cab driver to continue on past the cemetery and the assembled circus outside. She had telephoned her apologies to Chubby's parents from the airport before catching a flight to her own hometown where she had avoided the media by laying a wreath on her father's grave at night. There was not, as yet, any final resting place for her mother or younger brother whose bodies had yet to be recovered and identified.

The navy public relations department would dearly have loved to have paraded Nikki to the media as the female warrior who had downed four confirmed enemy aircraft and survived the destruction of the *John F Kennedy* battle group, but the circumstances surrounding the death of her father had made that impossible, even had she been willing.

Nikki had declined the navy's offer of extended leave, choosing instead to return to active duty where she reasoned she would be too busy to dwell on her loss; however any ideas she had harboured about an immediate re-assignment had proved overly optimistic.

For several days Nikki had found herself kicking her heels in the B.O.Q at Nellis. The trouble with Bachelor Officers Quarters when you were in transit through a base was that they were basically four walls and a ceiling, a motel room without the TV. She had been assigned an aircraft but lacked both a RIO and a carrier to fly it to.

For the most part she had kept to herself, and either the vibes her mood projected or the unjustified suspicion that others regarded her as a Jonah served to deter company. Either way, the USAF pilot's, Marine and Navy aviators who also awaited assignments kept their distance from the newly promoted Lieutenant Commander who wore a face like a week's worth of wet Mondays.

Two nights previously in the Officers Club, she had been sat on her own and trying to ignore the conversation going on nearby. A quartet of reservists were trying to out bemoan one another on the woes of being plucked from the cockpits of 747s and finding themselves back in uniform.

From the far side of the club had come derisive laughter and the chant of 'bullshit', which had pulled her away from her own brooding thoughts. With some annoyance she had at first turned to see what the commotion was about and then had been drawn toward the large knot of men and women who had gone quiet again as they listened to whomever was sat in their midst.

"I'm telling you straight, every time one of the bastards got on my tail they overshot when I put the anchors on, and I shot them in the arse."

"Five bandits?" asked one of the onlookers.

"In the same fight?" another asked

"Och aye, one after the other. Bang, bang, wallop, wallop, wallop!"

Nikki had eased through the throng and seen Sandy sat at a table with a dozen brews in front of him and a vivacious Afro-American honey sat on his lap. Clad in skin-tight jeans, denim shirt and cowboy boots she was the only one in the room not in uniform and Nikki assumed the Fleet Air Arm pilot had smuggled her on to the base.

"Hey, Sandy."

Sandy looked at her smirking at him and rolled his eyes, his face dropping.

"Hey, Nikki."

Nikki addressed Sandy's audience.

"I had the misfortune to be stuck in a life raft for several days with this guy, and I was ready to feed myself to the sharks rather than hear that line another time...only back then it was *two* Mig-31s, not five."

The beers sat in front of Sandy were obviously war beers, tokens of appreciation for his service and warrior status, and their donors reclaimed them swiftly from a protesting Highlander.

"Och, come on now guys...the heat of battle and all that..."

Even the beer in his hand was snatched away

Sandy's audience departed, leaving him crestfallen.

"Well thank you very much indeed Nikki, and after I shared the warmth of my Gaelic heart to keep you alive too!"

She bent to plant a peck on the top of his head.

"Your liver will thank me when you're in your fifties, Sandy." She took a now vacant seat at the table and they caught up on events since arriving at Pearl.

Sandy had discovered that the Royal Navy's Fleet Air Arm currently had over twenty pilots apiece waiting to fly their dwindling inventory of Sea Harriers. So, as he was still shown as attached to the US Pacific Fleet he had offered his services to the Navy and would be ferrying an AV-8B out to the USS *Essex* very early the next day, via a stopover in Hawaii.

"So are you a ferry pilot or something?"

"No Nikki, I'm joining one of your VMA Harrier squadrons. I'll be showing US Navy aviators how the Fleet Air Arm does it."

"VMA doesn't mean Navy Scotty, they're Marines."

"Oh, grief!" Sandy groaned.

"It'll do you good." Nikki had said. "Spending all of your off duty hours running around, and around, and around the flight deck with a pack on your back."

Sandy looked crestfallen.

"Sounds just like our marine pilots, wasting time by training to walk to war when they've got perfectly good aircraft to carry them there at a fraction of the effort."

She hadn't seen or spoken Sandy since the *Hood* had docked, so she was gratified to learn that he at least had been at Chubby's funeral.

Very little was said about her late RIO, she had done all her crying aboard the *Hood*, and she had learnt that the Brits deal with the death of a colleague in combat in a very stoical fashion. There are no group hugs; no tears spilt into one's beer, and in fact little outward displays of grief. They raise a glass to toast their fallen friends' memory and that is all until the war is over, when the business of proper mourning begins.

Sandy's friend had re-seated herself on a chair and listened quietly while they talked, merely nodding a 'hi' to Nikki when Sandy had introduced her as

"And this is Candy, she's delicious."

Not until Sandy had excused himself to visit the john had the girl really spoken.

"So you're Triple 'A' then?"

Nikki had been unsure what the she was talking about, but if Sandy's line shooting had included herself in his scoring then she was going to do some facial rearranging once he got back.

"Excuse me?"

"Lt Cmdr. Nikki Pelham, four kills...Almost an Ace."

Much relieved, she had allowed a laugh to escape.

"So Lt Cmdr. you know Sandy pretty well, huh?"

"I guess as well as you can after sharing a life raft, a sub full of sailors and a three birth sailing boat occupied by six."

"Okay, then at least that part of his story isn't total BS, but did he really disarm and capture a Chinese aviator?"

Nikki laughed again.

"Sorry but no, the guy had already surrendered to an elderly English couple before they picked us up. There was absolutely no hand-to-hand combat involved. The guy was just a kid really, not much different from one of us."

She saw Sandy emerged from the door leading to the head and decided to find out what relationship he had with this snake-hips-in-denim civilian before he returned.

"So, are you and Sandy, *good* friends?"

"We only hooked up this afternoon, but if I see you at breakfast I'll let you know." Candice had added a wink for emphasis, so on the premise that two's company and three's a crowd, Nikki had left them to it and retired for an early night.

The phone in her room had woken her just after she'd dropped off to sleep; informing her that she had a RIO, one Lt (jg) LaRue. C and they were to be in the briefing room at 1000hrs. This was to be her last night at Nellis AFB.

Sandy hadn't been at breakfast in the mess hall, he had flown out at five a.m. Nikki went easy on the coffee and ate only toast and jelly, natural bodily functions were no respecters of long range flights and she loathed the pee tube. Having taken the edge off her appetite, she picked up her small canvas bag of belongings and headed out.

The shock of finding Candice, now in flight suit and sipping coffee, had caused Nikki to pause half way through the briefing room door, and check that she had in fact found the right room.

On seeing Nikki, Candice put the cup down and stood to deliver a smart salute.

"Ma'am, Lieutenant LaRue. I have been assigned as your Radar Intercept Officer, Ma'am."

She had looked over at the briefing officer who had given a wry smile, shooting his eyebrows up in confirmation that this was no joke.

They had been briefed on their route through the air defence zones, radio frequencies, IFF codes and the tanker plan, where Nikki had kept an eye on her RIO, ensuring she was getting every detail down correctly and being reassured that this girl whom she had suspected the previous evening of being some kind of aviator groupie, seemed to have the competence she would have hoped for.

It had not been until after they had disconnected from a tanker 500 miles off the West Coast and Nikki had set a course for the tanker they would meet several hours hence that they could relax.

"So tell me lieutenant, how did that hot date go?" There had been a few seconds before a reply had been forthcoming.

"Begging your pardon ma'am, but that friend of yours is one sick puppy."

It had taken her back a bit.

"Say what?"

"My momma didn't bring me up to get butt naked with no cross-dresser with a shiv." Nikki had been lost for words until Candice had explained.

"We sneaked back to his room and he went into the bathroom, so I got comfortable, if you know what I mean?"

Nikki had a fair idea.

"You got naked?"

"Yes'm...and then he came out the bathroom in a skirt..."

The scene, or how it must have been, jumped into Nikki's mind.

"A kilt."

"Whatever ma'am, but he had some dead animal hanging off the front of it...."

"A Sporran."

"Okay, it looked like road kill, but if you say it was a dead Sporran, then that's what it was. He had a knife too, a shiv, stuck in the top of one of his socks."

"It's called a Dirk, Lieutenant...Sandy was wearing traditional Highland dress."

"Well I don't know why their women folks put up with it. A man should be a man and not go dressing up in women's things!"

Nikki killed the intercom and sat there with her shoulders shaking in helpless laughter for several minutes.

When she had gotten it out of her system she'd flicked the intercom back on.

"Hey, LaRue?"

"Yes, ma'am?"

"They call you Candy or Candice?"

"I prefer Candice, Ma'am."

"Okay, so do I, so from now on unless there's brass or unfamiliar company about, then I'm just Nikki, okay?"

She had decided that this RIO would do but she had ensured the intercom was switched off before saying a final goodbye to her previous RIO.

Across the room Candice murmured something in her sleep that snapped Nikki out of her reflective mood and then she too closed her eyes and slept.

RAF Gütersloh, Casualty embarkation area:

Despite the pounding head, throbbing shoulder and broken ribs that made each breath painful, Ray Tessler felt like a fraud as he sat amongst more seriously wounded men and women who waited for the Royal Air Force Tri-Star air ambulance to begin loading. He reasoned it out for himself in his head, frequently, that with broken fingers he couldn't handle a weapon so he would be a liability on the firing line, but having told himself that he took one look at a seriously burned corporal from the Royal Tank Regiment, hooked up to saline drips on a gurney nearby, and felt like a fraud all over again.

The hospitals nearest the fighting were shedding themselves of those already in the beds, in order to cater for those that would soon require them. Ray was going back to the UK on a civilian aircraft pressed into service to evacuate those wounded who didn't need the air ambulance facilities, but they shared the embarkation area, a large hangar that the heaters struggled to warm.

A door opened at the back of the hangar to admit more evacuees, and Ray saw a friendly face, that of the driver of the Warrior he'd been in when he'd been injured. Ray raised an arm to wave, and immediately regretted it, but the Guardsman saw him and made his way over, one arm heavily bandaged and limping as he went.

Ray had come to the battalion as a battlefield replacement, vacating a desk job at RHQ to join the unit just before it was relieved at Magdeburg, for its advance to contact towards the Soviet airborne drop zones. The Warriors driver on the other hand, had been with the battalion for three years and had seen every fight it had been in since the start of the war.

"How you doing, sir?"

"Not bad. I feel like I've been stuffed into a washing machine and put through a fast spin cycle, but otherwise I'm okay...how's yourself?"

"They dug a half dozen bits of metal out of me, but apparently the grenade that did it was far enough away it'll just leave some interesting scars I can blag a few free beers off of in the pub back home."

Ray nodded.

"You going to St George's too?"

The young Guardsman looked at the label tied though the buttonhole of a breast pocket on his combat jacket.

"Yes sir, looks that way but the doctor thinks it shouldn't be long before I get a few days leave."

Ray had been told something similar, and there was nothing he was looking forward to more than holding his wife and kids again. St Georges' hospital in south London was only a few miles from the family's married quarters, and if for some reason the doctors there kept him in then his wife could easily find her way there.

The line for the seriously wounded began to move as RAF personnel wheeled the patients out to the waiting aircraft, and an hour later it was their turn.

Ray managed to get himself seated beside the other Coldstreamer, over the objections of an Airman with a list attached to a clipboard. Ray switched on his Sergeant Major persona and the airman hurried away, amending the written seating plan with a biro as he went.

The flight into Gatwick airport passed swiftly, but they found they still had to go through Customs when they got there. Ray and the Guardsman had only the dirty and rather ragged combat gear they wore, but they still had to go through the 'Nothing to declare' channel and submit to a body search to ensure they didn't have some lethal souvenir from the battlefields concealed about them before they joined the queue being checked off at the exit to the Customs hall.

It wasn't as if anyone could have gone missing between Germany and Gatwick, but Forces Movement Control has their way of doing things, and that includes head counts at every opportunity, checking the face and the photo on the individuals I.D card, the MOD Form 90, matched the details on the clipboards.

Ray didn't pay any attention to the military policemen stood near the exit until his name was checked off the list by a Staff Sergeant with the cartwheel emblem of Movements worn on an armband. The man looked over his shoulder at the nearest RMP.

"Got another one here, corporal."

He had not returned Ray's I.D card, but had stuck it under the spring clip of his clipboard instead.

Two RMP lance corporals started towards him, and Ray asked the Staff Sergeant what he had meant by 'another one'.

"Just go with them when they get here, sarn't major, sir." The Staff Sergeant put up a hand to rest on Ray's chest, preventing him from passing the checkpoint.

Bringing his good hand up to the restraining hand on his chest, Ray curled his fingers around the Staff Sergeants thumb and bent it backwards, just enough to elicit an "Ow!" from its owner.

"I said, *what do you mean by 'another one'*, Staff?" He kept a hold on the thumb, adding a touch more pressure.

"Coldstreamers...fuck sake sarn't major, leggo of my hand!"

Ray let go of the thumb and the Movements NCO tucked the clipboard under one arm in order to massage the offended digit. "The RMP are picking up all members of 1CG when they come back to the UK...I don't know why and I don't think they do either."

The RMP NCOs arrived and one stood by Ray without speaking whilst the other spoke to the Movements Staff Sergeant, discussing Ray as if he wasn't present. He consulted a list of his own, and upon it were two columns, naming those who had been at Leipzig and those who had joined after that particular battle. Finally he took the I.D card from the Staff Sergeants clipboard.

The figure in the ragged combat jacket and trousers, stained with blood and ingrained with dirt did not look a lot like the picture on the I.D card.

The left side of Ray's face was swollen and bruised black and blue, with shades of yellow thrown in. Somewhere between the makeshift mine going off under the Warrior and here, Ray's solitary badge of rank, a smaller version of an RSMs coat of arms, had been torn from the front of his smock, but his rank was clearly displayed on the lists both the Staff Sergeant and the RMP carried.

"Is your regimental number, 27130087?"

Ray looked at the military policeman and felt his temper start to rise, but he didn't reply.

"I said, is your number 27130087?"

The line of servicemen from the flight had come to a halt, and whilst some were impatient to get on there were others obviously curious about what was unfolding.

CSM Tessler felt embarrassed about being questioned in such a fashion by an arrogant junior NCO who's own uniform was pressed and pristine, having been nowhere near a battlefield.

Ray's companion on the flight, the young Guardsman, had now been stopped by the same staff sergeant, who again signalled to more of the waiting military policemen. However, having double-checked his identity another RMP lance corporal withdrew a pair of handcuffs from a pocket, and made to put them on the Guardsman's wrists.

Confused at the turn of events the Guardsman resisted and a small scuffle broke out, during which the wounded soldier let out a cry of pain as his injured arm was grabbed.

This was too much for Ray who pushed past his own pair of RMPs, who were still waiting for an answer to their question, and placed himself between the Guardsmen and the RMP trying to cuff him.

"This man, *unlike yourselves*, has fought in every one of our brigades actions since day one of the war...so you *will* treat him with some fucking respect or I'm going to start back-squading teeth!"

This young NCO wasn't used to having his authority questioned. He hadn't managed to cuff the Guardsman either, who had managed to get free and now stood a half dozen paces away looking angry and not a little frightened. Another ragged form had placed itself in the way, obstructing him and he was now in no mood to mess about. Setting his feet, his hands started to close into fists.

Ray wasn't exactly in his best fighting form, although as he saw the RMP prepare to take a swing he resolved to go down throwing punches and to hell with Queens Regulations, but he was reprieved when their audience began making angry noises at the treatment of wounded soldiers by the forces of military law and order. Surging forward they placed themselves in front of the wounded Guardsman, and Ray found himself flanked by men who like himself carried injuries from recent combat, but who were fully prepared to give the Red Caps a good kicking if they forced the issue.

Angry jeers brought a young lieutenant from a side office where he took in the tableau of impending mayhem, and cursed himself for not being present when the flight had arrived. His RMP detachment was made up of young men and women rushed through training at Chichester and then given their single stripe at its conclusion. The Corps more experienced soldiers were across the channel, keeping the MSRs in operation and even manning traffic points in the middle of air raids. His detachment lacked seasoning and experience; otherwise this confrontation would never have come to pass. As he viewed the servicemen facing off against his young military policemen he noticed the figure stood front and centre. Despite his appearance he had the air of command about him.

The RMP lieutenant pulled on his beret and he strode over to the exit.

"What's going on here, and who are you?" He addressed the question to Ray, who gritted his teeth as he pulled his feet in as best he could, coming to attention and identifying himself, before explaining what had occurred.

The RMP officer let him finish before swivelling around to take in the junior NCO with the handcuffs, and then turning back.

"It seems that someone got a little ahead of themselves...however, we have orders to detain you for questioning about matters of which I have not been given the details."

"Thank you sir." Ray answered, impressed with the RMP officers calm disposition when a small riot had been in the offing just moments previously.

"Are we under arrest, sir?"

"Not to my knowledge, sarn't major...but that may well change later once we've handed you over to SIB." Looking levelly at Ray he went on.

"I really don't know what this is about, but if I were you I would get legal representation before I spoke a word to *anyone*, if you get my drift?"

Ray looked into his eyes and could see written upon them that contrary to what had just been said, this lieutenant had a pretty damn good idea about what was going on.

Nodding his thanks Ray first turned to the lance corporal with the handcuffs.

"Put those things away before I stick 'em where they'll smell!" He then turned to the first pair of RMPs, snatching back his I.D card and pointing a stiff digit at his interrogator.

"And in future, Lance *Corporal*, whenever you address a Warrant Officer you'll stick a 'Sir' somewhere in the sentence, or I'll drop kick you into the nearest empty cell...understood?"

There were few civilians out and about at the airport, but those who were present were all maintenance workers, only Heathrow catered to those few who still needed to travel by air. They had seen returning soldiers being escorted by the military police on a number of occasions and it had lost its novelty value by now, so the sight of Ray and the Guardsman being driven away to Her Majesty's Military Corrective Training Centre at Colchester attracted little interest.

1 Mile east of Devils Island: French Guiana.

Twenty two gallons of water is shipped daily aboard the Juliett class submarine *Dai* when in the tropics and all of it as a result of condensation even when she is submerged, mainly in the bow where the hull was coolest. Captain Li knew this as it was one of the myriad of statistics associated with being captain. It was flushed out of the bilge each day after being measured.

No doubt one day a discrepancy in that amount would be the first clue to some mechanical fault.

He made a mental note to check on how much was in the bilge tomorrow because the whole crew were hushed as they listened to the sound of propellers approaching from the starboard side.

With the memory of the depth charging by the Brazilian frigate still fresh, even the coolest calmest crew members were already breaking into a sweat.

Dai was at 200 feet and moving forward at a bare three knots with all ancillary equipment shut down to minimise their audible profile, or Silent Running to the picture house audiences.

The quiet within the vessel served to magnify the sound of the approaching enemy corvette. The water being thrashed by the blades driving it towards them, louder and louder with each revolution of its propellers, the audible thump of the bow smashing through the waves along with the higher pitched whine from the ships twin screws was causing a nervous gesture here and there.

Eyes fixed on the starboard bulkheads and traced the sound, heads raising as it drew closer and louder, and then they were staring straight upwards as the corvette was overhead, the whine of the screws now almost as shrill as a dentist drill, their whole bodies braced and ready to flinch, but no warning call of depth charges hitting the water came from the sonar shack. The heads continue to follow the sound to port as it forged away, diminishing in volume as well as in threat, leaving a hundred sets of gratefully relaxing shoulders clad in sweat darkened shirts.

Li had no doubt that there were nervous eyes watching *Bao's* bulkheads also, even though they had yet to suffer the character building and brown adrenaline producing experience of a depth charge attack.

Bao was off their port quarter and in the process of moving into position a quarter mile behind them as *Dai* aimed for the gap that lay between the three islands that formed an unequally sided triangle off the coast of French Guiana.

The submersible was still riding piggy-back as they edged closer to the islands, seeking both traditionally chain anchored mines and bottom seated magnetic mines.

The Juliett carried shortwave ultra-low frequency sonar that was first devised by a clever man in a shed as a means of avoiding reversing ones car into walls or other cars when parking. The invention was then stolen by an even cleverer lady who adapted it as a tool for ships and submarines to find sea mines without being overheard at a distance by the people who had planted them. China called its own pirated version the Mouse Roar.

For thirty minutes they cautiously closed on the notorious islands.

"There isn't such a thing as a stealth mine is there?" whispered Jie who was now clad in black wet suit, and with his hands and features painted for war, daubed dark green, grey and brown with greasy waterproof camouflage paint.

"Thank you *so* much for inserting that seed of doubt." The captain murmured. "But no, there is not."

There was a long pause as the soldier thought about that.

"But if there was, we wouldn't know about it would we, because they are stealthy, right?"

The captain glared at him.

Jie shrugged. "Just saying."

They crept on in silence, feeling their way closer to the land.

Just as Li was beginning to think the French were very lax with their security an urgent voice declared otherwise.

"*Conn, sonar*...stationary object, range zero six five, bearing two nine nine...classify as anchored sea mine...conn sonar, stationary object range zero nine nine...bearing three one five, classify as anchored sea mine...conn, sonar...stationary object..."

"Both engines back slow together...!"

Already barely making headway the *Dai* lost way almost instantly and backed off from danger. Behind her the *Bao* did likewise as its hydrophones tracked the Juliett and heard the brief flurry, knowing what it must mean.

...all stop, helmsmen hold this position."

He and the Exec studied the chart with Jie Huaiqing close by.

"Well we knew they probably had one and indeed they have, off our starboard quarter..." Li carefully marked the mines discovered by the Mouse Roar sonar. Li suspected that going active with their main search sonar would reveal a dense minefield and possibly one that also contained magnetic proximity mines.

"Bring us slowly up to sixty feet...raise ECM."

They remained there for ten minutes with the ECM sensors listening to localised radio and microwave transmissions as well as feeling for radar energy.

The ECM board warrant officer swivelled in his seat.

"Captain, four brief bursts of microwave transmissions, all from landward and all digitally encrypted, otherwise the board is clear, no radar energy seaward or landward at this time."

Jie looked at the chronometer above the chart table; it was set to Beijing time. He did a quick mental sum and smiled to himself.

"Exactly 7pm local time, five digitally encrypted transmissions..." he muttered and then raised his voice enough to address the ECM operator.

"Range and bearings?...I'll bet the first and fifth transmissions were from the same point inland and the other three are spread out along the shore, back in the undergrowth somewhere?"

The two naval officers were watching him quizzically.

"Encrypted microwave transmissions of short duration, that'll be from man-portable battlefield radio sets." He enlightened them. "Radio checks on the hour to observation posts or patrols watching the beach."

"Major?" responded ECM. "Approximate ranges only, based on signal strength..." he rattled off four sets of ranges and bearings which the captain marked on the chart.

"I think you were right Captain." said the Exec. "If he'd gone to my school I'd definitely have bullied the smug, swatty bastard."

Jie grinned, and noted the approximated locations whilst the captain stepped over to the periscopes.

"Raise 'Search'." It slid smoothly up and he grasped the handles before pressing his face against the eye shield, switching to lo-lite TV and swinging the device around through 360°, 'Dancing with the Grey lady' as it is known, his hand cranking the prism elevation upwards as he looked for aircraft as well as surface craft. After several revolutions he was satisfied they were in no immediate danger and turned to study the land.

During their journey north along the Atlantic coast of South America Li had noted the twinkling lights on the shores of the neutral countries, Argentina, Uruguay and Brazil. In towns, cities and ports the lights blazed away, illuminating shipping to landward of the *Dai*, silhouetting them against that carefree absence of blackout regulations. It had been enough to make a grown predator weep, all that tonnage there for the sinking but being unable to do so without compromising the mission.

Here though, French Guiana was in total darkness, a sinister dark mass on the horizon.

He took a step backwards.

"Down 'scope, lower the ECM, come left to two zero zero ...port motor back slow, starboard motor ahead slow...now slow ahead together, helm amidships."

Again they inched forward and Li stared hard at the chart as if trying to divine whether the French had also mined the deep water to seaward of the ancient volcano that Ile Diable and her two sisters sat atop of.

"I assume we know that there isn't some kind of enemy position or listening post on those islands?" asked the Exec.

"It's a bit late now to be worrying about that, but no, the islands are directly beneath the launch path of the rockets and were abandoned because of that...as our resident anorak on western health and safety laws can confirm?"

Captain Huaiqing's blacked up face suddenly sprouted a set of pearly white teeth.

"Conn, sonar, sharp rise in the sea bed...six hundred feet... five fifty...five hundred...." The granite pinnacle arose steeply from the depths, its sides almost sheer in places.

"All stop."

"Conn, sonar, *Bao* is matching us Captain."

"Thank you" answered Li. "Raise the ECM... raise 'Search'."

Again the area was clear of detectable threats and as the periscope slid back down again Li looked at the chronometer.

"Half an hour to high tide Major, and there are no mines in the vicinity." He turned and faced the soldier. "The French had a six hundred foot long cable car affair running from Royale to Devils Island as the tidal race is too fierce for boats in the channel so don't hang about...and the very best of luck to you Major." He held out his hand.

"Thank you for the excellent job of getting us here Captain, and whether or not we succeed I hope to see you on the dock in six hours." The handshake was brief but firm and Li hoped it did not betray the guilt he felt.

If the troops failed to take the pads out of operation then he would not be seeing Jie or his men again. His orders on that count were precise, allowing no room for manoeuvre and were marked for his eyes only.

Four of the troopers entered the submersible through the after hatch and Jie Huaiqing with five men departed one at a time from the escape hatch just aft the conning tower to attach themselves to its outer hull.

The submersible's batteries, motor and air supply had been tested regularly on their marathon journey from China, and its pilot ran through the start-up, instruments lighting up one at a time until the board was fully lit with green lights over 'Air', 'Battery', 'Propulsion' and 'Manoeuvring'.

Jie rapped on the submersibles hull with his knifes hilt to signal they were all secured outside upon which the crew of the *Dai* heard the sound of the securing clamps releasing. The sound magnified by the water.

Once the Mouse Roar sonar showed the submersible was clear and entering the channel between the three small islands *Dai* remained in place knowing that *Bao* was launching her submersible too.

To their left, the south of the islands was almost certainly a continuance of the dense minefield but there was no need to seek it out now.

Li had been correct; the channel was the chink in the armour protecting the satellite launch facilities.

It took several minutes for the second special forces team to reach them and then pass into the channel also, after which the passive sonar told them *Bao* was moving back out to sea and *Dai* followed.

Major Huaiqing was attached to the casing of the small vessel by a rubberised carabiner and a firm grip on the foot and hand holds as he watched the submarine that had been 'home' for six weeks disappear into the ocean blackness. He gripped the regulator between his teeth, breathing calmly into his re-breather as he returned his gaze to the way ahead, where lay the channel between the small islands that had been more the gaoler of the prisoners incarcerated there than any gun totting prison guard. But surely he thought, they must have thought the risk worthwhile at such times as this when standing on the shore watching the maelstrom relent twice a day?

The submersibles spot lamps snapped on as the mouth of the channel approached to show rock walls covered by razor edged barnacles that would flay the living flesh from any unfortunate swimmer caught in the currents grip, and then he was startled by the black soulless eyes and evil, jagged fanged grin of a Tiger shark that entered the circle of light created by the spot lamps. It deferentially ignored the submersible that was larger than itself, and the Chinese troopers clinging to it like pilot fish.

That at least answered his question.

Beyond the channel his submersible ceased forward motion and held station awaiting the second submersible to emerge safely. It appeared after a little more than five minutes and turned north, to head parallel to the shoreline for fifteen miles.

The Captains submersible though came to a heading of 280° and continued for the shore.

An hour later the submersible settled to the bottom well short of the low water mark, its purpose fulfilled.

According to the ECM data they were now at worst about five hundred metres from a Foreign Legion O.P

Captain Huaiqing slipped out of the rebreather while still submerged but retained the weights belt about his waist for the moment to prevent bobbing to the surface. He partially emerged from the sea to lie in the surf with just passive night goggles and the muzzle of his French FAMAS assault rifle visible.

A downpour of tropical dimensions was pelting down from above raising a low lying haze of flying spray as the droplets burst upon impacting the sea and already sodden sand. It roared down, smiting the wide palm fronds like a constant drum roll. Even with PNGs, passive night goggles, the visibility was greatly reduced.

The beach was exactly as expected from both satellite photographs and tourists holiday snaps incorporated in the original briefing back in China.

Pale grey cadavers lay strewn and entangled upon the beach where storms had tossed them, their rigid bodies going brittle in the intense heat of the sun, in the seasons when it shone. These once proud trees did not hail from close hereabouts though. Overhanging the myriad rivers and waterways that drained the South American rainforest they had eventually succumbed to age or to undermining by flood waters, the rivers carried them away, out to sea eventually and thence to a timber cemetery such as this.

Once upon a time the shore had not been so crowded. Once it has been sun dried, the dead wood made excellent fuel for cooking fires at the many hamlets and fishing villages along the coast of French Guiana. The remains of the villages between Kourou and the border with Suriname were now as grey and lifeless as the trees on the beaches, the inhabitants moved on in the interests of un-burst eardrums, such was the thunder of the rocket launches.

Two men crawled slowly forwards, hesitating only once to peer at their commander.

Jie Huaiqing gave them a reassuring nod and they squirmed forwards through the sand, wasting no time looking for mines or trip wires. The scouts disappeared into the jungle lining the shore and separated, searching left and right for any waiting legionnaires manning OP's or laying in ambush.

After a few minutes one returned to give the all clear and they all of them still in the shallows shed their weights belts, hoisted heavy, vacuum sealed bags and sprinted from the sea heedless of their footing.

Nobody with half a brain would waste mines on a beach where a few thousand heavy Leatherback turtles were going to be digging holes to lay their eggs.

Once in cover they stripped off the wet suits and opened the bags, pulling on boots, camouflage clothing, weighty bergen's and combat equipment.

Captain Huaiqing took a fat barrelled 7.62 calibre handgun from the bag. The Norinco Type 64 was purpose built for silent dirty work at greater distances than a sound suppressed 9mm. He looped a lanyard through the trigger guard and hung it suspended around his neck, tucking it out of sight down the inside of his smock.

Next Jie pulled on a green beret, setting it just so. He had practiced this many times in the dark onboard the *Dai* during the voyage.

The last item out of the waterproof bag was his map case. A French military map of the area and a wildlife reference book were squeezed inside. Expertly forged orders authorising their presence within the security compound were tucked inside the pages of the book, fastidiously clean and uncrumpled. A legionnaire may drag himself out of the jungle in rags with six months' worth of beard, too weak to salute and no one will think the less of him, but to produce an illegible *Ordres écrits*? Unforgiveable! It was part of what made the legion different. Romantics continue to seek out the recruiters, and grizzled recruiters continue to sort out the romantics.

"Fools fight for idéaux, professionals fight for Orders!"

P.C Wren has a lot to answer for.

The *orders* are everything to the legionnaire, the romantic ideals, simply nothing.

In the wet and dripping jungle near the ocean the professionals of another country's army adopt a veneer of that which defines a legionnaire for the purposes of subterfuge.

"Remember, any civilians we meet we treat with polite disdain and any army, navy, air force or marines encountered will be ignored as if they are a sub species, comprendre?" It would be completely out of character for a legionnaire to so much as greet a member of any countries military with any level of civility.

"Oui, mon Chef!"

He paused for a moment to hold the PNG's to his eyes, looking them over and checking the prized *Béret vert* on their heads was sat correctly as any true legionnaires would be.

It was not unusual of course for Orientals to be serving in the Legion, but possibly a whole squad could raise a curious comment. However there was nothing else for it but to trust in luck and a little bluff to get onto the site.

Tucking away the PNG's he nodded approvingly and then lifted a heavy bergen onto his shoulders.

"Bonne."

Their communications were a problem in a country this size with only ESA, the military and the gendarmeries having access to anything above cell phones. Any transmission made could come from a relatively small number of known sources, so secure encrypted transmissions were out. They would stand out like a sore thumb. Likewise plain speech, that would also register as being 'off' so no *"Broadsword calling Danny Boy?"* on the air waves and microwaves tonight.

Using the cellular system was too easily spiked by its being simply turned off once the French woke up to the fact they were under attack.

The solution was pre-arranged text in apparently accidental transmissions of seemingly innocuous material, the greatly annoying 'open carrier', 'open channel', or 'Permanent Send' momentarily, if you prefer. Jie's chosen offering was a classic, of the musical variety, as he informed Senior Sergeant Yen, the unit's warrant officer and the senior amongst the eight troops remaining with the *Dai* that they were ashore without incident and proceeding.

Jie sang softly to himself apparently absent minded and depressed the transmit button on his Thales tactical radio.

"...La mer...Qu'on voit danser le long des golfes clairs
A des reflets d'argent...La mer...Des reflets changeants
Sous la pluie..."

He certainly did not do Charles Trénet full justice but following a calculated pause a single flick of Senior Sergeant Yen's radio transmit button acknowledged receipt of the message.

Jie turned directly away from the sea, heading towards the highway known as Route de l'Espace.

"Allons-y!"

Kourou Map and Key

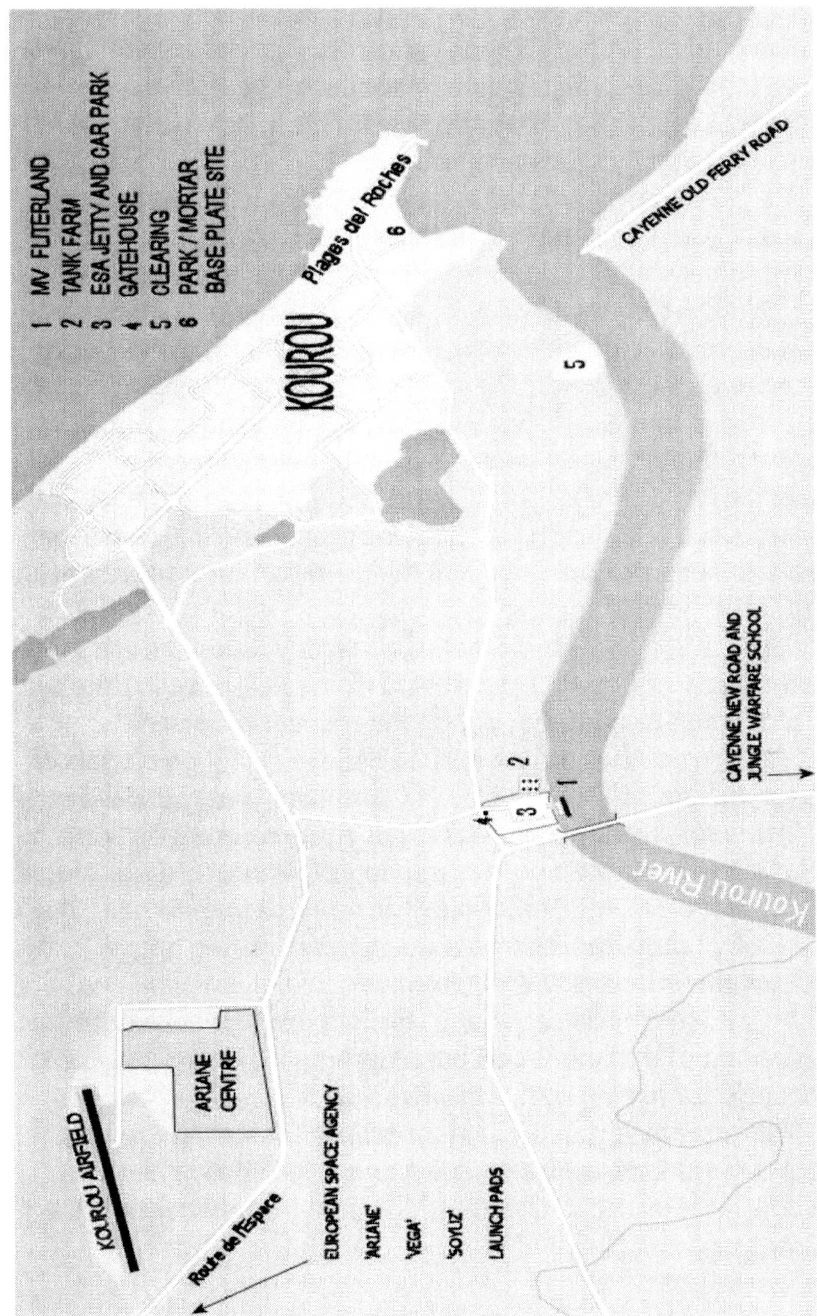

The Kourou estuary: French Guiana.

It would be with extreme caution that Li approached Paracaibo Wharf, the European Space Agency dock sitting three and a half miles downriver from the coastal town of Kourou at the river's northern lip.

No intelligence updates had been received for over a month. The last they had received merely stated that pair of Atlantiques was at that time believed to have been attached to the colony defences along with a pair of corvettes. There was nothing to indicate where the French naval flotilla was basing out of, either Kourou or the capital? The colony's main port of Dégrad des Cannes, which had grown to become the southern suburb of Cayenne, housed a permanent detachment of marines in a barracks beside a jetty extending into the Mahury River estuary. It was easily deep enough for even a destroyer to dock there and the river was wide enough for it to turn even without the aid of tugs.

Their intelligence briefing included only that of an armed civilian security guard was present at the ESA dock in Kourou except when freighters carrying the rocket sections or satellites were due, or had docked and were still unloading. There was nothing in the way of warehousing at the ESA dock to interest a thief, that all took place at the colony's main port. All the ESA dock boasted was a solid, modern jetty and a crane on the river. The quayside was little more than a car park, half covered to provide relief from the sun for waiting heavy duty transporter vehicles and their crews.

A small tank farm sat to one side in a jungle clearing, it was connected to the jetty by all the plumbing necessary to accept deliveries of petrol, Avgas and diesel fuel.

Tall security fences topped by razor wire surrounded the dock and tank farm. Motion sensors and CCTV provided a second layer of security, monitored from a guardhouse at the main gate.

Unlike the port at the capital, Kourou required the regular services of a dredger to keep the main channel deep enough for the freighters to navigate their way safely. When completely unloaded the freighters had to be towed stern first back to the sea by tugs.

As such neither *Dai* nor *Bao* could remain completely submerged for their eventual jaunt downriver.

Li did not imagine that storming the dockside facilities would be anything but counterproductive, and so the low key tactics Captain Huaiqing had suggested were being employed.

Having dropped off the submersible, *Dai* flooded two forward torpedo tubes and two rear tubes. He also opened the outer doors so as to be fully prepared for a surprise encounter with one of the warships, if in fact they were indeed operating out of the ESA dock.

Half of their YU-6 21" torpedoes were armed with the new sodium hydride warheads which released the sodium on impact, producing 2000°C of heat as the compound reacted with the hydrogen in the seawater, or at least that is what it said on the tin.

Li had four forward tubes loaded with conventional warhead torpedoes because everything new has unforeseen bugs somewhere in the system. If he was going to be at knife fighting distance with the French flotilla then he wanted proven technology to hand. The last two forward tubes contained YJ-12 anti-ship missiles. Useless within the confines of the river but they would be ready for immediate use when they returned to the ocean. No time costly unloading and reloading of tubes to delay their immediate use.

The rear tubes were also loaded with conventionally tipped weapons but he only had four of the smaller, and aging, 16" torpedoes. There were four rear tubes in a torpedo room a third the size of the one forward as there was no storage for reloads, the stings-in-the-tail sat in their tubes ready for use during the entire duration of deployments.

All the torpedoes were set to run shallow.

Thus, suitably prepared for the worst, *Dai* moved along the coast to within five hundred metres of the town itself without encountering any further mines.

This part of the operation was lacking several ingredients from the rehearsed plan they had trained for in China. The loss of *Tuan*, her submersible, the special forces detachment and their explosives would mean some ingenuity and adaptability on the part of the much smaller force that was taking on their tasks.

Captain Li was reassured by the quality and enthusiasm of the men.

No cannon fodder, these.

He watched them prepare themselves and their equipment to knock off the Kourou police station and night duty personnel, to render useless any air assets on the small airstrip outside the town, blow a bridge and lock horns with a fearsome regiment of jungle fighters.

Each man would be carrying a FAMAS F1 5.56mm assault rifle, bayonet, three APAV40 rifle grenades, a bespoke detachable sound suppressor, smoke grenades, CS gas grenades, plastic explosives, detonators, an anti-armour mine they could adapt with electrical detonators or simple use as a mine, various 'switches' for booby traps, cheese wire garrottes, ropes and a host of other items that made the submariner feel fatigued just imagining having to carry it all.

Half a kilometre off Les Roche Point the eight remaining special forces troopers exited through the rear escape hatch and swam ashore.

Kourou was a very modern place given its moderate size. Thanks to the commerce and cash associated with the space centre it had good roads, street lighting and orderly housing. Microwave masts for the local cellular telephone system were visible, as were the satellite dishes that linked the residents to the motherland via the internet and satellite TV. Had it not been for the war the street lights would be lit, the bars neon signs ablaze and the populace would be enjoying themselves, but blackouts did not engender good nights out so most stayed home and only a lone police car had been visible on the streets through the search periscope's lo-lite TV.

Li felt a little self-conscious as he had strode from his cabin with a webbing cartridge belt, holster on his hip and camouflage cream on his face. His men nodded respectfully but one unseen wag mimicked the sound of clinking spurs.

"Laugh it up boys." He'd responded. "If it gets so that me and this gun are the only thing between success and swimming home, you'd better be wearing your water wings." His expertise with small arms was limited to one day a year when he was required to demonstrate safe handling drills on a range. The ten rounds he fired during that process did not in any way count towards his annual requalification, which was fortunate for him.

Bao remained submerged beyond the river mouth with her Lo-Lite TV equipped search periscope raised along with the ECM and communications masts.

Dai entered the estuary at periscope depth; a bare twenty feet of water beneath her keel.

The control room was now illuminated with red lighting in order that the bridge crew and landing parties eyes would already be acclimatised to the dark.

Li was glued to the periscope until he saw a broad slipway off to their left. The road that served it was the remains of the original main highway to Cayenne.

"All stop."

The slipway belonged to the old ferry service that had existed for centuries in progressively modern form, and profited at that spot since the Portuguese had first claimed the land. Frenchmen, Dutchmen, Spaniards and Englishmen had also fought over ownership of this country but the Kourou river ferry had survived and prospered despite them all. Only when a Swiss built a bridge downriver did the fat lady finally sing for the ferry. It sat abandoned now, a mere marker for a Chinaman at the point where the river started and the deeper estuary ended.

Dai slowly arose, her masts emerging from the waters like a clutch of Excaliburs.

Brown, silt laden, water flowed off the Juliett's bridge and down the grey steel sides of the conning tower, but her bulk stayed hidden beneath the surface, giving them the radar profile of a small boat.

Li undogged the top lid and locked it in place as he emerged into the rain. Lookouts took post and four ratings strained to haul a 23mm cannon up the ladder from the control room and mounted it as quietly as possible, loading a belt of ammunition but not cocking the weapon as the harsh metallic sound would travel far across the water despite the rain.

It was a snug fit now in the conning tower with look-outs, the Strela air sentry, 23mm and Captain Li.

The Strela had a back blast area which limited its arcs of fire. The ideal was for two sentries on the casing, one forward and one aft of the conning tower. In heavy weather though, the best-of-a-bad-job position was aft of everyone on the conning tower, perched above them all and attached to the ECM mast by a safety harness. This position was of course not conducive to engaging targets approaching from the rear. Nevertheless, Li had his air sentry assisted up there to allow more freedom of movement on the bridge.

Captain Li squinted against the downpour and pulled up his collar to minimise the discomfort of having water running down the back of his neck. He had a hood but he preferred keep his hearing unhindered.

Raising night glasses to his eyes he picked out the channel marker. They remained on electrical power, draining the batteries precious charge but preserving the element of surprise as Li conned the vessel slowly forwards keeping diligently above the deepest part of the rivers dredged channel.

His nose wrinkled as the salt tang of the ocean became polluted by the scent of the jungle, the rotting vegetation and wet mud from the mangrove swamps that lay just outside the small towns influence.

The trees, the creepers and dense jungle undergrowth closed in on them, overhanging the river banks as soon as the town had slipped behind them in the darkness.

A nightscope picked out a wooden dugout canoe drawn up on the bank, the Stone Age existing just a stone's throw from the twenty first century and all its internet broadband glory.

Their world became that of the tropical downpour and the ominous dark mass of the jungle, picked out by a fractionally lighter sky.

It was claustrophobic. They were out of their comfort zone, away from the deep waters they were designed to hunt in and this added to the diligence with which the bridge crew kept watch.

Li allowed himself to swing his glasses up and down river every so often, taking in the black and impenetrable gloom of the banks.

Amid the leaping strikes of raindrops upon the river two bright dots appeared beside the bank, he kept his glasses upon them as he tried to work out what they were, a surveillance device? He lowered the glasses and they disappeared, invisible to the naked eye in the darkness but with the glasses raised once more he immediately picked them out again as they were now moving towards his command, creating a faint V of a wake in the rivers surface. A seabird swam into his vision and into the path of the glowing dots, its own head pulled back into the protection its furled wings afforded against the rain.

There was a splash, a flurry of movement and both bird and dots disappeared with the swish of a caiman's leathery tail, leaving only a few floating feathers. Li shivered despite himself at the suddenness with which death had visited this primeval place.

The river bent around to the right and Li leant over the side of the conning tower so as to more quickly sight the ESA jetty, glasses held to his eyes with one hand and the other clutching a microphone to his mouth, thumb just touching the transmit switch and the order to open fire ready on his lips. The rating on the 23mm cannon clutched the weapons cocking handle tightly, his knuckles white and bracing himself to ratchet the lever to the rear.

Below decks the tension was palpable. In engineering they were awaiting the call to throw the engines into full reverse for a fighting withdrawal back to the ocean under fire from surface warships. The torpedomen stood ready, and between them and the control room waited the armed ratings who would be their sentries along with the Fassing party in the central passageway. All were bathed in red light, clutching small arms with the awkwardness of the unfamiliar, but ready to carry out the fuelling procedures from the novelty of a rock steady surface for once.

The darkness of the jungle on the northern bank altered with the appearance of a silhouette that possessed straight lines. It separated from the unruly mass of the night time rain forest to sit stationary a hundred metres off the north bank. As it came into the view of the 23mm gunner he immediately took aim.

"Belay that!" Li commanded sharply. "It's the *Fliterland*."

Bulky, specialised derricks sat above the elongated ships hold where the *Soyuz* rocket sections and delicate payloads were stored but the freighter was riding high in the water, empty, her last cargo unloaded weeks before.

Rust streaked here and there, the freighters blue hull and white superstructure loomed over them as they slowly motored along her cliff-like port side.

The dock beyond the freighter was empty of warships too. Li was not as relieved as he might have been. He still did not know where the French corvettes and fast patrol boats were.

"All stop."

The rain showed no sign of relenting as the *Dai* sat motionless in midstream. Li took up his glasses again, to peer downriver at the road bridge, and to look for any sign of sentries.

It was both a modern and no frills, functional, construction for carrying a two lane highway as well as an effective barrier preventing anything more substantial than a large motor launch from progressing downriver beyond that point.

Ten prefabricated concrete supports had been sunk into the riverbed to carry the highway. Li guessed that a minimum of three spans would need to be dropped for it to hinder a determined engineer beyond a week. Ideally those supports should be destroyed too but they were substantial and solidly built. It would require the services of a demolitions expert and more time and explosives than they possessed.

As for sentries, Li saw a shape midway across in a rain slick waterproof cape slowly pacing about; head down in the manner of the truly bored and thoroughly miserable. He looked slightly hunchbacked on account of his weapon hanging by its sling off one shoulder beneath the cape to keep it dry, the muzzle pointing downwards and of no immediate offensive use to man nor beast.

This was not what he expected of one of the vaunted legionnaire jungle fighters of *3e Régiment étranger d'infanterie.* This must be either a student from the jungle warfare school or one of the local reservists

As Li watched the soldier suddenly leaned back against the guardrail and sat down heavily upon the bridges tarmac surface. He did not move again.

Two more figures appeared from the north end of the bridge, and in contrast to the sentry the butts of their weapons were in the shoulder and they were up in the aim. Bulky sound suppressors panned from side to side as they moved rapidly in that odd gait that keeps the upper body and shoulders level and stable, the knees seemingly joined together. They did not pause on drawing level with the slumped figure, they did not tarry to feel for a pulse or to offer aid, the nearest of his SF detachment briefly lowered his aim and Li saw two flashes at the muzzle as he double tapped his victim in the head, just to be certain.

They continued on across the bridge, walking rapidly and looking for further targets as they disappeared from his view.

Two minutes later they returned at the jog but this time they did stop at the supine figure. One stood guard as the other stooped, getting a good hold before straightening up with his arms under the sentry's armpits and draping him over the guard rail. He bent again to grasp the ankles and upended the body into the river. The splash of it hitting the water was followed by others with the forms of eager caiman sliding down the southern bank. Long tails propelled them swiftly through the water in a race to claim their supper.

On the road bridge, the Chinese trooper peered over the side at his victim before looking up and into the darkness, directly at the otherwise invisible shape of the Juliett's conning tower. He raised a hand to give a little cavalier salute to the submarine and then both jogged back the way they had come.

Li looked away from the bridge and what was about to be the disquieting sight of large reptiles feeding on a human corpse.

"Open main seawater valves... vent ballast, blow one and two."

High pressure air displaced the water in her ballast tanks, forcing it out into the river and *Dai's* casing rose up out of the muddy brown waters.

The sound of a car engine swiftly drew all eyes back to the dock in time to see a police car, 'Gendarmerie' emblazoned on its side, approach the jetty, flashing its headlights rapidly.

"Captain?" asked the rating on the 23mm cannon, again in the aim.

"It's okay, just two of our supercargo arriving in borrowed transport."

The car halted on the jetty beside the freighter. Two special forces troopers exited the vehicle.

Li depressed the transmit button on the microphone, updating his executive officer before getting busy putting the *Dai* alongside the jetty fuel valves, one of which was connected to a storage tank a high grade diesel.

"All back dead slow...get the sea duty and the security details topside."

The *Dai* moved past the *Fliterland* again, with the sea duty linesmen taking post as Li skilfully backed them up against the jetty behind the freighter's looming stern.

Lines were thrown to the two troopers who made the lines fast, securing the *Dai* to the side of the jetty.

An extending ladder was brought up from below and laid against the jetty's side, and the dockside security party hurriedly climbed it and hustled away to form a perimeter.

The senior NCO commanding those SF troops re-boarded and reported that all was going to plan at their end. The dock was secure; the logging company's Chinook at Kourou's small airfield was being booby trapped even as they spoke and the other two detachments were ashore without incident and approaching their targets.

At the bridge, ropes were being tossed over the sides as a preliminary to wiring the road sections for demolition and the rain stopped as suddenly as if someone had turned off a tap.

"Fasser's topside and begin fuelling operations…oh, and make to *Bao*, *'Come and join the party'*."

As the fuelling crew appeared on the casing he shook his head in wonderment and spoke aloud to no one in particular.

"Damn me, but I think this could actually work."

Route de l'Espace: 'ESA Space Centre facility: French Guiana.

There is a road that runs from Brownsville USA, going south along the Atlantic coast all the way until it ends suddenly on the shore of the Beagle Channel at Tierra del Fuego. Pretty much as far as you can drive on continental America, clocking up thirteen thousand miles on that twisting and turning road from Texas. It follows the coastline for all but a twenty mile section where the original road runs straight through the cluster of rocket launch pads on the equator.

A newer section, a wide sweeping detour now cuts through the rainforest keeping traffic far away from the ESA and *Soyuz* sites. The no-longer-public section was renamed Route de l'Espace and came to represent the single most valuable item in the entire country.

Low lying and low profile reinforced concrete pill boxes at the side of the road command the approaches to the launch pads, each with five sets of twin thirty calibre machine guns spaced to provide 360° of overlapping coverage. The guns were set to fire at shin height, and anyone hit would then fall into the thirty calibre stream. It was a method first devised by the German Imperial Army way back in 1912 as the most effective method of despatching multiple attackers, rather than leaving some wounded, and still a threat.

At the southern entrance to the complex a rattrap gate allowed one vehicle at a time into a controlled search area with optical underside scanning built into the roadbed and ESA security staff checking for vehicle borne IEDs, weapons and stowaways. The exit gate could not open whilst the entry gate was closed.

Concrete lined drainage ditches had a dual anti-vehicle role, and outside the entry point a concrete blockhouse/Guardroom controlled access.

Captain Jie Huaiqing and his nine troopers moved along the roadway in Indian- file with its staggered spacing making fire from the flanks less likely to take out pairs of troops. It was basic fieldcraft.

They held to the roadway, not avoiding the occasional approaching vehicle. Trucks, cars and vans splashed past, adding a little more to their already soaked camouflage uniforms as the tropical deluge had not relented.

It suited Jie's purpose, bad weather was better in his chosen line of work.

They moved with deliberateness and they moved as if they belonged, leaning forward slightly at the waist as that best allowed them to balance themselves under the burden of the 15 kilo cratering charges each carried.

After thirty minutes they saw stationary red tail lights ahead of them. After several minutes more Jie got the impression there was more than a single vehicle, the sound of idling engines confirmed that, but they were still well short of the ESA controlled area, now visible far ahead, its access point lit up.

Jie knew, in detail, the procedures that were in place here and a holding area was not included, that is to say one hadn't been included six weeks before.

This was where fresh intelligence would have assisted.

A hundred yards on and he saw the lead vehicle in the queue move off slowly, continuing for the facility but the remainder sat there a quarter mile from the entrance and Jie left his squad in the undergrowth to recce ahead cautiously.

Half way along the column of trucks, vans and cars he was able to see that they were being held by two soldiers who were clearly not legionaries' as one carried the shoulder flash of the 110th Infantry and the other wore the maroon beret of the airborne forces.

The driver of the baker's truck at the end of the queue was listening to a music CD and jumped as legionaries appeared at each window, faces blacked with camouflage cream.

"Autorisant passé!"

The night and the rain hid them from the legitimate articles at the head of the queue but they had to work quickly before a further vehicle arrived to silhouette them for possible discovery.

The driver handed over the pass and then left the vehicle to open the truck for inspection and the troopers kept him busy with queries about his load and his movements.

Alone by the cab Jie leant in and ejected the music CD to surf the channels until he found the local news station.

Delivery men worldwide consistently collect polystyrene coffee cups, polystyrene fast food containers, cigarette packets and newspapers with which to decorate the front dashboard.

Between the news channel stories and speed reading newspaper articles, ignoring the obvious tabloid favourites' of who-is-screwing-who by identifying the cliché' bylines', Jie gleaned an insight into local events in French Guiana since they had departed from China.

The plan to tie up the troops chasing illegal gold miners from Brazil had worked well, much better than expected in fact.

A television news channel had persuaded the gendarmes to allow a news crew to embed with one of their jungle patrols to better cover this increase of the illegal mining problem. The presence of a young pretty reporter may possibly have had some bearing on the gendarmes becoming a little over eager to please in the execution of their duties.

They not only turned away would-be miners they encountered at the border, destroying their tools, but they also stopped and searched *Garimpeiros* crossing back into Brazil, seizing any gold they were carrying.

If the eight man patrol of gendarmes believed the *Garimpeiros* would meekly accept the loss of their earnings and would not seek retribution and restitution at gunpoint then they were at best optimistic. The gendarmes had soon reported the TV crew and themselves were surrounded by ten times their number somewhere near the Surinam, Brazil and Guiana borders. Nothing more had been heard of them in almost two weeks. Under pressure from the media and the ministry the governor had taken what action he could, bearing in mind that he had zero chance of reinforcement from Europe.

By replacing the jungle fighting expert legionnaires' at the ESA and *Soyuz* sites with the as yet non jungle qualified, but conventionally trained soldiers undergoing courses at the jungle warfare school, he had two hundred more boots on the ground searching for the missing reporter, cameraman and policemen.

This was good news Jie decided, far less chance of an awkward "Who the hell are you?" moment from one of the genuine articles before they got inside.

Only here, out of all the locations in sight of the ocean was the blackout not in place.

The ESA perimeter was covered with pressure sensors, ultra-sonic movement alarms and lo-lite CCTV which required no illumination, but the checkpoint at the entrance was lit up as bright as day and it was towards this oasis of spot lights and 200 watt bulbs that Jie led his troopers.

The approaching squad were under observation as they approached, the barrels of a pair of 'Thirties' tracking them unerringly from the moment the holding area soldiers had informed the guardroom of armed 'friendlies' on the way.

Before them was a long stretch of straight, level road with the jungle and undergrowth cleared for twenty five metres at either side. That was a long way to go to reach any kind of cover from view if they should need to.

They were committed.

Three and a half miles beyond the entrance it was possible to make out the Italian *Vega* launch pad with a tall slim column in place and illuminated by floodlighting. The lighting was not for the benefit of the press, although it does make for eye catching footage and career defining photography, the primary purpose is simply to spot problems such as leaks and loose or missing inspection panels because at the end of the day even rocket scientists can screw up.

Unlit and invisible in the rain and night but only three quarters of a mile from *Vega* was the more substantial *Ariane 5* pad. Accidents can happen so at no time was their dual activity taking place at both *Vega* and its relatively close-by neighbour.

Soyuz though, was six miles distant and an *Ariane 5* rocket was in place there. Rain pelted its length, rattling off the casing of its fantastically expensive payload package with a sound identical to that which it was making on the rusted corrugated tin roofs of dilapidated and abandoned fishermen's huts near the beach.

Two miles closer but half hidden behind jungle not yet cleared was the tall white final assembly building. The *Ariane* pads next customer was stood outside on a giant transporter that would deliver it at 3mph, slowly but surely once the *Vega* had lifted its package into orbit.

Jie and his men arrived at the illuminated entrance point just as the downpour came to a sudden end.

Once more 'accidentally' depressing the transmit switch of his radio Jie sang softly and tunelessly. "...voyez...Ces oiseaux blancs...Et ces maisons rouillées..." He waited for the acknowledging 'click' from the other end before he removed his bergen and left his men standing in a group, chatting quietly together in a non-threatening manner on the side of the roadway but studiously ignoring the French army regulars who were in evidence.

A junior NCO checking the driver's documents of the vehicles that arrived and a second soldier ostentatiously covering him gave the newcomers an appraising look before 'blanking' them in return.

Captain Jie Huaiqing wore the rank of a '*Sergent Chef*', a Colour Sergeant equivalent, owing to ninety percent of the legions officer corps being French regular army officers on secondment he would have been asking for trouble if he had posed as one of the ten percent raised from the ranks.

At the guardroom window though, he found not a senior army NCO in charge, but a marine lieutenant with a broken wing.

A fall during the descent of a slippery hillside on one of the jungle warfare courses cross country navigation exercises had put the marine out of action, but at these 'all hands to the pumps moments' even the walking wounded can be found a task within their limited abilities.

The officer nodded and pointed to his right arm in a sling by way of apology at not returning Jie's salute.

"It's always the one you can least afford to do without eh, sir?"

"The essential 'W' arm, Chief. Writing, waving and wanking." The marine officer replied ruefully.

"And what brings you to these parts instead of seeking out beautiful reporters in distress over by the border?"

By way of reply Jie fished out the waterproof pouch from his map pocket at his thigh, withdrawing the book and thence the written orders from between its leaves.

Instead of opening the orders the officer turned the book, which Jie had placed on the sill and peered curiously at its cover, a picture of a sea turtle was self-explanatory as to the books purpose, the script being in Chinese logograms.

"You are a wildlife enthusiast, Chief?" he asked. "Plenty of that around here."

Idly opening the front cover he looked at the stamps on the inside for the briefest of moments before turning to the colour glossy photographs in the centre.

Clearly not a fellow Herpetologist he closed the book.

"Well each to his own eh, Chief." He said with a smile and returned it, opening the orders with a flick of his left wrist whereupon he held the creases flat with spread fingers against the writing shelf on his side of the window and began to read.

"Additional perimeter patrol, huh? I hope you are familiar with the ground so you know not to venture between the yellow markers and the fence?" he said glancing up from the orders.

Jie nodded in affirmation, emphasising it with a respectful "Yes, sir."

"Or every damn alarm on the place will go off, *again*." added the officer.

With a shrug the lieutenant handed the orders back.

"You need to book yourself and your men in, I can't do it myself." He added, nodding again at the limb in a sling.

"Not in that book!" he warned as Jie reach for an open binder nearby on the sill. "That's for civilian cleaning staff...you need to unload your weapon and come inside. The binder is in the corner and a bit heavy for a one arm bandit to carry across." He grinned. "I'll buzz you through."

Jie duly carried out an unload and looked across the road to his men, making a surreptitious thumbs up gesture out of sight of the marine officer at the window and the soldiers nearby as he placed the ejected magazine in a pouch and secured it.

A faint nod in reply came from Corporal Chui, his senior NCO.

On pushing open the door at the sound of the harsh electronic buzz he found himself in a guardroom typical of those anywhere in the world. Institutional light green paint from floor level, up to above average shoulder height and then cream up to and including the ceiling. A narrow rubber mat ran across a shiny floor and he knew without being told that to step off it onto the gleaming and highly buffed linoleum would not be met well. It smelled of floor polish, coffee and Gauloises cigarettes.

The marine officer had his ear to a telephone when Jie appeared.

"On the table in the corner, Chief." he nodded to neatly arranged binders and logbooks on a shelf.

Jie however could see all manner of labelled registers and books identifying the contents as Fire Drills, Mileage Returns and archived Incident Logs, but he could see nothing to indicate a booking in and out register.

"Sir, I can't seem to find it...?" he turned and the marine officer put down the telephone and smiled affably but ignored the question.

"So tell me Chief, how you come to have an April date stamp in a Shanghai library book when the war started in March?"

Time seemed to freeze, as it does at those times of discovery for the kid with his hand in the cookie jar, the burglar half inside the window when the light comes on, and the soldier with an empty rifle.

He froze for a heartbeat as realisation hit him. Somehow the French officer had been on to him from the start, and by allowing him inside he had both lulled Jie and his men into a false sense of security, and separated the leader from his men. The sudden roar of the thirty calibre machine guns outside jarred him into action.

Jie drew back his arm to fling the weapon at the marine, to buy time to reach the Norinco inside his smock.

The marine officer had a Glock 17 held with confident ease in his left hand and shot Jie twice through the chest before the captain could complete the throw.

Jie's legs folded beneath him, all strength leaving his limbs he found himself on his knees, too weak to reach the smocks zipper.

The marine officer crouched over him, the pistol in his left hand.

Jie stared at it.

"Ambidextrous..." Said the officer in a slightly apologetic tone "...and two years with the Embassy guard in Beijing, in case you were wondering." He continued in good, but slightly accented Mandarin.

Jie felt the floor tremble and a thunderous sound announced the *Vega* rocket launching another replacement military communications satellite into orbit.

The roar muted that of the thirty calibre machine guns and its tail flames light even invaded the guardrooms interior noted Jie, but at its height, darkness came.

ESA Jetty, Kourou River: French Guiana.

Locating the valve for the diesel storage tank took but a moment but getting power to the pump in order fuel the *Dai* took long minutes before the switches were found in an electrical cabinet in the gatehouse but before that happy event a more worrying one occurred.

Snatches of gunfire were heard on the wind just before a column of fire rose into the heavens with a rocket and satellite riding upon it.

Captain Li queried the SF detachments warrant officer, Senior Sergeant Yen who tried without success to raise the two other teams on their tactical radio, looking a little comical, armed to the teeth yet in a singing voice that would strip paint from the walls he canted his head to one side, over the Thales radio microphone on his left shoulder and gave voice to a lullaby.

"Frere Jacques, frere Jacques, dormez vous? Dormez vous?"

There was no response from *Dai's* or *Bao's* teams, no indication that they had entered the site or not though either.

Unbeknownst to the captain, the *Soyuz* team had been approaching the northern entrance to the site. There was no issue with new procedures as signposts directed anyone with business with ESA or *Soyuz* to follow the detour to Kourou and use the southern gate.

They had not heard gunfire as the wind was at their backs. The launching *Vega* had of course been a very spectacular last view.

A bare fifty metres lay between themselves and the guardroom when the *Vega* launch took place. Ten faces could not help but follow its fiery splendour upwards, its tail flame illuminating them rather conveniently for the thirty calibre crew at the north gate who were now stood-to and on the lookout for bogus legionnaires.

"Night ranges, sir? Local gun club perhaps?" the warrant officer suggested to Captain Li.

"At this time, when rockets are launching?" Li responded. "No, that is not very likely. The 'big sky' theory is frequently disproved by stray rounds and ricochets." He shook his head. "It would be prudent to work on the assumption they are blown, and the brown stuff is about to hit, I think."

The two troopers tasked with ensuring there was nothing on the small Kourou airstrip that could be used against them arrived back at a fast jog.

"Something is stirring in town, sir." One reported.

"Quiet as the grave when we went through it the first time, but there's people moving about and cars starting up now. Some fat bastard in pyjama bottoms and combat jacket nearly trod on me on the way to his car." The troopers had been moving quickly and quietly along silent streets when they had been surprised by house lights coming on and the sound of car engines starting up. Dropping prone in someone's flower bed and remaining motionless had been instinctive.

"Seven bellies he had." Put in his mate. "Like a stack of jellies jogging, they were, and he farted at every other step!"

"What is it with you guys?" asked Captain Li, his face screwing up in distaste at the description.

"Is there some 'Instilling graphic and unpleasant mental images, course' you all attend or something?"

He gave consideration to what he had just been told. The out of shape resident in combat jacket hurrying out to his car was more than likely a member of the reserve platoon formed from retirees.

"Where were they headed?"

"North, sir." The first trooper replied.

"So, good news for us here but not so good for the launch pad teams." muttered Li. Not good news for the town either, he thought, knowing that the orders in his safe would have to be carried out regardless of his personal feelings.

The captain of *Bao* would have a sealed copy in his safe, to be opened on the death or incapacity of Li, the next senior officer in the flotillas chain of command.

His executive officer also knew, Li had briefed him of course. The only other member of the crew to be intimate with that part of the mission would of course be his own 'steward', who may even have received a briefing by the admiral himself before the orders had even been written.

However, there was still time, they did not know for certain that the launch pad teams had been compromised, and even if they had it did not automatically follow that they were prevented from completing their missions?

He had his fingers crossed for Jie and those nineteen men to show before the refuelling was done and the bridge dropped into the muddy Kourou.

Across at the bridge the demolition preparations were well under way. Two troopers stood watch, one for trouble approaching from Cayenne and one keeping an eye on the quartet of caiman in the river. The biggest and strongest had claimed the sentry's corpse so the others were watching another pair of troopers hanging by ropes below the bridges roadbed, wiring it up.

An adult caiman's tail can lift 80% of its body vertically upwards, clear of the water for just long enough to snatch unwary birds and monkeys from the lower limbs of overhanging trees, and Li could imagine what was going through the minds of the hungry trio as they watched the troopers suspended below the bridge, working swiftly and methodically like temptingly dangling Piñatas.

The trooper watching the trio of reptiles obviously thought they were thinking the same thing as he suddenly fired a long burst, the spent cases hitting the tarmac road surface and making more noise than the fired rounds had. One of the beasts reared up, threshing and twisting...the other two immediately turned on it, sinking their teeth in and instinctively rolling their wounded brother, seeking to subdue it by drowning before tearing off chunks and devouring it.

"That'll keep them busy until we're done." Senior Sergeant Yen observed aloud but broke off as an armed rating relayed a message from the front gate, shouting across that the telephone was ringing non-stop at the gatehouse.

"Well." Said Captain Li. "If they answer it then whoever is on the other end will know something is wrong and they will come in force, or they can leave it and maybe just a few will come to see if anything's wrong in which case you can thin out the opposition a bit...but it's your call Senior Sergeant, you are the on-site authority on dry land combat."

Twelve armed sailors and the four troopers who were not engaged at the bridge was hardly a substantial force.

Senior Sergeant Yen departed to arrange what he had called a greeting for the unwelcome with some of the Type 72 light anti-tank mines they had brought. Not as effective as bar mines they were good for wrecking a tanks tracks and a road wheel perhaps. They could temporarily incapacitate any current main battle tank and devastate soft skin vehicles. As the French in Guiana had none of the former and plenty of the latter the relatively small but powerful AT mines could prove useful.

As *Dai*'s fuel tanks reached absolute capacity the *Bao* arrived, holding station in midstream as *Dai* cast off, and again moved beyond the dark and silent *Fliterland*, still operating on battery power in the hope of keeping their presence a secret as long as possible.

The maw-like air intakes and even larger exhausts' covers remained closed and hopefully would remain so until they were again back out to sea.

Perhaps the telephone call was the guard's wife? Perhaps it was a wrong number or even his bookie...?

It arrived with a thunderous roar, its undercarriage just clearing the white painted roof of the covered parking area, overflying the *Fliterland* and the two Chinese submarines to disappear in a shock of noise and downwash beyond the jungle canopy of the southern bank.

Neither *Dai*'s or *Bao*'s air sentries fired, so suddenly had the big Chinook appeared and departed that only *Bao*'s 23mm and a trooper on the road bridge fired a shot. The 23mm cannons gunner failed to aim ahead of the aircraft before letting rip so naturally he missed by as much as four aircraft lengths, the tracer curving harmlessly behind it. The troopers lighter and sound suppressed rounds 'lacked the legs' as they say, falling short.

"I thought they booby trapped that bloody thing?" Li shouted across the warrant officer on the dock who had paused to duck and watch the big shape cross the river.

The sound of the big rotor blades drowned out the reply as the machine cleared the trees downriver, flaring as it crossed back over to the north side and obviously aiming for some open space four hundred or so yards away around the bend. Li could barely make it out in the dark.

It was impressive flying by a military or ex-military pilot with plenty of experience in heliborne assaults. Flying so low as to minimise the opportunity of effective ground fire.

Li realised that his own air sentry was unable to engage it with the Strela as the submarines bridge was in the back blast area of the weapon. It was his own fault for not repositioning the sentry on the casing when the opportunity arose and he cursed himself for a fool now.

Don Caldew had been flying for the 'My T Oak' logging and lumber company for over two years, since right after getting out of the service in fact, flying the companies surplus Boeing CH47 Chinook.

The pay cheques were fatter than the ones Uncle Sam had given him but the work was as dull as ditch water. He missed the excitement, the adrenalin rush of flying into a hot LZ, he missed the guys and he missed something else too, the mission purpose, the sense you were doing something important. He recognised that that was what had made him sign on the dotted line in the first place.

Don came from a little town in the American Midwest where he was born in the same hospital his folks had been born, went to the same High School his folks and their folks before them had attended, and was expected to get a job at the local plant, just as his parents and their parents had. They hadn't even considered setting up a college fund for him. Why should he want or expect anything more? Don did want more, but he didn't know quite what it was that was missing from the life plan his parents had presented him with. The answer, when he found it, had changed his life forever.

The army recruiter at the local county fair had seen a light appear in young Don's eyes as he looked at the glossy photographs in the pamphlets and the poster with the 'Be All You Can Be' title. Most of the first questions the recruiter got from visitors to his stand were "What's the pay like?" or "Did you ever shoot anyone, mister?" The first category, if they signed on, would wash out in 70% of cases, the second would come back in ten years when they were old enough and ask the same question as the first category. But Don's had been "Do you make a difference?"

With his level of education, Don joined the infantry as a rifleman and he loved the life, the camaraderie and the sense of doing something with a purpose.

Another life altering experience was his first flight in a helicopter, a Blackhawk. While his buddies were staring out at the ground Don had been craning his neck to watch the AC, the Aircraft Commander, and his co-pilot.

It had just been an air experience flight, an introduction to the drills required to get on and off without walking into a rotor blade or grabbing hold of something you shouldn't in order to climb aboard when fully loaded down with weapons and equipment. They had a short cross country hop to a wide green meadow where the aircraft had landed and shut down while they all had lunch, army style of course, but Don had sought out the AC, asking him about what it took to be an army helicopter pilot. The answers had been a little sobering but Don was not one to be easily put off.

Back home at that time his friends were marrying high school sweethearts and making babies, although not always in that order, and buying houses on the same street where their parents and grandparents lived. Don went home on leave after passing basic, but apart from attending his sister's wedding the following year that was it, he never went back again.

The army ran further education courses and Don applied himself with a will. His first tour in Iraq was as a rifleman, but his second was in the left hand seat of a CH47 Chinook.

A chunk of metal taking off Don's right leg below the knee during a hot extraction in Helmand province ten years later was the only reason he had left, not because he wanted to but because the army was downsizing and younger, 100% fit AC's were preferred over the prosthetic limb owning variety.

Lifting tree trunks out of the woods kept his mind focussed but flying personnel and equipment from A to B was as interesting as watching traffic signals change, at least he was still flying though.

'My T Oak' won the ESA contract to clear the jungle from around the facility and other small jobs appeared in-country too, mainly at the behest of the Governor's office to clear trees around the small marine bases on the Suriname and Brazil borders, and the legion camps of course. Being a Vet and having seen combat went a ways to establish a cordiality with the normally frosty legionnaire's that led to a respect for his flying skills, so it was to him and not his boss, that they had come to request assistance with boarding the fleeing freighter *Fliterland* a hundred miles out in the Atlantic. Don's 'Pinnacle' manoeuvre, keeping station on the moving vessel without making contact but close enough to drop off troops, had allowed fifteen Legionnaire's to step off the lowered rear troop ramp and straight on to one of the bridge wings and seize the vessel.

Tonight, at the logging camps accommodation near the airstrip outside Kourou, Don had been dozing in front of the communal TV set with his prosthetic limb beside him, lightweight, strong alloy tubing instead of something pretending to be a living lower leg. The false leg sensibly allowed one handed operation in its attachment and removal as the designers realised the owner may not always be in a position to sit whilst performing those tasks. The free hand could prevent the owner from falling on his ass.

Don was called to the telephone in the office and told it was urgent, so having hopped one legged to the 'phone Don attached it as he listened. On the other end was the legions operations centre and the duty watch keeper, a major, explained their Puma was still tied up on the border so could Don take the platoon of reservists from Kourou up to the *Soyuz* site as there had been an attempt to infiltrate all the launch pads. Once he had dropped them off he wanted Don to collect one of the Cayenne reservist platoons and deliver it to the ESA final assembly building.

Don was practically rubbing his hands together. All he needed was assurances that the company had been informed because they had torn him a fresh one after the *Fliterland* incident.

He roused his co-pilot and crew chief, a pair of French Canadians with attitude, that is to say they considered themselves more French than the French. It would be fair to say that Don's enthusiasm for the evening's unscheduled flying was not shared by them on any appreciable level.

Half a dozen members of the Kourou platoon were already at the airstrip when Don arrived, hobbling on his false leg but keen as mustard nonetheless.

The Chinook was only a half dozen years younger than Don but older than both his co-pilot and his countryman. He set them to carry out the pre-flight walkabout as he settled himself into the right hand seat.

Checking that nothing had fallen off since the aircraft had last been used was a job he had once carried out himself, religiously, but he was not that nimble anymore.

Don attached night vision goggles to his flight helmet; they were absolute essentials here in the equatorial tropics where day does not gradually become dark over a couple of hours, the transition will occur in scant minutes. Airfield lighting with a backup generator was also in short supply in these parts so that was another good reason to be able to see in the dark whenever necessary.

Cars were arriving all the time now, a pick-up truck with eight middle aged men crammed into the back was the last to arrive.

The platoon commander, a grossly overweight baker, and possibly his own best customer, was pulling on combat trousers over pyjama bottoms as the senior NCO got the men in three ranks and called the roll.

Don counted twenty three men in total, the Chinook seated fifteen but he would bend the rules under the circumstances and deliver them in one trip.

His co-pilot took his seat and buckled up as the crew chief finished seating *'Pères Armée'* and stood outside the aircraft ready to spot any problem visually during the start-up.

Don spoke aloud as he ran through the 'before engine start' and start-up checklists because even under the circumstances he wasn't about to bend the rules for that!

It was only thirteen miles to the *Soyuz* site, but forty five from there to Cayenne. He left the troop ramp down for the three minute hop to the launch pad.

No sooner had they left the ground when they were diverted south to check the jetty and bridge guard across the Kourou River. The four man guard of reservists were not answering their radio and there may be a problem at the gatehouse to the nearby ESA dock. The local gendarmerie patrol car was not answering its radio either or they would have sent that instead, he was told.

Don was enjoying himself. Not a problem, had been his response, he banked around and overflew the gatehouse and jetty.

"I found your police car...a bunch of armed men and two for-goddamned-real submarines...we got ground fire from the bridge and the subs!" he reported a minute later.

"Far be it for me to tell you your job, but do you want me to put these guys on the ground at the clearing between the town and the jetty and then go fetch the rest from Cayenne?"

The Governor had been alerted to the Chinese troops in Foreign Legion garb and now on learning that there were two surfaced submarines at the jetty with more troops on the ground he could be forgiven for wondering, just briefly, if an invasion force had somehow been missed?

There were troops guarding the launch pads and they had destroyed two groups attempting to infiltrate. They were stood to and that was the best he could hope for under the circumstances. This 'new' force though, for that is how he thought of them, needed to be engaged, to spoil whatever they intended or delay them until regular forces could be brought to bear.

The nearest regular troops to the Kourou river bridge and the ESA Jetty were the commandant of the jungle warfare school who was in a little Peugeot P4 utility vehicle, the French 'Jeep', enroute to check up on his students. However, he had only the schools sergeant major and his driver with him.

The legions commanding officer was ordered to start moving troops to the ESA launch facility, and his Puma and small Gazelle were the obvious means but the process would take over an hour before the first men arrived.

One corvette was at sea and had been turned about, its sister ship was preparing to sail.

The corvettes were on detached duty from Toulon and their crews enjoyed the Cayenne nightlife when on a stand down. The gendarmeries visited the bars with commandeered taxi cabs in convoy behind the police cars, spreading the word, rounding the crew up and filling the cabs.

The patrol boats were based at Cayenne though; the crews had homes in many cases and were summoned by a telephone call. One boat readying to leave, the second patrol boat was on the slips having a shaft replaced as the old one had been struck by a hidden deadfall whilst manoeuvring in the Mahury estuary. It was a constant hazard, colliding with the dead falls, the trees that had toppled into the river to be washed out to sea. The most dangerous were those waterlogged trunks that were not yet so saturated as to settle to the bottom, but instead sailed just below the surface, invisible in the muddy brown river water, mother nature's own malicious timber torpedoes.

She wasn't going anywhere for a few days.

Both Atlantiques had only returned two days before. Losses to the NATO maritime patrol fleet had seen them called away to assist with fighting the convoy's through the waiting wolf packs. Staging out of Shannon airport in the Republic of Ireland they had flown around the clock.

Since their return the crew's had been on a maintenance stand-down as both hard working aircraft and crew members received essential TLC.

Now of course panels were being secured, and pre-flights already underway before the ground crews had even finished securing engine covers back in place.

So Don was told to put his load on the ground at the clearing where the reservists would receive radio orders. He was then to lose no time in bringing the other reserve platoon, currently mustering on a football pitch at Cayenne, to join with the first load of reservists.

"This is what makes life worth living!" he whooped, and laughed at the expression on his co-pilots face.

The sound of the Chinooks twin engines echoed through the jungle and along the river. It was a typical moonless tropical night, the jungle seeming to suck every iota of light out of the universe.

It was on the ground now, that much was certain, but what was it doing?

Unloading troops was a safe bet, and probably the Kourou reservists, but although they were potentially less of a threat than they probably had been twenty years before when the men were in their prime, Li would have been a lot happier if whatever his two troopers had done to the helicopter had worked.

Neither of the Strela operators was in position yet. But the helicopter would not be likely to turn back towards the jetty on take-off, not unless the pilot was an idiot. It was a case of stable doors and horses already bolted.

As soon as the reserve platoon had disappeared down the troop ramp and into the trees Don applied power and pulled gently on the collective, lifting the machine straight up until he saw the rotor blades were clear of the tree tops whereupon he eased the cyclic forward and slightly right.

Down through the chin windows at his feet the jungle canopy was all varieties and shades of green in his night vision goggles, the dense jungle slipped just beneath the Chinook as he banked it carefully around, away from the guns at the jetty and as the trees gave way to the surface of the river below them he raised the troop ramp, aiming to make as fast a run as possible to Cayenne and back.

A blast of heat and a shockwave threw him violently forwards against his harness and suddenly he was starring vertically downwards at the river rushing up at him.

The impact was indescribable, his co-pilot screamed all the way down and then the river burst in.

Don was on automatic pilot, carrying out ditching drills he had never before had to perform for real but which he had undertaken many a time in dunker training at Fort Rucker, Alabama. What made this different though was that the disorientation was complete. The bone jarring contact with the river, the shock, the absolute blackness as the silt heavy water engulfed them and the voice at the back of his head which whispered. *"No safety divers this time!"*

He released his straps and felt to his right for the door release but the door was gone, ripped off in the impact and his hands instead met the uneven and slippery surface of a deadfall tree trunk, covered in weed and algae, barring the way. He groped straight ahead, where the front canopy screen had been and again he touched slimy bark. To his left was a body, his co-pilot still strapped in and so with panic threatening he pulled himself back into the troop compartment, or at least where the rest of the fuselage used to be.

The cockpit was upside down at the bottom of the river, facing back the way it had come, the heavy front rotor assembly having obeyed the laws of gravity and had turned turtle the front half of the aircraft.

The rest of the aircraft, the troop compartment, simply was not attached any more.

Air trapped inside Don's helmet showed him the true way up and he broke the surface coughing and sputtering.

The night vision goggles had been ripped off in the crash but there was some light, the flickering of flames and he turned to face the north bank, wreckage only recognisable by a broad rotor blade standing straight up out of the river like a grave marker.

The crackle of flames from aviation fuel doused jungle growth and black, oily smoke gave no clue as to what had brought them down, but then Don spotted something moving in the river, something which had already spotted him.

His artificial limb was not designed as a swimming aid but primal fear, the dread of being eaten alive spurred him on, desperately making for the south bank with the damn thing acting like an anchor.

The jungle overhung the banks, jagged branches seeming to seek to both impale him and also to fend him off like medieval pikes thrusting at unwelcome horsemen. Beneath these was a steep bank, perhaps three feet high, its lip beyond his grasp even if he could reach the damn thing.

In the flames light he saw a dark gap in the cover and made for it, seeing an unobstructed path to a sloping but muddy route out of the river and away from the closing caiman.

Don's good foot touched the semi-solid riverbed at the shallows and he sobbed with relief but he knew he was far from being out of danger yet. He stood; leaning forwards, wading towards safety, his arms outstretched and his right hand grasped a thick protruding tree root when the caiman's jaws snapped closed.

He screamed aloud and got his left hand on the root also as the creature tugged, hard.

It then occurred to Don that he should be in agony right now, but he was not. The caiman had a firm grip on the boot laced onto the prosthetic limbs 'foot'.

He was hanging on for dear life with both hands and if the beast had continued to pull back towards the deep water then it would have eventually won the tug-o-war.

The caiman rolled, it did so instinctively and suddenly Don was free as the artificial limbs retainers gave way.

Scrambling up the muddy slope until clear of the water he paused for the briefest moment to look back. The creature was not in sight; only turmoil on the surface gave any indication of where it was.

Turning back towards safety he saw sudden movement above him, smelled warm fetid breath and saw the layered teeth on the jaws that closed on his head.

Captain Li had raised his night glasses to peer downriver as he heard the change in the Chinooks engines pitch.

"Standby Strela... aim slightly above the trees, you may get a lock-on even if you can't see the bastard!"

The sound seemed to roll towards them in waves as the power came on to lift the aircraft out of the clearing.

He caught a glimpse of the rear rotor, set above the fuselage and the forward assembly, but it then banked away out of sight for a second, reappearing over the river a few seconds later.

The flash made Li take an involuntary step backwards and there followed a thunderclap of sound that echoed across the jungle.

The helicopter came apart in mid-air, plunging into the river.

Li lowered his glasses and leaned over the conning tower to congratulate the air sentry but the man was looking back up at him with a don't-look-at-me expression and pointing to the tip of the launcher, where the surface-to-air missile was still very much attached.

"SIR!" called a voice from the dockside.

Sergeant Yen was cupping his hands to his mouth.
"As I was saying...they stuck a Type 72 in the engine compartment and wired it up electrically to the troop ramp locking mechanism...worked at treat, eh sir?"

ESA Jetty, Kourou, French Guiana.

Greasy smoke drifted down river on the breeze and the flicker of flame was still visible on the water, a reflection from around the rivers bend of the Chinook's final resting place.
It had been quiet for almost twenty minutes, a lull but one that was obvious to all as the quiet bit that comes before the other thing.
Small arms fire broke out from the south side of the road bridge as the troopers finished their task of preparing it for demolition and climbed back over the guardrail. The muzzle flashes were visible from the bridge of both *Dai* and of *Bao*. One of the troopers was hit and started to topple backwards, but his mate grabbed him and in the act of pulling him over was himself hit, falling screaming to the roadway. Both vessels 23mm cannon opened fire, tearing up the area where the shots had been fired, ripping splintered chunks out of the trees and amputating branches that fell with a splash into the river, silencing the firing from that quarter.
The injured were dragged to safety under the cover of the automatic cannons fire.
"Cease fire! Cease fire!" Captain Li called out. "Only shoot at what you can see from now on." They had only a limited amount of 23mm cannon ammunition. The Russian *Admiral Potemkin* had gone down with all the supplies.
He peered into the darkness but it was impossible to tell how effective the fire had been.
Shots next came from the opposite direction, from the eerily dark and foreboding jungle on their side of the river, it started with a single weapon, and rapidly increased into a vicious fire fight.
"How much longer?" he shouted to *Bao*'s bridge.

"Another hundred gallons give or take!"

The wounded troopers from the road bridge were taken aboard the *Bao.*

From downriver there came the sound of other helicopters rotor blades, growing louder by the moment but he caught no sight of them at all through the night glasses or weapons sight.

"Raise radar."

Up it went, twenty eight feet above their heads.

"Go active...one sweep, no more."

It was the equivalent of keeping phone calls short so the call could not be traced, in pre digital technological terms anyway. These days in the same way the callers ID is instantly displayed on screen so too is the radar type and location to within three metres on anti-radar weapons systems.

Modern weapons would target the origin of the source location even if the radar were to be turned off, or stooge around waiting for it to reappear.

How else though was Captain Li to see what the enemy were up to?

Just the two slow moving track of the helicopters showed, and no sign of the fixed wing threat yet.

"Double up the air sentries, I want one on the forward casing immediately." He called down.

There had been nothing from Jie's or the *Soyuz* team, no sounds of cratering charges, no nothing. No more lullabies were sung by the tone death senior sergeant. What had been a forty strong unit had first been cut to twenty eight with the sinking of the *Tuan*, and was now down to six effectives. The two other teams were dead or captured and the mission had well and truly lost the advantage of surprise.

An explosion beyond the fuel storage tanks brought a sudden end to the attack from that quarter, the versatile Type 72 anti-tank mine and white phosphorus smoke grenades turned into an anti-personnel claymore mine by Sergeant Yen incorporating a pile of hardcore left over from the laying of the car park. The screams of those caught in its blast provided all the judgement necessary on the mines effectiveness.

The firing slackened for several moments before redoubling in intensity as the wounded reservists mates extracted them using proven CASEVAC, casualty evacuation methods.

Under the cover of this weight of fire five pairs skirmished forwards. Nylon waterproof capes were tossed down, the three wounded casualty's screams were ignored as they were quickly rolled onto the capes and dragged away far more swiftly than would otherwise have been possible, the smooth material of the cape providing minimal friction with the wet jungle floor. The dead were left where they lay to be retrieved after the fight.

Once back in cover the veterans with the middle aged spreads drew on the experience of years, from Kolwezi and a dozen bushfire wars in Africa, treating wounds from first aid packs stocked according to lessons learned on those battlefields. WP is small grains of phosphorus that burn in contact with the air to produce white smoke. It burns skin and bone too; in clumps it can burn clear through a limb. The best treatment is immediate immersion in water whilst the grains are removed with wooden implements. Metal tweezers will only increase the injury, rapidly heated by the same grains they picked at, glowing red hot within minutes, so the tools of choice are tiny wooden spoons, the type you can still get in some cinemas and movie theatres in small individual tubs of ice cream, suitably wetted before application of course. These were in the packs, so too was Colgate toothpaste, the original white paste but in the small sachets sold in third world supermarkets and shanty town shops. Spread thickly over the injury it took the heat out of the badly blistered surface burns, preventing further tissue damage and bringing relief from the pain.

Puncture wounds, the entry wounds, these were plugged with female sanitary tampons pushed into the entry wounds, swelling up and keeping the wound clean. Bacteria will complete a bullets job so the wounds needed to be kept clean from the outset particularly in germ rich environments such as a jungle.

Screaming men had rifle slings forced between their teeth to bite on as field first aid was applied.

When the mine had been fired by Yen he knew how the legionaries would react and made sure heads stayed down on the friendly side. He knew the reservists ammunition supply was just what they carried in their pouches, so what the hell, let them brass up the bushes as their mates were retrieved, wasting rounds and reducing their options regarding further offensive moves.

He had killed two and wounded another three, and those three would have at least six uninjured troops carrying them to the rear.

He did not know how many they faced from that direction, but he figured that it was more than the fifteen a Chinook could officially carry, but either way the reservists were now short eleven weapons and a bundle of brass they could not replace any time soon.

The road bridge suddenly blew with a flash and a boom that must have carried far further than the sound of the Chinooks demise.

The black and acrid by-products of high explosive, the smoke and stink of burnt almonds was carried away on the wind as two out of the three spans prepared for demolition fell into the river. The third just stayed stubbornly where it was, the explosives wedged into the joins between the span and the supports were visibly still intact.

Rubble fell back to earth, splashing into the river, onto the surviving sections, and into the jungle with a crash.

There was no obvious explanation as to why the third road span had not joined the other two but that was all academic now, thought Li.

They needed to be gone from here, and the arrival of a belt of two 81mm mortar roads just short of the road in front of the gatehouse added further emphasis.

"Back together both, dead slow." Li ordered.

two more rounds arrived, uncorrected, merely bedding in rounds to set the baseplates solidly, but in that the baseplate position for each barrel was good for only a half dozen rounds apiece as each round fired drove the mortar baseplate deeper into the sodden earth.

The legionnaires had been put down on the Route de l'Espace by the Puma and Gazelle, and set up their mini mortar line on the verge.

Had they a rifle platoon nearby the mortars would have been sited on the solid but unyielding tarmac with a riflemen acting as a shock absorber, fingers in ears and with both feet on the baseplate.

"Une prochaine!" would summons the next rifleman when the former rolled off the baseplate in pain with one or both ankles broken.

Riflemen were good for an average eight rounds, even on a bad day.

The *Bao* cast off whilst still fuelling; hungry for every drop of precious diesel they could get into the *Kilo*'s tanks.

The fuelling probe ejected itself, the hose at full stretch it sprang from the intake valve, clanged against the starboard main ballast tank and flopped into the river with a splash.

Slippery diesel made life interesting for the FAS party but they quickly secured the intake valve and riser.

Something struck the *Fliterland*'s hull, ricocheting away with a whine. The shooters from earlier on were back, lying prone on the southern side of the now wrecked road bridge, taking pot-shots at *Dai*. The *Dai*'s 23mm replied, its gunners first burst going 'over' through lack of practice, allowing the jungle warfare schools CO and RSM to make it into cover speckled with shredded leaf matter. Like an evergreen wedding party, plastered with matching confetti, crawling rapidly backwards heedless of gravel-rash on skinned knees and elbows, back beyond the roads camber as cannon shells diced and sliced the overhanging trees canopy. It is doubtful though that the wedding party analogy was befitting the language being issued by both thoroughly alarmed men, especially from the sarn't major who had a far greater vocabulary along those lines from which to draw on than his colonel.

Aboard the *Bao* a linesman dropped with a cry, the muzzle flashes of a half dozen FAMAS assault rifles in the jungle on the north bank were temporarily extinguished by the joint efforts of *Bao*'s 23mm and several armed ratings on the casing.

Dai's casing doors slid open, the forward pair sucking in oxygen and the after pair coughed, spluttered and gave vent to a throaty roar as her diesels kicked in.

Captain Li's putting the Juliett alongside the jetty was not as neat and pretty as the first occasion. A screech of steel against concrete announced her arrival and the 23mm gave one last burst towards the bridge before swinging dockside to cover the withdrawal.

They fell back in bounds, working in pairs with one firing as his mate moved back to the next available cover, but harassed by fire from the jungle bordering the car park, and more seriously by an old sweat with the reservists tactical radio.

The still ringing telephone in the gatehouse was at last silenced as the building blew apart and began to burn. The next rounds sent the prefabricated roof sections of the covered car park sailing, only to fall spinning like lethal Frisbees' amongst the armed ratings. Behind them Sergeant Yen and a trooper lay behind a low wall, liberally dusted in debris from the nearby gatehouse which now silhouetted them in its flames. Incoming fire cracked passed, just overhead or struck the brickwork to ricochet away whining, sending brick splinters flying. Yen cursed, a long cut down the length of one cheekbone from one such shard of red brick. They fired rifle grenades into the jungle shadows, attempting to silence the spotter but the next rounds were 'on' and the orderly withdrawal became a sprint to safety by the survivors.

Six of *Dai's* crew members lay unmoving on the black tarmacadam, the neatly and precisely painted white lines defining the car parking spaces now marred by flecks of blood.

Crewmen stood on the casing helped their messmates down, dropping off the edge of the jetty where they were grabbed before they could topple into the water from the curving convex ballast tank.

Bao's 23mm was still firing into the jungle but she had not slowed, the cannon's fire becoming less effective with each turn of her screw.

Sergeant Yen and the trooper arrived last, *Dai's* 23mm working over the darkened jungle as they threw smoke grenades into the undergrowth before running hell for leather down the sloping car park, shouting to cast off and that all who could were already aboard. They pounded along the jetty and arrived as the gulf between it and the submarines casing was widening, caught as it was now by the current. Not slowing as the seamen had but leaping long and high, risking broken bones but they made it and grimaced on sprained ankles as they were helped below.

Dai's 23mm cannon fell silent, all ammunition expended.

Captain Li looked over at the fallen crew members as the *Dai* backed away from the jetty, illuminated in the flickering firelight from the burning gatehouse they were unmoving, the wind ruffling tattered and torn uniform clothing.

"All back slow...special sea duty men below!" he leant over the coaming to shout at two armed ratings and the air sentries standing upright on the after casing.

"Air sentries kneel behind the conning tower...you riflemen there, *get down*!"

The throb of *Bao's* diesels reverberated as she too switched from her electric motors. She had reached the bend in the river, her 23mm silent too, either out of ammunition or out of effective range.

The next rounds arrived, fired from mortar barrels pointing up at a high angle, the baseplates now sunk almost two feet.

High angle equals greater flight time equals greater variation of error. One round struck the now empty jetty whilst the other landed well 'off' in the small tank farm to perforate several of the cylindrical containers.

"Standby tubes One and Two...helm, give me five degrees to port...'midships, steady, all stop!"

Dai's stern pointed not safely mid-stream but angled toward the southern bank.

The *Fliterland* was now once more a darkened silhouette, sat silent and aloof from the mayhem.

Dai's bow pointed directly at the dark shape.

Li raised the microphone.

"Fire one!"

The gunner dropped without a sound and a lookout screamed. Perhaps a dozen points on the north bank lit up with the muzzle flashes of the Legionnaire reservists determined to exact revenge.

Rounds struck the coaming, the mast cluster and the sides of the conning tower to produce a sound like pebbles flung on to a tin roof.

The 21" torpedo, set shallow, broached the surface on leaving the tube, porpoising but unswerving it struck the *Fliterland* amidships, exploding and flinging fiery debris every which way.

The tank farm blew in spectacular fashion, a great fireball climbing high into the sky.

The scene was now lit, the darkened field of battle not such an unknown now. The submarine in mid river bathed in the light of fire, picked out by the shadow her bulk cast on the jungle behind.

Li's jaw dropped momentarily as he witnessed the spectacle, and then on seeing the reservists on the north bank likewise frozen in shock, weapons still trained on his vessel but heads turned, witnessing the destruction of freighter and fuel tanks.

Li's jaw closed with a determined snap and his right hand dropped, fumbling under his oilskin coat and unbuttoning the flap on his webbing holster. Drawing the weapon, he dropped the microphone in order to pull back the slide, aim, pull the trigger and frown when nothing happened. The slide was still glaringly to the rear, and an empty magazine housing in the pistols butt the obvious cause.

He swore, hurriedly located the magazine in his trousers pocket, inserted it sharply and the slide sprang forward with a satisfying snap. Li pointed it shore wards once more only to find his targets had gone, slipped away back into the shadows.

A corpsman took the wounded gunner and lookout below and their replacements, heaving up a metal box of 23mm ammunition took post.

By now there was no sign at all of the *Bao*.

The *Fliterland's* sterncastle was on fire, her hold a furnace. The freighter was listing to port and settling by the bow, the tops of her copper plated propeller blades reflecting the firelight from the tank farm.

With a shriek of tortured steel her aftermost derrick sagged forwards and toppled into the red maw of the hold sending a cloud of burning cinders aloft like emigrating fireflies.

No second torpedo would be required. She was now a major obstruction to any future use to this dock or to this jetty.

"Five degrees starboard...slow, back together."

They edged away, back from the flickering firelight on the water, back into the dark of a river crowded in on two sides by the jungle at night.

Around the bend in the river a small area of the north bank still burned, the Chinooks grave marked by the upright rotor blade protruding from the water.

"Look sir!" announced a lookout, pointing into the trees on the south side.

Captain did not need his night glasses, the flames provided enough light.

"You don't see that very often do you sir? A one legged pilot, sitting up a tree."

The company's silver wings caught the firelight and stood out in stark relief on the breast of the wet one-piece flight suit.

At the foot of the tree a caiman, possible eighteen feet in length was gnawing at a pilot's helmet.

Li straightened and raised his hand in a formal salute.

Don Caldew shifted his grip to hold the branch with his left, extending his right with knuckles downwards toward the Chinese submariner and raised a single upright digit.

Forty eight miles south east a pair of Breguet Atlantiques taxied. One behind the other, *Poseidon Zero Four* and *Poseidon One Eight* followed the glistering wet taxiway as their operators established communications with all elements involved, on land, sea and in the air.

Bombing-up had taken place on the taxiway itself, five hundred metres from the nearest airport building without the blessing of the airport manager who had been overruled by the governor. By prior agreement this potentially hazardous procedure was to have taken place outside the perimeters chain link fence via a pair of extra-width security gates, gates that opened on to a hard standing where the airport fire brigade practiced its art on a prefabricated concrete aircraft facsimile. But it was late and no one knew who had the keys.

Both aircraft carried four depth charges apiece, *Zero Four* also held two Mk 46 torpedoes whereas *One Eight* carried only one, but beside it in the bomb bay was an MM40 Exocet anti-shipping missile.

Ordnance expenditure in the Atlantic had been high, as the three quarters empty bomb bays testified.

In addition to the low loadout of offensive weaponry the defensive variety was also thin on the ground with the appearance of the Soviet's Launch-At-Depth anti-aircraft system. It produced an uncalculated psychological effect on air crews, despite the small number of hulls that had carried the device. The bad news spread fast.

NATO's maritime patrol aircraft crews had quite understandably made rather prodigious use of counter-measures, exhausting many NATO members stocks of flares and chaff.

Parachute flares for illumination they had aplenty, but both aircraft were reduced to prayer, a box of cartridges and a crew member with a Very pistol by way of surface to air counter measures for heat seeking missiles.

Zero Four turned onto the end of the runway, lining up on the centreline, her twin Rolls Royce Tyne turbo prop engines ran up with the captain holding it on its brakes.

Something caught the captain's attention, turning his head to look out of the left side window he could see an area of the cloud base above the horizon in the north that was glowing red.

The journey back to the ocean, stern first, seemed to Li to be taking an interminably long time, far longer than it had been to originally reach the ESA dock, and indeed it was, out of necessity.

A lookout was posted over the stern for deadfalls which would cause far more damage to the rudder and screws if they collided, than would a bow-on encounter.

Bao was visible ahead, engines stopped as crewmen hanging over the stern used brute force to manoeuvre one such hazard to the side.

"All stop."

The chant of the diesels had a way of negating the fear of the unknown that this jungle held.

Rather than be reassured though, Li looked about him, peering at the banks, alert, aware that something was amiss.

"Go to electrical power."

The throb of un-muffled diesels gave way to a drone, a murmur inhibited by a wind blowing in the wrong direction.

It came from up on high, above the lofty jungle canopy and above the cloud base.

"Bridge...ECM; we've been painted by radar Captain, airborne source bearing 120 degrees!"

"Stand to, air sentries!"

A green flare, not of the para-illumination variety, emerged from the clouds, falling rapidly, a red flare followed before harsh white magnesium produced light dropped swinging into view, the wind carrying it as it hung suspended on a small parachute.

Dai's air sentries pivoted, the Strela launchers at their shoulders and eyes squinting down the open iron sights atop the launcher as they attempted to judge the position of the hidden aircraft. Fingers took up first pressure on the triggers to engage the missiles seeker head.

The 'lock' lights flickered and the tone was intermittent, confused by more coloured flares falling from the clouds, as they turned slowly from north to south.

Li too was peering upward at the sound of the Atlantique's engines as a lookout called "Aircraft action, *forward*!"

The second aircraft also came in from the direction of the ocean, but a scant hundred feet above the trees, its wings tilting as it followed the lie of the river, the bomb bay doors gaping open.

The same parachute flare dropped by *One Eight* which had illuminated the submarine's also revealed the pale grey shape of *Poseidon Zero Four* at the moment an object fell from out of the open belly, followed immediately by a second.

Bao's air sentries were taken by as much surprise as were half of *Dai's*.

The sound of the Rolls Royce engines passing above them and the roar of *Bao's* and *Dai's* 23mm automatic cannon's made Li flinch but his eyes did not leave the two falling objects, blunt nosed depth charges, not tumbling but semi stabilised, oscillating at the finned tails as they fell at an angle towards their target.

Tracer chased the Atlantique, spent 23mm shell cases rattled and rang against the metal deck of the submarines bridge.

The first depth charge crashed into the trees near the south bank of the river some fifty metres beyond the stationary *Bao* but the second struck the Kilo's forward casing.

It sounded a lot like two cars colliding, without the desperate last moment screech of brakes. Black acoustic tiles flew aloft like crows startled at the sound of a shotgun, and the depth charge bounced, spinning end over end now, the tail section stabilisers parting company in the impact, flying off into the darkness.

The dented casing grew larger in Li's sight, like a dustbin flung by a petulant giant it arced up and towards the Juliett.

The air sentry on *Dai's* bow fired, engulfing the conning tower in white exhaust gases as the slim missile left the launch tube. The smoke robbed Li of his view of the approached object.

The depth charge on the river bank blew with a blinding flash, its 200kg warhead felling two trees and sending wickedly barbed wooden splinters outwards in all directions, the detonation echoing for miles around.

The Strela's success went almost unheard in comparison. It flew straight and true for the greatest heat source, striking the starboard engine exhaust. The effect of the small 1.7kg warhead and a secondary charge detonating the missiles remaining fuel was visual, rather than audible. A small flash followed by much smoke.

Poseidon Zero Four instantly lost altitude, the starboard wing dropped, the wingtip clipping a tree top and it seemed to be all over bar the shouting for the aircraft and crew.

The port engine roared as its throttle was pushed through the gate in an effort by the captain and co-pilot to compensate, to ward off a threatening departure from controlled flight.

They clawed for height, the tree tops so close, waiting snares to drag them from the air to a fiery end in the jungle but the prey won the battle as its remaining ordnance load was jettisoned. *Zero Four* bounded up and clear of the tree tops, disappearing into the night towards the west.

Li coughed and waved a hand ineffectually as if warding off unwanted cigarette smoke. He stood upright to peer through the missiles exhaust fumes, to see where the charge would land, and so the deluge of filthy brown river water, heavily laden with mud struck him from behind. Bouncing clear over the *Dai* the depth charge had plunged into the river beyond to lodge in the silted bottom where it went off.

Declaring an emergency *Poseidon Zero Four* shuddered in flight, a vibration increasing by the moment.

It was missing three feet off its starboard wingtip, and the propeller was continuing to spin despite the engine now being shut down and denied fuel. Refusing to be feathered, the rogue propeller spun on, and at a higher rate than that of the still functional port engine. The reduction gearbox had been damaged and the blades could not be turned into wind to reduce drag.

Fire retardant compound was pumped onto the engine but as the propellers RPM spun ever higher, the propeller nosecone glowed red, and the vibration worsened.

A flicker of flame necessitated the fire handle being pulled again and all the while the aircraft was in a gentle sweeping turn so as not to overstress the damaged wing.

The captain aimed to bring them back to Cayenne, it was after all the closest airport with a runway long enough to accommodate them.

Ten minutes on and the propeller was rotating at 120% of the maximum recommended RPM, and again the fire handle had to be pulled to extinguish flames.

They were dumping fuel from the port wing and transferring fuel from the starboard. The risk of the flames reaching the fuel tanks in the damaged wing was very real indeed.

Over the ocean now and continuing their left turn, lining up for an approach to runway 26. The captain gave due consideration to the options available, to attempt a landing or to ditch?

By day the Cayenne fishing fleet could be seen at its moorings due to the scarcity of fish. There were no civilian boats abroad that could come to their assistance and the nearest navy vessel was laid up, the rest were rushing north to do battle.

A ditching rarely had a happy ending anyway, so he announced to the crew that he was committed to a landing at Cayenne. They buckled up and a few peered out and down at the dark ocean. However, it was too dark to see anything unaided. Obligingly the starboard engine provided some, and the flicker became a tail that could not be extinguished now, the fire retardant compound having been completely expended.

The second Atlantique, *One Eight*, could be heard stooging around up above the clouds, and the Legion's two helicopters could be heard also, as they raced low towards the town of Kourou, dropping the two mortar teams at Pont Les Roches, the mouth of the estuary that the Chinese raiders must pass on their way back to the ocean.

The *Bao* and the *Dai* were underway again, backing down the river to the estuary where they could at last find room to turn and face their tormentors.

"Radar, one sweep only."

Above them the Atlantiques threat warnings sounded as the *Dai's* radar swept across them in return.

"Capitaine... I would advise chaff right about now...but."

"But...we have no chaff..."

Unwrapping a stick of spearmint gum, popped it in his mouth the pilot unlatched the side window, ejecting the gums silver wrapper.

"That will have to do." He muttered to himself, resigned to fate.

Severe vibration was shaking *Zero Four*, severe enough to throw off her captain's voice, giving him an induced stammering which at another time would sound a little comical.

"Fifteen degrees flap...gear down."

Had the circumstances been different he would have overflown the runway in order that the control tower confirm the right gear was fully down, but the nose and left gear had green lights.

The starboard engine was aflame, consuming itself, the flames streaming behind.

Ahead of them the tarmac was lit up, and emergency vehicles were sat off to one side, well clear of the runway but awaiting their arrival.

Zero Four crossed the outer marker, the approach lights whipped below them and suddenly there was the threshold.

He missed the touchdown zone, holding off as he allowed the left gear to touch first, sweeping along with the nosewheel and right gear just clear of the tarmac. There was no chance of going around again, no chance of reaching the ocean for a ditching now either, too late to change his mind. The right gear touched and the nose settled, he chopped the throttle and held the aircraft to the centre line. All there was to do now was stop the damn thing before they ran out of runway.

The wind was blowing the flames along the wing toward the fuselage but captain and co-pilot were busy standing on the brakes. One life threatening crisis at a time, s'il vous plaît.

At the far end of the runway the threshold markers were beneath the front wheel as he pivoted the aircraft left with the last bit of momentum, to buy a little more time before the flames reached fuel tanks that were still filled with vapour.

With brakes applied the captain pushed out the left side window as he unbuckled.

The cabin was filling with choking fumes but he had to check the crew.

Crewmembers were vacating the aircraft rapidly; the senior operator was last, coughing on toxic fumes. His co-pilot exited through the captains opened window and the captain himself followed the senior operator, dropping to the tarmac and running as fast as he could.

As the fire trucks arrived the open hatches were belching smoke. Fire could be seen inside the cabin as internal fittings caught alight. A thunderous bang sent flames and pieces of the starboard wing soaring as the vapour filled fuel tank gave way. A pair of less violent explosions announced the tyres of the right gear bursting.

The damaged wing sagged and the Atlantique leaned to the right, grey smoke pouring from the pilots open side window like a chimney, the fuselage completely engulfed in flame..

Cayenne airports fire crews had at least a proper subject to test their skills on now.

A signaller handed Li a message form, the *Bao* had sustained damage to her forward pressure hull where the depth charge had struck the casing. Submerging in that condition was possible but not advisable in ordinary circumstances. She had a double hull, but that pressure hull was not just there by idle design.

"Damn all we can do about that now, anyway." He mused.

Bao was still on diesels but *Dai* remained on electrical power despite the chief engineer complaining the batteries were down to a 72% charge.

He used the radar sparingly as that was a double edged weapon, but he could hear the approach of threats without the enemy using that against them.

A flash off in the jungle caught his attention and a fraction of a second later he heard the sound of mortar rounds detonating.

Those damn bloody French mortars again! He thought.

They had to be firing blind though, possibly alerted to their approach by the sound of *Bao's* noisy diesel engines.

Two more rounds landed, well short, one on the bank and the other splashing into the river without going off. There was only mud and silt where that particular mortar round had landed, nothing solid enough to crush the soft nose cone and fire the fuse there.

Captain Li gave a moment's thought to the weight of a mortar round. How many could those helicopters carry?

Jie would have known of course.

To be on the receiving end of a mortar attack was doubly hazardous as they made no sound, no advance warning to dive for cover, unlike the mournful drone he know heard!

Bao's radar mast was fully extended and rotating.

A 100mm shell from a naval gun smashed into the bank between the two submarines, digging deep into the soft earth before exploding.

Li shouted down the open hatch.

"Make to *Bao*...they are ranging in on your radar energy, but at least we know there is a surface warship in gunfire range."

The rotating radar ceased but three more rounds impacted in the vicinity, white hot steel fragments striking the *Dai's* conning tower.

He raised his night glasses once more, looking back towards the river mouth. The river was widening now.

Dirty water sprayed over the conning tower from more mortar rounds landing in the river.

A round struck the bank beside *Bao*, the air sentry on the Kilo's after casing screamed and fell, sliding down the curved steel pressure hull into the river. *Bao* did not heave-to, and the rating was floating face down as the *Dai* reached him. Li watched the corpse disappear behind them in the darkness.

"Engine room...switch to diesels once more. We need to run on the surface for a little once we regain the estuary."

The mortar rounds continued to harass, raining down around them but the naval gunfire had curtailed with the cessation of the *Bao's* radar sweeps.

A rating appeared at the top of the ladder looking a lot like a caricature of a Mexican bandit, draped across the shoulders with belted ammunition for the 23mm.

"This is the last cannon ammunition, sir."

Li nodded in acknowledgement and instructed him to start throwing empty cases over the side once the new belt was attached to the end of the existing one.

If they had to run silent it would not do to have brass shell cases rolling around and knocking into each other and the steel sides at such times.

Bao chugged backwards past the old and abandoned Kourou ferry.

In the distance, highlighted against a black skyline, the sparks from the plastic augmenting charges that fitted about a mortar bombs 'tail' hung in the air like fireflies before dying. It was of no use to the gunner though as it is almost impossible to judge the distance to a light at night with the naked eye. What may appear to be the light from a farmhouse window on a hillside two miles away may in fact be a glowing cigarette end six feet off, and vice versa of course.

Coloured flares again reappeared, falling though the cloud to be followed by another parachute flare. They were trying to assist the mortar crews and whatever warship was out to sea but instead its light revealed on shore the tiny figures of the French Foreign Legionnaires serving the two mortar barrels at Pont Les Roches.

Bao's quick eyed gunner had seen the sparks and now he was on it, the barrel aiming up at an angle of perhaps as much as forty degrees.

Dai's 23mm joined in, working the stream of tracer left and right, wreaking a terrible revenge upon the mortarmen. Plunging fire dropped upon them wherever they crawled to seek cover, behind protrusions in the ground or the crudely crafted logs, laid out as park benches. The automatic cannons shredded the logs, reduced the protrusions in the earth and annihilated whatever was hidden behind.

No more mortar rounds came their way.

Bao's helm came over as her captain sought to turn bow on to the ocean again, at long last.

Dai now motored past the old ferry slipway too and Li put his glasses to the southeast, looking for the French warship.

The captain of *One Eight* finished his flare run across the estuary without himself or any of the crew catching sight of any action on the ground.

It was the fast patrol boat, *La Capricieuse,* which informed the Atlantique that the enemy submarines were emerging from the river into the estuary.

As sophisticated as they were, the Atlantiques onboard systems were unable to separate the submarines from the ground clutter while they were on the river. They were built to seek out targets on the surface or peeking up from below.

The patrol boats greatest asset was her speed, but this came at the cost of armament and armour. Her plywood hull was light and tough enough to deal with stormy seas, and her weaponry would be devastating against drug and gold smugglers vessels, but they had limited value against other warships.

"'Poseidon One Eight' this is La Capricieuse...enemy sighted!" Her commander was a young lieutenant not long out of the Brest naval academy.

"Attacking!" was the next message, the young man's voice not disguising the underlying excitement.

Five miles beyond them was forging in the corvette *Premier-Maitre L'her,* the second corvette still another ten miles further off.

The patrol boat made a magnificent sight, turning in and racing towards the surfaced Kilo at 25 knots, a great white bow wave standing out in the darkness. She had two automatic cannon, a 40mm and a 20mm, along with two 12.7mm machine guns, all were firing, and throwing out arcing lines of tracer, but speed and accuracy are not the same thing.

Crashing through waves, *La Capricieuse* opened fire at eight hundred metres, the gunners aim being thrown off by the action of the waves. The slowly moving and steady *Kilo's* single 23mm cannon remained silent, until the range had closed to three hundred. The patrol boat was obligingly bow-on and the cannon fire ripped through her from stem to stern. None of the patrol boats guns were firing as she tore past the *Bao.*

On the horizon there was a flash followed by a low moan overhead. A shell burst in the sea behind them.

Dai was some five hundred yards behind the *Bao* when she herself finished her turn.

The patrol boat *La Capricieuse* had been deliberately run aground on the shore at La Pont Roches and was settling low in the water but there was no sign of movement on board.

Bao fired again, but this time there was a geyser of water erupting from just forward of her bow as she launched on the fast approaching corvette, first one and then a second RPK-7 anti-ship missile was launched from her forward torpedo tubes.

"Full ahead together." Li ordered. "Dismount the 23mm and get it below...bow air sentry to the bridge."

The chugging growl of the big diesels increased apace.

There was another flash on the horizon but it was followed by a far larger emission, as the first anti-ship missile flew into chaff flung out by the corvette.

The first missile detonated in the chaff cloud and then the corvette exploded. It was initially a very visual, yet silent event, until the sound of the double explosions reached them.

There was cheering from the *Bao*, and then *Bao* blew up too.

A flash, smoke and a sound that made Li cringe, followed by wreckage falling all about and into the sea.

The air sentry was just appearing at the top of the ladder, he could not have seen the explosion but he did hear it and his eyes were as wide as saucers.

"Get below!" shouted Li to the man.

"Lookouts below... clear the bridge...*sound the diving alarm!*"

Poseidon One Eight's onboard systems had tracked the Exocet all the way from their bomb bay to its terminal impact.

Wary of surface-to-air missiles the Atlantique banked hard to port so as not to overfly the second submarine and instead her captain headed for the now stopped and burning corvette.

"Ready the life rafts!"

Captain Li removed the outer clothing and the ridiculous gun belt as he reached the control room, holding them out for his steward.

"He's gone captain." His exec said. "He was one of the landing party who were caught by the mortars."

Li faltered momentarily, not because he had any affection for the man, but because it may have a bearing on his future actions.

The launch pads had not been put out of action by conventional methods, which had been a complete failure as far as Li could tell.

His orders in the case of the special forces mission being a failure was to stand off and nuke the ESA site from the sea.

To fail to do that was a certain death sentence for himself and every member of the crew, including family members.

"Range to the *Soyuz* site?"

"Thirty point eight miles, captain."

The French aircrew were currently engaged in aiding the stricken warships survivors, but that would not last.

They had a small window in which to act and still be able to clear datum.

"Bring the boat to launch condition one, please."

Poseidon One Eight did not notice the launch of the single weapon. It burst from the depths with its protective cocoon falling away and its short stubby wings extending.

The cruise missiles ramjet propelled it at a respectable 467mph towards it target, the *Soyuz* launch pad, where the 320 kiloton warheads detonation would obliterate the *Ariane* and *Vega* sites in the same blast.

Such self-sacrifice, such effort by the inshore raiding flotilla.

Four submarines and three hundred and sixty one men had set off on this mission. One submarine and seventy four men remained now.

Far quicker, at 879mph, three Mistral high velocity surface-to-air missiles left the mobile launchers of the Legions air defence section and rendered all that effort null and void, obliterating the *Dai's* cruise missile before it had even crossed the coast.

Operation 'Early Dawn'

Battle of the Kourou River chronicle of events

'DAI' and 'BAO' avoid detection by French ASW corvette 'Premier-Maitre L'her'

Submersibles successfully penetrate minefield and land raiding parties.

3rd raiding party swim ashore at Kourou, neutralize local police and Kourou River Bridge sentries.

' DAI' and 'BAO' seize the ESA jetty along the Kourou River and refuel.

First two raiding parties destroyed by French troops guarding the ESA perimeter.

'DAI' and 'BAO' detected by Chinook helicopter at the ESA jetty.

Chinook helicopter brought down in the river by booby trap.

'DAI' and 'BAO' attacked by staff from the Jungle Warfare School.

3rd raiding party successfully blow Kourou River Bridge.

3rd raiding party defends against ground attack by French Foreign Legionnaires.

'DAI' and 'BAO' come under mortar attack, raiding party returns and vessels make fighting withdrawal.

'Dai' torpedoes and sinks MV Fliterland.

'DAI' and 'BAO' attacked by French maritime patrol aircraft. 'BAO' damaged.

'BAO' attacked by fast patrol boat and corvette 'Premier-Maitre L'her'. Patrol boat damaged and corvette sunk by 'BAO' anti-ship missile.

'BAO' sunk by air launched Exocet. 'DAI' launches cruise missile at ESA

The Battle of the Kourou River - 1

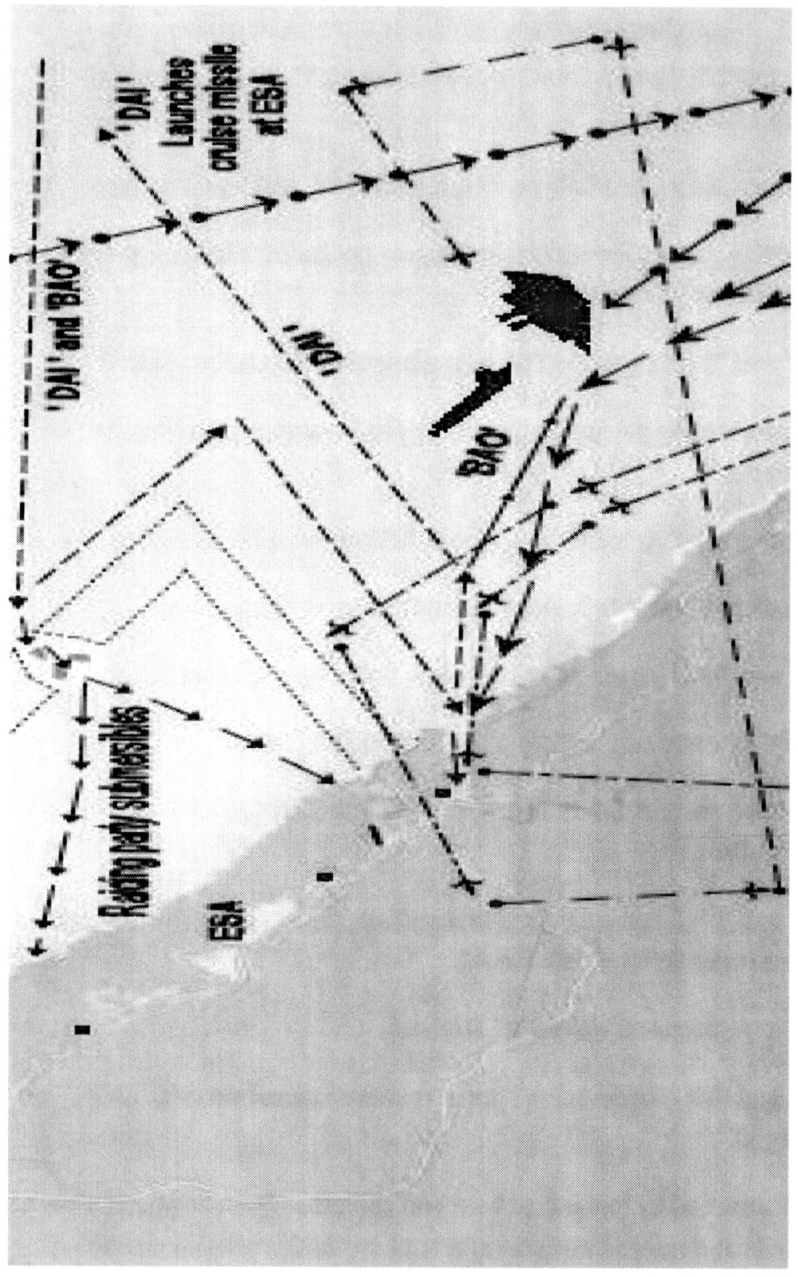

The Battle of the Kourou River – 2

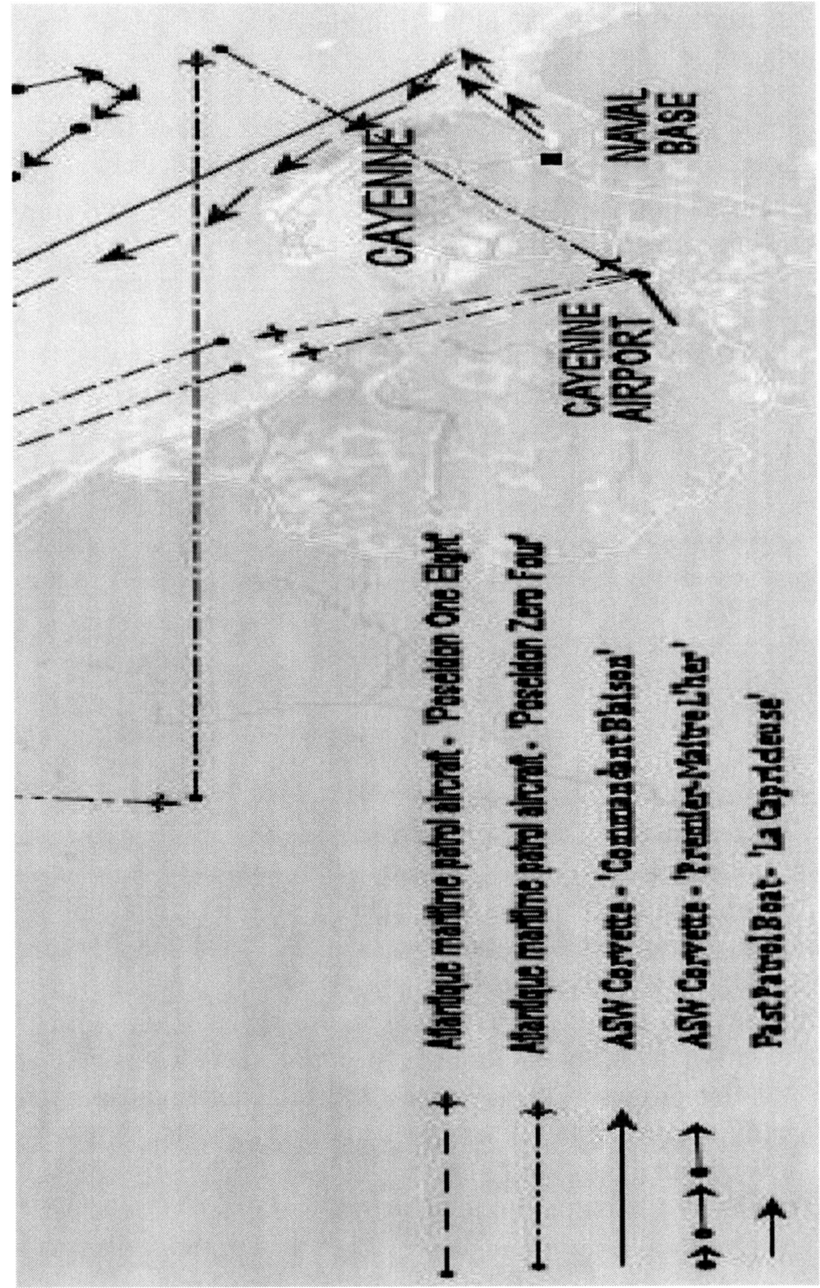

CHAPTER 3

Arkansas Valley, Nebraska, USA: 2057hrs, same day.

The return to the subterranean haunts that had become the homes for the President since the Washington bombing was depressing for Henry Shaw. Rubbing shoulders again with proper, down to earth troops who said it as they found it without the addition of spin had been a breath of fresh air. He already missed being with those who performed their duty as required and without catering to hidden agendas.

A not quite junior aide had met Henry on his return and managed to be respectful whilst still giving off a distinct coolness toward him. It was only to be expected; Henry would not have been surprised had a posse of MPs brought him back from Europe to face the President's wrath.

In stark contrast to the civilian, the marine guard had been more than happy to see him back. In their eyes the Corps top Marine had gone off to the battlefield instead of staying in a hardened shelter with the army, navy and air force brass. It was a simplistic and erroneous view of the situation, which unfairly slighted the other services, but since when did a Marine ever pass up on the chance to strut that little bit more in front of the rest of the armed forces?

The President looked up when the Chairman of the Joint Chiefs entered the Situation Room, giving a perfunctory nod of welcome to Henry but his eyes held no warmth.

"Has General Carmine fully briefed you on what you missed while in Europe?"

He nodded.

"Yessir, Mister President."

Henry took his seat and returned the greetings from CIA and FBI; apart from the service personnel at the table no one else so much as met his gaze. Terry Jones and Ben Dupre did not involve themselves in the office politics of whichever administration happened to be in power. They both knew Henry was on the Presidents' shit list and they both knew why. They also quietly admired the Marine for the balls he had shown doing what they both believed to be only right and just.

Henry thought back to when he had last been in the presence of the President. It had only been a week ago, just seven days that had been filled with briefings and hurriedly arranged meetings before moving on, on to another headquarters or out of the way location.

Looking back on it now it seemed far, far longer.

The President cleared his throat, bringing Henry Shaw back to the present.

"General, will you now present your briefing please?"

ETO, the European Theatre of Operations, appeared on the screen set against the far wall. Henry centred the picture over the channel ports

"As you can see, units of the US 4th Corps and Canadian 5th Infantry Division have now begun leaving the forming up points outside the city ports and begun the drive towards Germany after delays in offloading due to air attacks, and in some cases sabotage of dockside facilities." The view changed to show a map of the parallel routes the Corps would take across the Continent and into Germany on the same autobahns the Soviets were trying so hard to reach.

"4th Corps is leading as the Canadians are top heavy with leg infantry in trucks, but those are being dropped off along the way to secure bridges and key points against further Soviet airborne drops which would cut the service support routes."

"*Again.*" The President grumbled.

"Precisely, Mr President" Henry said in agreement.

"The Canadians have four such battalions in two brigades who will retain a small degree of artillery support but the remainder of their two brigades' artillery units, an armoured regiment and the two mechanised battalions, will proceed as part of the 4 Corps reserve."

"What of their logistics and support units, General." The President interrupted. "I do not see any of those?" his hand waved at the clusters of military symbols on the map.

"Rail priority has been given to ammunition and stores for units already at the front, and in particular the division straddling the autobahns to the channel ports, Mr President. The combat units are travelling by road and every MP, and every civilian cop we can muster is employed in keeping them moving and keeping refugees clear."

Henry paused to briefly underline the situation.

"This is a race we are engaged in, and if we win it the reds will still be engaged in fighting other NATO units when they arrive and 4th Corps can immediately launch a counter attack. If we lose then the Corps will take a defensive stance and we will again be reacting to the enemy instead of taking the fight to them."

The picture on the screen altered as Henry brought up the image of the German battlefield, focusing initially on the units either side of the Saale and Elbe rivers. The symbols depicting the types and size of units, lined on both banks, coloured blue for NATO units and red for the Red Army, but there were far more red symbols stacked behind each other to the east than there were blue ones on the west.

Two red coloured parachute symbols still remained in place on the western banks, despite NATO's best efforts to dislodge, and then annihilate them.

"Mister President, just before dawn this morning the Red Army began a massive rocket and artillery bombardment of NATO lines from north of Haldensleben, down to the southern suburbs of Magdeburg."

He stepped closer to the screen, his back to the wall and gesturing with his right hand without looking, without needing to look as he had memorised each screen of the briefing.

"The units being targeted are the US 5th and 12th Mechanised Brigades, the British 1st Armoured Brigade and the German 5th Panzer Grenadier and 4th Panzer Regiments." Henry paused to look the men and women present.

"SACEUR informs me that by midnight tonight at the latest, those units will have ceased to be combat effective and the Red Army will in all probability begin an assault river crossing against minimal ground opposition."

Grave looks were exchanged around the conference table, it was not unexpected news but that did not make it any easier of hear.

"General?"

Henry looked to his President, who had lowered his head to peer at him over the rim of his glasses.

"Yes, Mister President?"

"You have been to that sector have you not?"

Henry nodded in affirmation. "Yes sir, it was my first stop after meeting with General Allain."

"Is there anything that could have been done, or was there anything left undone...anything you feel may have prevented this from happening?"

General Shaw had been to all the sectors, not just that one. He had met with the commanders of the units mentioned and also been to the positions to see for himself the state of the defences, the level of training evident amongst the troops, and of course to judge the morale of the men and women in the fighting positions. Henry had squatted in the bottoms of trenches and shivered with the cold along with humble riflemen, speaking in English with British, Dutch and their own troops, in passable bier hall German to Panzer Grenadiers and schoolboy French to Belgian infantrymen and French Foreign Legionnaires.

It hadn't been his brief to crawl through a frozen wasteland at night, to spend three hours just a rifle shot from a fortified pile of rubble that had once been a factory, but he saw it as his duty as a commander of troops to share some of the hazards faced by the men and women he had been ordered to send into harm's way. The troops in that foxhole hadn't known who he was until the next day, hours after he had departed for another sector of the line. For an hour he had listened to the sounds of a wounded man, a Soviet paratrooper, crying for his mother in those ruins on the perimeter of one of the Red Army footholds on the west bank of the Saale.

In all it had reinforced something he and a good friend had discussed and agreed upon many years before, and that was that the only person to have the moral right to send men and women to war was someone who had themselves been in harm's way in the armed service of their country. If that simple fact became a matter of law then there would be far more talking around tables and fewer body bags, but that discussion had taken place in disreputable bar cum brothel in Southeast Asia, where even the flies had sense to swerve to avoid the bar girls. They had been young lieutenants then, and he at the end of a three-month attachment to his friends unit to see why Britain was winning its jungle war when at the same time America was losing hers.

Over many bottles of Tiger and in increasing degrees of intoxication the two men had written a new constitution on the backs of beer mats, built around the foundation of his friends somewhat slurred words

"You shouldn't be in a position to start a fight unless you've been in one yourself...no high office without first joining the brown adrenaline club."

A campaign slogan for their bid for world power had read 'Vote for me, I've not only shit myself in battle...but look here *I've even got the soiled shorts to prove it!'*

Henry had left the next day to return to Saigon with a hell of a hangover and little recollection of the previous night's events, his friend however had a better memory and over the years whenever they had bumped into one another and shared a drink or six he would speak whimsically of one day making 'The Beer Mat Constitution' into a reality, and had even worked out how it could be achieved.

When at last the wounded soldiers cries had faded and gone forever it had given Henry a greater determination, the co-author of the beer mat constitution may be dead at the bottom of the Irish Sea, but the idea was very much alive.

"Mister President, those men and women are outnumbered fifty to one, they have fought and held this long despite the inadequate equipment and war stocks their governments provided them to do the job, and the fact that they are about to be over run, and where the blame lies for that, is no fault of theirs."

A pin could have been heard dropping in the seconds that followed, and Terry Jones was not alone in realising a line had just been crossed. The President had been questioning whether there was fault in the ability of the men and women in uniform at the battlefront, but the Chairman of the Joint Chiefs had laid the blame squarely at the door of government.

The Joint Chiefs are free to criticise the Chief Executive, but on a one to one basis behind closed doors, not in front of onlookers even if they were on the staff.

The President became very still, and his eyes narrowed a fraction as he looked at his top soldier. Henry met the President's gaze and held it calmly in the knowledge that if he were to be relieved now it would matter not one iota.

The President broke the silence.

"A simple yes or no would have sufficed, General."

Henry went on to outline what they believed the enemy would do once they achieved a breakout.

"We expect the Third Shock Army to head for Amsterdam, Rotterdam, Zeebrugge and Antwerp, with their Sixth Shock Army following on behind through the breach and to then swing south west for the French ports. What remains of Second Shock and Tenth Tank army will probably hook left and right to roll up the rest of our lines. These are their last, first class outfits and they about used up their second-class units in keeping up the pressure on us and trying to force the rivers up to this point in time. Which leaves third class units to assist in the mopping up, whilst the fourth class...those manned by troops in their forties and early fifties, will in all probability be used to secure the lines of communication."

The President had rested his elbows on the table before him, and his hands were clasped together, the fingers entwined and he rested his chin on the spire they formed.

"What, may I ask, does General Allain intend to do about that?" The President followed on before Henry could answer.

"There is just a cobbled together, infantry heavy division sat in the way of god knows how many tanks so does he honestly believe that will hold them until our new Corps arrives on the scene?" with that he sat upright and raised a coffee mug to his lips while he waited for the answer.

Henry responded with four words.

With a snort that sent coffee splashing across the papers in front of him, the President choked in mid swallow. An aide hurried over and began mopping up the spilt coffee before him, and the President coughed whilst fishing out a handkerchief and dabbing at a growing stain on his shirt. Leaning to one side to see past the charring aide he stared at Henry.

"What?"

"He's going to attack." Henry Shaw repeated.

The President knew what forces were in Germany, and so he had to ask himself, and Henry, if SACEUR had taken leave of his senses.

"General Allain is quite sane Mr President; he is just faced with desperate choices at a desperate time."

Turning back to the screen Henry continued his explanation by highlighting two NATO units sat slightly to the rear of their own lines and at either side of the expected breach.

"These two units, the 2nd Canadian Mechanised Brigade and the French 8th Armoured Brigade, are currently in hide positions and have been brought up to strength as far as possible as regard reinforcements and supplies. Once the lead enemy manoeuvre units have passed through the breach they will close it behind them, sealing the breach."

"General?" The President was pointing the end of a pen towards the screen.

"If memory serves, that Canadian unit was over a hundred miles away two days ago and holding a section of the line to the north, and the French brigade was a lot further south, so who is in those positions now?"

"The King Alfonso XIII Light Infantry Legion Brigade relieved the Canadians in place thirty hours ago, and the Lusitania Light Armoured Cavalry Regiment took over from the French 8th Armoured about this time yesterday. They are both Spanish rapid reaction units and as such carry little in the way of excess baggage so the move took very little time."

The President was about to ask another question, clearly surprised that these moves and the Spanish units involved had not previously been even hinted at. He wasn't certain that the Spanish units in question were even under SACEUR's control. However, General Shaw had already turned away.

The map on the big screen panned back to encompass the south of Europe and the UK. Blue parachute symbols were clustered about the locations of airfields far from the fighting.

"Tomorrow morning at 0300hrs GMT, elements of the Belgian, Turkish, Greek, Spanish and Italian airborne forces, along with three battalions of the 82nd and the British 1st and 2nd Parachute battalions will drop into occupied Germany to attack enemy airfields and supply lines."

Henry paused before finishing and looked at all the faces peering from him to the screen.

"This is a one shot deal and there will be no reinforcement or re-supply."

The President sat listening with raised eyebrows as Henry spoke, and when he had finished the President looked around the table.

"Why is it that this is first that I have heard of it? Why haven't any of the European leaders spoken to me about this? Why General, *was I not consulted*?"

Henry gave him that answer.

"I think you will find sir that General Allain felt that the other leaders would only have seen it as throwing good money after bad, and would have wanted to preserve those forces for the defence of their own borders. He may also have felt that by consulting you sir, it would have put you in an awkward position."

"No shit." The President replied with much irony, and then as another thought occurred to him his brows knotted together in confusion.

"So how did he get those airborne units, General?"

"He didn't consult the national leadership's sir."

Henry answered.

"Only the Generals'."

What Henry had revealed was a deliberate subversion of the lawful chain of command in those countries, and the President could only assume that General Shaw had no part in it. As to the use of their own airborne the President did not have any cause to gripe, they were troops already 'in theatre' and under SACEUR's command, as were 1 and 2 Para. Some of the Spanish and Italian unit symbols were centred over RAF Lyneham in England, as were Danish, Swedish, Norwegian, Dutch and Canadian air transport units, the means to carry those paratroopers to war. The President was at a loss as to why *no one* in the British Ministry of Defence had noticed a sizeable foreign force drawing rations.

"General Shaw, is the British government mixed up in this, are they colluding with SACEUR?"

Henry gave a short laugh.

"*Mizz* Foxten-Billings is so wrapped up achieving her own secret agenda she can't see beyond her own little conspiracies, sir."

The President looked hard at Henry Shaw, trying to judge the truth of his words. After a very long moment he gave up.

"Win or lose, the elected governments of those countries are gonna have that damn Canadian by the balls when this is over, and they'll pin 'em up right alongside the ones they cut off their own general staff's." The President shook his head slowly as he considered the fall-out which would surely come about.

"Mister President." Henry Shaw interrupted the President's chain of thought, bringing his eyes back to the end of the room.

"If the reds reach the coast then it is game over, and those governments won't be able to touch him because some KGB troops will already have put him against a wall and shot him...but if it works and we stop them, do you really think Pierre Allain, or those general staffs, will give a flying fuck what the food will be like in whatever prison they may choose to toss them into?" The President and everyone else present were silent as Henry spoke, lecturing them as if they first graders who needed the rules explained.

"General Allan's job is to defeat the enemy." He went on. "That is a soldier's job, and General Allain is one hell of a good soldier. He will be a sneaky sonofabitch if that is what it takes to save lives and do his duty, and if that means pissing off a few politicians, then so be it."

Henry looked at everyone sat around the table.

"Pierre has more honour in a single finger nail then that silly English bitch has in both her little boy breasts."

Terry Jones felt the President's eyes upon him but his poker face remained in place. He had received a report from his chief of station in London, qualified by another from Paris that Henry Shaw had been getting about, probably by covert means during his fact finding mission to the embattled continent. Henry had even been present at the London police commissioners' home when a veritable who's who of military men and senior police officers, some of whom were retired, who had come calling. Art had cobbled together a hurried surveillance operation and had himself chosen to spend an uncomfortable night in a covert vehicle near the commissioner's home rather than be present when the SAS arrested the cell responsible for Scott and Constantine's deaths, which was indication in itself that his London stations chief had a gut feeling that something was amiss.

Terry had not had the chance to fully analyse the possibilities that the report could be indicating. There was every chance that Henry Shaw had been avoiding the time wasting that the meet and greets of announced visits would have entailed, but his presence in England at that gathering, and his apparent previous knowledge of SACEUR's plans could put a very different spin on it. Had Terry known then what he had just discovered at this briefing then he may have read more into it if he had not also received information of a possible intelligence break through that had taken preference in the order of importance. That particular information was being analysed right now, and he could only give the President a heads up on what may, if it was genuine, be of considerable help to them. However, back in the here and now his President wanted answers.

"Mister Jones, did you know anything about this? Didn't the Central Intelligence Agency have any hint that NATO armed forces were about to give their elected governments the finger and do their own thing?"

Now was the time he should have produced Art Petrucci's report, but instead Terry shook his head.

"No Mister President, and to the best of my knowledge neither have the intelligence agencies of the European countries either."

A very annoyed President looked back to the screen. He would consider what, if anything, he would do about this revelation after the briefings, and after a showdown he planned to have with General Shaw. A single sheet of paper lay inside a folder before him. The President had ordered it typed by a secretary but it was addressed to himself from Henry

"Okay then, let us move on."

Henry briefly went over the events involving the destruction of the Soviet airborne brigade, chiefly because there was evidence that one of the Russian Premier's shakers and movers in the starting of this war had been killed in the fighting.

"Serge Alontov was probably their most able airborne and Spetznaz commander; he had also performed a fair amount of intelligence and espionage work as a military attaché in London during the eighties. We also know that he entered the States illegally on at least two occasions in connection with Project October, which was a Cold War plan to cripple America on the outbreak of a war with the USSR, by espionage, sabotage and the assassination of key figures. We know he was a patriot and with his knowledge and experience he would be an obvious choice to carry through their plans. I believe Mister Jones has some related information on this for later in the briefing."

"I am a little puzzled, General Shaw, as to what this man was doing in combat if he was such a close aide to their Premier?"

"Uriah, Mister President." It was the first time Ben Dupre had spoken at the briefing. "Look up the Book of Samuel in the Old Testament. King David wanted to get rid of one of his generals without getting his own hands dirty, so he put Uriah in the front rank during a battle. It got him out of the way permanently."

Looking back at General Shaw a moment, the President lowered his voice.

"Don't tempt me Benjamin," he growled before then returning his attention once more to Terry Jones.

"I assume the late Comrade Alontov did not leave a grieving Bathsheba for that bastard to covet though, and this was his way of disposing of future threats to his leadership?"

"Wife and only child, a son aged two years, killed by a drunk driver while he was serving in Afghanistan, sir. He never remarried." Terry did not have to refer to any notes on Serge's private life, there was little to tell.

"It would seem the Russian Premier was merely cleaning house, sir."

The President grunted before gesturing at Henry to move on, and five minutes later having finished the brief that this particular audience were cleared for, he relinquished his spot to a navy officer and returned to his seat.

The President already knew about the PLAN invasion fleet in the Indian Ocean, having been summoned from his bed for a video conference with the Australian PM three hours after its discovery. One of Admiral Gee's staff, an earnest and slightly bookish looking officer took them through the preparations Australia was making, and the progress of the *Nimitz* battle group to get underway and intercept it.

"Mister President, at the outbreak of war you may recall that the USS *Nimitz* was undergoing refit. She left the yards with a great deal of work unfinished and with over a hundred civilian workers still aboard, who have continued that work whilst she was enroute to Australia and it is in fact still on-going whilst she is tied up in Sydney. She also left without her full complement of crew or a complete air wing, so we have had a ways to go to restore her to full combat readiness.

Personnel and aircraft have been flown out to Australia where her air wing is dispersed for the moment to bolster the Aussies air defence, but another two, three days at the most should see the *Nimitz* and *Bonhomme Richard* putting back to sea." The briefer was unused to the President's ways, and columns of facts and figures replaced the view on-screen of the Pacific Theatre of Operations.

"Owing to a shortage in naval airframes, particularly of the latest model of F-14, we have had to refurbish and hurriedly add upgrades to mothballed aircraft from storage at the boneyard, which we are still in the process of flying out to her. However, if I can draw your attention to the graph I am just putting up on the screen...you can see that the speed at which these airframes are being refurbished, is increasing exponentially as the work crews become more proficient with practice, and..."

The President cleared his throat loudly, interrupting the officer in mid flow.

"Commander, er...Donnelly?"

Caught unawares the officer blinked and gaped at the President before fully turning from the screen to face him.

"It's Donkley, sir."

"Did Admiral Gee leave you any notes before he left?"

The commander looked confused

"Erm... like his itinerary, sir?"

The President smiled tightly.

"I was thinking more along the lines of a piece of paper with the heading, 'What pisses the President off most'. It would be a short list, I'm sure. However, somewhere near the top would have been Facts, Figures, Statistics and Graphs...just keep to the good stuff and I'm sure we will get along fine, Commander."

For a long second the briefer was motionless

"The good stuff?"

"Anything that doesn't make me feel that I am being forced to watch an Open University math and chemistry programme."

The briefer didn't watch British TV, but he got the message anyway and after somewhat regretfully turning over half a dozen pages of notes, the graph was replaced by the Pacific once more.

"USS *John C Stennis* and the USS *Constellation* battle groups have left the Hawaiian Islands along with the USS *Essex,* USS *Boxer* and the amphibious assault vessels of 2nd Marine Expeditionary Brigade, but it is likely that any landings may already have taken place by the time they arrive. USS *Saratoga* and USS *Kitty Hawk* are in the final stages of reactivation from the reserve fleet and will be ready to accompany the 1st and 4th MEB's, which are forming up at San Diego. All three MEB's will constitute the 1st Marine Landing Division for any future offensive moves in PTO. Units of the Royal Australian, Royal New Zealand and allied navies are proceeding at best speed from their former positions covering the Pacific approaches to Australia, however it is doubtful that they will be in a position to intercept before the invasion fleet nears land."

The President interrupted once more. "Any intelligence as to which part of the coast they are aiming for?"

"No sir, their course is still due south, as of last reports at noon today." Commander Donkley moved back to his prepared text.

"We have detached the USS *San Sebastian* from the battle group and she is also making best speed to intercept and assist HMAS *Hooper*. The *Hooper* is currently experiencing difficulties with her sonar suite and as such at risk of detection, or losing contact."

"How long before *Nimitz* can get underway?"

"She will not clear port for several more days Mister President"

An hour later the room had cleared of all those without the need to know the rest of the briefings topics, leaving Terry Jones with the floor.

His first item was not one of great secrecy, but it was not of sufficient import for the previous session, however it was of personal interest to the President, Henry Shaw and of course himself.

"I received news several hours ago that the cell that carried out the killings of Scott Tafler, Major Bedonavich and the two

British police officers, has been arrested after a raid by the Special Air Service. They are all Russian, all are KGB Spetznaz forces officers………"

The President cut him off mid-sentence.

"Do they know that we want them?"

"Mister President, they do know and they also point out that the killings took place on British soil."

"Those bastards not only killed an American intelligence agent, but they also killed two of the people responsible for ensuring we did not lose the war before it had even started. I hope their Home Secretary realises that?" He was determined that the United States was going to have its pound of flesh, and he wasn't prepared to standby whilst the individuals concerned sat in a warm cell for the next twenty years. Terry Jones did not give a direct reply, but continued with what he had been in the process of saying.

"After the raid the building was thoroughly searched, and the police found pretty conclusive evidence that the same cell were responsible for the missile attacks on London, Portsmouth and the oil refinery at Canvey Island." Terry paused for a moment.

"Over a thousand people alone died when Canary Wharf collapsed, so when the Met Commissioner promised me they would hang for it once they'd been tried, I believed him, sir."

The President was not as convinced as Terry Jones, but that was something he would take up with the prime minister himself, always providing of course that the United Kingdom wasn't a newly conquered Soviet state, in a month or so. There was nothing further to be said on the subject and Terry Jones had inserted a USB into the drive running the plasma screen, he was now waiting for a signal to begin his briefing proper.

"Okay, Mister Jones…what else do you have for me?"

In the entire time that the war had been in progress these were the first images the President had really looked at. He was either far too tired or occupied with the business of running a country at war to have much inclination to watch the tube.

The news agencies war correspondents footage appeared several times a day on TV, and it was almost constantly on cable, but such was the agreement his government had forced upon the networks there was nothing truly graphic. Americans could no longer watch news from virtually any source they chose, since the Internet had been locked down as it, and all forms of communications, had come under tight Federal control.

Early in the war the news agencies had of course screamed blue murder when the emergency powers had come into play and they had taken their argument before a Supreme Court judge. As an ex–serviceman, and the father of two sons and a daughter who were in war zones, the judge had listened to their hackneyed argument that 'the people have a right to know', and after due consideration, which lasted all of thirty seconds, he had announced his decision.

"A wife has the right *not* to know she is a widow because you first showed her kids their Father's body 'live and as it happens' on national television...case dismissed!"

As the battalion of lawyers had stood to leave, confident that their employers would find certain ways to circumvent the ruling, the judge had banged his gavel once more to get their attention.

"And before you go people, that gentleman at the back of the court tells me that selling uncensored footage to an agency in a neutral country would be a very *bad* idea." Having filed past the figure in air force blue wearing the rank and insignia of a colonel in the USAF Space Command, they had duly conveyed the judge's comments to the network chiefs.

Twenty-four hours later a two billion dollar satellite owned by a Brazilian network had been broadcasting a live report from a well-known US network correspondent of the fighting at Leipzig airport when the satellite went off the air permanently.

After that incident the US networks couldn't even give away uncensored footage.

Pressing the key, the plasma screen had filled with the image of combats aftermath. Idly noting that the picture taker had not been a professional photographer, the President took in the scene.

British infantrymen and Soviet paratroopers lay in those postures that only the dead can achieve whilst American troops either stood about either watching the cameraman work, or were in the background gently lifting the bodies of the dead Brits they had soldiered alongside of into body bags. The angle changed with the next half dozen shots, and the President got the feeling he was watching a crime scene being recorded. The last four photographs were of a Soviet paratrooper; two were of him lying on a forest floor, quite obviously dead. An American paratrooper was knelt behind in the last two, propping up the body. The young American was looking into the camera as he held the corpses head steady for the picture, and the President found himself staring at the living man rather than the subject of the photograph.

"How old is he?" he asked quietly, almost in a whisper.

"Forty nine, Mr President." Terry answered.

"No Terry, I mean the 82nd trooper."

Terry paused, taken back momentarily before consulting photocopied sheets of information. Everything connected with the incident had been recorded in long hand, and even a list of all the allied troops involved, the dead and the living, was available.

"I believe that is Specialist First Class Tony Beckett, US Army Reserve and a New York cop. He is twenty four, and he was responsible for evidencing the incident."

"His eyes look older." Said the President, looking hard at the tired face, streaked with dirt and camouflage cream.

"He looks a little like your son, Henry," but General Shaw didn't reply, he also was looking at the screen but his mind was far away with the USS *Nimitz* battle group in Australia, where both his son and daughter were right now.

"Is that young man still alive, Terry?"

He got a nod in reply.

"He is in New York having accompanied the body and the evidence stateside. I believe he is currently on a twenty four hour pass before returning to his unit."

The President looked again at the young American before turning his attention is the dead Russian paratrooper.

"So if this guy is Colonel General Alontov, where are the rank badges, and what proof do we have that this is him and not a set up?"

The next two pictures were of the same dead Russian, but this time he was laid out naked on a slab.
Without a beating heart to circulate the blood about the body it had settled, drawn downwards by gravity to give his back a purple, mottled look, whilst the rest of him wore the pallor of death.

"The finger prints taken from the corpse in the forest, and again in New York match the several sets we had already acquired from his time in London and the States."

Terry elected to skip the rest of the photos of the post mortem that had been a necessary part of the investigation.

"That was the easy bit, Mister President."

Scanned images of the first of the pages recovered from the forest appeared on the screen alongside the English translation.

"The hard part is deciding if this is disinformation..." The screen changed again to another page, where several well-known names appeared along with their code names and contact details.

"...or if at least one of these names has been feeding the enemy details of what he has been privy to on senate oversight committees for the past decade?"

A light on the top of the telephone receiver in front of Henry Shaw began to blink and he picked it up, identifying himself in a low voice before covering the mouthpiece so he could listen to the caller without any of the briefing being overheard at the other end of the line.

Scrolling through all but the last two pages bearing Peridenko's writing, Terry revealed eighty-three names of men and women of many nationalities, and resident in neutral countries as well as the warring ones.

The President recognised more than a few of the names and others he had actually met at one time or another. Before he had gained the presidency two of those individuals had been on first names terms with him, although in the business sense rather than social.

"So what are we going to do about this, arrest the ones in this country and inform the other governments?"

"Neither, Mr President." In the world of espionage there was very little that was black and white, in fact the best they could really manage was various shades of grey.

"This list, if genuine, is by no means every agent they have in the world, if indeed they are agents, and we may never know why it was written or why a soldier had it hidden in his clothing." Terry went on to explain.

"Handwriting analysis proves that this was written by Anatoly Peridenko, but is it his list of his best agents, his worst agents or is this the membership list for an online dungeons and dragons web ring?" The President was pondering over Terry's words, listening to his spymaster.

"The bottom line is, we arrest no one today and we tell no other government today. It would only take one slip up, one mistake, for this knowledge to be compromised. As it is we can watch these people and assess this list's value, and if they are working for the enemy camp then we can use that knowledge to control them, the information they have access to, or we can even feed them what we want them to see. Either way, it is of no immediate use to us knowing if..." Terry looked up the screen.

"...if for instance, *'Tuscan Ranger'* is a KGB master spy or the equivalent of Woody Allen as 007."

"Or just," Put in Ben Dupre, "A fifth level Barbarian warrior with level two spell casting abilities."

The President shook his head slowly.

"It's bad enough that we could have been penetrated so seriously, but now I know we're in trouble if my FBI chief is familiar with nerdy role playing games."

Ben shrugged as Terry chuckled, but then the President returned to the business at hand.

"So, it's a case of, *better the spy you know than the spy you don't*, then?"

Terry nodded in agreement, which hardly pleased the chief executive.

"So is that it?"

"No Mister President, there is more and I believe that it could possibly be of practical use to us, if not against the new Soviet Union, then certainly against the PRC." He brought up on the screen the last two page of Peridenko's list, and these bore names of individuals from the PRC, North Korea, and all the countries of the new Soviet Union, including Russia.

"If I were a gambling man, I would be willing to bet all my money that Peridenko had plans to achieve high office, and had already put into place the means to acquire the Premiership."

The names on the screen were all military men, and all in prominent positions in their countries armed forces.

"Which I think you will agree indicates an element of foresight and forward planning." He highlighted a trio of Chinese officers.

"For instance, if you weren't willing to share power with your principle ally then the positions these characters hold could give you the knife to stick into the PRC's proverbial back." One name in particular stood out due to his apparent position in the Peoples Republics equivalent of America's National Security Agency.

The Chinese text appeared and with it a translation. Terry removed from an inside pocket a copy of the CD Rom which Serge had carried, placing it before him on the conference table.

"Alontov also carried a CD Rom sewn into his clothing and this is booby trapped with some very aggressive viruses, however despite this and the fact that the software and hardware to play this are rather specialised, NSA is confident that they can tell us what the hell it is exactly within a few more hours."

The rest of the room were looking at the translation, but most of it was apparently referring to the CD Rom.

"Mister Jones, why would he be carrying a CD and not a USB? And do we have any ideas what it does?"

"The first is simple sir; a CD is more resistant to electro-magnetic pulse, EMP, than a USB. Secondly, there is a chance that this disc is something that may get us access to somewhere that would be of advantage to us. I cannot say more than that at the moment, because we just don't know for certain."

Lord knows we could do with some luck, thought the President.

"So what are we going to call this thing? And who will have access?"

"The codename for the CD's location and its standalone systems is *'Church'*. All matters related to the contents of the CD will be known as *Choir Practice*, and we in this room, plus the three specialists who are cracking the CD, are *'The Choir'*."

"Spare me!" grunted the President, disparagingly under his breath.

"Is there an issue with the choice of code name, sir?"

"No, I am sure that is adequate, Mr Jones...but I won't hang up the bunting until we know more."

He looked across at Henry who was replacing the telephone receiver.

"General Shaw, are you ready with the *Guillotine* and *Equaliser* updates?"

Terry cleared the screen and ejected his disc, handing the floor back to the CJC.

Henry placed his own disc in the drive, bringing up Gansu Province and zooming in the picture on to a range of mountains southwest of the Gobi desert.

"We, or rather the men on the ground behind enemy lines in the PRC, have met with a serious set-back and they have taken casualties."

Leaning forward in his seat the President interrupted.

"Are they compromised?"

With a shake of the head Henry explained.

"There has been a great deal of snowfall in the past week out there, and the storm that had them socked in added a shit load more. The teams were scaling a rock face of about 500 feet in height when a passing PRC helicopter triggered an avalanche. Two men are dead including one of the team leaders, another three have injuries that will prevent them continuing, and in addition to this, three of the laser designators have been destroyed."

The President breathed the Eff word.

"Can they continue as planned?"

"That's a negative, sir."

"How long do we have before we need to give them a revised plan?"

"It is not necessary sir; Major Dewar is going for the ICBM field. He has left two of the slightly injured behind to look after the fracture cases and he has taken the remainder, plus the remaining designators westwards toward the silos."

"Is he authorised to make that decision, General?" The President had been trying to visualise the condition the teams were now in, and the adverse weather conditions they had encountered he assumed that with their losses the commander would have requested instructions.

"Firstly, he is the commander on the ground and knows their capabilities better than we do, and secondly he is British." Henry shrugged.

"He doesn't work for us Mister President."

The President glared at Henry.

"You know I didn't mean that General. This is a joint operation, but doesn't he have to ask permission before he writes off half of the mission goals?"

General Shaw nodded an apology.

"It is a simple matter of arithmetic, and Dewar knows he doesn't have enough to do both jobs anymore so he's going to neutralise the greatest threat."

"Okay then, okay. Is there anything else on that particular element of *Equaliser*?"

There was nothing more from China and Henry moved on to the North Pacific.

"In stark contrast to the previous item, I now have some feel good news for you, sir."

The picture was quite hard to make out, mainly owing to the lack of light, but then a darker shape appeared from the left of the screen, travelling right across to disappear out the other side, but the President was unable to make out what it was.

"That was taken by HMS *Hood* and it has now been digitally cleaned up and enhanced."

This time everyone could make out the shape of a submarine, and it was not one of their own vessels. It carried a conning tower similar in design to that of a Russian Delta III, but sat much further forward on the hull than on the Russian design, however, the flat topped SLBM compartment, sitting platform-like above the after hull was also a feature in keeping with a Delta.

"The *Hood* had a firing solution locked down twelve hours before they took these hull shots, but as you can appreciate it was necessary to get close enough to see if it was the *Xia* or the *Chuntian*, and they struck gold. They have returned now to tailing the *Xia* and are about four thousand metres from her."

The President cleared his throat.

"General, I know you and Mister Jones have given me your assurances already, but are you absolutely certain that this is the only one that they've got?"

"Mister President, there was the *Changzheng 6,* which was also a converted *Han* but she was lost at sea in the eighties. They don't have any more, sir."

"Let's hope."

"Roger that."

It was the best he could have hoped for and he had to settle for that.

"Has the *Chuntian* been located yet?"

"It cannot be entirely comfortable out there, sort of like being in the woods at night and knowing you are not alone, however Mister President, although we have not yet located the *Chuntian*, the *Xia* is now boxed on three sides. We can take her anytime we want and the skippers are one hundred per cent in agreement that they will find *Chuntian* before she finds them."

Leaning back in his chair the President signalled for a refill of his coffee mug before speaking.

"So one part of *Equaliser* is in place, and *Guillotine* just awaits a location…or do you have something from Russia?"

"No Mr President, only to state that we have three RORSATs dedicated purely for *Guillotine* that are sat on pads ready to go and that India and Pakistan have begun sabre rattling at one another, as have the Vietnamese and Kampucheans. They have got to the stage where their artillery can be heard sounding off and the casualty reports are quite believable."

The President was quiet for a while as he thought about the 'What if's', the question marks associated with any operations chances of success or failure.

"What, if anything, can go wrong with those satellites" the President queried "…tropical storms? Sabotage?"

Henry shook his head but in a non-committal fashion.

"Sir, in order to guard against weather problems we will have one at Vandenberg and two on pads down south, on the *Ariane* launch pad and also on the *Soyuz* pad."

The President gave a cold smile.

"Strangely fitting I feel…but please continue General."

"Hurricanes up here or typhoons down there do not have predictable seasons any more, not since the nukes cooked off in the Atlantic so we are hedging our bets by covering for those eventualities. At worst we will have one RORSAT up when Major Nunro goes after the Premier's scalp, but we are robbing Peter to pay Paul as it leaves only the smaller commercial European launch pad available down there, and of course Kennedy and Canaveral free for the normal business of keeping satellites up long enough to be effective over the battlefield ." Henry paused to glance at some notes for a second.

"Security is tight at our end and an indefinite lock down is in place but that is going to cause issues soon."

The President frowned.

"How so?"

"The French have the benefit of a handy jungle and mangrove swamps full of things that will eat you, whereas we have troops on full alert with nothing to keep their highest level of alertness going indefinitely, and with the best will in the world and the best NCOs kicking ass, an unused knife will go dull through lack of use."

Never having been in that situation the President could only take Henry's word for it and so he moved along to the mock war between India and Pakistan.

"What are they firing at?"

"Nothing." Henry shrugged. "Blank rounds only, but the media aren't being allowed close enough to know the difference."

"Okay, anything else?"

Henry cleared the screen and held up both hands, crossing his fingers and stating

"No, Mister President."

The President accepted his coffee with a smile of thanks and consulted his wristwatch.

"Right then people, that will be all for now." Henry stood along with the rest but felt the President looking at him.

"Stay a while General, I'd like to speak to you about Australia." Henry regained his seat and sat with his hands together on the table in front of him.

Remembering something the President called over to Terry, halting him half way out the door.

"Oh, Mister Jones?"

Terry stepped aside to allow Ben to exit.

"Yes, sir?"

"Do your people have a contact number for SFC Beckett?"

"Yes sir, Mister President?" Terry nodded.

"Good, extend his leave to forty eight hours and then get him on a plane here. I'd like to meet him before he returns overseas."

Terry hesitated.

"Why, sir?"

"Why not?" Putting his mug down he turned sideways in his seat to face the door.

"I have not met anyone who was directly involved in the fighting yet, and so I would like to speak to this young man about his experiences...and I am after all the Commander-in-Chief so I can do stuff like that, and you as a minion should obey without question and back away to the door, bowing as you go to see it is done."

Terry smiled.

"I thought the bowing minion thing was the reason we threw off the yoke of imperialism?"

"I thought it was because we didn't want to pay for the war against Napoleon?"

"I'm pretty sure bowing and scraping played a big part, Mr President."

The President dismissed him with a wave of the hand. "Whatever."

His Secret Service Agent was stood inside the door, hands crossed in front and seemingly taking no interest in the goings on of government.

"Mike?"

"Yes, Mr President?"

"Could you give us a moment; I want a private word with General Shaw."

"Certainly Mr President, I will be right outside."

The doors closed, shutting them off from the outside world for a while.

"That was a nice thing you did just then, Mr President." Moving his folder into the centre of the table in front of him, the President looked back at Henry.

"Why, because I didn't want Mike to witness what I am about to say?"

Henry shook his head.

"No sir, keeping that young 82nd man, Beckett, away from Germany when the Reds hit his unit."

"I thought you believed that everyone should do their share, no matter what their status in life, General?"

Henry had been fairly sure the showdown couldn't be far off when he had read the Washington Post three days ago. It had been a two day old copy and although an article on a Congressman's daughter starting boot camp had been on page five, he had begun to look over his shoulder for a high ranking military policeman, and an armed escort walking with purpose toward him.

Fishing a copy of Das Spiegel from out of his briefcase he slid it along the table to the President.

"Centre spread, Mr President."

Opening the magazine the President read the article's headline and looked at the glossy photos of rich American's enjoying the snow in Aspen.

The article was in German but President read aloud in English.

"America's rich and the beautiful aren't training for arctic warfare here, they are partying whilst members of their own countries lowest wage brackets are dying on the firing line............"

He closed the magazine and pushed it back.

"You have an issue with this, General Shaw?"

"I have several issues, Mr President. That one vies for the top slot with my other pet bug bear."

"Which is?"

"Millionaire football players, Mr President. Despite earning more in one year, than an entire team of scientists trying to find the cure for cancer will ever see in their lives...they strike for even more pay."

Henry was toying with him and he knew it, but he played along anyway.

"General, there is a football season and there is a baseball season, but there are no biology or chemistry seasons that millions will pay good money to watch, but if there was then we would have millionaire test tube jockeys by the score. This is not an ideal world, or hadn't you noticed?"

Henry ignored the reply and continued on.

"My other 'issue' dates back to March 3rd 1863. President Lincoln signed the Federal Draft Act in the full knowledge that there was a clause included that allowed the rich to dodge military service for the sum of $300." He fixed the President with an enquiring look.

"What's the going price today Mr President?"

"You are being simplistic, General." He took a sip of coffee and Henry sat waiting.

"The reason we, as a democracy, win wars is because we make a trade off. Some people, those with the means, build the weapons we need and others use them. They keep the wheels turning by doing what it takes to keep the unions sweet and looking the other way while corners are cut. If you piss off those with means you don't get the same cooperation."

Henry countered, speaking very deliberately.

"Or the funds for the war chest come election time."

"For your information General, I have goals just as you have goals, and before I leave this office I would like to see full education, education for one hundred per cent of the population, and the poverty line knocked back another five per cent if not eliminated altogether." The President's face was becoming flushed.

"I do not happen to like even a small fraction of the people I have to deal with in order to get even the smallest worth of good out of the shit I have to put my seal to."

Henry sat back and regarded his commander in chief.

"You are the President, and you tell them that you serve the will of the people and what's good for the people is good for them." The President was shaking his head at the naivety of the man.

"Do you know how much it costs just to get nominated? Let alone run an election campaign?"

Henry didn't respond, but it wasn't because he didn't know, it was because he didn't care.

"It's a fallacy that 'just anyone can be President'. You have to get sponsors to foot the bill, and they all have agenda's."

"Mr President, we have reached a point where a line must be drawn. As the leader of democracy you are supposed to be the last word in integrity, yet you sold your soul to get here." It was the last straw for the President, who was well aware of the situation without having to be reminded of it. His temper had been held in check up to this point, but now it snapped as he swept away the mug before him with a violent sweep of the hand.

"God dammit Henry...you're a Marine, and you took an oath and so you do not ever, ever, *play politics while you are in that*

uniform!" The coffee mug flew across the room, shattering against the wall.

With a bang the door flew open and Mike took a step inside. Balanced on the balls of his feet and in a half crouch, he had his jacket open and a hand on his firearm. He took in the room and then focused on Henry, his eyes narrowing slightly. Behind him stood two Marines, their hands were on the cocking levers of the M-16s they held.

Raising his hands the President calmed them.

"It's okay, it's okay.... just an accident"

Henry had remained seated and calm, as unruffled by the exhibition of temper as he was at being considered a physical threat to the President in the eyes of the Secret Service.

When they had backed out of the room and the door was again closed the President took a deep breath and allowed the anger to settle.

"My eldest son got his call up papers today. He turned eighteen just three days ago and his mother is pissed as hell at me. Added to which, some long standing friends of ours have stopped calling her since their sons and daughters got call up papers, she's pissed at me about that as well."

"I was eighteen when I first put this uniform on, Mr President."

"You volunteered and there wasn't a war going on at the time."

"The advisors were in Vietnam and the writing was already on the wall." Henry sighed.

"If it's any consolation, my father was entirely pissed at me."

"Why, he fought in Europe and again in Korea?"

"He had a saying Mr President, what do you call a rifleman with a six figure checking account...a member of the National Guard. He was done with fighting wars for the benefit of all, when a noticeable percentage of the 'all' consistently failed to show up to do their bit. He thought the time had come for the poor working stiffs to stay at home in front of a TV and see how the rich boys handled it on their own for once. There were a few times over there where I thought he had a point."

"You didn't stop your son and daughter joining the service, though?"

"They had the chance to listen to their fathers and their grandfathers' experiences and views. It's a free country, and after listening they both entered following college. Matthew joined the Corps and Natalie the Navy."

The President knew this, but he didn't know where they both were.

"Matt's the CO of VMA 223 aboard the *Bonhomme Richard,* and Natty is in Sydney too as TAO on the *Orange County*."

"*Bonhomme Richard* was damaged in the first missile attack on Japan and was in dock at Sasebo when Japan surrendered wasn't she?" asked the President. "And *Orange County* is providing air defence for both the *Nimitz* and *Bonhomme Richard* while the Aussies fix them up in Woolloomooloo Navy Yard?"

"Yessir, *Bonhomme Richard* is in the dry dock there and they aren't going anywhere until the rest of the *Nimitz* group arrives."

Only part of the *Nimitz* combat group had sailed with the carrier, the remainder were making their way with *Essex* or were stood out to sea as a precaution.

The President smiled, pleased with himself for remembering weeks old briefing items despite the masses of information that flowed in constantly for his eyes.

"Is your father still alive?"

"No sir, we lost him in '92, a few months after my mother passed away, but I think he was proud of the way his grandchildren turned out." Henry looked the President in the eye.

"My youngest is in the same draft as your son Mr President; they are both going to Parris Island."

The President opened his folder and looked at the single sheet that lay within. He stayed that way for a moment before closing the folder and standing.

"I think we are done for now, General."

CHAPTER 4

2 miles north of Magdeburg.

Colonel Leo Lužar's 43rd Motor Rifle Regiment led the way for the rest of the reconstituted Rzeszów Motor Rifle Division. It wound its way past wrecked and burnt out fighting vehicles of all types. The twisted, fire warped and shattered remains of aircraft, the fighters, fighter-bombers and helicopters from both sides were evident in the green hues of the colonel's night viewing device. Multi-millions of the people's roubles and dollars reduced to scrap value where they had fallen.

The Rzeszów Motor Rifle Division had been rebuilt from the remains of two other divisions following its abortive attack on the British 3rd Mechanised Brigade.

Second Shock Army, to which they belonged, along with Tenth Tank Army had been worn down by constant attacks upon NATO since the start of the war. They had been reduced from seven divisions to just three, and were no longer capable of the shock they were supposed to deliver.

Lužar's 43rd MRR had done better than the rest of the division by actually getting across the river. Only the Mitterland Kanal had separated them from the flesh and blood defenders, the US paratroopers and British guardsmen.

For the lack of bridging sections the attack had failed, and that was the only reason he had not been taken into the woods and shot in the back of the neck with the other regimental commanders. His defence of the efforts by the engineers to complete their task had saved another life, that of their commander.

This time they were doing it differently, a battalion of infantry had preceded them under the cover of heavy artillery pounding the far bank with H.E and smoke. Both they and the light assault boats they had dragged forward were concealed amongst the detritus of war, the armoured vehicles and ruined bridging equipment from the past two attempts to cross at this spot.

This was familiar terrain for Lužar, his previous attack had taken place three miles south of this point, and his job tonight was similar, that of securing the far bank whilst the first ribbon bridge was put across. The perimeter would be extended until the entire division had crossed and the Polish 9th Division had achieved a similar goal to the south of them. The Polish and the Hungarian Divisions were the door stoppers, they would re-orientate, facing along the NATO line to the north and south, keeping the breach open for Third and Sixth Shock Armies to pass through, followed by the rest of their own formations before rolling NATO up from the flank.

Lužar had deployed his regiment from road march five miles back, and it was now had the tactical spacing between his vehicles to minimise damage from all but an MLRS strike. He had been given assurances, once again, that NATO's multi launch rocket systems had been neutralised. Half a mile from the river he gave the signal to the infantry who began their assault river crossing covered by a renewed artillery barrage.

It was too far away for him to see the men dragging the aluminium boats down the steeply sloping bank and seating the outboard motors. Feeling extremely exposed the infantrymen attempted to offer the smallest possible targets as they laboured, before entering the fragile craft and pushing off towards the opposite bank.

At the halfway point each and every man was wondering at point the defenders would unleash a withering storm of artillery followed by small arms.

Colonel Lužar briefly changed frequencies to the Poles command net. His Polish was limited, but good enough to note that there were no contact reports or calls for help being put out. Always assuming that they had jumped off on schedule, at the same time as the 43rd Motor Rifle Regiment then the opposition they were encountering was apparently light.

He turned back to his own net and as the river came into sight he heard the infantry battalion's commander reporting that they had reached the far bank without loss. The man sounded anxious, as if he feared they had stepped into a trap that was going to close at any moment.

"Where the hell has NATO gone?"

"Colonel?"

Lužar had spoken aloud without realising, and he looked down at his sergeant.

"Nothing, let us just keep alert, okay?"

Germany: Same time.

Two fierce air battles broke out over the skies of Europe, one over NATO's rear areas and the other over the Red Army's.

The Red Air Force's build up in the skies over the Czech/German border was watched by Lt Col Ann-Marie Chan and her controllers orbiting above the German countryside west of Bielefeld. Lt Col Chan and her squadron had arrived at Geilenkirchen AFB whilst the wreckage was still being cleared. The bodies had all been removed but there had still been blood stains on the concrete of the dispersal they had been allotted and the dispersal's former occupant had lain where the bulldozers had left it, tens of millions of dollars' worth of scrap with its tail number still visible despite the fire scarring.

Tonight she counted the regiments of strike aircraft and their escorts and advised the AC to begin extending their orbit to the northwest in preparation for repositioning.

The Soviet's knew that 4th Corps was on the move and their sorties today would be at the road network and not at the docks. There were more of them in the air this morning than had been over the past few days but she wasn't fretting. Popping a mint into her mouth she then sat watching her screens and let her fingers softly drum on the surface of the workstation and murmured to herself.

"Come on boys, momma's got a surprise for you."

The moment that her screens indicated that the Soviet strikes were inbound she scrambled German Tornado's, Dutch,

American and Belgian F-16s to intercept, whilst at the same time starting several other balls rolling.

The *Charles De Gaulle's* air wing had made a low level run from the North Cape several hours previously. Keeping the coast of Norway over the horizon and avoiding radar contact it had eventually turned to enter the Kattegat and passed the small island of Anholt before landing at the Swedish Air Force base of Angelholm-Barkakra, set beside the stormy waters of the bay known as the Skalderviken.

Refuelled and carrying a heavier weapons load than would have been possible to lift of the short deck of a carrier, they had sat on the runway waiting for the signal to launch.

At Satenas to the north of them and at Malmo to the south, the taxiways were lined with Swedish, Danish and Norwegian aircraft configured for Wild Weasel and air-to-air interception.

Satenas launched first and the aircraft skimmed above rooftops on the journey south, being joined enroute by the French at Angelholm-Barkakra and finally the wings from Malmo. The multi-national force, one hundred and seven airframes strong, crossed the coast and lost even more height as it headed for the shoreline across the Baltic. Along the way the massed formation slimmed down as groups broke off and headed for their own primary targets.

In the south of England an even more diverse force took to the air and set course. Greek paratroopers rode in Danish C-130s, the Turkish airborne brigade in its entirety were carried in French C-130s plus their own Turkish built CN-235s and their ex-Luftwaffe C-160D Transall's. Spanish and Italian paratroopers were carried aloft in USAF C-141s whilst their own C-130s carried pallets packed with their heavier gear. For the British this was to be the first time since Suez that they would jump into action, although both 1 and 2 Para had been fighting in the line as infantry until a week before. The Territorial battalion, '4 Para', had provided the replacements to bring both battalions up to strength; much to the disgust of 3 Para's CO who had argued unsuccessfully for his own unit to be relieved in the line by the Territorials and so be able to take part also. The two British battalions were aboard RAF, USN and USAF C-130s which made the three battalions from the 82nd and the Belgians the only countries who shared a common language with all their aircrafts crews. The British and Americans are united in their beliefs that other is speaking Martian.

RAF Tornado GR4s and Jaguar's loaded for flak suppression preceded the transport stream with USAF F-15s providing cover. USN F/A-18s and F-14 Tomcats of the USS *Gerald Ford's* air wing rode shotgun for the transport aircraft while their E-2C Hawkeyes provided the force with all seeing eyes and the ability to provide ECM when the time came.

Ann-Marie blessed SACEUR for whatever strategy he had used to pry loose the next group of assets. The attrition rate over the past weeks had been frightening, and today she would have been left with only helicopters and a newly arrived A-10 wing, operating with minimal fighter cover to try and stem the tide of enemy armour pouring through the breach in the NATO line.

The Indians were on the rampage and NATO ground forces were circling the wagons.

In southern Europe at the foot of the Italian Alps, the bulk of the cavalry were lifting off from Trento and Bergamo. The three F-16 wings from Italy, Greece and Turkey took to the air, followed by four squadrons of Turkish F-5As and venerable F-4E Phantoms. To the west of them Spain's F/A-18 wing formed up and headed north also for the first of two rendezvous with tankers. None of the aircraft carried external fuel tanks; their hard points carried ordnance that would be expended before they touched down on the tarmac of designated airfields in France, Germany and the Low Countries.

Thick fog had settled upon the hill along with a fine drizzle, which soaked the hessian strips of the ghillie suits the snipers wore. Big Stef and Bill halted at a challenge from the battalion CP's sentries, holding their arms and weapons well clear of their bodies as they complied with the requests made of them. Having answered the challenge correctly they squeezed through the sandbags and soggy blankets to enter a dug-out that smelt of damp earth, in the side of a steep sided gully that served as a shelter bay and briefing room. Removing their Bergens they sat upon them as they awaited Major Popham to brief them on their task of the day; however the next person to enter was not the 2 i/c but the battalion padre. He wore the same combat clothing as they did but no webbing and no camm cream on his skin either.

"Good morning boys, the 2 i/c sends his apologies and he will be a few minutes yet."

Stef knew the man fairly well, muttering a

"G'mornin' Padre," as he lowered himself onto a bench made of empty ammunition boxes on the opposite side of the dugout to themselves, Bill on the other hand gave a half nod and stared unseeing at the earth wall opposite, lost in his own thoughts.

The padre had once been a colour sergeant in the Scots Guards before something had happened to change his outlook on life. He had come to the battalion as a captain in the Royal Army Chaplains department, and usually he was a fairly normal kind of guy, but now and again a kind of overbearing zeal seemed to come over him and he would seek out his spiritual charges whether they wanted his counsel or not. In barracks it was not unusual to see soldiers climbing out of windows to avoid him if he was seen entering their accommodation block.

Their current situation as a unit had not been kept a secret; the CO had not made light of it. They were within a whisker of losing the war in Europe, but the remnants of the Guards regiment that had held Hougoumont Farm, and the paratroopers who boasted Saint Mere l'Eglise amongst their units past achievements were not used to running. All the same, the recent loss of an entire platoon had hit both the Brits and Americans hard. Colin Probert and his men had been acknowledged as pretty damn good soldiers and although no one could have been expected to prevail against such odds as they had faced, there was a feeling that if Probert's platoon could be overrun then what chance did the rest have. Since the over running of 1 Platoon the padre had been getting around the positions, doing his job as he saw it, offering the services of his office to bolster those that may need it.

Bill was vaguely aware of Stef and the padre conversing in low tones but it wasn't until his partner gave him a dig in the ribs that he realised the priest had addressed him.

"I was saying that I haven't seen you at my services, since you were attached to the battalion?"

Bill shook his head.

"I tend to catch up on sleep whenever we are back in the battalion lines Padre...it's nothing personal."

The padre studied him for a moment before replying.

"Are you an agnostic young man, surely you have heard the word of the Lord?"

Stef had got to know Bill quite well, and knowing him as he did he gave another nudge by way of a warning, but groaned inwardly when it was ignored.

"No Padre, not personally."

The gauntlet, as far as the padre was concerned, had been flung down. Using what he considered to be reasoned examples, he sought to put doubt into the snipers mind but found instead that Bill had long ago formed his own views on the subject of the established churches of all faiths on the planet.

"Don't get me wrong padre, I believe in a Supreme Being creating the universe and I believe in good and evil, I just don't happen to believe, or trust, the interpretation that humankind gives it. In case you had not noticed, we seem to be a bit shy of miracles around here"

"God is all around us, Staff Sergeant. Haven't you ever witnessed the miracle of birth?"

Bill smiled wryly. "I've had occasion to actually deliver a baby padre, so yes I have witnessed that. I often give to charities for famine relief...but I have never witnessed a starving bishop, or even a malnourished mullah for that matter, though."

After another five minutes the padre accepted that Bill was not about to join the ranks of the born again, and having made his excuses he started to leave, but Bill sent him a parting shot.

"Let me know when they find the missing page to the original bible, padre."

Pausing before the blackout the padre looked back at the sniper.

"Missing page?"

"Yes Padre, the page at the beginning where it says 'Names, places, characters and incidents are a product of the authors imagination and any resemblance to any living person or real events is purely coincidental'."

Bill had gone too far and he realised that fact as soon as he had spoken, so he muttered an apology.

The padre looked at him for a moment, ignoring the attempt to make amends.

"*You* may not believe but I'll thank you not to mock those of us that do, Staff Sergeant."

Stef saved his comments until the padre had disappeared.

"For a copper, your people skills suck at times."

Bill and Stef had been inside the battalion lines since it had begun to dig in on the hill, but they were now to relieve a sniping pair forward of the battalion perimeter.

The American paratrooper from the 82nd, Major Popham, came to give them their orders and although both Stef and Bill knew the location of the hide, Major Popham opened a map to show them where the 40 Commando positions were in relation to it.

"To your ten o'clock, about six hundred metres off, is a small copse with dead ground behind it. This is the marines gun line for a battery from 29 Commando Regiment's 105mm guns, and fourteen hundred metres to your front you will see a small farm with a sunken lane just visible at its left hand edge. The farm is the most visible mark for the rear perimeter of 40 Commando's real estate, and that sunken lane runs diagonally across your front." He paused to point out the features on the map.

"Your marines will withdraw along that lane and I need you to report that movement, because if communications between us and them go to rat shit then we isn't going to get much warning, is we?"

"If Ivan plays it smart, he'll use that lane too." Bill used the edge of his thumb to measure the distance on his own map from the foot of the hill to the point where the lane came closest; it was only eight hundred metres.

"When you get on the ground you will see the lane is lined with trees. The marines have prepared most to be dropped behind them as they go, so it will prevent vehicles using it and allow them some breathing space to pass through 1 Argyll & Sutherland Highlanders and set up shop again in pre-prepared positions a mile back. They have a troop of your Hussars with them which will break off and rejoin us once the pass through is complete." The map showed the Royal Marines fall-back positions backed onto the autobahn that was the Soviet's goal. There were no such positions beyond that for the men and women of 3 (UK) Mechanised Brigade, beyond the autobahn lay the gun lines, headquarters and support units.

"What's the timescale sir, when are they expected to make contact?"

Jim knew the answer to that one.

"If they haven't hit the anti-tank mine field in front by 10am, then they stopped for breakfast somewhere or the...what the hell is a Wimik?"

"It's the Royal Marines trying to prove they can use words consisting of two syllables." Stef told him, but seeing the American major was looking blank he quickly added.

"A Wimik is what the marines call a Landrover with 'fifty cals' and a Milan post bolted on."

Jim shrugged and went on.

"Well, they have a screen of Wimik's out forward a couple of miles beyond the mines to shoot and scoot

"Is there any chance that your 4th Corps will beat them here, sir?"

Shaking his head Jim folded the map and put it away.

"I doubt it, we are in for a hard fight but if we can hold them long enough, well..."

He left the sentence unfinished and reached across to shake both soldiers by the hand.

"Good luck to you both."

They pulled their bergens back on and checked for anything rattling before pushing their way back outside and heading for the 3 Company sentry position where they would take the winding route through the field defences to exit the location.

The sound of aircraft passing to the south of them came as they were at the trench that guarded the safe route. It was still foggy and far too dark for them to see the air armada, but the drone of the transports and the fighter escorts were apparently heading east, so it was a toss-up whether they were friendlies on the way to make mischief, or enemy aircraft returning from dropping yet more airborne troops behind them, this time to block 4th Corps.

They arrived at the hide in plenty of time for the relieved pair to be back in the battalion location before first light, where they would get perhaps a couple of hours of sleep before the Soviet armies arrived.

SACEUR's Gambit

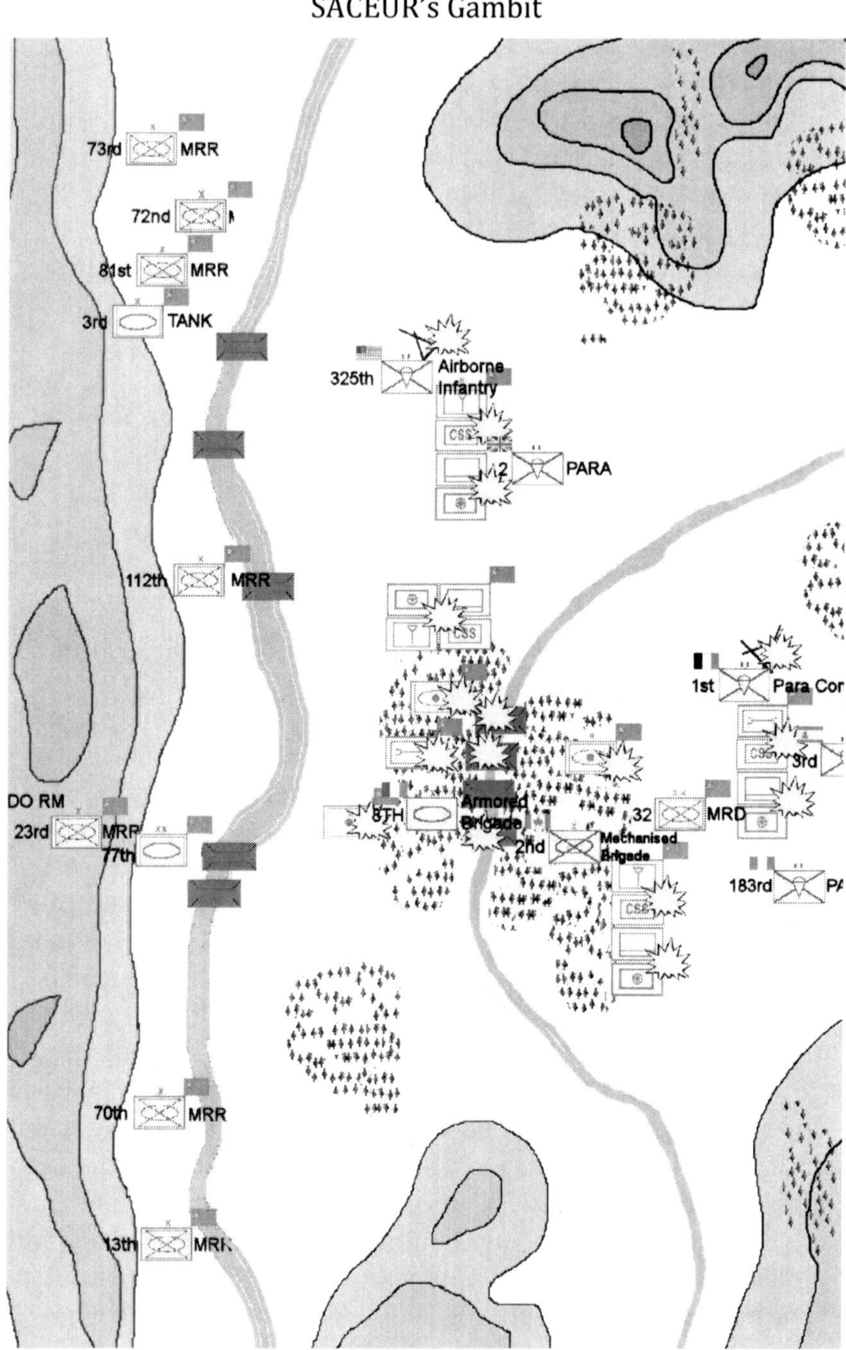

The hamlet of Struhn, 25 miles east of Magdeburg, had never been much more than a cluster of buildings that other people passed through, even before the autobahn between Berlin and Magdeburg had bypassed it.

With the autobahn a kilometre south and a railway to the north the world passed Struhn by even faster than before. That had changed to an extent when NATO had avoided being outflanked by withdrawing from this part of Germany and a company of Czech mechanised infantry, assisted by an anti-aircraft unit, had arrived to guard the major rail junction three quarters of a kilometre to the north.

The only inhabitants who still remained were an elderly couple, the remainder of the hamlet's residents having joined the tide of refugees following in NATO's wake. Their tiny cottage had been looted as they huddled, terrified in one corner. They had little to start with, but the invaders had first emptied their larder and then returned later to steal the furniture to use as firewood when the snow came and the temperatures plummeted.

The couple had survived, sharing body warmth beneath piled blankets and on vegetables ignored by the thieves. The old man augmented this fare by defying the curfew to set snares in nearby woods and hedgerows, and again before the dawn to check them for catches. He dared not leave the snares in place during the day in case some enemy patrol happened across one and stole his catch.

A solitary, skinny, rabbit was the nights total haul and after bashing the creature on the head and dismantling the snare he was carefully making his way to the edge of wood, stopping often to listen for patrols, when something came crashing down through the branches behind him, striking the ground with a dull thud.

The old man turned in panic, clutching the scrawny animal to his chest, and then took a pace backwards as something else; something larger followed it even more noisily.

A dark shape came to an abrupt halt two feet above the ground, bounced and swayed and began to mutter expletives. It fumbled for a moment inside its smock before finding and switching on a pair of passive night goggles, which it held to its face for a look down at the ground. Satisfied that it wasn't suspended above an abyss by its snagged parachute it used them to slowly pan around its surroundings, and froze when it reached the old man.

"'Mornin'." It said after a pause.

The old man didn't speak English, and stammered back a query whilst still clutching the rabbit in both trembling hands.

"Bitte?"

"Yer not wrong there mate, it's just this side of bleedin' freezin'."

The British paratrooper wriggled free of his harness and crouched for a few moments before standing with difficulty, hunched over under the weight of a bergen he had just struggled into.

"Nice meeting yer mate but I can't be gossiping with you all night now can I? So, I've got to be off."

After several moments the old man slowly followed in the direction the paratrooper had taken and stopped at the edge of the wood. He couldn't make out the soldier anymore, the meadow beside the wood was dotted with abandoned green parachutes and their former owners were hurrying off into the darkness. The 1st and 2nd battalions of the Parachute Regiment had arrived to put a clot in two of the Red Army's main supply arteries.

Lt Col Reed and Arnie Moore left the battalion CP to visit each of the locations, starting with 4 Company on the left. He had held another O Group for all the company commanders just the last evening, but today was going to be a busy one and he wanted to get around and speak to as many of the men under his command as possible.

4 Company was one of the 82nd's and was tied in with their neighbour's right flank, 2LI, 2nd Battalion Light Infantry. To make things more complicated the Light Infantry's shortages had been made good with a platoon on loan to each of its rifle companies from 2 Wessex.

A small stream with high banks provided a physical boundary between both units, and although it was too dark to see it, Pat could hear the rushing water faintly from the entrance to the company's CP.

The first thing that caught his attention once inside the CP was an 82nd signaller wearing a beret, not that there was anything wrong in that, they were under cover and not under fire, however, behind the paratroopers badge was sown a Guards flash, the blue, red, blue rectangle his own men wore behind their own regimental cap badge. Pat let it go without comment; this was after all a battlefield in Germany and not Horse Guards Parade in London.

The battalion was stood-to half an hour before first light whilst he and Arnie were at 4 Company, and they remained there until it was stood down without incident a half hour after dawn at which point they crossed the stream to say a quick hello to the neighbours, and of course to also run a professionally critical eye over who was essentially guarding their flank.

They were too far from the stream to easily get back into cover behind its bank when they were challenged and both Pat and Arnie stopped and held their rifles one handed and away from their bodies as they peered toward the sound of the voice.

Pat could not make out the position though until he was told to advance a few steps and halt again, close enough so that the sentry covering them did not have to shout out the number to which Pat responded correctly.

Lying behind the sentry's trench Pat and Arnie were impressed to discover the soldiers were 2 Wessex territorials and not 2LI regulars and they couldn't fault the position.

Passing back over the stream to 4 Company's turf they went from trench to trench, knowing that this was to be a day of days for them all and an end of days for some.

The normal day in the field, once stand-to is over, starts with weapon cleaning and personal administration, but only one man at a time stripped and cleaned his weapon per trench, his mate's was ready for use during this time. Pat and Arnie exchanged a few words with the men as they worked and found nothing to cause undue concern. For some of the men, those who had arrived in the past five days for the large part, it would be their baptism of fire when the Soviet's arrived, but each of these men had been paired off with a seasoned soldier.

Leaving 4 Company they came through a jumble of boulders to 1 Company's left hand platoon, and these trenches had been dug by CSM Probert's platoon but were now occupied by a mixture of 82nd men and Coldstreamers taken from the other three rifle companies. The majority of Headquarter Company were Guardsmen, as were Support Company, he had an additional Mortar Platoon there from the 82nd, but Pat Reed only had one rifle company remaining that was made up entirely of Guardsmen, 2 Company. The brigade commander, true to his promise, had made enquiries as to the low numbers of replacements for the Guards battalion under his command, and had been informed that the regiments' second battalion, 2CG, was being reformed and had priority call. As to the question of the lack of recognition for 1CG's efforts, he was informed that the Defence Secretary herself had reviewed each of Pat Reed's recommendations and found they lacked sufficient merit for gallantry awards.

The Americans viewed Lt Col Reed's recommendations in a different light as regards their own soldiers and the previous evening he had been pleased to announce the names of men from the 82nd who were receiving medals for gallantry. He couldn't give the same news to his own regiments' officers but he did announce promotions that included those on the casualty lists. He could create NCOs from buckshee guardsmen, give existing NCOs the next rank and make Warrant Officers out of senior NCOs, but it took higher authority to approve and confirm the raising of men to commissioned status, or giving an officer the next rank. However, pending confirmation by that higher authority, Captain Sinclair received his brevet majority, young Mr Taylor-Hall became a Lieutenant and a signal was sent to RHQ requesting that they inform CSM Probert of his brevet promotion to 2Lt, as soon as his surgery permitted of course.

Arriving ahead of the US 4th Corps, a large amount of ammunition and stores had arrived the previous afternoon and a newly promoted Colour Sergeant Osgood was busy with a fatigue party distributing 1 Company's share of it.

All about the battalion location their own defences had been thickened up with US made bar mines and Claymores. The division had replenished ammunition stocks and had more to spare, all they needed now was luck.

Whilst the Iron Curtain had stood, the Red Air Force occupied former WWII Luftwaffe bases in East Germany during its decade's long face off with NATO. After the reunification, the modern Luftwaffe inherited a dozen airbases that had changed little since the 1940s and promptly closed the majority. Cottbus, to the south east of Berlin was retained and modernised, unfortunately the recent withdrawal from the region had been so rapid as to make the Soviet's a gift of a fully functional airbase with modern facilities.

The former airbases of Sperenberg, Welzow, Falkenberg, Wittstock, Merseburg, Altenburg and Holzdorf were quickly reoccupied and the runways patched up. It was from these airbases that the close air support against NATO on the Elbe/Saale line had been provided, and would continue as the Red Army began its latest drive for the Channel ports.

Cottbus airbase was of particular interest to NATO due to its proximity to one of Europe's main east/west trading routes and the roads and rail lines that followed it.

At 0433hrs the bulk of the Belgian Para Commando Brigade had landed at three drop zones around the Twelfth century town of Bad Rouen.

Belgium's 1st and 3rd Parachute Battalions in company with 3rd Lanciers-Parachutists Battalion and twelve of its jeeps on pallets, landed along with the 14th Parachute Commando Engineer Company south of the town, on either side of the river Spee. Meanwhile 2nd Commando Battalion and 35th Parachute Commando Anti-Aircraft Artillery Battery dropped on Cottbus airbase itself, five miles beyond the town's northern suburbs.

The fighting at the airbase was bloody, swift and still taking place as the C-130s of the Belgian Air Force's 15th Transportation Wing landed the GIAT 105mm guns and crews of the brigade field artillery battery.

To the south, the 1st and 3rd Parachute Battalions carried out a simultaneous assault of both ends of the A15 autobahn bridge where it crossed the Spee on the edge of the town.

Being over a hundred miles from the fighting, the reservists protecting the bridge had mounted only a small guard whilst the remainder slept. They were all men in their forties, recalled after twenty years of civilian life and given the minimum of refresher training. The Belgians took out the sentries without a sound before moving on the trenches and fighting vehicles occupied by sleeping reservists. It wasn't a completely bloodless victory; apart from the sentries, three other members of the bridge guard fell to silenced rounds or cheese wire garrottes.

With the bridge secure the Belgian Paratroopers' 3rd Battalion, less its mortar platoon, remained on the eastern bank whilst the engineers prepared the bridge for demolition, and the 3rd Lanciers special forces company, *1'ere Compagnie d'Equipes Specialisee de Reconnaissance* mounted their jeeps and went north into the town.

Bad Roulen has two rail lines which enter it and join at a small marshalling yard on the western side of the river. The bridges that carry the railway lines lie at either end of the town park on the eastern bank.

The town fathers had been working hard over the past few years to undo the damage the communists had done by industrialising the city and ignoring environmental controls. The riverside park had been cleaned up, landscaped and beautified, but the heavily polluted river still had a long way to go. The park had become a tented city housing the lower ranks of the two companies garrisoning the town, and it was the job of the jeep company to prevent them from interfering by causing chaos and mayhem, whilst securing the railway bridges.

By the time the jeep company reached the first rail bridge the alarm had been raised by the airbase, not by radio but by landline as the Belgians carried portable jamming sets that flooded their known frequencies with silent noise, a means of cutting communications without alerting the victims.

The commander of the jeep company watched through a night scope as an officer emerged from a sandbagged CP and listened for the sound of gunfire before hurriedly pulling on his fighting order as he ran to rouse his men.

Before the running officer could reach the park a jeep had drawn level with him and a well-aimed blow across the back of his neck with an entrenching tool sent him tumbling. The jeeps raced for the bridge, cutting down the sentries at the western end and driving across, the vehicles bucking wildly on railway sleepers. The sentries on the eastern bank shared the same fate as their mates on the opposite side, and the bridge was in Belgian hands.

A jeep and its crew equipped with 40mm Mk-19 automatic grenade launchers were left to secure either end of the bridge, along with a Milan equipped vehicle. Two of the company's snipers found themselves spots where they could best observe the tented area in the park whilst the drivers set up GPMGs. Once he was satisfied his men were in position the Belgian company commander established radio communications with the brigades mortar line, and then settled down to wait for the Engineers to blown the autobahn.

Dropping the solidly built bridge into the Spee wasn't a particularly scientific event, but the engineers were not looking for marks for grace and artistic interpretation. Cratering charges had been laid on the on-ramps for good measure and when the spans were dropped the ramps were wrecked also.

The roar of the demolition charges reverberated upriver and on hearing it the seven remaining jeeps entered the park in column and accelerated down the main 'street' of the tented area, firing into the canvas structures as they went.

The sound of the autobahn bridge being destroyed had brought men stumbling from the tents into the darkness. They could hear the sound of speeding vehicles but the blackout was in force and they were unaware that NATO troops were amongst them until the jeeps opened fire.

As the jeeps cleared the tented area the commander called for mortar fire on the centre of the park, and the Belgian's on the first railway bridge opened fire. Anyone the snipers saw who appeared to be attempting to establish command and control were singled out and despatched, whilst the grenadiers and 'gimpy' gunners began expending rounds as fast as they could fire.

Before the smoke had chance to settle the paratroops to the south were seeding the area with booby-traps and moving north to their next objective. It is far easier to take a bridge by assaulting both ends at once hence the 3rd Battalion remained on the eastern bank. Apart from the two railway bridges there were four road bridges spanning the river within the town limits, hence the 3rd Battalion had remained on the eastern bank.

On the northern edge of the town park the jeep company met its first real opposition. The company commander elected to take the second railway bridge in the same fashion as they had taken the first; using the speed of the vehicles and the firepower they carried to best advantage.

The previous rail bridge had been at street level with barriers to stop traffic whenever a train was due, however the second bridge was raised above street level, crossing 29° above the Spee and the streets running beside it. Access for maintenance vehicles to the top of the steep embankment at the eastern end was via a ramp behind a row of buildings, with a tight turn at the top before a narrow gateway.

The jamming that had blinded the air defences to the presence of troop carrying transports had dissipated with the departing E-2C Hawkeye that had accompanied them. It wasn't an unusual occurrence for NATO deep strikes to venture out this far and the AAA detachment had learnt by experience that trying to burn through the interference only earned you an anti-radiation missile for your troubles. So the radars had been switched off until the crews were certain that neither they nor the town had been the NATO aircrafts' target.

The sounds of the autobahn being dropped and the attack on the park alerted the detachment that a ground assault was in progress. They attempted to broadcast an alert by radio but when this failed the crews buttoned up their vehicles, and the ZSUs lowered their quad barrels to the anti-infantry position.

The ZSU, or 'Zeus', mounted as it was on a PT-76 amphibious tank chassis was as deadly to infantry and light armour as it was to rotary and fixed wing aircraft. Each of its four 23mm water-cooled cannons fired mixed belts of explosive, fragmentation and armour piercing tracer rounds at a rate of 1000 rounds a minute from a high speed, hydraulically stabilised armoured turret, making it very accurate and very hard to kill without anti-armour weapons.

Bad Roulen had two AAA detachments assigned to its sector, one at the airbase and one covering the rail junction and marshalling yards where the coverage there encompassed the autobahn bridge also. Both detachments were standard in size and equipment, four ZSU-23-4s and four mobile SA-9 Gaskin launchers in each to provide short and medium range cover.

As the first Belgian jeep appeared at the top of the embankment there was one seconds worth of ear splitting cacophony as it was engaged and reduced to jagged scrap by a ZSU that had driven out onto the tracks at the western end of the bridge. It was guarding against just such an eventuality using its night sight to watch for any enemy approach. The jeep had not quite cleared the gateway so it was now blocking the way for the remainder, and as it began to burn it illuminated the remaining jeeps which were nose to tail on a narrow ramp with no hope of getting past.

The sentries on the bridge were not equipped with night viewing devices and although they heard the Belgian vehicles rushing up the ramp, they leant across the stone parapet beyond the bridge and were able to identify them by the light from the burning jeep reflected off the buildings backing onto the embankment. The stalled line of vehicles in flickering light, were then taken under fire by the sentries. A second jeep was lost in the act of reversing back down the incline when its driver was hit and lost control. The vehicle veered off the narrow ramp and rolled down the side of the embankment, spilling out its occupants as it went.

The Belgians carried out a hasty retreat, withdrawing back the way they had come, and on finding cover in a side street they dismounted and called for mortar fire support.

Back in the park the neat rows of tents had been reduced to torn bundles of canvas, many of which were burning fiercely. A mortar man working in the dark had in error selected a WP, white phosphorus smoke round, which had burst in the centre of the camp, landing amongst the jerry cans of petrol and kerosene the cooks used to fuel the field ovens. Burning particles of white phosphorus and burning fuel had splashed outwards to set alight not only tentage, but also soldiers who had been using the tents as cover from view. The sight of human torches in their target area had made even the tough professionals of the Belgian airborne pause, easing their fingers off triggers for a moment, but then the snipers ceased looking for leaders and began shooting the burning men, and the remainder resumed the job they were paid for.

3rd Lanciers normally provided the brigades dedicated anti-tank support, but today they had unshipped four of the Milan's from their jeeps and left the remainder along with the jeeps, back in England. One pair of the Milan's was sited to cover the autobahn approaches to the bridge, whilst the other two covered the flanks of the mortar line. Fighting as infantry the remainder of 3rd Lanciers provided the protection for the combined mortar line from the 1st and 3rd Parachute Battalions and a tactical reserve for the brigade commander whilst the two parachute battalions advanced north into the town.

Blocked at the second railway bridge the jeep company commander watched with a sense of frustration as mortar rounds exploded on the railway embankment, on the street behind the bridge and on buildings next to it, in fact the rounds were landing everywhere but on the intended target, the western end of the bridge where the ZSU had been.

The Belgian's, like all the other NATO airborne forces behind the lines this day had only the ammunition stocks they had jumped in with. They were wasting mortar rounds and the commander called an end to the fire mission and concentrated on finding another solution. The jeep company had started with four Milan equipped vehicles, of which one was at the first railway bridge and a second was lying on its back at the foot of the embankment. He had one of his remaining Milan vehicles on standby, and sent two more of his snipers to the three storied corner house at the end of the side street they had taken cover in. Forcing the street door open the pair made their way to the top floor but they were unable to find a window that allowed them to see the far side of the bridge. They were in the process of dragging a sideboard onto the landing below the attic hatch when the house's lawful owner appeared at the top of the stairs. The sight of the elderly housefrau made the paratroopers pause in what they were doing.

Clad in a floor length nightgown and wearing a yellow builders hard hat for protection, she was carrying a tray upon which rested a silver coffee pot and her best china cups and saucers, with slices of cake on a matching plate.

"Kaffee, junges?"

Several minutes later the commander entered the attic where his men had removed roof tiles. A sniper had to swallow a mouthful of chocolate cake before reporting that they could now see the ZSU and it was still at the end of the bridge. Returning to the street he dispatched the waiting Milan equipped vehicle with another jeep for support. Driving out of the side street they turned into the road running parallel with the embankment and floored the accelerators. Bursts of small arms followed the vehicles, fired by the sentries on the bridge, but the ZSU was too far from the parapet to engage.

Three hundred yards along the street, the jeeps halted in front of a haberdashery store and dismounted the Milan launcher. Ignoring the solid looking shop door they followed a litterbin through the store window and made their way to the rear. No damage was required to exit through the rear; a key was sat in the back door lock and after drawing the door's bolts they clambered over a wall at the back of the yard to find themselves on the embankment.

The snipers confirmed by radio that the ZSUs barrels were still pointing unerringly along the track and the Milan crew stayed out of sight below the stone parapet.

At a range of only 200m from the bridge the helmeted heads of the two sentries filled the snipers telescopic sights whenever they popped up for a peek over the parapet. Unwisely both enemy soldiers chose to take a look at the same time and both snipers fired as one before turning their attention to the tracked flak vehicle. Distracting the ZSUs crew proved to be a simple matter, though not without certain hazards. It took ten rounds fired at two second intervals to get the attention of the ZSUs commander. Irritated at the rounds ricocheting off the turret he looked through the viewing blocks until he saw the muzzle flash of the weapon which was no threat to his vehicle or its occupants, but the regularly spaced rounds smacking off the 3" thick armour would seriously get on their nerves if it continued.

The Belgians saw the turret begin to swivel in their direction and knew it was time to go. Unfortunately, having scrambled over the roof ties to the narrow attic hatch they found it was impossible to negotiate as quickly as might be desired. The leading man was still squeezing himself through when the first 23mm rounds struck the far edge of the roof, and then began to move towards them as the ZSU continued to traverse. Stranded until his mate could get clear, the second sniper took one look over his shoulder at the stream of cannon shells that were demolishing the roof and stepped off the joist he was balanced upon, crashing through the plaster ceiling into the room below.

Having effectively blown apart the roof the ZSUs gunner started on the top floor, lowering the barrels and reversing the turret's traverse. Now clear of the attic the first sniper took the stairs five at a time whilst his mate, liberally covered in plaster dust and lagging behind on the landing, dived headfirst over the banister rail as the first baseball sized holes appeared in the walls.

With all their attention on the task in hand neither the vehicles commander nor the gunner saw the Belgian Milan crew rolling off the top of the parapet to land beside the track. The ZSUs driver on the other hand could see them clearly in his lo-lite screen and shouted a warning over the intercom as he put the vehicle into reverse.

It was a hundred metres to the railway station and a further hundred before the stations raised platforms gave way to the marshalling yards, and until it reached them the ZSU was hemmed in on both sides.

The jeep's driver passed the launcher and three rounds across the parapet to its crew and then ducked when the ZSU opened fire. Seeing his first burst miss the gunner shouted at the driver to stop, his weapon was not self-stabilising and the uneven surface was throwing off his aim, but the driver could see the paratroopers attaching a round to the side of the launcher and was in a funk. They clearly weren't going to make it and he forgot about what he should have been doing, focusing instead on the threat along the railway line. With a screech of tortured metal the ZSU veered off its straight line, hitting the edge of a concrete passenger platform and with a shudder its engine stalled. The driver threw open his hatch and was halfway out when the wire guided missile passed beside his head and struck the vehicle's turret ring.

The leading company of the 3rd Battalion met little resistance when it reached the park. They found thoroughly demoralised Soviet soldiers hiding behind trees and anything that could provide cover. Those that had weapons tossed them away and knelt with hands clasped behind their necks when called on to do so.

Dawn was beginning to break as the last man from 3rd Battalion crossed the only remaining bridge across the Spee for twenty miles, but ten minutes later it too had been dropped into the polluted water.

The brigade commander used the light from the flames of the last of the Soviet anti-aircraft vehicles to be hunted down to study his map before ordering his force at the airbase to pull out and head for their next objective.

2nd Commando Battalion had suffered far heavier than the rest of the brigade's dozen dead and wounded, but they had been faced with regular troops in prepared positions that had to be attacked across open ground.

The commando battalion had captured the airbase motor pool intact and had sufficient transport to carry the troops, the wounded and pull the brigade's 105mm guns. From where he was standing the brigade commander could see a glow across the rooftops to the north from the fires at the airbase tank farm. All that remained to be done at Cottbus was to destroy the stored munitions, much of which had been moved from the bomb dumps and placed in stacks on the runways where they would be detonated once the troops were clear.

An aide intercepted the town folk who were making a beeline for his commander, armed with a bottle of Schnapps and wanting to greet the town's liberators. The commander felt a sickness settle in his stomach. His brigade was mounting captured and commandeered vehicles in preparation to pull out, and he wondered what revenge would be exacted on the town when the Red Army reoccupied it.

Two explosions to the south jolted him from his gloomy thoughts and he turned to his radio operator. The signaller finished acknowledging a message and reported that a pair of BMP-2 fighting vehicles had appeared on the eastern side of the autobahn. The Lanciers Milan's had engaged both but only succeeded in destroying one of them.

It was time to go.

CHAPTER 5

Russia: Same time.

Following Svetlana and Caroline's visit to the Russian girls contact, the routine at the farmhouse had sunk back into more or less the same monotonous routine as previously.

Svetlana no longer had to listen to the radios constant programming of folk and classical music from dawn to dusk. From 1900 to 2100 were the times she now draped herself in an armchair next to the old couples' radio set, the rest of the time she and the Americans helped out around the farm.

The previous afternoon Patricia had left once more to perform maintenance on the Nighthawk; it left the pilot and the spy to help the farmer and his wife until the evening.

At 8pm Svetlana had listened to the hourly news report, hearing how the courageous Red Army had forced the Elbe and Saale rivers and NATO was in full retreat, which to her reckoning made it the seventh time in the past two weeks. Even the wording of the item was identical to that of the previous bulletins.

After the news the music programme had resumed with *Wait For Your Soldier*, sung by a well-known baritone and Svetlana had sat upright. After all the previous so-called good news reports, the audiences had been treated to stirring performances by the Red Army Chorus singing the likes of *The Brave Don Cossacks*. The piece tonight had been followed by *Ochi Chornye*, Dark Eyes, but the romantic gypsy melody had stopped after twelve seconds with an announcer apologising for technical difficulties before it had restarted.

Caroline, sketching the Russian girl once again had noticed the body language change and paused in what she was doing.

The same baritone who had performed the song, informing already faithful and patriotic womanhood that their men would return and to keep faith in inevitable victory had then sung *Dubinushka*. The sequence of the first two songs, with the *technical difficulties* had been the signal from Elena Torneski that the Premier's present location followed. Torneski had allotted each of the secure locations the title of a song and Svetlana opened a map, finding Saratov on the river Volga, and then tracing a finger westwards to a river valley twenty-six miles from the town.

"Here's your target Caroline."

Major Nunro had looked at what was marked as a disused mineshaft set in a re-entrant off a narrow river valley.

"Can you hit it?" Svetlana had asked.

"Oh we can hit it honey, we just got to get there first."

It was only a little under 400 miles as the crow flies, but it meant an initial circular route to avoid overflying the Moscow air defence zone, after which they would need to pick their way around four fighter bases that lay on the way.

Leaving the Russian girl, she had set up the satellite transmitter, sending the location to the US and informing them they could not attack for at least eighteen hours, allowing for the time it would take to return to the forest strip once Pat had returned.

Svetlana was no longer in the living room when she'd returned. The water was being run upstairs so Caroline lifted a floorboard and false section of pipe below it to bring out a laptop. The USB she had inserted contained what had been the most up to date intelligence on AAA locations in Russia at the time they had left Kinloss. With the machine powered up she'd begun the business of plotting a route.

Patricia had an uncomfortable journey, as usual, concealed within their contact's ancient van. Patricia had been trying to learn basic Russian and used a flashlight to read the children's textbook she had found in a box at the farm. It was one way to pass the time, repeating parrot fashion such useful phrases as "*Ya zhyvu na marskom paberezh'e*", as if a KGB guard at a checkpoint could give a damn that she allegedly lived at the seaside, though! Twenty miles from the forest the contact had stopped the van and left the cab to stand beside it, looking for all the world like a man tending to the call of nature. Being inside the rattling contraption she could hear little of the outside world so it came as a shock when he spoke loud enough for her to hear, informing her that there were helicopters in the area and about a mile off one was hovering, the light reflecting off the lenses of a surveillance device it carried. No doubt the crew were watching them as he spoke, his head carefully away so they could not see him speaking.

"How long have they been watching us?" Pat had asked.

"Off and on for about forty minutes."

"And you only tell me now?"

She hadn't been able to see him shrug as he did up his fly buttons.

"I didn't need to pee until now. Their cameras are very good; they would see I was just pretending if I stopped when I first saw them."

They had continued the journey and the helicopter, apparently satisfied had vanished for the time being, no doubt checking on other vehicles in the area.

At a small hamlet the driver had stopped the van and left her there whilst he went to make discrete enquiries.

On his return the news had been nearly all bad, deserters had taken over one of the more remote farms, remaining until the food had run out before moving on, but not before killing the family that lived there, to prevent them from sounding the alarm as soon as they were out of sight. The bodies of the family had been found that morning, and the word around the hamlet was that they had been related in some way to the regional military commander, who had drawn on resources from surrounding regions and begun a manhunt. All properties were being searched and roadblocks were up on all the roads, slowly extending out from the scene. The only good news was that the helicopters were on loan to the region for just today, and of course the contact knew of another route to the forest, always providing it wasn't too muddy for his van.

"How far is this commander extending his search, as far as our farm?"

"Possibly, and possibly they will search the forest also, it is an obvious place for deserters to hide but only now are there enough militiamen available to do that."

"How did you find out all of this?"

"The baker, his son-in-law is a militiaman, and they both like people to know they are in the know."

Lying in the darkness with the contact leaning against the vehicle's side, eating Tvarok and Chyorny Khlep, local cottage cheese and black bread purchased from the talkative baker, Patricia was silent for a moment as she weighed up the correct course of action to take.

"We have to go back, collect the others and get to the forest."

"Da." He wrapped the remains of his snack in a tissue to be finished later, and fished out the vans keys. Five minutes later they were heading back.

A thousand feet above the forest one of the helicopters in question slowly quartered the area. In the observer's monitor, the heat sources showed up as lighter outlines. Birds, small animals, silka deer and wild boar, all left their traces on the screen, but humans thus far had been the only cause of excitement all day. It had landed in a clearing to drop off five militiamen before taking to the air once more, ready to provide fire support. It had proved an anti-climax to find two elderly men from a local village cutting wood, and after collecting the militia the patrol had continued.

The presence of the helicopter was of great concern at the airstrip. The Green Berets positions were all covered with heat sensor defeating material, grey woven, man-made fabric that could be cut to size. Even up close the strip looked disused, its surface fractured by the hardy bushes and grasses growing through the cracks they had made, but the downwash of the helicopters blades would literally blow away that deception, if it landed there or even hovered a few feet above.

The entire detachment had stood-to when the sound of the aircraft had reached them, moving to the dug in positions circling the strip, but it was almost an hour before anyone saw it. The detachment commander had picked up the field telephone and received the report. The report had been concise and accurate, identifying the threat as a single a Mi-8R Hip with military markings. The detachment commander had questioned the observers identification because of the similarities between the Mi-8, the ageing workhorse of the rotary wing fleet, and the Mi-171 which was more heavily armed, carried more armour and also a modern ECM suite, however the soldier qualified his identification of it by stating the tail rotor was on the right of the tail assembly not the left, and there was an absence of the bulbous additional filters, a feature of the Mi-171, on the turbine intakes above and slightly aft of the cockpit. The Mi-8R was a reconnaissance aircraft and as such could only carry eighteen troops, six less than its troop carrier sibling, but the Mi-171 could carry twenty-four also. Either way, if properly trained and handled, those troops could tie down his men until reinforcements arrived.

The Green Berets could easily bring the machine down but that would be letting the cat out of the bag and at the end of the day, if the enemy discovered their presence then the mission was a failure. If Major Nunro was not able to fly the F-117X out then the weapon would have to be removed and the aircraft destroyed. What would then follow that course of action would be the E&E from hell, and the detachment commander didn't give a lot for their chances of survival if that came about because the priority would be to keep the weapon out of enemy hands, and that meant staying together as a unit rather than scattering in pairs.

The American Special Forces troops watched the helicopter, kept their FIM-92A Stingers close to hand, and settled down to a long day.

The journey back had been a nightmare, thanks to a broken hose that had been temporary fixed with a roll of duct tape, and a puncture and further complicated by a frozen wheel nut, which had sheared off, consequently it was gone midnight before the van had halted a quarter of a mile from the farm. Patricia, stiff from the long confinement left the van and made her way cautiously across country, her heart pounding in the expectation that the militia had beaten them here and were just lying in wait for her return.

Like most aircrew Patricia had posed for a photo in flight school, clad in flight gear with helmet under one arm and a Beretta 9M featuring prominently in its shoulder holster, it was the warrior bit, but like most aircrew she hadn't spent a great deal of time at the range. The two English police officers had made her and Caroline put several hundred rounds down the range before taking them through CQB, close quarter battle scenario's to gain familiarity with the weapon, and therefore confidence. She wasn't bubbling over with confidence as she'd set off with a handgun supplied by the contact, reminding herself to make use of shadow and remain still when the clouds gave way to the moon, using the time to memorise the ground between her present piece of cover and the next.

When cloud covered the moon once more she moved cautiously forward with her Beretta held before her, straight-armed and the weapon in a two handed grip. The bulbous, six-inch long sound suppressor destroyed the balance and she had been warned that both range and stopping power would be inhibited, so she had to be close for it to be of any use. Where her eyes went the weapon followed and after several hundred yards she was feeling a lot better about this, the Lara Croft of the flight line, but then she swore under her breathe, calling herself some very unflattering names as she knelt and cocked the weapon, wincing at the noise it made before standing once more and continuing. Why the hell hadn't she thought to make the weapon ready whilst still inside the van?

The house, when it came into view, was in darkness and she paused for a few minutes to listen, realising that ears were at least as important a sense as the eyes at night, before moving around the house in a circle. Once she reached the side of the house where the old ladies herb garden lay she paused again, waiting for the moon to appear through a gap in the scattered cloud covering in order to look at the well-tended and raked surface for boot prints, there were none. Surely anyone surrounding and then searching the place would have walked across it at some point, wouldn't they? Off in the direction of their nearest neighbour a dog barked, its sound carrying across in the nights stillness, Patricia couldn't remember hearing that before and peered in the direction of the disturbed canine but the other farm wasn't visible from ground level.

Inside the dark house she paused inside the kitchen to listen, but found that her heart rate was so high the coursing blood in her veins was inhibiting her hearing and she had to wipe the sweat off her palms, rubbing them against the material of her jeans whilst holding the Beretta one handed, before fishing out a pen light.

She had experienced problems with this back in Scotland, holding the weapon with sound suppressor in one hand and the torch in the other before finding what Pc Pell had called 'her girlie solution', resting the suppressor on her other forearm whilst holding the penlight cack-handed.

Trying to remember all she had been taught she checked each of the ground floor rooms, but all appeared in order, the signs of a search were not evident. Keeping to the edge of the stairs to minimise the risk of creaking floorboards she made her way upstairs. The first bedroom was Caroline's, and Patricia had to put the pen light between her teeth in order to turn its handle before resuming her stance. The penlight revealed an unmade yet empty bed with the sketchpad lying open upon it.

It wasn't what Patricia had expected to find and she remained motionless for a second with a bemused expression on her face before entering the room and kneeling to check under the bed. She didn't know what she expected to find but she didn't know where the hell else her pilot could be. No USAF pilots were hiding beneath the springs and she stood, the light from the penlight illuminating the sketchpad as she did so and Patricia did a double take. There was a full length nude study of the Russian girl, impressive in its capturing of Svetlana's features and of the expression on her face, it was also extremely graphic, the pose was obviously post coital but Patricia's attention was snatched away from it as the distant barking sounded once more. Stepping to the window she opened the curtains to see that their neighbours lights were on, which in itself was a very unusual event for a farm at this time of night, but also there were the headlights of at least three vehicles beside the building too.

She left Caroline's room at a dead run, turning along the corridor to the back of the house and racing for Svetlana's room. She didn't slow when she reached it, just barged the door open before stumbling to halt inside. Svetlana and Caroline were together on the bed, their faces turned towards her in alarm before the tangle of naked limbs hurriedly unravelled. Patricia ignored the nudity and the confirmation of a relationship she had only suspected a few minutes before on seeing the sketch pad, her pilot was ashen faced and seemed to be trying to find the right words but Patricia no time

"The militia are searching all the farms...get dressed!" Caroline opened her mouth to speak but closed it again as she realised what she was about to say was as inane as it was futile. Svetlana was already moving, pulling on underwear and jeans, so Caroline followed suit.

The commotion had roused the elderly couple who had appeared on the landing outside their room and Patricia managed to make them understand that they could not switch on the lights and that herself and the other two young women were leaving, she then retrieved the satellite phone from its hiding place in the orchard, sending a brief sitrep before placing it in a rucksack.

Although their few belongings had been kept packed for a quick exit should it be necessary, it still took several minutes for them to gather downstairs. Caroline removed the laptop from its hiding place and replaced it with a bottle of good vodka, as an excuse for the hiding places existence if a search should discover it. Svetlana came down last, having ensured that there were the odd items left in the bedrooms and bathroom that would reinforce the farmers story that a niece and her friends from Moscow had been staying, but had decided it was safe now to return to Moscow, and had left the previous day. She kissed first the wife and then the farmer, wishing them well and promising to visit once the war was finished. For her part, the farmer's wife hugged and kissed all three before shooing them out into the darkness with a prayer for their safe journey.

Svetlana took from Patricia the Beretta and also the lead, walking point as they headed back the way the American had come. She set a fast pace that had them breathing hard by the time they reached the van and the, by now, extremely anxious driver.

Once they were concealed within, their contact pulled on a pair of PNGs and off they moved, back towards the forest, but only for a few hundred yards. In the dark confines within the van they were alarmed at the sudden stop the van made, followed by its reversing fast and then turning sharply. The smooth surface of the road gave way to ruts and holes as the contact backed into a field and concealed the van behind a high hedgerow before switching off the engine.

The Russian and the USAF aircrew had no way of seeing out of the vehicle and could only sit in the darkness with beating hearts. At first they could hear nothing at all, just the sound of their own breathing, but then came sound of engines and the clank of tracks on the road surface.

A pair of BMP-1 fighting vehicles passed by the field without stopping and then came a third BMP leading a convoy of three trucks, which also drove by without stopping or slowing.

Further down the road the leading pair turned off the road, demolishing a section of fence and driving across the crops so laboriously planted and tended by the farmer and his wife, to take up positions where they could intercept anyone fleeing from the farmhouse.

After a few minutes their contact left the van to listen, but apparently satisfied that there were no more militia following on he returned to the cab and the journey resumed.

Arkansas Valley, Nebraska, USA.

An apologetic marine lieutenant shook Henry Shaw into wakefulness, but at least he had the decency to have a mug of java in his hand.

There was no contact yet between the Red Army and the forces charged with denying them easy access to the autobahns, and neither *Equalizer* nor *Guillotine* had reached critical mass. Henry would need his strength and wits about him when that happened. Accordingly he had taken the opportunity to return to his bunk after the President, under protest, had been ushered off to bed by his doctor for a minimum four hours sleep. The Presidents' blood pressure was sky high prompting an immediate ban on coffee, and the prescribing of beta blocking drugs. The doctor was an admiral and didn't give a damn that his patient was the leader of the free world. He had left his private practice and put on the uniform again to replace his predecessor, killed in Washington DC like so many thousands of others. The President had tried charm and bullying, all to no avail in his attempts to get the physician to leave him alone.

In the end, when the coffee embargo had been declared the President had asked the admiral outright why he was so persistent in making his life difficult.

After a moment the admiral had answered.

"Perhaps I'm just pissed because I voted for the other guy last time around, or maybe I just think your wife is too nice a lady to be a widow....but to get back to the business at hand Mr President, if I see you with coffee one more time I will dump the entire stock down the John, and throw whichever guy or gal who gave it to you in the brig."

Concerns in the shelter were naturally for the President's health and welfare, but becoming collateral damage in the caffeine conflict was truly alarming for some of the dedicated worshippers of the little brown bean.

The mug in his hand was at least an assurance that the Java tap had not been turned off in the intervening hours.

"Mr Jones is waiting for you in the conference room, sir."

Henry straightened up, rubbed his eyes and ran a hand over his chin. There were the first signs that he should shave again at the first opportunity before the heads of the bristles that were just beginning to appear had a chance to develop into a five o'clock shadow.

General Shaw had never had the good fortune, or looks, that had early bristles looking 'cool' on him, they always appeared more disreputable than 'designer'.

Terry Jones looked up at the electronic buzzing that heralded the arrival of the United States Marine Corps top soldier.

"Good morning Mr Jones." Henry mumbled, a portable electric shaver restoring order for the time being.

"Pardon me but a chin follicle massacre was required."

He silenced the device with a flick of a switch on its side and ran fingertips over his lower face, inspecting the results.

"I remember the very first flop house hotel I stayed at." Henry said conversationally.

"On my first ever weekend pass from Parris Island I caught a bus over to Beaufort where I could get gloriously drunk and sleep it off in peace. The landlady pushed the register over the desk for me to complete and asked if I had a good memory for faces?...well I naturally asked her why and she replied..."

"There's no shaving mirror." Terry finished the story for him.

Henry laughed. "Oh, I see you stayed there too?"

Terry was smiling back, but the smile did not reach his eyes.

"No, I was never in the service and I think our lives have taken us on pretty different courses General, and that doesn't make for too much common ground, shared experiences or mutual friends." His look was steely, and the crocodile smile remained.

Henry seated himself opposite, to all intents unaware that the CIA Directors remark was anything but a casual observation.

"There was Scott, I liked that young man."

Terry Jones did not reply immediately, his eyes remained unblinkingly on Henry.

"Yes, indeed." He eventually allowed. "There was Scott Tafler."

"So what is occurring now that could not wait until the Presidents next briefing?" Henry asked.

Terry at last looked away and used a remote to switch on the plasma screen at the foot of the long table.

There was a segment of a cable news programme regarding Argentina's claims to have responded to an attack on one of their maritime patrols by sinking a pair of surfaced submarines.

Henry didn't dog the news channels, despite them often bearing bad tidings well before the intelligence services got wind that there was even a problem.

Scraps of uniform and a short length of hose had been recovered from the surface of the ocean and were displayed for the cameras. The hose bore stencilled Cyrillic lettering and the uniform items had been identified as being of Russian and Chinese manufacture.

"This footage is from the Argentinian aircrafts cameras." Said Terry as the item drew to a close.

It was a very grainy view, made worse by the weather conditions and low altitude; two hundred feet below the cameras minimum focus height.

Terry pressed 'Freeze Frame', capturing the blurry shapes of the *Tuan* and the *Admiral Potemkin* in the harsh magnesium glare of the aircrafts dropped flares. The Chinese Kilo was dwarfed by the bulk of the Russian submarine.

Terry opened a folder and passed over a clutch of still captures from the footage, digitally enhanced and showing the STREAM rig clearly joining the vessels in a replenishment at sea operation.

"Well I'll be..." Henry shook his head incredulously. "Ingenious little fuckers, aren't they?"

Terry flipped across a fourth enhanced still and Henry was silent for several minutes as he studied it.

"If you'd just shown me the first three I would have said it was a long range hunting party, but what is this submersible doing here...do they have a sub down somewhere down that way?"

Henry then looked up and glanced around as if realising for the first time that the two of them were alone. He turned the photograph over and saw its point of origin was Naval Intelligence, not the CIA.

He looked up at Terry, noting the stare and that cold half smile had returned.

The CIA was briefing the military on something the military were already aware of, and furthermore it would be aired by the navy in a few hours' time for the President with Henry present.

"You want to tell me what this is all about? Why am I really here Mr Jones?"

"Well, that is indeed the sixty four thousand dollar question isn't it?" Terry said. "What *are* you doing here, General?"

Henry stood, looking across the table at Terry.

"Well I'm not playing mind games with a spook when I could be sleeping, that's for sure and certain, Jones."

He crossed the room to the door but before he could turn the handle Terry Jones spoke again.

"I liked Scott too, and if I had been in London last week I sure as hell would have been present when his killers were picked up...so I have to ask you Henry, what was it that you were doing that night which was so all fired important that you stayed away, huh?"

General Henry Shaw paused momentarily, looking at the CIA Director and returning his stare before turning the handle and departing.

General Shaw had a small bunk all to himself with a locking door to add a little security for sensitive papers. It wasn't as if sneak thieves were likely to be a problem in such a facility though.

A standard metal lined documents case held what papers Henry kept, and that sat below the single metal framed bed.

On arriving back at the bunk Henry reach beneath the bed and drew out the case, lifting it and checking that its locks were still secure. Satisfied, he crouched to slide it back in its place and that is when he paused, seeing the faded beer mat that was no longer with its five brothers inside an internal compartment, laying where it had fallen unnoticed during an otherwise professional search.

Germany.

Well before dawn the 43rd Motor Rifle Regiment had oriented towards the south west in hastily prepared positions, guarding against a possible counter attack by NATO. They were now three miles inland and five from the bridgehead, out of earshot of the roaring of engines as tanks, APCs, self-propelled guns and all the hardware of armoured warfare crossing the ribbon bridges to the western bank of the Elbe.

At the bridgehead a tenth bridge had just been completed. By the time dawn arrived a further five would also be carrying the weight of the Sixth Shock and Tenth Tank Armies fighting and support units as they moved forward into the offensive.

As yet no work had begun on the autobahn bridge; the combat engineers were still clearing the booby traps left by NATO, a dangerous task at the best of times but doubly so now in the dark. The platoon of engineers tasked to perform the clearance had already lost three men, one dead and two wounded, but had no option but to continue. The schedule called for prefabricated bridging sections to be laid between the spans starting at first light, and to that end a detachment of field police were ensuring that the engineers did not waver from their explosive ordnance clearance duties.

In order to fulfil the role the planners of this campaign envisaged, Colonel Lužar's regiment had been re-equipped with whatever equipment had been left over after the two, mainly Russian, armies spearheading the drive to the channel had been refitted. His battalions consisted of a mixed bag of MBTs and APCs of differing types and marks. The latest types to be added to the regiment's inventory were not new; indeed his own command tank wore the tell-tale signs of previously having been knocked out. A crudely patched area on the outside of the turret had its twin on the inside, an area of scorched metal and blistered paint

His battalions' main battle tank companies now consisted of T-62, T-72, T-80Bs and T-80Us, plus the inferior T-90s. As for his APC companies, well they were also a mixture of BDRMs, BMP1s, 2s and 3s with ancient BTR-60s in evidence here and there. It was hardly a first class unit anymore but he had been assured that NATO units were in a worse state, and any moves made against him would be half-hearted efforts.

Only one company of his faithful PT-76 amphibious tanks remained of the battalion he had first attempted to force the Elbe with. The survivors had been reformed into one large company the next day. So many of his men had fallen that night without knowing that they were merely a diversionary attack, a side show to divert reserves from being able to repel the Red Army's main effort, which itself had proved a long drawn out affair and an eventual failure.

For Colonel Lužar the shooting of the other unit commanders after that night had been monstrous, they had not been expected to succeed and yet they died for failing.

Thus far Colonel Lužar had not seen a single enemy fighting vehicle and the only reaction to their presence had been several artillery strikes. Taking all things into account the resistance they had met had been pathetic, although the artillery had been highly accurate, and up to that time he had begun to wonder if they had killed all of NATOs brave young men and women, and the rest had run away.

To his right sat the charred remains of a BRDM infantry fighting vehicle. Flames still flickered in the molten rubber of what had been its tyres. An entire infantry section had perished with the vehicle and its crew, without so much as firing a single shot. It was just one of the eleven AFVs he had lost in that thirty minute attack, and the way the enemy fire had been corrected, to walk across fighting positions pointed to the presence of a spotter in close proximity.

Patrolling had discovered the spotter's location in the ruins of a building only 300m in front of the colonel's own position, but sloppy command and control by the infantry patrol's commander had left an escape route open. His infantry came under effective automatic fire from the ruins, which allowed the enemy troops to slip away in pairs until only a single weapon remained. Frustrated by the lack of aggression shown by his infantry, Lužar had ordered his own vehicle forward to break the impasse, but if he had thought the sight of his approaching T-80UK command tank was going to intimidate the remaining enemy soldier he was mistaken. The enemy soldier had continued to pin down the infantry with short economic bursts, buying more time for his comrades to make good their escape. Lužar had been forced to drop down inside the turret to avoid the fire directed his way, after which his gunner had fired a single main gun round into the ruins, silencing the weapon.

Colonel Lužar had left the tank after unclipping from its storage place an AMD 65, the tank crews folding stock version of the AKM. His loader, similarly armed, had accompanied him into the ruins where Lužar had half hoped to find his enemy still alive. It had taken courage to remain there all alone and in the knowledge that the best you could hope for was to be captured once your ammunition ran out, but you had to be a real optimist to count on that as an outcome.

His enemy had been lying face down in the rubble, one leg at an unnatural angle and the material of the camouflage trousers soaked in blood. Lužar gently rolled him over onto his back and using a penlight he'd looked at the face of a young man in his early twenties. One side of the soldier's head had a strange uneven look about it; the result of being crushed by flying masonry but the colonel had felt for a pulse anyway. The half lidded, dead eyes stared back at him as Lužar had looked him over. The uniform and equipment were British, and he had read the name on the tag above his victim's breast pocket before removing the 9mm Glock from its webbing holster on the dead soldiers fighting order.

Returning to his command tank he had climbed inside and closed the hatch, turning up the internal lighting before unloading the pistol and stripping it for inspection. He'd found the weapon had been recently cleaned and lightly oiled, which were hardly the actions of demoralised troops at the verge of breaking. With the lighting doused once again Lužar had unbuttoned the hatch and watched the infantry place inside a shallow grave the body of 2Lt Reed. J, Royal Artillery.

Back in the here and now the colonel was still mulling over the significance of apparently well-trained and motivated troops, and their conspicuous absence from the field.

Russia: Same time.

The van passed through the talkative baker's hamlet, the buildings all in darkness and not a soul was in sight. So far the roads had been empty of civilian traffic that were for once complying with the curfew, thanks to the extra militia drafted in from surrounding regions, but those extra men not employed on enforcing the curfew, they were committed to the house searches and cordoning suspect areas such as the forest the van was heading for.

Five miles from the edge of the forest, the van turned onto a farm track and from then on its passengers were treated to a rough ride. Caroline powered down the laptop she had been plotting their course on, it was impossible to work whilst being jolted about. True to his word the contact knew another way, the network of tracks linking the fields of various farms, but after two miles in low gear the engine was overheating badly and the makeshift repairs on the hose gave out. Steam enveloped the van, preceded by a loud report as the hose burst and followed by curses from the driver's cab.

They arrived at the airstrip tired and muddy, having crawled along a ditch to avoid a pair of sleepy militiamen. Any hopes of rest were dashed when Caroline and Patricia were informed that their target was to be attacked as soon as possible

Germany.

Black, oily smoke rose above the emergency landing field as Lt Col Arndeker turned onto finals and brought the speed down to 160knots. Without any effort on his half, the flaperons lowered in response to the lower speed setting and Arndeker peered ahead. There was a lot of activity on the grass to the left of the single runway. Fire trucks were clustered together near a burning aircraft but it was too far to yet see anything more.

A country lane, bordered by hedgerows, ran across the bottom of the landing field and Arndecker's F-16 passed a few feet above it before touching down. He had seen the fresh scars in the grass as he had gotten closer to the field, pointing like a finger to the wreck, which he now identified as a German Tornado F3. It had apparently slid along on its belly for some distance before performing a ground loop, ending up on its back and facing the way it had come. Silver suited firemen on two of the fire trucks were pumping foam from nozzles mounted above the driver's cabs, covering the aircraft in a white shroud. Arndeker swept past, getting a momentary glimpse of two bodies, covered from head to foot by blankets, laid out side by side next to one of the fire trucks.

Turning off the runway he followed the perimeter track around the field, passing the mobile control shack before turning off onto a prefabricated road made of perforated aluminium strips that led to an orchard. Amongst the trees were parked a dozen aircraft, which like him had run low on fuel and now awaited the field's solitary fuel bowser.

Arndeker's eyebrows rose as an airman guided him to a spot next to an aircraft wearing the Triple Crown insignia of Sweden. Having intervened in the Soviet attacks on Norway and the North Cape the Swedish government had back peddled somewhat, aligning itself with NATO 'in principle' but ducking the question of committing forces outside of its own borders. The presence of a JAS 39A Gripen indicated something not included in any of the briefings Arndeker had attended.

On shutting down, Arndeker clambered down the ladder an airman had put against his cockpit and took a look at the neighbours. The Gripen was the only Swedish aircraft there; the remainder consisted of another Luftwaffe Tornado, a pair of RAF Jaguars and eight F-16s in the liveries of Norway, the USA, Belgium and The Netherlands.

The airman, a Royal Air Force aircraftman, informed him that the bowser was refilling and that a NAAFI wagon would be coming around with tea and sandwiches. Thanking him he then headed for the cluster of men and women in flight gear sat beneath the Tornado.

None of the American's was from Arndeker's squadron but he knew them by name and introductions were made all round. The German's were grim faced having witnessed the death of two of their squadron mates, and said little. He sat beside the pilot of the Gripen, a good looking blond with high cheekbones and striking blue eyes who introduced herself as Lojtnant Ulrika Jorgensen. Ulrika's flight had been responsible for taking out the Red Air Forces AWAC cover far behind the Elbe, clearing the way for airborne drops. It was the first Arndeker had heard that NATO had taken offensive action, and he thanked her and her country for finally stepping beyond the border. Her response had been curious, laughing and telling him he had better make the most of it because the air force would as like as not be behind bars this time tomorrow. He was about to ask what she'd meant by that but the promised NAAFI arrived and there was a scramble to be at the head of the line. Over plastic cups of sweet tea and cheese sandwiches, which the RAF crews called 'mouse meat sarnie's', they had all described their experiences of that morning. Arndeker congratulated Ulrika on the Il-76 and Mig-31 she had brought down that morning, bringing her score to three when added to a Flogger bagged on the day the Soviet's had overflown her country to attack Norway.

Arndeker himself had brought down his fourteenth enemy aircraft and the thirteenth of this conflict. On being scrambled before dawn he had led his entire squadron, numbering just seven aircraft, against a Red Air Force regiment heading for the main highways from Antwerp. For the first time in two weeks they had taken to the air fully loaded with ordnance, courtesy of the newly arrived convoy from the States. Being able to carry more than just one AMRAAM per sortie had been a joy to the NATO pilots and an unwelcome shock to the red fliers who had become accustomed to their opponents increasingly limited offensive capabilities.

His F-16s had broken up the formations of strike aircraft before their escorts had intervened and from there on in it had become a fur ball. Arndeker's wingman, a young woman from Idaho, had been on her second mission had mid-aired with a Mig-29. The two aircraft had exploded, the wreckage locked together in an obscene embrace as they'd fallen towards the German countryside. Arndeker had watched until they disappeared into low cloud but no parachutes had appeared.

His last AIM-9L had been a clear miss, defeated by a combination of his intended victims ECM suite and some damn fine flying. He'd lost contact with the rest of the squadron and was almost entirely defensive, loosing off snap shots at fleeting targets of opportunity until a Mig-29 had unwisely shown him its rear end, flying straight and level for just a little too long and offering a minimum deflection shot. He had put a long burst of cannon into it, watching the shells explode in a line from the tip of its port wing to the wing root. The wing had folded up, sending the aircraft into a spin. Just before entering the low cloud that had swallowed his wingman an object shot clear of the crippled aircraft before blossoming into a parachute. Finally with his HUD warning him of a fuel state approaching critical and a pair of Mig-31s, also shy of air-air ordnance but hard on his tail, he'd dived for the ground somewhere north of Duisburg, losing them in the ground clutter.

Everyone there had similar tales to tell, but not in the tones of bravado, rather in a matter-of-fact manner that sounded almost bored.

All the aircrew in the orchard, with the exception of the Swedish flier, were showing the signs of fatigue, a weariness that ran as deep as the bones and permeated the nerves. It was the result of flying ever more sorties each day as losses reduced the numbers of men and women available to fly the missions. It was also through watching that band of colleagues who had been the core of the squadron, thin out or disappear altogether, leaving the survivors to wonder when it would be they who failed to come back.

By unspoken agreement the talk of combat and lost friends petered out, turning instead to peacetime flying, famous gaffs, non-fatal yet spectacular screw-ups and the like. For a time at least the war was pushed aside, replaced by the laughter the recounting of these tales and anecdotes caused.

The fuel truck returned, its own bowser now refilled and the small international tea party finished up the lukewarm beverage and the sandwiches that were curling up at the edges.

Arndeker was the last in line and the other aircraft had already departed by the time the fuel truck had given him enough to get back to his own field. He was alone in the orchard and the warmth of the other flier's spirits had departed this place. There was eeriness about it now and he was eager to be gone. Fifteen minutes later he was airborne again and heading home at treetop height to avoid trouble.

Australia: Ian McLennan Park, Kembla: New South Wales.

Australia's immensely long coastline had but eighty thousand full time and reserve personnel of the Australian Defence Force to guard it against invasion at the outbreak of war, but this had swollen to two hundred thousand men and women under arms. In addition they welcomed others to the task.

Japanese, Taiwanese and Singaporean personnel wore a French design behind their cap badges, a fleur-de-lis, signifying volunteers from Chinese occupied counties. These were in main service personnel who had escaped in order to fight on when their own countries surrendered to the People's Republic of China. There was even a Moro commando brigade in training near Brisbane, its instructors were Australian SAS as a deal of suspicion existed between the available US instructors and the Muslim's from Mindanao in the Philippines.

Two divisions of the US 2nd Army, plus air and sea assets, had arrived from evacuated South Korea and a further division from the USA, 5th Mechanised. Along with major units of the US Pacific Fleet this went a good way to having a credible defence force to face off the invasion force that was heading their way.

3rd Marine Expeditionary Force and the majority of the former USFJ army and air force units relocated to New Zealand from Japan.

There were no force relocations from Taiwan. All US units that had fought on the island had perished along with the Taiwanese armed forces on that last terrible day.

A very small component from the British Army was also present in Australia, albeit accidentally despite the current British Defence Minister's attempts to spin it as largess.

Four British Mk2E Challenger main battle tanks of the 1RTR, Royal Tank Regiment, were sat in hull down positions on the high ground above the Princes Highway and Kembla Grange Racecourse, the temporary 'home' of the 5th Mechanised Division, to which the troop of British tanks, an infantry platoon of 3rd Battalion Royal Green Jackets and support troops were attached.

The division had the daunting task of defending a stretch of coastline from the port of Kembla, situated forty miles south of Sydney, to Bateman's Bay, ninety miles to the south, and west as far as the northern edge of the city limits of Canberra, in all a mere seven hundred and twenty square miles.

Officially the British troops were part of the divisional reserve and therefore had no pre-prepared forward fighting positions.

Having been at Fort Hood on exercise *'Commanche Lance'* at the outbreak of war the small British contingent known as unofficially as 'The Queen Elizabeth's Combat Team' had embedded with their hosts, the 52nd Infantry, for a return to Europe via Atlantic convoy's with 5th (US) Mechanised Division but the division had been turned around on reaching the docks in Texas and entrained again to be sent west as reinforcements for Australia.

'Heck', Captain Hector Sinclair Obediah Wantage-Ferdoux, RTR, Lt Tony McMarn, RGJ and Captain Danny King, their US liaison, walked together across the dusty and uneven hilltops west side of Ian McLennan Park, a bike scrambling and off-road dirt track area beside a football ground and small covered spectators stand, the home of the South Coast United Soccer Club.

In appearance the hill was spookily similar to that of an ancient Briton hill fort of the stone age, the camouflaged twenty first century armoured fighting vehicles whose barrels poked outwards at its crest somewhat at odds with that. However, as the Brits had dug in they had found nothing to excite viewers of the Discovery Channels 'Ancient Aliens' but plenty of evidence of landfill. The terraced sides engineered for stability rather than defence.

Both officers carried mess tins, mugs and 'scoffing rods', knife, fork and spoon clanking in one hand as they headed over to the covered football stand to join the breakfast queue.

The stand was the cookhouse and feeding area for the combat team, the changing rooms were the 'barracks' for the cooks and REME L.A.D, Light Aid Detachment, and the car park sported a covered workshop constructed of scaffolding with a 'wriggly tin roof', which means 'corrugated metal sheeting' to civilians.

"So we have a spare barrel and a bunch more rounds per tank?" Tony asked.

When the Australian Defence Force was looking to replace its ageing German Leopard 1s it had tested the contender's main armament. The German Leopard 2s L44 main armament also 'gunned' the US M1A1 Abrahms, and an L44 was tested for comparison beside the British L30 tank gun. The rifled British gun could throw a HESH, shaped charge road, 8,000 metres, a full five miles, with great accuracy and twice the range of the smoothbore German gun. But accessibility to spares and upgrades from the other side of the Pacific as opposed to the other side of the planet was a factor in Australia's choosing the American tank over the German and British MBTs. It also meant that in a magazine in Darwin there was sat 144 rounds of ammunition left over from that testing.

Heck's troop of Challenger 2s had arrived in Australia with just their 'Front Line loads' of forty nine rounds per tank and the commander of 5th Mech, 'Duke' Thackery, had little use for the Brits other than as a forlorn hope and as casualty replacements as the Abrahms and Challengers ammunition was not compatible.

"In the big scheme of things we have thirty six reloads per vehicle, which is good for one engagement perhaps...still, it's better than jack-all, isn't it?" Heck responded.

"Not enough for General Thackery to change his plans. You are still a throw away quick reaction force to plug any penetrations."

"Throw away?" Heck muttered aloud. "Penetrations?" he continued. "I am not sure I like the parallels with those of a 'spent johnnie'." he concluded.

Danny frowned.

"Pardon?"

"A used, prophylactic." Tony informed him.

They joined the end of the queue, standing behind Sergeant Rebecca Hemmings and Master Sergeant Bart Kopak. Rebecca still wore a drawn look on her otherwise pretty features. Becoming a widow early on in the war was not a matter that she had fully come to terms with yet, but the ever hopeful Bart was there if and when she did.

Bart was 'not on rations' with the British unit anymore. They no longer warranted a liaison team, just Danny King the captain from the 11th Armoured Cavalry. The three officers were aware of the situation but none of them made any comment. Rebecca and Bart were good people.

The line shuffled on, closer to the heavy ' Hay Boxes', the insulated metal containers for transporting cooked food to the troops. Such containers had once been lined with dried straw to retain the heat and as such the name 'Hay Box' had remained.

Eventually each officer was served and found a spot to sit together in the stands to eat.

A slice of fried bread, a fried sausage, a fried egg, two tinned tomatoes, half a dozen tinned mushrooms and a half ladle of baked beans.

Be it Chelsea Barracks or Camp Bastion, Catterick or Kembla, the high cholesterol breakfast was an even surer sign than a bugler sounding reveille that the British Army had started a new day.

Russia.

A day, which had started badly, was steadily getting worse for the deputy commander of Militia Sub-District 178. His boss had been slightly vocal when the men had not been in position and ready to go a half hour before dawn, rather vocal when the dawn came and no move was made, and screaming dire threats into radio microphones thirty minutes after that.

The trouble was, the thousand and twelve men they had were policemen, not soldiers, and lining them up twenty feet apart along the forest's edge was not as easy as it sounded.

Shortly after they had stepped off, the real difficulties had become evident. Gaps appeared where men elected not to push through heavy brush, but rather to walk around. Men walked alongside friends chatting, and where the going was easy the line surged forward, leaving others struggling through underbrush far behind.

It was not happening as the sub district commander had envisaged, the evenly spaced line of his briefing was not going to sweep evenly along at three miles an hour, uncovering the killers as it flushed them from hiding, and apparently it was all his deputy's fault.

The commander had been unwilling to listen to other opinions, which was nothing new; he was an arrogant individual at the best of times.

The deputy had put forward the possibility that the culprits could have put a *lot* of distance between themselves and the scene of their crime, which was why the search of farms and buildings in the region had come up empty, and why the reconnaissance helicopter the previous day had not uncovered any clusters of skulking humanity in the trees of the forest.

His opinions and theories carried little weight at the best of times, and these earned him a contemptuous rebuke.

The deputy had initially been in charge of the line of militiamen, then humiliated in front of the men by his superior when all did not go according to plan, he had been despatched instead with two BMP-1s to check on the men cordoning the forest.

It had taken an hour for the deputy to accept that he was better off away from the line of 'beaters' because things would only get even more fraught as time went on. His boss, the commander, was an idiot and what is more everyone knew he was an idiot, so what did it matter that he had treated his deputy like an imbecile in front of the lowest ranks? All he had to do was ensure there were no problems with the cordons, and generally keep his head down for the duration of the operation. It would take several days to comb through the forest so he would take the opportunity to enjoy the time away from the overbearing buffoon who held the next rank, savour the independence and autonomy whilst he had the chance.

The deputy commander directed the driver of his vehicle to head for the nearest roadblock, after that he would look at the map for the best way through the forest. An easily navigable route would cut time off the journey from one side to the other, and would serve to avoid crossing the commander's path.

Gansu Province: China.

Those men engaged in the preparation of the Cadre's 'accommodation' were stripped down to just their arctic white smocks, which were providing only camouflage, not warmth, in the sub-zero temperature. Despite the freezing air the men were warm from tunnelling into the snow, and had removed upper layers of clothing to prevent sweat forming.

Richard worked along with them, preparing the location for an indefinite stay, or at least until all the pieces were in place, and the attack could go ahead. The major knew nothing of the other elements involved, and had he been asked about Operation *Equalizer* or Operation *Guillotine* he would have shrugged his shoulders and asked in all truthfulness what they were. He wasn't a fool though and knew that in all probability there had to be at least one other operation working toward achieving the mission's ultimate aim. Logic dictated that there had to be an operation running to take out the PRCs other means of waging intercontinental nuclear war, that of the submarine threat. He had spent many hours aboard submarines during his career, but always as a passenger enroute to or from some covert operation or other, he had no idea how they would go about finding China's vessels in the Pacific and Indian Oceans. Driving submarines was a complete mystery to him, and yet some people were remarkably good at it, as testified by the blinking 'message' light he had just noticed on his communicator.

When Richard had been a boy of four his parents had bought him a Scotty, a Highland Terrier that Richard had named Jack. There hadn't been anything particularly outstanding about the animal but it had been his first dog and therefore memorable to Richard alone. The message, once decompressed and decrypted comprised of a single word, the name of Richards very first pet. He was a little taken aback at having received the Go word so soon; it was after all just a few hours since the bulk of the force had departed for the extraction point. A few men rolled their eyes skywards, having come near to completing their snow holes only to be informed that they were now to 'paste up, patch up and piss off', but no one complained aloud. The entrenching tools were packed away and warm clothing was once more pulled on,

The batteries in the RERs and laser designators were almost brand new but Richard had them changed anyway, before he led the Cadre out, back along the ridge and abseiling down to the canyon floor at the avalanche site. There was nothing left to indicate that troops had been there, except of course the small holes in the rock wall where the pitons had been driven in. Once the snow thawed it would doubtless uncover the bodies of the two dead men, the smashed equipment and abandoned kit, but for now the still falling snow was covering over all signs that men had passed this way.

The Cadre crossed the canyon and scaled the face on the opposite side without a single appearance by PRC helicopter patrols. Richard wasn't about to look a gift horse in the mouth, if the PRC aircrew felt the weather was unsafe to fly in then that suited him just fine. He knew that the enemy now was time, getting clear of the area before the manhunt began in the wake of the, hopefully, successful attacks on the silos. Once they had cleared this particular ridge and the valley beyond then their chances of successful evasion were greatly increased. With luck Garfield's men and the Mountain Troop contingent would already have gotten the injured men across this ridge and down to the valley floor. Richard was not about to break a radio silence maintained since setting foot in China, they would find out how well Garfield had done when they caught up with them. He wanted to be on the valley floor before midnight and across it before the dawn, which would mean some gruelling cross-country skiing. Passing the word that there would be no rest stops tonight; Richard led the men past the site where they had weathered the blizzard, and onwards toward the valley.

Germany.

Commanding 3rd Shock Army's point Division was a fifty two year old Romanian from Piatra Neamt, in the foothills of the Carpathian Mountains. He had been a Lt Col commanding an artillery battalion during the last years under Ceausescu and had never envisaged reaching Staff rank; all those places had been earmarked years in advance for officers from Romania's communist elite. With the fall of the tyrant however, the new government deemed him too lowly in rank to be tainted by association, and yet capable enough to handle the responsibility of a sudden elevation in rank, in order to help fill the vacuum created by the former general staff's sudden retirement.

The division he led today was a different creature to the one he had brought over to the communist cause during the coup that had preceded this war; over a third of the original number had become casualties to NATO's fierce defence by the time his division had reached the Spee. Originally the division had consisted of a reconnaissance regiment, a tank regiment and three MRRs, motor rifle regiments, each made up of three battalions; a rotary wing aviation battalion, an artillery regiment consisting of a heavy, a medium and air defence battalions, plus the usual engineering and logistic support units. All had been native Romanians, and a full two thirds had at least two years recent service under their belts. NATO had almost annihilated his reconnaissance regiment and all that had remained were two companies worth of men and vehicles, which had lately been reinforced and brought up to the size of a superannuated battalion. Shortly after reaching the Spee the division had been taken out of the line and sent to the rear to reconstitute, his three battered motor rifle regiments had amalgamated to become two, and the tank regiment now numbered two battalions instead of three. The arrival of a Czech and a Bulgarian MRR to bolster the division's ranks had been a mixed blessing because it caused distinct communications problems, but they were already blooded and were therefore preferable to units consisting of green conscripts. Cold bloodedly, the division commander had assigned the Bulgarian's the duty of walking point where NATO could dull its edge, and once the newcomers had become combat ineffective as a unit it would be broken up and absorbed by his Romanians whilst the Czechs took up point position and remained there until a similar fate befell them. It did not occur to him that the commander of 3rd Army had been thinking along exactly the same lines when he written his own orders, using the Romanian division as the expendable tip of a mainly Russian spear.

At a midnight O Group the division commander had deployed his Romanian MRRs, the 111th and 112th, on the left and right rear of the Czechs, who were to follow directly behind the Bulgarians. His tank regiment, the 93rd, was to follow on behind and in this fashion the tanks would be in position to exploit any breaches that might appear, passing through the lead units to either widen the breach or to punch deep into the enemy's rear. The division's axis of advance took them straight at a linear feature that lay like a natural barrier to the all-important Autobahns to the English Channel. According to his maps this feature was called Vormundberg, and according to intelligence it was occupied by a ragtag unit of British and Americans with a forward screen of French and British light troops, which he had described to his officers at the final O Group as, 'hardly something to lose any sleep over'. It was therefore with a degree of optimism that the O Group had broken up and his officers had returned to their units to deliver their own orders. A large bite had been taken out of that optimism a few hours later, just as the division was about to jump off. NATO launched massed air raids on the Soviet armour west of the Elbe and for reasons unbeknownst to the division commander their own air cover had been conspicuously absent. As a result, all of the divisions units had taken casualties but the Bulgarians, being at the forward edge, had been hit particularly hard and had taken 70% casualties, including their regimental headquarters. Under threat of arrest from his own superior the divisional commander had been forced to abandon the casualties, policing up the remainder and revising his plans so that the Czech regiment lead the way.

After the first forty minutes of an unchallenged advance he had felt some of the earlier optimism restore itself. At the top of a rise he had dismounted from his command vehicle to look back along the way they had come and was moved by the awesome spectacle that met his gaze. His unit may have been under strength but it was still impressive for all that, and beyond his divisions vehicles he could see those of other units, but as moving dots against the landscape. Surely NATO had nothing left with which to deny them their march to the coast?

But five minutes later Milan missiles and expertly called in air strikes had begun exploding his precious reconnaissance vehicles.

Reports from the roving troublemakers of 2REP, *2e Regiment Etranger de Parachutiste's* Anti-Tank Platoon, and the Anti-Tank Guided Weapons Troop of 40 Commando RM, had charted the progress of Third Shock Army's lead elements as they advanced westwards away from the Elbe. The French Foreign Legion paratroopers and the Royal Marine Commandos had used every opportunity to inflict harm and delay upon the enemy. Wire guided anti-tank rounds and air strikes called in by the NATO troops shredded the reconnaissance screen that preceded the armoured units, forcing the enemy to deploy forward other fighting vehicles to plug the gaps in the screen. The larger fighting vehicles were no substitute for the smaller, quieter and more agile specialist reconnaissance vehicles and were easy prey to the Milans of the French and British. Battle tanks costing millions of roubles were left burning in the fields and roads, falling victim to soft skinned vehicles that cost mere thousands. To counter this, the Soviet's called in helicopter gunships to ride shotgun and range ahead of the tanks, and where they caught the NATO troops in the open the helicopters 23mm cannons tore up both the un-armoured vehicles and crewmen alike. The next air battle began as a direct result, with the marines and paratroopers calling for CAPs to deal with the threat from the air and the Soviet rotary wing crews quickly doing likewise once air-to-air missiles began thinning them out.

Arndeker was listening to events taking place overhead but not getting involved in the dogfights. He was at 150 ft. and banking to the left to follow the contours of a hill whilst keeping an eye out for a chimney stack on the horizon. The chimney was a visual marker, once seen he would steer a few degrees to the right of it until he reached a disused and weed choked canal which he could follow, making use of the man-made defile's cut for it through the low hills. It would bring himself and the four F-16s with him down the right flank of the enemy armoured thrust heading for the autobahn. The mission called for them to RV with two flights of three Swedish Gripen's and following hot on the heels of a Wild Weasel sortie by French Armee de l'air Jaguar, Mirage F-1 and 2000Ds, they were to make as many sweeps of the armoured formations as Arndeker felt were advisable. Right now he felt a suitably safe and appropriate number was probably zero, but he wasn't able to say what he felt, i.e., "I'm tired of this game and I don't want to play anymore," because he was the squadron commander, an officer in the armed forces of his country and the one who set the example for his subordinates to follow. It just wasn't acceptable to announce that he vomited at the thought of going into combat again, that his nerve was close to being shot, or that it took five fingers of vodka just to get him off to sleep at night. It wasn't acceptable in the eyes of his peers and it wasn't acceptable in his own either. Lieutenant Colonel Patrick Arndeker, USAF, loving husband and proud father of two was racing toward burn out and he couldn't see it, he couldn't see it because to open his eyes to that possibility was not acceptable either.

This sortie was a maximum effort by his squadron, with all available airframes taking part, and Lt Col Arndeker who had decided to rest his pilots where possible between sorties had no option but to comply. The first mission of the day, intercepting the inbound strike against 4 Corps, had cost the squadron his wingman, and whilst he had been at the emergency field his Exec had led the remainder against a second strike. His Exec had not returned from that one, which left his squadron with exactly five operational airframes left out of the fifteen there had been at the outbreak of the war.

Quite apart from the slowed reactions induced by fatigue, Arndeker had witnessed for himself of late a phenomenon that he had read of in pilots during the First and Second World Wars, that of a recklessness in some of his pilots, as if they were resigned to an untimely end and therefore did little to avoid it, such as flying straight and level through ground fire when they should have been jinking to throw off the gunners aim.

The German hillside flashed past and then he saw the distant concrete column pointing heavenwards. The wings of Arndeker's F-16 came level and he checked his aircraft were still with him, they were and in anticipation of a right turn to follow the old canal the five moved into an echelon left formation.

Arndeker almost missed the canal, so choked with weed was it that it almost merged with the undergrowth on the banks. He took the flight around in a hard turn to starboard and settled down to just seventy-five feet above it with four aircraft moving into trail behind him.

"Chain Gang lead, this is Lion Dog Zero Three?"

Lion Dog was the call sign of their controller for this gig.

"Go, Dog."

"Gang, you got Steel Talon, a flight of four Gripens approaching from your 8 o'clock, fifteen miles out."

"Roger Dog, they're late and there was supposed to be two fights of three?"

"They got bounced, Gang."

It was a very clinical way of stating the fifth and sixth aircraft were spread across the countryside somewhere.

"Roger Dog, have the French guys adjusted to compensate?"

"Negative Gang, their timetable is not variable so I suggest you continue as planned and on time, but it's your call."

The plan called for five different formations of aircraft to arrive over the battlefield at designated times in order to carry out a coordinated attack. The timing was important to maximise the shock effect of the layered defences being stripped away and leaving the enemy armour open to attack. First in were to be the Armee de l'air Mirage F-1s, engaging the Red Air Force Top CAP to allow the Jaguars and Mirage 2000Ds to destroy or force off the air the AAA radars, and by so doing opening the way for Arndeker's F-16s and the Gripen's to carry out attacks with Rockeye's and Gator's. The window of opportunity would be scarce minutes, in single figures, before the Soviet's recovered.

Arndeker didn't want to delay until the Gripen's arrived and he didn't want to leave the Swedish fliers to brave the Soviet's anger on their lonesome either. He informed his flight and the AWAC he was switching frequencies.

"Steel Talon lead this is Chain Gang lead on TAC Six, over?"

After a moment's delay the Gripens flight leader responded in accented English, and it took a second for Arndeker to realise he had spoken with the owner of that voice only a few hours before.

"Gang this is Talon, sorry for the delay, begin your run without us, we'll be a couple of minutes late."

"Talon this is Gang, we will hold for your arrival but we can only make a single pass over the target."

"Roger Gang, I appreciate that...however, my higher has briefed us for a minimum of four passes."

On his second radio Arndeker heard the French going in, and they lost an aircraft to ground fire almost immediately.

"Hey Ulrika, I'm sure your higher had no idea you would be delayed, but four passes is way beyond sensible...it's a bad neighbourhood we're visiting so hold it down to two passes and we'll stay with you."

Talon's leader knew that the delay would give the Soviet's the recovery time necessary to concentrate their fire on whoever was in the air, and it was better that their guns be divided up on nine targets rather than four.

"Roger Gang, you got a deal...and again, we do appreciate it." Arndeker could hear the smile in her voice and felt good about himself for the first time in several days.

His F-16s passed through the final cleft in the hills and he took them in a shallow turn to port, orbiting just above the treetops as they waited for the Gripen's.

Arndeker listened to the radio chatter; he couldn't speak French so he tried to judge from the tone of the pilot's voices how it was going for them.

"Chain Gang lead this is Lion Dog Zero Three, the 2000D's and Jag's are doing a first rate job. I'm watching radars going offline all across the target area and I advise you to begin your run now, it doesn't get much better than this, Gang?"

"Roger Dog, we'll hold for Talon anyway."

There was a hint of 'Don't say I didn't warn you!' in the AWAC controllers voice as he acknowledged Arndeker simply.

"Roger".

If all had gone as planned the Armee de l'Air aircraft would still have been overhead when the Swedish and American aircraft went for the tanks and APCs, but the French had expended all their anti-radar ordnance and were already departing the area as the Gripen's finally arrived. The two leaders hurriedly agreed on a simple plan to replace the original, the Gripen's and the F-16s would make a north to south pass over the head of the column in extended line, four hundred metres between aircraft, with the Swedes on the left, they would then all swing left and make the second pass further down the column before egressing to the north.

The American and Swedish aircraft hugged the contours of the earth as they began their approach. Flying below electricity pylons and between trees, they headed for the pillars of black smoke in the distance that marked the positions of the victims of the French HARM missiles. On cue from the AWAC they popped up to 500 feet and began looking for targets of their own on the ground below.

The Wild Weasel sortie by the French had destroyed more than half a dozen AAA vehicles and intimidated the remainder into shutting down their radars, but it had not slowed the armoured advance. The scene that met Lt Col Arndeker was of a countryside crawling with machines of war, and all of them headed west. His first thought was that there were not enough munitions in the armouries of the west to deal with even half of the fighting vehicles spread out before him. Tracer began curling up towards him, travelling slowly at first but seemingly heading right for him. The tracer grew larger as it approached and suddenly seemed to accelerate, only to flash past harmlessly, but Arndeker still hunched his shoulders and tried to make himself smaller. Each F-16 carried a pair of Rockeye II's, slung in tandem down the centreline hard points and a Gator mine dispenser on each of the inside wing pylons. Arndeker touched the rudder to line up on a company's worth of tank's advancing in line abreast and pickled off a single Rockeye. The weapon fell clear of the aircraft before splitting open like a clamshell and releasing the 247 bomblets it contained, which fell like an ever expanding, elongated cloud. He wasn't aware of what effect the bomblets had, he saw a road crossing ahead of him and selected the portside mine dispenser, leaving a trail of small munitions across the road and the fields either side of it.

Either his sensor suite was malfunctioning or none of the AAA vehicles within engagement range was emitting because the only sounds coming from his earpieces were voices, one female and seven male as the other pilots shouted to one another on the radio. Apart from the tracer there was little in the way of nastiness being directed their way, but the urge to be far from this place was very real. He pickled off his last mines in the path of a mass of self-propelled artillery emerging from a wood, and held his breath until the armoured spearhead had dropped away behind him and only open fields lay ahead. A quick call on his radio confirmed that his wingmen had also emerged unscathed, as had the Gripens, so he felt a lot more comfortable about the next pass.

The nine aircraft turned in a line to the left and then turned north once again, this time with the F-16s on the left. Arndeker found himself flying toward a line of poplars, and pulled back the side stick to clear the tops of the trees. Immediately a loud warbling sound in his headset told him that a SAM radar was illuminating him, and he felt the vibration as his ECM suite automatically punched out chaff. The warble changed, becoming a frantic two-tone siren as the transmitter locked him up. More chaff was ejected and the siren reverted to warble, and then cut out altogether. Arndeker was soaked in sweat and his stomach rebelled, churning in reaction.

Exhaust trails from ground to air missiles criss-crossed the sky, tracer from light, medium and heavy automatic weapons as well as from 23mm cannon slashed in front, beside, and all around the attacking aircraft. An aircraft hit the ground in a welter of fragments, careening through a potato field before exploding, but Arndeker couldn't tell if it had been American or

Swedish and his mouth went dry with the realisation that in the space of mere seconds the hunters had become the hunted. The pilots were shouting warnings to one another over the radio, spotting for one another the deadly ZSUs and mobile SAM launchers, but if they were close enough to identify the vehicles visually they were close enough to be engaged by them and the voices carried a sense of panic.

"Smoke in the air!"

"Watch out for shoulder launchers by the farm!"

"Oh fuck...SAM's! SAM's!"

"Zeus on the low hill, Zeus on the low hill!"

"I'm hit! I'm hit! Jesus Chri...."

A warbling returned to his headset and he ejected chaff himself, not waiting for the ECM suite to do the job. He caught his breath as he saw a ZSU-23-4s turret tracking him and kicked the rudder savagely whilst pushing the side stick forward enough to avoid the four seemingly solid streams of 23mm cannon that would otherwise have nailed him.

The warbling in his ears changed to a siren and then became a monotone that turned his blood to ice. His HUD told him a pair of SA-9s had been launched at him, and were guiding on his F-16 despite the chaff and automatic track breakers engaging. To go up into the clouds would only be to invite other launchers to attack as he entered their engagement envelopes, his last manoeuvres had brought him down too low for him to engage in drastic turns so the only direction left to him was downwards even more. Arndeker eased the side stick forwards, and the F-16 sank earthwards until it barely cleared the tops of hedgerows but the tone continued without missing a beat. The chaff was still being discharged, but the bundles were breaking on contact with the ground instead bursting apart in his aircrafts wake. The jet wash and his slipstream did kick up strips and scatter them, the foil strips swirled about before settling to the ground or snagging on branches of bushes and trees, but they did not provide the degree of radar reflection their normal deployment would have achieved. The fear was a physical force within his chest, squeezing his heart and compressing his lungs whilst reaching up to grasp his throat. He caught a brief glimpse of something fast moving that left a trail of dirty white exhaust behind as it passed a few feet above his canopy without exploding, and he looked about frantically for the second missile, where the hell was it! The second missile had flown into a tree but Arndeker was unaware, he never saw it, not a single visual clue as to its whereabouts, and then the warning tone in his ears ceased as the SAM launcher lost radar lock.

Arndeker had heard stories about airmen whose deaths had been so swift that they apparently never realised they were dead, and their shades appeared before the commanders who had sent them to their deaths, shocked and confused and asking for explanations. Arndeker took the flesh of his right bicep between the thumb and index finger of his left hand, squeezing it through the material of his G-suit until the pain made him wince. He let out a gasp of breath in relief but realised three things, firstly his legs were shaking uncontrollably, he had urinated without realising it, and thirdly he was staring at a Soviet tank commander stood upright in a tanks turret and gaping right back at him. It could only have been for the merest fraction of a second but the moment seemed frozen in time. With a start Arndeker realised the F-16 was still slowly losing height and he pulled back on the stick, rocketing up and over the T-80. Arndeker let out a little laugh in relief, but even he could hear the hysteria that edged it. Once back at 500 feet he pickled off his last Rockeye above a mix of tanks and armoured personnel carriers, looking over his shoulder as he did so and noting on the way the holes in his port wing. When the hell had that happened?

He was about to head down again but instead he broke hard left, avoiding by a hairs breadth a mid-air with a flaming comet that cut right across his path. The pilot of the stricken aircraft had an open radio channel, and over the roar of the flames could be clearly heard the pitiable screams of intense pain, the screams of a trapped animal enduring unbelievable searing agony. The burning aircraft wasn't losing height, if anything it was slowly gaining altitude and prolonging the suffering of its pilot, trapped and burning alive in its cockpit.

Arndeker unplugged his headset, tearing the lead out of its socket to cut off the awful cries before vomiting into his oxygen mask, not just because a human being was being burnt to death, but also because that human being was female. Something else struck his aircraft and this time he felt it, the F-16 lurched with the impact and he snatched away the oxygen mask to spit out the bilious remnants of his breakfast as he waited helplessly for flaming fuel vapour to fill his cockpit too, but nothing happened and no master warning lights flashed.

A red light blinked on the HUD, flashing the symbols '00' next to the Chaff icon. He was out of radar decoys, and on checking the store's inventory for flares he noted that he had only four of those remaining. His heart was in his mouth as he flew, oblivious to the whereabouts of the rest of the aircraft, determining only to get clear of what had become a waking nightmare.

Without realising it he passed beyond the Soviet armour and was above open country once more, but he was still shaking and in his mind's eye tracer was still seeking him out. He became aware of an F-16 at his left wingtip, its pilot looking worriedly at him, and beyond that F-16 was a single Gripen that was trailing smoke.

With great effort he pulled himself back to the present, attempting to replace the headset lead in its socket but only succeeding after several abortive tries, his hands just shook too much.

Beside his own aircraft, only the other F-16 and the damaged Gripen had got out. His No.2 was in the aircraft off his port wing, asking him for his situation and for further instructions. Should they make a third run, strafing with cannon, sir?

They had left dozens of enemy fighting vehicles in flames, scattered mines in the paths of others that would blow off tracks and hinder them, but they had not deflected the enemy one single degree from his purpose and the advance was continuing unchecked.

Arndeker could only respond to the radio requests with single syllable answers, and his voice sounded so weak, so frail, that his wingman assumed he had been wounded and took the lead, shepherding his squadron commander toward their home field.

The return flight was uneventful, which was just as well because there was no fight left within Arndeker's frame. The control tower slotted them for landing in order of damage and injury. The Gripen and its pilot were in no condition to return to Sweden so it accompanied them west to their field. The pilot was losing blood so he entered the pattern first, and Arndeker followed behind him, flying woodenly in jerky motions like a nervous pupil on his first solo.

The Gripen was a quarter of a mile ahead of Arndeker, grey smoke still leaving a thin trail behind it as it let down toward the airfield. There had been a raid whilst the flight had been up, and thick black smoke rose from a dozen places within the facility. The runways had been prime targets for the raid this morning, as they had for previous raids and the longest was now peppered with small craters along a third of its length. A second runway was blocked, and a bulldozer was shoving the still smouldering remains of a Red Air Force Flogger from the tarmac but the runway they were lined up on was intact, and soon they would be safely down once more.

The whine of electric motors announced his gear was lowering, and he felt the triple thumps as the gear locked into place. The flaperon's extended further as the airspeed bled off, and the F-16 followed the Gripen toward the tarmac.

The Swedish aircraft was above the outer marker when it exploded like a thermite grenade, and Arndeker gawped uncomprehendingly at the fireball, his brain not registering the warning shouts in his headset from the controller and his surviving wingman, or the tracer flashing past from behind, missing widely at first but zeroing in.

His ECM suite was silent, it hadn't warned him of an approaching enemy because no radar energy was being radiated and no infrared systems had locked him up. They had been caught at their most vulnerable by a pilot who had gone back to basics, relying on nothing more complex than a gun sight projected onto his HUD.

Bangbangbang! The impacts snapped him out of his trance-like state and he realised his danger. He selected Gear Up and pushed the throttle all the way forward to Zone One Afterburner, needing to recover some airspeed fast before he could manoeuvre worth a damn but there was no accompanying kick in the pants. 'AB Fail' flashed on the HUD, informing him the Afterburner was non-functional. Bile rose into Arndeker's mouth, it tasted acrid and he spat it out. His flight suit was already stained with vomit, and in truth he was past caring about such things as appearance. The turbulent wake of a Fulcrum shook the F-16 as it passed above him and to the right, its cannon still firing at him as it overshot. Arndeker looked down toward the Patriot site that guarded the base, but only a blackened, scorched area of earth marked where it had been when he had taken off for this mission, less than an hour before.

His heart was beating a tattoo in his chest as he watched the airspeed build, but far, far too slowly. Any drastic evasive action he took right now would only result in a stall but he tried a shallow bank to the right, to avoid being a sitting duck for anyone else that may be back there.

His F-16 wallowed drunkenly despite his gentle touch on the side stick and rudder, so the Fulcrum had damaged some control surfaces at the very least. He could land, and save his aircraft for the repair shop, or punch out here and now. What remained of his self-esteem rose to the surface and he determined to stay with the machine, to put it down in one piece.

He was at 400 feet as he crossed the airbase perimeter and his airspeed had risen to 200 knots. He couldn't see the Fulcrum any longer and maybe it had cleared off back to its own lines. Arndeker called up the controller, telling him he was going around before trying to land once more.

230 knots and Arndeker was muttering aloud to himself, mouthing encouragements to the F-16 like a coach egging on a flagging member of a cross-country team.

"Come on, come on, that's it, good girl, push it a little more, give me a little extra, that's it, that's it, not much further now."

The canopy exploded into a thousand fragments and the cannon strikes sounded like a sledgehammer hitting a trashcan as the rounds struck the fuselage. Arndeker screamed in pain and fear as something struck him hard in the side of the chest, he felt ribs snap but then a sheet of flame filled the bottom of the cockpit, lapping around his feet, ankles and lower legs. The Neoprene of his G-suit may be fire proof, but it didn't prevent him feeling the heat of the flames.

The master fire warning light shone a bright crimson on his panel and the stall warning whooped in his ears as the nose of the F-16 rose drunkenly, announcing its departure from controlled flight and began a sideslip toward the earth. Arndeker blacked out momentarily as the blood was forced from his brain by the acceleration of the ejector seat throwing him clear. He was oblivious to the sudden release of pressure to his shoulders and waist as the safety harness that bound him to his seat fell away, but he registered the nauseous vision of ground then sky, ground then sky, before his parachute opened. At a height of only fifty feet the canopy fully deployed, arresting his head over heels fall to deposit him on the grass beside the far end of the runway, the shrouds of the parachute settling behind him.

It took him a second to realise he was down on the ground and still alive, and he ran his hands over himself as he sought injuries. He felt pain in his chest whenever he breathed; shrapnel from an exploding cannon shell had come through the side of the cockpit but struck the 9mm Berretta he wore in the shoulder harness. The pistol had probably saved his life in a way not intended by the manufacturer, but it would never fire again. Arndeker was peppered with minor wounds from tiny pieces of shrapnel, including shards of Perspex but he was ninety nine per cent good to go, in body at least. There was nothing to prevent the flight surgeon from applying some sticking plasters and marking him fit for duty. He removed the Beretta from its holster and stared at it, perhaps he couldn't put a round through some fleshy part of his body but maybe he could bludgeon a knee cap, and then they couldn't make him fly again could they, at least not for a while?

He heard the pounding of feet approaching and looked over his shoulder. Men were running toward him, running past the dispersals in which sat the twisted and the charred skeletons of two A-10s. The blast walls on three sides had not protected them from the liquid fire of napalm.

The wreckage of his own F-16 belched smoke and flame a few hundred metres away and at the opposite end of the runway the Gripen burned fiercely, whilst in the field beyond was another burning F-16, that of his wingman. He was a squadron commander without a squadron, a pilot without an aircraft to fly or any nerve remaining to fight. The nearest man was too close now for him to be able to incapacitate himself without what he saw as his own cowardice being plainly obvious. He allowed the damaged firearm to fall from his fingers and sat, with shoulders slumped in abject despair.

Arkansas Valley, Nebraska, USA.

The stresses of this day of days showed upon everyone present in the room.

All stood as the President entered and took his seat, waving everyone down.

"Sit, everyone please sit."

General Shaw remained upstanding, his briefing notes laid out before him with thick red marker pen annotations here and there.

"Mr President?"

"Go ahead General." The President wagged a message slip in his hand.

"I got this a couple of minutes ago so start with Guiana, how bad is it and how badly does it screw up *Guillotine*?"

A map of South America appeared on the screen behind Henry and he cleared his throat.

"As you are aware Mr President, the ESA facility on the equator has been attacked but it was not a result of a security leak?"

Henry addressed the President's question by bringing up the aerial photographs of the surfaced Typhoon and Kilo. His eyes flicked momentarily to the CIA director but Terry ignored the look.

"No Mr President, there is no possible way that this attack could have been put together within the timeframe of our formulating *Guillotine*." He pointed to the huge Russian submarine.

"This is a Typhoon, that is to say that 'Typhoon' is NATO's designation for Russia's largest class of submarines carrying ICBMs. However this one has been extensively modified to provide at sea refuelling and replenishment for diesel electric submarines such as this Kilo class beside it."

The picture altered to the computer enhanced photograph that clearly showed the fuelling hose connecting both vessels.

The next photograph was of the submersible upon the Kilo's rear casing.

"These were taken a week ago by an Argentinian P3 Orion out of Tierra del Fuego which attacked and sank both vessels. But the sinking's were only made public after a delay of several days."

The President stared long and hard at the photograph on the screen.

"What is the sailing time for a diesel submarine from China?"

"Three to four weeks the cross the Pacific with refuelling along the way, Mr President." Henry replied.

"The conversion of the Typhoon was most certainly carried out pre-war sir, so it is entirely possible that this was being planned as long ago as two years." He did not need to add that the infiltration by Chinese intelligence agents had made discovery of this preparation by the NSA or CIA highly unlikely.

At last the President nodded, satisfied that their best hope was not already doomed.

"The attack failed and we can still provide satellite support, sir." General Shaw assured him.

"I spent a half hour on the phone with the French Premier." The President said. "I have to say that I was having trouble reading his reaction. I expected Gallic rage but he was surprisingly reticent for someone who has almost had some of his sovereign territory nuked, he certainly seems to be taking it better than I did." The President had a gut feeling that the French were not likely to just shrug off a nuclear attack, even one that had been defeated.

"Our people in Russia almost had the difficulty factor of their mission doubled Joseph, so look at it from that angle instead." The President took a sip of water.

"Now, as you will notice there are just we few of us members of the choir present, so go ahead Terry, the floor is all yours?"

Terry smiled at the President.

"Did you ever get one of those discs through the mail from a company offering free Internet time, where you load the disc into your PC and it connects you to the company's server?"

It had taken a little longer than Terry Jones had predicted for the secrets of the CD-ROM to give themselves up.

The President nodded in agreement to Terry's question of course; there had been a time when the things had been a modern day plague with the postman delivering the unsolicited offerings from various competing companies almost daily.

"Well this disc lets us in through a backdoor to the PRC's space and satellite program." Terry held the item aloft.

"Is this true?"

"Yes sir, indeed it is, however as a spook I prefer this feature..........." The plasma screen on the wall of the briefing room had been showing western Germany and the positions of the opposing units; it now changed to depict the Philippines and events there from the Peoples Republic's perspective.

"Oh my word..." The President found himself on his feet without consciously rising from his seat.

"How are we seeing this, how is this possible...can we look at all area's their forces are engaged in?"

"Each operation is password protected but they can be cracked, as we have in fact already begun to do." Terry pointed out.

"The late and probably very little lamented Comrade Peridenko, was no fool Mister President. I have already said that I think he was planning a coup, and I now think he was planning on dissolving the partnership with China once he had attained the Premiership. This disc could give a wise man one hell of an advantage."

The President's response to his CIA chief's observation was one of unsubtle sarcasm.

"Oh really, you think!"

Terry had been in the business far too long to let something as minor as a President's sarcastic retorts faze him.

"Yes sir, I do." Terry responded. "Just as I know that he could just as easily have blown the whole deal by being too obvious, because if the PRC get the slightest suspicion that someone is reading their mail, they'll change their access codes and encryption in a New York minute."

The President was quiet for a moment as he thought about that and Terry allowed him the time to let it sink in before gesturing toward the screen.

"All we are doing at the moment is looking at the data feed from the Peoples Liberation Army's, Sixth Army headquarters on Leyte, to the Central Committee headquarters." Terry explained.

"That doesn't effect the outcome of the war by one iota, because we're merely spectators, we are not doing anything with the data. However, once we act on what we see, or even start to feed disinformation to them on the basis of what we can see here, then from that moment on in we are running the risk of them changing the locks on us, or god forbid, they feed *us* what they want us to see."

The President was silent as he looked at the board.

"So what exactly have we got here, what does it give us?"

"We know where every single satellite of theirs is, what each one does and we see and hear everything that they do. We can read all the data passing through them, we know where every single PRC military unit is, what its equipment and supply state is and where it's heading to." Terry had asked these exact same questions of his experts only an hour before.

"We know what hardware they have scheduled to go up and we can see precisely what they know about our own satellites, for instance, I now see that we need to start producing more communications satellites, because they will start prioritising their destruction in the next forty-eight hours."

"Won't that affect our RORSAT and photo reconnaissance satellite replacement program?"

"Of course it will, but we don't need them as desperately as we did before Mister President, because we can utilise the PRC's own satellites now, but of course we will still need to put some up for them to shoot down, otherwise they may get suspicious. All we do is keep sending up something that emits radar waves, I'm sure there must be a warehouse full of 1960s and 70s satellite technology gathering dust somewhere?"

"We are also working on the possibilities of a hack, perhaps to shut down their communications totally, or even write a disinformation program similar to the one they stiffed us with." Terry had already ordered the writing of several programs, but although they may never be used, it always helped to have something available if the opportunity came up.

"We couldn't just do that now?"

"No sir, we are peeping over their shoulder, that's all." Terry said.

"Our safest bet is to continue to do so, too." He added with feeling.

While the President and the CIA boss were speaking, Henry was studying the screen. It was all being downloaded elsewhere by NSA and Henry could look at it again anytime he wanted, so he wasn't too vexed when someone in China pushed a button to bring up the Indian Ocean and Australia. He nodded to himself after taking a moment to see where the PRC thought the allies ships, aircraft and land forces were in that region, and he conceded the PRC had a pretty accurate picture of their deployment, they even had his kids' ships up there but something else caught his eye and made him feel cold all over.

The President saw Henry stood close to the screen and apparently taking a professional interest in the PLAN and Red Fleet ships heading south across the Indian Ocean. He didn't know the names of the ships although they were right there on screen, right next to the icon representing the vessel in question, but it was all in Chinese characters of course.

From where the President was stood he could make out a solitary icon trailing along at the rear of the invasion fleet.

"What ship is that Henry has it got engine trouble do you think?" he moved from his seat to stand beside the big marine.

"Looks kinda lonely all by itself back there." The President removed his glasses from a pocket and polished the lenses before putting them on and leaning forward, peering at the solitary vessel.

It was a small submarine icon and lacked any I.D beside it accept a tiny Australian flag.

"Oh my god, Henry..."

Henry's expression was grim.

"Yes Mister President, apparently they have discovered that the *Hooper* is shadowing them." The exact course, speed and depth were displayed beside the icon.

"It must be difficult to move about without being heard if you're half deaf, yourself?"

Terry Jones took a look at the screen and then at his boss, he knew exactly what the President was thinking, and as soon as he opened his mouth Terry cut him off.

"We can't warn them Mister President."

"But they'll sink her if we don't, the Chinese will kill them all!" The President looked from one man to the other, but neither showed anything except grim acceptance. He tried anyway though.

"Those men and women probably won't hear them coming in time to escape!"

"We can do nothing to help them Mister President, not whilst there is the slightest chance that the enemy may guess how we knew that they had discovered the presence of HMAS *Hooper.*"

"But...."

"We have here a tool that could help us defeat the Chinese, *IF* we use it right Mister President. We *will* take direct action as a result of what we discover, but only if the stakes are high enough sir, because the more often we do so increases the chance of the enemy guessing how and why we did what we did."

The President looked from CIA chief to top soldier, but Henry shook his head sadly.

"He's right sir, the only reason the enemy hasn't sunk her yet is because they are waiting for the right opportunity, probably when the time comes to change course for their intended destination. Until that time arrives they will try and use her to deceive us as to their real intentions, and we also have to let them think we are buying it. If they change course for New Zealand we are going to have to do something there, just to make them think we don't know any better ...I'm sorry Mister President, but we can't do anything to save them."

The President took a last look at the tiny icon that was far from home and forcing himself to ignore the men and women it represented, he strode from the room.

The Vormundberg

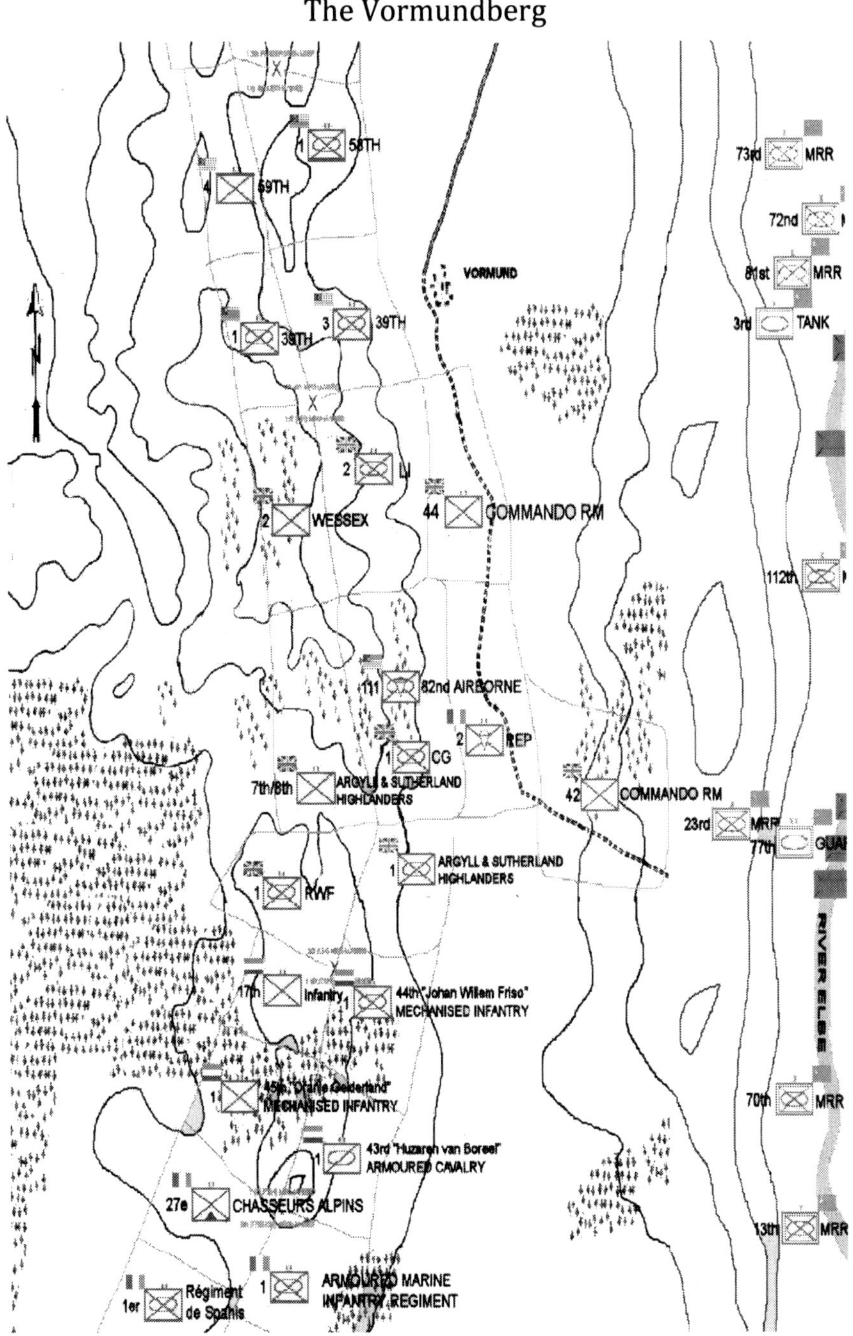

Vormundberg, Germany.

The commencement of a massive artillery bombardment announced the arrival of the Red Army at the last line of organised defence that NATO had. Shells and rocket artillery began pounding the Royal Marines of 40 Commando in their fighting holes to the front of the wooded feature, and also isolating them from help by laying a wall of exploding steel to their rear.

On the marine's flank the Foreign Legionnaires were also receiving some serious attention.

In his battalion CP, Pat Reed could feel the detonation of the nearer high explosives through the soles of his boots, and despite, or maybe even because of having endured the attentions of the Red Army's guns at Magdeburg, he felt a sense of apprehension growing. The marines to their front were the buffer, the thing on which the Soviet's would expend valuable munitions, and of course time upon, whilst the lightly armed and equipped British troops picked away at the Soviet fighting vehicles as best they could.

Pat was aware that the new men, the US Paratroopers and British Guardsmen who had arrived in the last couple of days would be listening to the sound of the guns and wondering how they would fare once 40 Commando gave ground and fell back through their lines. He would have liked to be able to tour the positions once more but his place was in the CP now.

Jim Popham was having the same thoughts at the battalion's alternate CP set 500m to the rear of Pat Reed's location. Ptarmigan showed the latest sitrep from brigade, 40 Commando was reporting the return to their lines of sub units of their ATGW Troop, anti-tank guided weapons. 40 Commando didn't expect any more of their anti-tank element would be re-joining owing to the losses they had sustained. The forward screen of the leading MRR had reached the edge of the first obstacle; a deep ditch dug part way across their frontage by the Royal Engineers in the apparent hope of channelling the Soviet's into a prepared killing ground. An update by the brigades' intelligence cell identified the leading unit and Jim Popham wondered why that particular unit should ring bells with him. A field telephone near him buzzed for attention, Lt Col Reed was on the other end of the line.

"James dear boy, have you by any chance seen the latest on the opposition?"

"Yes sir, the point unit is Czech, their 23rd MRR according to the brigade G3."

"You may or may not know all the ins and outs of this battalion's first battle of the war, but it was against a Czech division that consisted of three regiments. The 21st MRR, which were annihilated whilst a second, the 22nd MRR, took heavy losses from this battalion before it, and the 23rd MRR, overran the battalions' positions."

"Ah, these are the guys who killed your wounded and the prisoners, aren't they sir?"

"No Major, these are the guys who *butchered* our wounded, and the men they captured."

There was a moment's silence from his CO and Jim wondered exactly what was going to be asked of him.

"I want someone to go around the positions one last time before we come under direct attack. Talk to the new boys and give them a little reassurance, and spread the word that we play rough but we play by the rules...even with these bastards!"

If word hadn't already got out, *well there's a first time for everything*, Jim thought, he was going to have the impossible task of stopping this turning into a grudge match.

Arnie Moore had been looking for an excuse all morning to get out of this bunker and mix with the men on the firing line, and so he didn't have to be asked twice. The RSM even managed to look sincere when Jim extracted a promise from him that he would be back before the Soviet's reached the forward slopes of the location.

Arnie Moore took a tri of Guardsmen with him, and ignoring the FV-432 assigned for his use, he took Jim Popham's Warrior and its three-man crew instead. He wasn't planning on returning to the bunker any time soon, and if he were going to take part in the fighting he would require something more substantial than a bulletproof taxi.

There was a brief lull in the artillery falling upon the RM positions, and a Wimik broke from cover close by to a Soviet O.P to dash back into friendly lines, chased by small arms fire and mortars that fell wide. No sooner had the vehicle made it to safety the artillery fell once more, keeping the marines pinned in their holes.

Fifteen minutes later, brigade informed 2REP and 1CG, the units closest to the Royal Marines, that 40 Commando's CP had gone off the air and the RM's senior surviving officer, the O.C. Bravo Company, had taken command but his company CP was not set up to run the whole unit, so there could be command and control shortfalls. It was not an unheard of occurrence to lose a CP; 1CG had lost its own during its first defensive action of the war, so on the face of it the marines had hit an unlucky streak. Major Venables was passed the same message by the CP with an update by the C.O, and he in turn warned his troop commanders that they might possibly be leaving their hide positions for the forward fighting positions earlier than expected.

As well as warning the attached arms and company commanders, Pat Reed had the information passed to the OPs and snipers; Big Stef listened briefly to a signaller at the battalion CP and replaced the hides' field telephone receiver.

"Keep a good eye open to the sunken lane, the Green Machine lost its CP."

Bill removed his eye from the Schmidt & Bender sight. "They've got another, a fall back like we have, haven't they?" The infantry was not his chosen arm and despite the time spent with 1CG he found many of the ways of the infantry a mystery.

"What about the farm, that's a CP?"

"The farm's their support company CP, and they may not have an alternate...we only have one because of what happened before. It's not standard practice."

Bill returned his attention to the scope.

"The marines' gunners are back." Stef grunted an acknowledgement. Half an hour before, the gunners had fired a mission and relocated, vacating the gun line nearest the snipers just before Soviet counter battery fire landed. The 105mm battery had been changing location after every mission it fired in support of the troops on the ground, and was now moving back in to their original position. If there were a breakdown in communication between units, it would be hard to tell if the gunners were relocating or bugging out because they may know something their neighbours didn't. The only way to tell would be the sudden influx of traffic, foot and vehicular, onto the sunken lane.

"Keep a good eye out for any signs of the marines pulling back, mate. This could all go to ratshit pretty damn quickly."

Bill kept his eye fixed to the telescopic sight.

"There's movement in the lane."

Stef crawled back to his place beside the staff sergeant and took up the Swiftscope, training it to where Bill had the rifle aimed.

"You see a Landrover with stretchers along the back?" Bill said. "It's just to the left of the farm."

Stef adjusted the point of view and then brought the vehicle into focus, watching it as it moved slowly down the lane.

"Casevac run." Stef muttered. "And it's a Wimik, not a 'Lanny'."

Anything on the lane was visible to their hide for only a hundred or so metres from the point where it appeared beside the farm, and after a short while the Wimik's position was only identifiable owing to the vehicles radio antennae, sticking up above the lanes bordering hedgerow. They watched it for a few minutes because there was nothing else going on at the moment in their sphere of responsibility.

"Why do they keep on stopping?" Bill asked after the antennae began whipping energetically back and forth, indicating the vehicle had stopped again. It had done so twice within the space of a hundred metres.

"I dunno." Stef was no wiser than his mate. "Maybe it's knackered, or maybe there's obstacles in the road that need shifting...and why are you asking me anyway, do I look like the fucking oracle?"

Any answer, which may have been coming, was drowned out by the sound of three 240mm mortar rounds landing as one. Both snipers had been looking elsewhere at that precise moment, and on looking toward the source of the sound they found the view of the farm obscured by smoke and flying debris. When the smoke cleared, the farmhouse, barn and all the rest of the buildings had all but disappeared. The mortars had been fired from seven miles away and the rounds had landed within a foot of one another, square on the roof of the farmhouse, but to the casual observer it seemed that a single lucky, *or unlucky*, round had scored on another 40 Commando CP. Fractured stone, brick and splintered timbers were still landing far from the point where they had played there part in the farms structure as Stef called it in on the field telephone. Bill swung his weapon back toward the lane in time to see the last of the stretchers and the burdens upon them being passed across the hedgerow. So the vehicle had broken down then, he thought, and watched the half dozen stretcher bearers lift their loads and start toward the hill defended by the Coldstreamers. That wasn't the marines pre-planned egress route but Bill didn't know if casevac's had to follow the same route.

The first port of call for Arnie was 1 Company, to pass on the gospel according to Pat Reed and to look up his mate C/Sgt Osgood before the fight started. Directing his driver to park up in a 'garage', a prepared camouflaged area with camm nets thickening up the natural cover that vehicles could use without having to unravel and drape their own nets over whenever they stopped.

1 Company's stores had two locations, the main stores were well to the rear but a good stock of ammunition and munitions was in a bunker dug into a reverse slope two hundred metres from the company CP and covered with pine trunks before the earth was piled back on. Arnie headed for the hillside stores first and met the padre as he made his way through the trees; the padre was still doing the rounds, moving from trench to trench. The sound of battle nearby had instilled in some a

renewed interest in things godly. The American paratrooper was moving downhill, whilst the British padre was heading up, having visited the Hussars in their hide positions and was now intent on speaking to the men in the forward positions. Arnie paused, stepping to one side and extending a helping hand to assist him over a particularly steep and muddy patch.

"Thank you, sarn't major." The padre was flushed and breathing heavily.

"When I left the infantry behind I left the concept of 'infantry-fit' behind too...I'm regretting that now."

Arnie grinned at the man. Sure, he could be a bore and a pain in the ass with his bible punching, singling an individual out for some one- to-one attention, and usually when you had just come off duty, but he was sincere and meant well or he'd be in a shelter bay already and not still wandering around above ground offering spiritual support. Arnie was thinking of something to say in reply, but both men heard the sound of an express train approaching from the east. The paratrooper was beaten to a handy dip in the ground by the padre, and both men pressed their faces into the mud as the sound got louder.

"For what we are about to receive may the lord make us truly thankful!" said the padre with irony.

Taken slightly aback, Arnie chuckled

"Amen." and then the ground heaved.

The rounds had landed upon the hills top, shattering the trunks of trees and cleaving deep craters in the earth, but otherwise doing no harm.

The padre raised his head to listen; canting it to one side for a few seconds, if the belt had been to 'fire for effect' then more rounds would be following them in now.

"Ranging rounds, so they must be doing better than expected against the marines, sarn't major, and now they are thinking about us." He climbed to his feet.

"I'm thinking the Reds will be here in an hour or so, and that means they'll be stonking this hill in earnest a lot sooner than that!"

It was an ironic scene, the Man of God telling the professional soldier what was happening in the battle.

The Padre's first taste of incoming artillery had been as a buckshee Guardsman during the Falklands War back in 1982, but it hadn't been his last by a long shot. Arnie Moore, on the other hand, had seen his own share of conflict but until Magdeburg he had not been on the receiving end of medium and heavy guns, which made the padre the resident expert. Looking at his watch the RSM was troubled. It had been just a little over two hours since the Soviet's had hit the protective mine field to the front of the marine's positions, and 40 Commando's CO had been confident on holding for up to twelve hours, six at the very least. The Royal Marine's weren't some pussy, amateur outfit, he had served alongside them in Afghanistan and Iraq, and if they were about to be overrun, or pushed off the position early it wasn't due to bad soldiering or a lack of guts.

He cast a quick glance downhill towards Oz's stores before turning and following the padre back uphill. Social calls would have to wait.

The stretcher bearing party had passed through the Battery from 29 Commando Regiment, Royal Artillery, uphill into the trees and out of view from the hide who's occupants could hear the sound of combat from over the rise the farm buildings had occupied, in the dead ground beyond. In the last forty minutes the sound of small arms had increased, and shortly after that the sound of main tank guns could be discerned. The Royal Marines, unlike the USMC, have no armour of their own. Two Troops of Scimitar light tanks on attachment from the Blue's & Royals were the nearest thing they had, the Scimitars 30mm Rarden cannon was ineffective against medium or heavy armour but it could defeat APCs.

The marines had twice the number of Milan's that an infantry battalion carried and they constituted the units principle tank killer, reaching out 2000m at their extreme range. The 94mm LAW is meant to take over from the Milan when the targets reach 400m, which is the Milan's minimum engagement range; however the troops had found that opening fire with the LAW at anything above 150m was a waste of ammunition if the target was moving.

The artillery had ensured that the Milan teams had their work cut out, they fired a high percentage of shells fused for airburst and whereas these had no effect on troops in shelter bays with decent top cover, they were designed for use against troops in firing bays. Had the Milan teams had a free hand then they could in theory have destroyed eighty enemy AFVs between the minefield and the Milan's own minimum engagement range, but only twenty three of the lead assault battalions vehicles were stopped by the guided weapons.

Channelling the enemy into the prepared killing zone had met with only limited success. Engineer vehicles had bridged the vehicle ditch in several places, allowing the mine ploughs to clear paths through the narrowest parts of the minefield. Rather than having a target rich environment of fighting vehicles sat stationary behind mine ploughs destroyed by Milan, those anti-tank teams that were not being kept in the bottom of their holes by constant airbursts had found ranks of mine ploughs confronting them. In the 12.5 seconds it took the weapons to reach maximum range the Soviet artillery spotters were targeting the launch site and a hundred square metres of real estate around the firing points for some serious attention in case the missile launcher had been remote sited. They had the quantity of weapons to achieve their aim, and consequently fewer than a dozen mine ploughs and combat engineer vehicles were destroyed. Too often the anti-tank gunners had fired and were guiding the missile home when they were hit by shrapnel or just forced to take cover, even.

The LAW gunners weren't troubled by the Soviet artillery in the same way that the Milan crews had been, because as someone had once said, 'It's considered bad form to shell your own troops'. The AFVs were too close to the marine's positions and so the gunners switched from H.E to smoke. The LAW isn't equipped with thermal sights and that fact, coupled with the burning particles of white phosphorus that produced the smoke, reduced the ability of the lightweight weapons gunners to engage.

The loss of 40 Commando's command post so early on had robbed the unit of its practiced and experienced, dedicated artillery and close air support systems before the Soviet's had finished softening up their intended victim. The Commando units forward air controller, artillery rep and their staff's, died when a single and frighteningly accurate salvo of heavy artillery scored a direct hit on the CP. Bravo Company's commander assumed control but he had neither the staff nor the radios to take over the role of the CO and fulfil the duties the former CP had achieved so well. He delegated the passing of artillery requests to Alpha Company CP, and Charlie Company the air support liaison role, but Alpha and Charlie were over two kilometres apart and liaison between the two became disjointed.

To the front of Bravo Company an entirely natural feature was causing the enemy fighting vehicles coming their way to bunch up. A section of stream with particularly high banks on one side, and a dense stand of Sycamore trees on the other were spoiling the combat spacing between vehicles as they were forced to close up in order to get past.

Charlie Company CP received an airstrike request from a Section Commander and Alpha Company passed on a fire mission from a Troop Commander. Neither CP told the other about it, and so it was that a pair of RAF Tornado's arrived over the bottle neck that was thick with enemy APCs and Tanks at the same time as a full battery's worth of improved munitions discharging Skeet submunitions. The leading Tornado was hit by a submunition and exploded in mid-air whilst the second aircraft sucked debris from the leader into an air intake, and trailing smoke and fire it made it to the brigade's rear area where both crewmen ejected safely. From then on the NATO air force's insisted on double checking with the artillery before accepting missions from 40 Commando, and the ensuing delays were the cause of missed opportunities.

No amount of digging could have reduced the casualties amongst the Royal Marines in their trenches; the Red Army had built its armoured warfare tactics around the use of massed artillery and used it without compassion, the Royal Marines were being thinned out and NATO artillery's counter battery fire was wholly inadequate.

The frequency of calls from the battalion CP was evidence enough that they were concerned about events in the marines sector.

"We could do with an answering machine." Big Stef replaced the handset again and checked the progress of the brew he was preparing. The water in a mess tin was boiling away nicely and he took it from small stove to transfer to a mug but the ground bucked beneath him and half the water was lost.

"What...!"

The ground heaved again and he dropped the mess tin, holding on to the walls of the hide for balance.

"It's the gun line." Bill had been taken by surprise with the first explosion and had swung his weapon from the crest by the sunken lane, around to the dead ground by the copse. He watched the effects of a second round scoring a direct hit on a gun's ammunition supply; it obliterated the howitzer, its tractor unit and its crew.

Stef crawled back into place beside Bill, peering through his scope. A third round landed, and it also struck the stacked rounds to the rear of one of the howitzers.

"Three rounds and three hits." Bill observed.

"Bloody good shooting!"

"Good shooting, my arse!" Stef swung around the Swift Scope, looking for likely spots.

"Start looking for spotters mate, you can bet yer left bollock those rounds were laser guided!"

Stef informed the CP and the information was passed to the forward positions, where the Guardsmen and Paratroopers watched their fronts for the spotters and their laser designators. One by one the howitzers were destroyed but no one got the faintest sniff as to the spotter's whereabouts despite dividing up the ground between them and scrutinising all possible hide sites. There was nothing to suggest the enemy spotter could be anywhere except to the front of the battalion lines, and why would you look over your shoulder to check if the designator was being used from within your own lines, anyway?

Philippines.

The invasion of the Philippines by the armed forces of the People's Republic of China was proving to be a slow business. Thus far Cebu, Bohol, Negros, Siquijor and Palawan were the only islands of any size to have been taken. The largest islands of the archipelago, Luzon, Leyte and Mindanao where still being fiercely contested by the regular forces and Chinese losses were far and above those expected during the planning stage.

The PRC had amassed a huge army since the Second World War and had spent the previous decade modernising it, to the extent that they could drive their armoured forces like a vast steel encased carpet over any of their neighbour's borders, swamping all resistance with ease. The problem they had with the Philippines was that it was not a single landmass, but rather a cluster of over a thousand islands, mostly hilly or mountainous and covered in forest or jungle over a high percentage of their area, and they did not lend themselves favourably to armoured warfare. There were no freeways, motorways or autobahns, there were just roads that were generally inadequate for normal peacetime use and easily put out of action. The Chinese needed leg infantry who knew how to fight in the jungle clad peaks that the home team found so easy to defend, and although China did have such troops, they did not have anywhere near enough of them. They had tried using armoured tactics on Luzon and for their troubles were now stopped dead in their tracks halfway across, and a similar situation existed on Leyte where the commander of the invasion forces had unwisely asked Beijing for permission to delay the landings on Mindanao, and instead use the troops earmarked for there to complete the job on Luzon and Leyte first.

The new commander of the Sixth Army had been briefed to keep moving forwards always, and had moved his headquarters, rather than his units, a half kilometre nearer the front within hours of taking over. The Political Commissar believed this was a sound tactical move for some odd reason, and reported it as such to his superiors. The real reason for the new commander's decision was simply that his predecessor had been buried in too shallow a hole, upwind of the headquarters.

Guerrilla forces on all of the islands were sapping Sixth Army of manpower and equipment, as 'conquered' islands demonstrated that they were far from pacified. Forces that were sorely needed on Leyte, Luzon and Mindanao were instead being tied down patrolling or guarding against guerrilla attacks.

Air power was one area where the PRC should have had the upper hand, especially as their opponents had a tiny air force with which to challenge them for air superiority. U.S made Stinger missiles in the hands of both the Regular Filipino troops, and the Guerrilla's, were having the same effect on the morale of the Chinese aviators as they had wrought on Warsaw Pact pilots in Afghanistan two decades before.

The fixed wing assets of the tiny but professional Philippines Air Force existed only upon Mindanao, where its two squadrons of F-5Es, a half dozen ancient and only recently reactivated F-8H Crusaders, Agusta S-211s and piston engined T-28D Trojans were backed up by a trio of Taiwanese F-16Cs. The Filipino's had these precious assets spread about the islands fourteen suitable fields and the United States had provided enough Patriot systems to make a serious attempt at destroying the Filipino air force, a very costly business. As it was though, the PAF rarely sent these aircraft into harm's way, and the Chinese assumption was that logistical problems were the cause of this. The PAF's helicopter fleet on the other hand, was not restricted to Mindanao, and was supporting both regular and irregular forces on the islands. The machines use of small clearings as bases and the pilot's intimate knowledge of the ground made them singularly difficult to deal with. The AGM-114C Hellfire missiles carried by the Filipino aircraft had originally been bought to deal with an invader who used armour in *support* of infantry operations, the aircrews had never dreamt of having such a target rich environment, and between them and the terrain they had managed to halt the Chinese ground forces for the time being.

Considering the sizes of the forces involved such a situation could only be temporary. In terms of numbers, the strength of the regular forces defending the islands was 160,000 soldiers, sailors and airmen, whereas the invading PLA Sixth Army had twice that number in infantry alone. It was only a matter of time before the commanders returned the infantry to their roots by getting them out of the vehicles in order to continue the invasion on foot. In the meantime the Chinese controlled the waters around the Philippines as well as the air approaches and this prevented any resupply in quantity of any of the staples of a fighting forces life. The general staff of the Philippines armed forces knew that with current ammunition expenditure rates, within a month the Chinese would quite literally have more troops than the Filipinos had bullets to shoot them with. Patrolling warships and combat air patrols enjoyed a free-fire zone around the islands, and frequently attacked without warning any vessel larger than a rowing boat. The islands were under siege and only once had that been quite obviously breached, the previous week, and probably by aircraft that had destroyed the CAP south of the Zamboanga peninsula. The commander Sixth Army was not concerned by such occasional breaches, after all, how much could an aircraft carry? Certainly not enough to make a difference, but he had directed the navy to place an air defence frigate off the peninsular anyway in order to strengthen the picket there.

Today the PLAN Jiangwei class frigate *Anqing* was receiving radar data from a pair of FC-1s providing the CAP, and two fast gunboats, which accompanied her. A Haiqing class patrol boat held station five miles ahead and a second vessel, a smaller Haizhu class, kept pace five miles aft, allowing the frigate to engage without bring its radar out of standby and therefore revealing its own position.

The *Anqing* was cruising at an economic ten knots, twelve miles off the peninsular and in relatively calm seas when the data link failed. Her communications officer tried to raise both patrol boats first and then the aircraft, but when his hails received no response her captain ordered the radar to go active. In addition to the sea search and Eyeshield 2D air search radars the 6 cell HQ-61 SAM was put in active mode, the gun crews of the dual 100mm and all four dual 37mm mounts closed up and swung out to seaward. They heard their attacker and they saw it with the naked eye but the radar screens remained clear. The bat shaped aircraft was on the *landward* side and only a mile distant when it was seen, climbing to 1600 feet before rolling inverted and diving back toward the island. It had disappeared into the sea haze before the quickest 37mm crew could get a round off, and by then of course it was too late anyway to avoid the pair of laser guided 1000 pounder's the aircraft had toss-lobbed there way.

At Edwin Andrew Airbase the American bomber force took to the air first, leaving the Philippines for the foreseeable future as they made full use of the gap in the picket. They were followed by four transports, two USAF C-5s and a pair of Royal Air Force C-130s which flew just a couple of hundred feet above the waves until well clear of the land and well beyond the radar coverage of the remaining Chinese pickets before the C-5s set course for Guam. The C-5s carried away the technicians, ground crews and essential stores that were needed to keep the B-1Bs, B-2s and the F-117A force in running order, the fuelling stop at the tiny atoll was just the first step on the journey home. The two Hercules from 47 Squadron took a different route, and headed for the nearest tanker serving the silo strike. Squadron Leader Dunn and Flight Lieutenant Braithwaite's C-130 led the way, and they settled down to share the flying between them. They had a long way to go and at an average speed of 460mph it was going to take them a while to get there, so the 'Loadies', and the Royal Marines aboard for security, settled down too.

Russia.

There had been neither sight nor sound of a helicopter all day, and yet the runway was to remain covered until the last possible moment, and the troopers at stand-to in their fighting holes. The commander of the small unit was not about to let standards drop just because the job was nearly done. The militia were miles away and floundering, but in his experience it could take just one piece of bad luck to have the tables turn on them, so until the F-117X was away for the last time, he was keeping everything locked down tight. In his original thinking the airstrip would be abandoned within an hour of take-off, but Major Nunro had come to him with a request and an apologetic expression.

"The problem I have is that I'm not flying a USAF Nighthawk, and this aircraft doesn't have the legs."

"If it's not a Nighthawk then what is it?" he had asked. "Looks like one to me."

"It's experimental and it still belongs to Lockheed-Martin, not the air force."

He'd seen the humour.

"It's a loaner?"

"Nighthawks are single crewed if you didn't know, this one can do more than a pilot on his or her own can deal with, so a back seater was required but to accomplish that they had to lose an internal fuel tank." The pilot had looked very apologetic.

"The short version is, we can reach the target and do the job, but flame out inside enemy territory. Or we can return here, and refuel before trying to get out."

He had acquiesced of course, because they were too deep within the forest for the militia to hear an aircraft take off, and it was only for a few extra hours after all.

To the south west, the two men he had shadowing the militia reported that the current rate of advance was less than half a kilometre per hour, and the radio traffic they were intercepting didn't indicate any surprises, but he wouldn't let the men relax.

In its well camouflaged niche the aircraft sat like a dark, brooding thing awaiting the dark whilst its crew and Svetlana, dressed in flight suit purely for environmental practicality, sat about talking and waiting for the night to fall.

41" 28' N, 171" 29' E.

There was little to break the monotony of the endless routine that had been drilled into each and every crewman from the first day they had stepped foot across the threshold of submarine school. The only way was the Navy way, and there was a logical reason for that, the Navy way was quieter, quicker and safer, never mind that it turned the hands into automatons. No one aboard had felt fresh air on their face since before the start of the war, and although the captain had seen daylight it had only been through a periscope and the last occasion that had been raised was over two weeks before. There wasn't a man aboard who did not miss their families and the outside world as much as they loathed the steel shell that they were forced to exist in. The enemy was out there and their submarine required only their chief executives order to attack and destroy them, but what was taking so long, they had been here for days now?

They were not party to the command-in-chief's intentions, and did not know the orders were dependant on events elsewhere in the world, so they continued to tip toe in the dark so as not to alert the enemy as to their presence.

The captain ordered the vessel up toward the surface, so that the floating antennae to be streamed. It was a daily occurrence, listening for the order to attack and at first there had been an air of expectation whenever they had done this, but that however had palled with the passage of time.

At 100 feet the vessel had levelled off and 1800 metres of antennae cable had been streamed, but unlike past occasions a bell sounded in the control room this time to announce high priority incoming traffic.

The captain and the executive officer wore solemn expressions after reading the received signal, and accompanied the weapons officer to his panel where they supervised the input of amended targeting data, adding Davao and Melbourne to their existing strike package of Pearl Harbor, San Diego, Los Angeles, San Francisco and Guam.

Aboard the USS *San Juan,* 7500m behind, they listened to the Chinese boomer reel in the antennae and return to her patrol depth.

CHAPTER 6

Germany.

One mile to the rear of his forward companies, the regimental commander of the Czech 23rd MRR was feeling a whole lot more optimistic than he had twelve hours before. It had been expected that his regiment would lose anywhere from 20% to 60% of its strength in successfully attacking the British marines in their current defensive positions. The combat between his unit and that of the Britisher's was also expected to be a long, drawn out affair, and it was probably more to do with the time element than concern for the fighting men's welfare that had prompted the Russians to present him with the services of one of their Spetznaz units. The units commander had not looked the most terribly enthusiastic of warriors when he had been shown into the regimental commanders presence, but they were apparently quite recently returned from operations on the other side of the line and may have felt entitled to some rest. Despite his mistrust of special operations he had to take his hat off to the Spetznaz major and his handful of men, wearing the clothing and equipment of freshly dead Royal Marines they had infiltrated the Commando position in a captured vehicle and pinpointed high value targets for the artillery. They had wrought havoc with the marine units command and control before moving on, and without doubt saving the 23rd MRR, men, equipment, and above all time.

In the attack on the marines position he had so far only committed two tank and three APC companies, he still had one complete battalion and two more tank companies waiting in the wings. The first British positions were already under his control, including a slightly wooded rise, the control of which allowed them access to the marines left flank. An attack on that rise should have prompted reinforcement and priority of fire the second it looked to be in danger of being successful, but no increase in shellfire, airstrike's or fresh troops had been evident due to the destruction of the chains of command. His men had killed the marines in their holes before occupying the position, and he was now ready to roll forward along the marines flank prior to making a sharp right and rolling up the entire position.

The snipers were ready to vacate the hide as soon as the marines began to appear in the lane were it topped the crest ahead of them. So far they had seen only the casevac party, but neither man doubted that it could be too long before the Commando began to withdraw, with its forward companies beginning a reverse leapfrog, giving ground but always with two companies covering as the other pair moved. That was the way things were done, and nobody had told them to expect anything else.

Stef saw movement on the crest first, two hundred metres left of the lane where a handful of men, some plainly wounded, forced a way through the hedgerow there, hacking at it with machetes to widen a gap and then dragging the wounded through it. More men appeared, this time in the lane, and then the men at the hedgerow were joined by two Scimitars of the Blue's & Royal's, reversing into view whilst firing three round bursts back the way they had come. A pair of men each dragged a wounded marine towards the Guards lines, leaving a gun group and three riflemen to fight a rear-guard action alongside the light armour, which had now reversed over the hedgerow. It was a short, one-sided defence and both Bill and Stef watched open mouthed as the four marines and the wounded on the reverse slope were cut down by automatic fire, coming not from the front, but from the sunken lane. What they had assumed to be Royal Marines of 40 Commando withdrawing were in fact Soviet dismounted infantry using the cover of the lane to get as close as possible to the next line of defence.

"Why weren't the trees dropped across the lane, I thought they'd been wired to blow, Stef?"

"Fuck knows, mate!" Stef grabbed the field telephone receiver once again, to warn the CP.

The troops in the lane switched their attention to the tiny knot of resistance beside the hedgerow, but it was not until two of the marines had been hit that the remainder realised that they had been flanked, but from their position on the crest the tankers were able to look down the slope and into the lane. A Scimitars turret traversed to the right and it opened fire, its 30mm cannon creating carnage in the narrow confines of the lane, which was now seething with Soviet infantry.

The response from the lane was sudden and swift, a Sagger left a thin trail of dirty exhaust as it flew across the intervening space to strike the light tank squarely on the rear of the engine compartment, the Scimitar's cannon immediately fell silent and the vehicle began to burn without any of the crew bailing out.

The surviving marines used the smoke of the burning armoured vehicle as cover to make for a ditch running down the opposite side of the field to the lane, but the surviving Scimitar moved only to place its burning cousin between itself and the lane, gaining some protection at least to its exposed rear. Neither of the snipers could see what the lightly armoured vehicle was engaging, but its commander clearly felt that whatever it was, it was a more serious threat than even the enemy troops at his back. The Scimitar continued to engage the enemy in the dead ground beyond the hedgerow, but moments later it was struck by a main tank round and exploded in spectacular fashion, only its tracks remained.

Its killer emerged into view from out of the dead ground, the T-72s main gun moving from side to side as it searched for another target. The marine gained the ditch but not quickly enough to avoid being seen by the T-72s driver who altered course once the hedgerow had been negotiated, placing the armoured vehicles right hand track into the ditch and accelerating. Mud and grass, gauged out of the ditch's bottom flew into the air in the tanks wake, but then Bill vomited as he saw the airborne detritus turn red.

"It's time to go!" Stef pulled the ends of the D10 cable from the field telephones terminals and stuffed the instrument inside his Bergan beside the Swiftscope. More tanks were appearing on the crest and Bill wiped his mouth on a sleeve before crawling backwards away from the firing loop.

"We need to get a rift on, or those bastards will be using us to line their wheel arches too."

The 'door' to the hide was removed by Stef who emerged into the daylight before reaching back to haul out their Bergans, and once Bill had joined him they kept low and began to follow a pre-planned route, although indirect, that made use of the best available cover back to their lines.

Arnie Moore, assisted by the Padre, guided the Warrior into a natural fold in the ground that gave the vehicle total cover from view from the front, and yet by moving forward just ten feet it would be in a hull-down position and able to engage. He had noticed this spot several days before, it was too narrow to accommodate a Challenger II or the older Chieftain's that the attached tank squadron had, but from this spot a Warrior could cover the steeply sided stream that separated this battalion from its neighbour on the left. Both units had of course sited positions to cover the possible chink in the proverbial armour, but Arnie could visualise those positions being swamped before any reinforcement could take place.

On the whole he thought Pat Reed had worked marvels in motivating tired men into achieving the level of defence that they had. It had been the commanding officer whom had seen the potential of making men spend time with picks and shovels on the slope between 3 Company's platoon and the company positions. The hillside on the right of the battalion line was steeper than on the left, and with a lot of sweat and blisters the men had managed to make it damn near impassable to all but tracked vehicles with very, very skilled drivers. Anyone advancing beyond the bounds of 9 Platoon would find the gradient suddenly becoming quite severe and the natural routes blocked by the simple expedient of placing several pine trunks on their sides between two trees; on the uphill side of course. The trees braced the stacked trunks, which could not be easily bulldozed aside owing to earth that had been piled behind and hard packed. Beyond these obstructions the drivers would discover where the earth had come from, the troops had crudely quarried six to ten feet in depth in a band along the side of the hill. It wasn't much but it would probably mean the infantry having to debus and hoof it uphill whilst the fighting vehicles tried to find another way around.

It had been impractical to attempt the same over by 1 Company; the slope was too shallow so mines had been planted where they could be the most use.

With the Warrior in position there was nothing to do but wait, and the RSM felt the need for a mug of good Java, but he'd have to make do with British Army freeze dried coffee granules instead.

"Do you have time for a coffee, Padre?" Arnie commented, but he did not receive a reply. The Padre was squinting off to one side at a thicket a hundred or so metres away.

"Padre?"

"Sorry sarn't major, I thought I saw a stretcher being carried into some bushes." The battalion aid station and casualty collection point was in the opposite direction to the one the bearers he was sure he had seen had been heading.

Arnie was unaware that any of the battalion had yet been injured and said as much, but the Padre apparently was not so sure.

"It will only take me a moment to check, RSM."

Arnie was going tell his loader to grab a first aid kit and accompany the Padre, but he was already striding purposefully away and Ptarmigan was carrying the news that 40 Commando had been overrun. Arnie glanced after the retreating back before shrugging; he and his crew had more urgent work to be getting on with, but he told his loader to keep an eye out for the Padre from the commander's position, and then got busy himself.

The Spetznaz major had spent an hour and a half looking for a position such as the one he was now in, with line of sight to not two, but three prime targets, a company CP, an ammunition resupply point, and the enemy battalions principle command post. This spot was also sufficiently divorced from the enemy defensive positions as to be safe from all but an unlucky round from his own side's artillery, but they would not of course tempt fate and his six remaining men were hacking at the ground with entrenching tools. The only fly in the ointment was a nearby enemy fighting vehicle that had since turned up, and although he and his men carried only small arms and grenades, he had the means to make it disappear permanently if it did not move on. All in all, the major considered that he and his men had done quite enough for one war and the time was approaching for them to sit the rest of this one out. After the next three targets were taken out their communications gear was going to 'malfunction', and he had no intention of putting his ass in harm's way again. With continental Europe in Soviet hands there would be a period of chaos, where an intelligent man with a touch of ruthlessness could set himself up in business before the forces of law and order again appeared. Food shortages would be the most obvious of the woes about to befall the western Europeans, but the major had sufficient contacts in the army supply services to ensure sufficient stocks. After all wars, food becomes a more important currency than even gold, for a while at least.

Before 'Civilisation' was again fully restored; the major intended to be Europe's wealthiest. It was this dream he was focussing on when he suddenly noticed a middle aged, and apparently unarmed British captain had entered the thicket and was glaring at him and his men. Incongruously the British officer did not appear to have a personal weapon with him, and he wondered what kind of fool ventured out unarmed during a battle?

"Who is in charge here?"

The major allowed a surreptitious glance toward the enemy APC before answering, and noted that its turret was still facing to the front but a figure in its turret was looking towards this section of undergrowth with a pair of binoculars. His men had paused in their digging, and two were eyeing their weapons that lay close by, but by a barely noticeable shake of the head he conveyed to them that they were to make no sudden moves.

Under the current circumstances, killing this man had to be an act of last resort.

"That would be me, sir." The Russian officers accent was pure East End of London, and the captain was unaware he was conversing with the enemy, but he wasn't done with the major and his men either. The slightly portly captain was looking hard at him.

"And just who is *"Me, sir"*...I don't recognise you, Corporal?"

"Corporal Brown, sir." The major let a hand slide behind his back, where the fingers curled around the hilt of an ugly looking fighting knife with a serrated blade that he wore on his belt. "This is what's left of my section; we are all that remains of 40 Commando, sir."

Although the Padre had the greatest respect for the fighting qualities of the Royal Marines, there was something unsavoury, and distinctly seedy about this individual.

"The only survivor's Corporal, or just the fastest runners?"

The major allowed the right amount of indignation to show in his response.

"We was ordered out sir, ordered to evacuate these wounded." He nodded at the two stretchers, covered by ground sheets so that just the boots of the occupants protruded.

"They died before we got here, so we'll fight on with your unit sir." He gestured towards his men.

"That's why we're digging in...so we can give those bastards some payback!" He saw a hint of uncertainty in the captain's eyes.

"If we'd run sir, wouldn't we just carry on going?"

The captain considered those words, and the Spetznaz officer felt a sense of satisfaction when he saw the other nod in apology and begin to turn away. His fingers relaxed their grip on the knife hilt, but then the captain paused and asked who his officer was?

That the captain wanted a name was obvious, and for all the Spetznaz officer knew this Britisher might well be on first name terms with every damn officer in the Royal Marines, so he picked a name at random and hoped his run of luck would carry him through.

The Padre had thought that he'd find some confused or even shell shocked stretcher bearers stumbling around when he had first spotted these men, but having got to them it had occurred to him they may have 'done a runner' from their own unit once the going got tough. The marine corporal however, was looking him straight in the eye as he stated their intention to fight on beside his own unit, and the Padre regretted his earlier impression. He was about to leave when it occurred to him that a mention in the regimental diary might not go amiss at a later date.

"Who is your officer, corporal?"

"Second lieutenant Chartridge, sir…" The Padre knew only two RM officers and both were colonels so the name of a 'Subbie' meant nothing to him, but then the marine ended the sentence with, "…he's our platoon commander."

The Russian knew that somehow he'd screwed up because the British captain's eyes narrowed.

"The marines don't call their sub units *Platoons* corporal, they call them *Troop."* With surprising agility he suddenly sprang across to the stretchers and hauled off the ground sheet covering the nearest one.

"Good God above!"

The British officer was transfixed by the sight of the severed pair of legs and the laser designator lying upon the canvas instead of a dead body, and the major leapt, aiming for the British captain's throat but missing it, slicing into the side of his neck instead. A look of shock came across the captain's face and he jumped backwards, a hand pressing against the wound in an effort to stem the stream of arterial blood that was fountaining from it. The major couldn't let this man raise the alarm and went to grab him, to stop him from getting into the open, but the stretcher tripped him. One of the major's men bounded after the mortally wounded captain who was still moving backwards towards the edge of the thicket, his free arm extended towards his attackers in an effort to ward off further injury.

The loader saw the Padre stumble backward into view and then another figure appeared, swinging an entrenching tool with both hands. The flailing arm failed to parry the blow aim at the neck, and the loader shouted in alarm whilst reaching for the pintle mounted GPMG.

Alerted by the shout, the RSM raised his head above the rim of the turret hatch in time to see the Padres headless body topple over and his attacker dashing back into cover.

The Spetznaz major in the guise of a Royal Marine corporal was no longer speaking in the tones of east London, he was cursing in gutter Russian as he waited for someone on the other end of his radio to acknowledge the fire mission he had just requested.

The first burst of fire from the Warrior did nothing accept punctuate the fact that the jig was definitely up for the Spetznaz team. Pieces of bark and an amputated branch fell to the muddy ground but the Russians were all lying flat. The diggers pulled back on their equipment, lying on their backs to struggle into the webbing before turning back onto their stomachs. The major ceased his attempts to raise the gun line by radio, rolling onto his side and pulling a smoke grenade from his pouch instead.

"Boys, when this goes off we all run like hell into the trees uphill from here, the cannon on that fighting vehicle can't elevate above ten degree's and it is only equipped with iron sights so they will be firing blind." He had been their officer for over four years and they trusted him to get them out of this spot, he could see that trust in each man's eyes and it bothered him not one iota that he was lying to them now in order to save his own skin.

"Keep the trees between you and that machine gun, and keep on up to the top of the hill, we'll RV there and I'll lead the way through a gap in the lines I noticed earlier...any questions?"

They could see the Warriors turret traversing as the 30mm cannon was brought to bear, and in the headlong flight triggered by the detonation of the WP grenade, none of the runners noticed that the major was not with them.

The dense smoke proved to be no obstacle to Rarden's thermal sight, and the two soldiers not brought down by the first cannon shells were higher than the paltry ten degrees the major had told them of when the second burst of 30mm caught them.

Arnie was not familiar with the Rarden cannon so he relegated himself to the position of observer, and because he was not focused solely on the fleeing shapes in the smoke he caught a movement out of the corner of his eye.

The major had waited a few seconds until he was sure his running men had the full attention of the NATO troops, before snaking away on his belly in the opposite direction. He now needed to put some distance between the action and himself, so it was a little frustrating when a webbing strap became snagged on the lower branches of a sapling. The sinewy growth, barely six feet in height, bent slightly and the tiny branches and leaves at its apex dancing a wild jig under the influence of the majors efforts to free himself before springing back into the fully upright position.

On the hillside, three still forms dressed as Royal Marines lay in the mud whilst the other three thrashed and screamed, of these one would make it whilst the other two would succumb to their wounds.

Arnie memorised the spot where he had seen the agitation in the undergrowth before taking in the situation on the hill, the wounded were calling out in Russian so it didn't take a genius to work out what the Padre had stumbled upon. The six who had broken from cover were out of the fight, but there could be more of them.

"Gunner, cease fire...100 metres, half right, in the thicket, watch and shoot."

"Rog"'

"Driver, back up...stop, turn right...stop." The Warrior had pivoted about its axis and now the turret swung back until its 30mm faced the same direction as the vehicle. "Driver, take us forward slowly."

Arnie was relieved that the Padre's head was lying face down when they reached the body, but he spared the gruesome sight the merest of glances anyway. They passed the Padre, and the Warrior nosed into the bushes and saplings that had provided cover for their enemy. The weight of the armoured vehicle either crushed the undergrowth, or the younger and suppler growth bent to the inevitable, only to emerge from beneath the vehicles rear end and slowly straighten once more.

In the scramble to buckle on webbing and gather up their weapons, the contents of both stretchers had been bared to view by the Spetznaz troopers and the Warriors driver deviated from course slightly in order to crush the laser designators he could see upon them before continuing.

The major had paused momentarily on hearing the British armoured fighting vehicles engine alter from its low idling murmur. It rose in pitch as it approached and the major felt the first tinge of panic, and his features took on a hunted expression as he looked about desperately for a hiding place. He assumed that the commander of the vehicle would debus the infantry section it was designed to carry before driving on down to the bottom of this slope. The infantry, he thought, would then spread out in a line and like beaters, and drive him on to the Warriors guns.

A short distance ahead was a thick, chest high bramble patch some fifteen metres across with a tunnel-like badger run just visible and he crawled rapidly towards it. The webbing was a hindrance and so he rolled onto his side to unbuckle, and then shove it out of sight deep beneath the brambles before easing his head and shoulders into the run. The barbs caught at the material of his camouflage smock and trousers, pierced the palms of his hands and left bloody scratches in his skin, but he forced his way on, ignoring the pain and the barbs tore free. The run almost pierced the heart of the bramble patch before curving around to the down slope side where the major suddenly found himself staring at the entrance to the badgers set. It was an old and well-established habitat that many generations of badger had occupied. The creature that had first chosen this spot had found granite lay beneath the earth but had persevered, tunnelling down at an angle, following a slab of the rock for yards before it gave way to manageable earth, as such the rock formed the floor of the tunnel and now bore the marks of its occupants claws, past and present. Over the years the elements had played their part in eroding away at the exposed entrance, the upper reaches however, were reinforced by the mesh of roots of the overlying undergrowth and had therefore resisted better than the bottom and sides, so it jutted above the entrance like a shelf. The Russian majors feeling of panic gave way to one of relief when he took in the dimensions of the excavation, and he wormed his way inside to where it tapered down to the sets proper entrance, and four feet of deep shadow lay between himself and the open.

Regimental Sergeant Major Moore had not dismounted his handful of Guardsmen, he did not know what numbers or weaponry they faced, except that they probably had no anti-armour kit or they would have used it already. Arnie was at the ready with the Gimpy in the commander's hatch from where he had the advantage of height to observe, peering down into the brush, seeking out his quarry with a finger applying first pressure to the weapons trigger. He was getting queries over the air from the nearby platoons wanting to know the reason for the gunfire, coming as it did from the ground lying between the left hand depth and forward companies, so he gave a brief sitrep followed by a terse

"Wait Out!"

The major smiled to himself in the darkness when he heard the throb of the approaching engine and wiped at the sweat which had beaded his forehead before resting his face against the cool granite he was laying on. Only a diligent search by men on foot could have discovered this hidey-hole, so he was safe for the time being and with luck the hunters would assume he had slipped away and so abandon the search, so he could afford to relax.

The Warriors driver brought the fighting vehicle along slowly, stopping whenever the RSM told him to but these stops were fleeting, allowing Arnie only to satisfy himself that they had not overtaken their prey. On one such pause however, the twenty-four tonne Warrior had settled, quite suddenly to one side as the ground gave way beneath the left-hand track. Arnie grabbed the side of the hatch to steady himself but after the initial list to one side the vehicle now seemed stable. Looking over the side of the turret he saw that some animal or other had apparently made its home beneath the bramble patch their fighting vehicle had entered and the weight had collapsed its tunnel. The Warrior obviously wasn't going to tip over so he ordered the driver to proceed and transferred his attention back to the job at hand.

The collapse had grounded the Warrior; the brambles were crushed between its armoured belly and the earth. Its left track spun around, churning at the soft earth until it was able to find solid traction, but Arnie did not see the soft earth it churned at turn to a red paste speckled with white bone fragments. The Warrior continued on down the slope until reaching the line of field defences before the company in depth, but no sign was there of any other infiltrator's.

Soviet artillery was beginning to fall on the forward companies now. Arnie reasoned that the movement he had seen was probably that of a rabbit or a fox startled by the cannon fire, so he ended the hunt by ordered the driver to take them back to the position covering the stream.

Pat Reed came off the air from a conference call with the brigade commander and received a handful of messages from a signaller, which updated him on several incidents taking place whilst the brigade commander had held his attention. None of the items were awaiting a decision from him or needed him to okay the appropriate action; they were being dealt with already. The 155mm self-propelled SA90s of 40 Field Regiment were firing a mission against the sunken lane, its rounds fused for airburst to best deal with the enemy infantry there. A damaged Army Air Corps Gazelle carrying a Royal Artillery officer had set down in a clearing behind the in-depth companies, it had been spotting for the guns when a Fulcrum had come within a hair of splashing it with a missile. It occurred to Pat that thus far they had neither seen nor heard of any close air support by the Soviet's against either the Royal Marines or themselves today, so maybe SACEUR's 'forlorn hope' had paid off? More good news was that two of his best snipers, Stef and Bill, had regained the battalion lines via 3 Company. Stephanski had ensured that the CP knew the enemy infantry were not only fighting unhampered by the wearing of respirators or gas masks, but also they were not even wearing their version of NBC suits over their conventional combat attire. It was a fairly good indicator, though not iron cast, that the enemy either had no stocks of chemical weapons at hand anymore or they did not see the need to employ them. This information was passed up to brigade as well as to the individual units and sub units in 1CG's area of responsibility. Pat also received his snipers brief account of the final moments of 40 Commando, relayed to him by another signaller.

"One of 3 Company's Milan crews is tracking the tank sir, it is still in clear view and they asked for permission to move forward to extreme range and engage?"

Pat knew damn well that they had in all probability already gone along the *correct* chain of command and had been refused.

"Three Nine knocked them back because he quite rightly didn't want his assets exposed too soon, so do they honestly think I'm going to overrule one of my company commanders just because their blood is up?" Pat left the signaller to pass on the rebuke, and carried on reading, his eyes skimming over the words and taking it all in. The RSM's report of infiltrators and the death of the Padre were both saddening and alarming, but none of the emotions he was feeling could be read on his features by anyone watching at that moment.

"Has this infiltration business been acted upon, Timothy?"

The Adjutant was on the radio to Major Venables and he raised a thumb above his head without looking around, confirming that he had it in hand but then winced as Soviet artillery impacted none too far away from the CP. As the rumbles died away he took the radio headset off and glared at it in disgust, but the radio operators were already removing the various radios antennae coax cables and replacing them with others that led to an alternative antennae farm. Pat listened as Tim re-established communications with the Hussar squadron's commander and explained that artillery had just taken out one of the antennae farms.

All in all, Pat considered that things could have been far worse by now, but he mentally kicked himself for tempting fate because another message was handed to him. The Guardsmen and Paratroopers in the forward companies had been receiving artillery for the past twenty minutes, but not in a concentrated fashion, that had just changed now as both company CP's reported a drastic increase in the weight of incoming fire. Lt Col Reed could only guess at how long the enemy was planning to soften up his unit before continuing the assault.

23rd Czech MRR went firm on the positions formerly held by the British 40 Commando, in expectation of one of the Romanian regiments passing through to take up the assault, but any hopes of a breather were dispelled when 23rd 's commander gave his sitrep. 23rd MRR still had adequate fighting strength remaining and were ordered to carry out a quick reorg whilst the next NATO position was 'prepped' by artillery. Once the reorganisation had been completed, they would step off over the rise and cross the 3 kilometre wide valley to fight through to the summit of Vormundberg. The commander of the 23rd knew he had just had one easy victory and was ready for more, he knew the Spetznaz team had crossed over into the next enemy position, securing him the sunken lane, a route safe from direct fire down into the valley that a company of mounted infantry in BDRMs and a tank company could use.

He had lost the best part of a company of infantry in the sunken lane through NATO artillery, but they had been dismounted and vulnerable to such fire, away from the protective armour plate of their vehicles. So hyped up was he with success, he did not think to ask if the Spetznaz major was still sending fire missions to the gun line, he merely assumed that the division commander would inform him if all contact had been lost. On the other end of the secure communications link the Romanian General was a little relieved that he had not been asked that question because lying was a necessary, yet tedious art in this business of man management.

The distribution of fresh ammunition and the shifting around of personnel to even up the losses went swiftly, largely due to the lack of incoming rounds from NATO guns.

At Lt Col Reed's insistence the guns available to the battalion were being preserved until the Soviet's put in their attack, and the Royal Artillery had a Phoenix UAV aloft now, watching for that very move. He knew that there was a distinct possibility that the enemy would use the sunken lane to get an armoured force closer to his forward companies' unseen, and whilst that attack was being addressed a far larger force could use the distraction to close with the Anglo American unit.

Pat believed that the brunt of the attack from the lane would in all probability be borne by 3 Company, but he was confident that with the assistance of the section from the anti-tank platoon and a troop of Challengers who were attached, they would cope. He could not predict where the main attack would be focussed; it could drive on 3 Company as a second wave to the first attack, or come at 4 Company and thereby divide the fire of his artillery assets.

Pat Reed intended on giving 3 Company exclusive call on the battalions 81mm mortars, initially at least, whilst using the artillery to carry out counter-battery shoots and then switch fires to pound on the larger force once it was halfway to the battalions position. This final NATO line did have close air support on call, but even with the extra help it was limited.

SACEUR knew that the French 8th Armoured and Canadian 2nd Mechanised Brigades' would need all the help they could get once they put in their counter-attacks against the Soviet bridgeheads, so he was preserving ground attack capable airframes for that moment, which left mainly tank hunting Lynx and Apache helicopters, with just a few flights of fixed wing ground attack aircraft, available to the blocking force.

The Royal Artillery rep called 1CG's CO over and showed him the current download from the Phoenix, showing tanks and APCs beyond the rise in the newly conquered ground, filing into the sunken lane and heading towards Vormundberg. Pat estimated their strength to be between two and three companies worth.

The UAV operator steered the machine north, where at first the only vehicles to be seen were the burning hulks of the 40 Commando soft skinned Wimik's and the Blue's & Royals Scimitars, before passing over massed armour that was already formed up and ready to go. His FAC, Forward Air Controller, was also watching the downloaded images, and sipping at a mug of beef beverage with an air of apparent calm about him, however Pat could see in the man's eyes that he was really loitering with intent, staving off impatience as he waited for the CO to call on the services of himself and his troops. A signaller passed Pat a slip of paper and waited silently as he read the content; 2 REP was now under attack from a force of tanks with BMPs in support, but Pat had expected as much.

The attack on the French paratroopers was merely a supporting attack, one designed to prevent them using their Milan's to fire into the flank of the Soviet attack at extreme range, effectively denying 1CG any help from that quarter. It was solid military tactics and Pat knew that it was only a matter of time before his neighbours, the Argyll's and the Light Infantrymen, received similar attention, isolating his unit from help as the main attack clashed with his forward companies and tried to drive over them.

The air battle above the Soviet armoured vanguard had proved debilitating to both sides and the sky was, for the moment, relatively clear as both sides refuelled and rearmed. Pat ordered the artillery to begin counter-battery fire so that his own men could emerge from their shelter bays and prepare to receive the enemy. His FAC dropped all pretence of nonchalance and hurried back to his proper place within the CP once Pat had told him what he wanted the available 'air' to do.

In fields and woodland clearings to the rear of the fighting a host of British Army Air Corps Lynx and Apache helicopters had been waiting with rotors already turning, and they now lifted off and headed toward the fighting.

The barrage impacting on 3 and 4 Companies slackened once the British 155mm rounds began finding the Soviet gun lines. It gave the men a breather and allowed them to collect their wits and their weapons, and then to leave the shelter bays of their trenches.

Although artillery was still impacting on the forward positions it was at a greatly reduced volume. Artillery rounds criss-crossed the air above the trenches as the gunners of both sides sought to make the other duck. It was a duel that the NATO artillery could never win decisively due to the Soviet's numerical superiority, but it served the purpose that Pat desired.

L/Cpl Veneer and Guardsmen Troper had put a lot of effort into the construction of their position, sandbags lined the firing bay as insurance against cave-ins caused by the Stingers back blast, but many of these were now leeching earth from rents where they had been peppered with slivers of shrapnel by Soviet artillery rounds bursting overhead.

Troper had neglected to put everything under cover once rounds had begun incoming, so consequently his tin mug and brew making kit had vanished, scattered into the undergrowth by one or more near miss.

"Bluddy 'ell...them fucker's 'ave ram-raided us!"

No sympathetic words were forthcoming from his partner, who was listening to his PRC 349 and had a hand held up for silence.

Troper had a hangdog expression, but a thought occurred to him and he instantly brightened up.

"I suppose it could be worse, we've still got your brew kit, haven't we!"

"No, *I* still have *my* brew kit...if you want some you can *buy* a mug's worth off me for two fags."

An indignant Troper levelled an accusing, and somewhat grubby, finger at his oppo.

"You jack bastard, you don't even bleedin' well smoke!"

"'Course I don't, filthy sodding habit." Veneer paused to listen again at the earpiece but no one was yet speaking to them.

"When was the last time we had a NAAFI run, eh? The smokers are gasping and will pay a quid for a coffin nail, so every fag you give me I'm selling on."

He stuck a finger in his free ear to drown out the expletives aimed at him, and acknowledged in turn the radio message aimed specifically at the battalions air defence contingent.

"Stop whinging, you wanker...our choppers are coming forward, but we've to hold fire on all fixed wing stuff until informed." He pulled a launcher and a pair of reloads from the storage bay and then noticed a trio of green painted faces topped by US pattern Kevlar helmets peering at them over the lip of a fighting position to the left and slightly downhill. He stopped what he was doing and stared back at them, but no one said anything so after a few moments he involuntarily looked over his shoulder to see if they were looking at someone else before looking back.

"What?"

The painted faces looked at one another as if telepathically electing a spokesperson; the one on the right lost.

"Erm...yuze guys ain't thinkin' of lightin' one of them things off, is ya?"

"What?"

The spokesman from the former colonies and his mates waited for a more substantial reply.

In exasperation the young lance corporal responded.

"We're the air defence detachment for this company, wot the fuck do yer think we're goin' to do?"

"We expect ya to walk three hundred paces in any direction but this one, *before* you let one off." It was a different spokesman, but the message was the same, *not welcome.*

"If ya fire that thing, every motherfucker with a gun will be shootin' it in this direction, they hate triple A."

L/Cpl Veneer gave brief consideration to reasoned argument, but logical debate had never been a strong point of his and so he settled for giving the neighbours two raised fingers instead. The rigid digits seemed to tempt fate because suddenly there were aircraft a hundred feet above them and everyone dived for cover before noting they were outbound rather than incoming.

The trio of RAF Tornado's passing overhead belonged to 617 Squadron, one of the most famous units of the old Bomber Command, which despite its maritime strike role had left its home base at RAF Lossiemouth two days before hostilities had commenced, flying to Gutersloh with fifteen Tornado GR4s and had been in the thick of it ever since. Three of its five remaining airframes passed a hundred feet above the heads of the dug in Guardsmen and Paratroopers, loosing off high-speed anti-radiation missiles before breaking hard to the north. They lacked the numbers to either intimidate in a major way or eliminate the AAA, and a mixture of quad 23mm and SA-9s rose from the massed armour and followed earnestly in the wake of the departing aircraft. The squadrons remaining pair of aircraft arrived on scene at that juncture, coming in fast from the southwest and adding eight more HARM's to the twelve already in flight.

It was a textbook perfect attack and the first HARM's began exploding AAA vehicles even as they began to pivot to face the new threat. The effect was the one hoped for, no one 'predicted' results or actions anymore, the pre-war doctrines and assumptions had been found naïve and wanting. As had been hoped though, the majority of the anti-aircraft artillery assets radars were silent five seconds later as two pairs of Jaguars popped up over a rise to the north west and over-flew the waiting armour of 23rd Czech MRR, releasing cluster bomb units as they did so. Seven seconds later a further four Jaguars came in from west, but they were less fortunate, the enemy were now reacting to the presence of aircraft overhead and one Jaguar fell to a sustained burst of 23mm fire whilst an SA-9 found the number four aircraft before it could release its load, exploding it in a fireball from which flaming debris fell to litter the German countryside. The remaining pair ejected chaff and flares as they egressed to the south but a refuelled, rearmed, and angry Mig-31 CAP arrived hurriedly back on station and pounced, taking out both RAF aircraft with missile shots before NATO's own combat air patrol could intervene.

23rd MRRs commander stood in the turret of his T-80 and stared off in the direction of his units FUP. There were trees between the forming up point and his present position but he had no trouble knowing where to look, the black oily smoke rising above the treetops indicated where fourteen of his armoured fighting vehicles were stopped and burning.

He felt a tap on the leg and looked down into the vehicle, into the upturned face of his radio operator.

"Yes?"

"The division commander is offering fixed wing cover for the attack, sir."

He gave it some consideration before dismissing the idea. It would mean severely restricting his anti-aircraft assets rules of engagement, and from past experience he believed that they would see nothing of this alleged air cover until after NATO air strikes had come and gone, unchallenged by their own air force and by the his own AAA that had been ordered to hold fire. The idea of using air power for precision strikes against hardpoint's was extremely attractive – on paper – but this was the real thing, not a classroom exercise.

"My thanks, but no thanks." Instead of disappearing, the radio operators face remained looking up at him.

"Is there something else?"

"Yes sir, First battalion's commander is asking for a delay, to deal with the wounded and he is also asking for a company to be attached from Third battalion to make up for what First just lost?"

From beyond the trees the sound of ammunition cooking off could be heard and reinforced the urgency of the moment, the attack could bog down before it even began. He shook his head emphatically.

"No, he goes right now, right this instant, and with what he has...tell the companies in the lane to begin their attack, and tell the mortars to start laying smoke."

The face disappeared and he heard his orders being relayed before the face reappeared and he received a thumbs up, confirming acknowledgement by the sub units.

He checked the switch on his own communications panel was set to intercom before depressing the microphones pressel switch.

"Driver...take us forward, just short of where that farm was."

The sound of the T-80s engine raised by several octaves and then it lurched forward, picking up speed as it headed over the battered countryside in the direction indicated. The regimental commander's entourage, a trio of BTR-80 APCs, a ZSU-23-4 and another two T-80 battle tanks accompanied it, the vehicle commanders keeping a weather eye on the skies for NATO strike aircraft.

Back at the 1CG CP the artillery rep had ordered the Phoenix away prior to the Tornado's 'Wild Weasel' sorties and the Jaguar strikes, but now it was arriving back above the armour of 23rd MRRs first battalion. Pat Reed saw that the lead companies were now on the move, and then a signaller informed him that 3 Company were reporting smoke was being dropped to their front.

Major Venables and his mixed squadron of Challenger II's and elderly Chieftain's had endured the Soviet bombardment without loss, but not without mishap. On the reverse slopes the tanks sat in holes dug against the side of the hill and therefore safe from artillery pieces firing at maximum elevation, but as ever the Soviet mortars concentrated on the areas the guns could not hit. One of his Challenger's had been buried by a landslide caused by the massive 240mm mortar rounds and smaller, yet more numerous 120mm fired from the 2S9 Anona self-propelled heavy mortar, and RE Sapper's were working frantically alongside REME recovery troops to dig out the tank and its crew.

All but two of his squadron's crewmen had seen action, even though the last time any of his call sign's had fired a main tank gun in anger had been at Magdeburg. Between repulsing the assault river crossing there and digging in here on

Vormundberg it had been an infantry show, but Venables had ensured that his crews carried out dry training at every opportunity, to the disgust of those Hussars who had been on the Wesernitz and therefore thought of themselves as 'old sweats' and above such mundane activities. Despite such elitist attitudes he was quietly rather proud of his small command and the way they were meshed together as a team. He was confident they would do the business today, and if the Soviet's achieved a breakthrough it would not be due to any shortcomings from his men. He did have concerns regarding equipment, particularly with the Chieftains and especially with Tango One Two Charlie, a Mk 10 with an unreliable engine pack and a gearbox that would have been changed had a spare been found in time. His thoughts were interrupted by a voice on the battalion net.

"Hello all stations address group Kilo, this is India Zero, Cryptic Tuesday, *over."*

The Hussar squadron was half way down the list in order of priority and so Venables employed the time on the squadron net.

"Hello all stations this is One Nine, move now, I say again, move now, over."

All three troop commanders answered and Venables own Challenger got underway, heading for its own forward fighting position as he acknowledged the CP on the battalion net. "Tango One Nine, *Cryptic Tuesday*, over."

The word was passed down the line, the enemy is coming and anything to your front is now 'in play'.

The American Paratroopers and British Guardsmen waited for the enemy armour with a feeling in their stomachs that their forefathers had probably felt too, when the order in those bygone days had been, 'Prepare to receive cavalry!'

The small group of armoured vehicles stopped short of the skyline and the 23rd MRRs regimental commander climbed from the turret to the engine deck of his T-80, before making his way forward and then with a hand on the main gun for balance he lowered himself carefully down the front glacis plate to the ground, not wishing to turn an ankle on the shattered stone and brickwork that lay underfoot. Two of the BTRs carried his small battle staff but the third carried infantry, and these had debussed before their commander had left the turret of his tank, his aide, a signaller, the intelligence, air and artillery reps hurrying to join him whilst the infantrymen had deployed in all round defence, providing local security.

The last few feet to the crest were accomplished on hands and knees to avoid being silhouetted on the skyline, and the officers took up position to the left of their commander, lying in a line of diminishing rank or seniority with binoculars being trained on the sunken lane.

Several minutes had passed since the regimental commander had ordered the two companies in the lane, one tank and one APC, to begin their attack and yet despite a thick smokescreen having been laid there was as yet no movement from that quarter. An angry demand for compliance was snapped at the signaller, burdened down with a heavy manpack radio but whom conveyed the order and then likewise conveyed the senior company commanders apology, a mortar round had scored a direct hit on the thin top armour of an elderly BTR-60PB, the blazing vehicle was clearly visible to the staff officers, it had been blocking the narrow roadway to the vehicles following behind, however the combined efforts of two T-90s had muscled it over onto its side and allowed vehicles to brave the exploding ammunition for its heavy, 14.5mm turret mounted machine gun as they squeezed past. The 81mm rounds being dropped by the Guards and 82nd mortar lines were harassing the armour in the lane rather than doing any real damage, they were area, rather than precision, weapons and the knocked out eight-wheeler had been a fluke.

The regimental commander snapped a query at the artillery rep regarding the greatly reduced weight of fire landing on suspected NATO positions but the artilleryman was spared the need to reply because at that moment the tanks surged out of the lane, leading the way for the APC company.

The delay had proved a drain on the Czech mortars supply of smoke and the screen was growing patchy, which allowed those defenders without the benefit of infrared sights, to see the opposition with their Mk 1 eyeballs instead.

"Who are they, do you know?" The commander had lowered his glasses and turned his head toward his subordinates, directing the question at the Intelligence officer, who stammered a reply.

The regimental commander considered the answer for a moment before chuckling.

"So, the remnants of a regiment we beat in our first battle, and some American's who's own regiment didn't want them...hah!" The laugh turned to a sneer.

"This will be over in no time at all comrades."

Turning his attention back to his forces, he raised his binoculars once more to his eyes.

The charge of the Czech armour went unchallenged, the weapons in the NATO lines stayed silent as the tanks grew ever closer, passing through the wrecked and ruined gun line of 29 Commando Regiment and into the fields that ended where the slopes of Vormundberg began.

The CO of the Argyll & Sutherland Highlanders called up Pat Reed, he had a troop of the Royal Scots supporting his own left flank company, and both their tanks and a section of the flank company's Anti-Tank Platoon would be in position to assist 3 Company and the Hussar Troop. Pat thanked the Scots CO for the offer, but they had best stay masked until needed, as he was confident the attack could be beaten unaided.

Over a rise a mile to the right of the lead company from the 23rd's First Battalion appeared, motoring downhill across fields toward the same sunken lane. It was an obstacle that would cause them to slow in order to negotiate it, but the enemy should be fully engaged in trying to deal with the first two companies and the regimental commander was confident the First battalion would arrive like a hammer blow, rolling up or rolling over the defenders. Satisfied that the fight was as good as won the regimental commander stood, as a sign of contempt for his enemy he dispensed with basic fieldcraft, and turning his back he began to walk back to his command tank.

Major Venables kept his eyes firmly pressed against the sight as he keyed the radios send switch. When different Arms speak on the same radio network the simple use of a prefix avoids, for example, the number two troop of B Squadron of an armoured regiment from being confused with 2 Platoon, 2 Company of an infantry battalion. 'India' denotes Infantry, 'Tango' denotes armour/tanks, 'Golf' denotes artillery/guns etc. As Major Venables was communicating directly with his own unit, on their own net he did not use the 'Tango' prefix.

"Hello One Three this is One, over?"

"One Three, send over."

"One, as per my last briefing the signal to let rip will be me lighting up a command tank…." His gunner was already tracking the Czech tank company commander's vehicle, a T-90 that was easily identified by its additional antennae.

"…but right now I'm seeing an SA-9 vehicle amongst the tanks, at least two Zeus mixed in with the APCs and there are at least two plough tanks with the lead element." Venables did not have to elaborate for the troop commander covering 3 Company.

"One Three, roger out to you…hello One Three Bravo and One Three Charlie, over."

"One Three Bravo, send over."

"One Three Charlie, send over."

Major Venables listened for just a moment longer to the AAA targets being divided up between that troop, before turning to the 3 Company net.

"Hello India Three, this is Tango One, ready when you are, over."

"India Three roger, standby…standby…fire!"

The Challenger II rocked backwards on its sprockets with the recoil of its main gun and the tungsten sabot flew true, striking their target where turret met body.

Less than a heartbeat later three other tank guns fired and sent two HESH and a further sabot down range.

The sound of the onboard ammunition in Venables target exploding caused the 23rd MRRs commander to stop and look back towards his lead companies.

The Company commander's tank had already blown up but the sound had taken a little time to reach the regimental commanders ears. He was in time to observe a four wheel SAM vehicle and a pair of ZSU-23-4s explode in unison, and moments later the first Milan missiles struck the charging line of tanks.

Aside from the visible proof that NATO ground forces could still fight, something caught his eye, something had briefly popped up from behind trees on the crest of Vormundberg but it had been so fleeting that he had only the barest impression, and then the frighteningly swift passage of a Hellfire missile ended with the death of another of his tanks.

"Kurva drat!"

Another object, though not in the same spot came into view and he saw a British Lynx helicopter half visible behind the trees, but unlike the Apache that had loosed off the Hellfire, the Lynx had to keep the target in view whilst attacking with the older, wire guided TOW missile, but older technology or not the T-72 it struck was reduced to burning scrap. .

Tank rounds, Milan, TOW and Hellfire missiles were coming thick and fast, although not all hit or killed their targets first time. Some crews were still blessing the luck that had given them a glancing blow only, when their attacker re-engaged and destroyed them.

He glared at his aide. "Get me close air support!"

"You were offered it earlier sir, but turned it down...it may take time to get it back?"

Unable to do anything to silence the enemy anti-tank weapons himself, the regimental commander took it out on the junior officer.

"Ty debile zasranej...so why are you wasting time making excuses?"

The business of controlling the tank fire was not, at this precise time, the responsibility of the squadron commander. The attack was being directed against 3 Company and therefore his troop commander controlled their aspect of the fight.

Major Venables and his crew were in a position to assist and so once he had initiated the fire, he allowed his crew to become subordinate to the troop commander, 3 Troop.

Venables Challenger arrived in its second fighting position having fired twice from the initial location. It had reversed out of that hole and motored to its present one where it had crept up a muddy ramp to present only the smallest target area possible to an enemy and still be able to engage. The gunner was looking through his sight at the dwindling number of tank targets below, traversing the main gun as he tried to decide which to engage when Major Venables took over, using the commander's over-ride to halt the main guns wanderings and bring the elevation up a few degrees.

"Target BMP with antennae's."

The gunner took a half second to answer.

"Identified!" He thumbed the laser rangefinder and Venables released the over-ride, allowing the gunner sole control over the weapon once more. A sabot round was already loaded but there were more tanks out there then they had sabot rounds to kill them with, so each one counted.

"Load HESH."

His loader opened the guns breach, removing one of the bag charges along with the sabot before replacing it with a HESH round, closing the breach once more and sliding the safety gate across.

"HESH loaded!"

"Firing!"

Overall command of the two companies had been borne by the commander of the infantry company since the loss of his opposite number in the first tank to be taken out, and he would probably have managed it quite ably had he been given a few more minutes to settle into the job. Having been struck by a round fired a greater height than the BMP-2 enjoyed, its angled frontal armour stood no chance of deflecting the round away. The HESH round struck the armour plate square on, its hollow nose cone flattening against the 9mm thick armour even as the projectiles rear mounted fuse fired. Roof hatches, gun ports and the rear troop door blew off, sent spinning away by the expansion of white-hot gasses from within the armoured vehicle. A second later the heat set off the 30mm cannon rounds stored within the vehicle and it blew up.

Venables did not dwell on the vehicles destruction; he was looking for more targets.

"Okay, let's find anoth..." and then the suns reflecting off a smooth surface caught his eye, drawing it to the insect-like body and bug eyes of a machine hovering just above the ground a half kilometre beyond the APCs, but it took a moment for his brain to register the thing was pointing unerringly at them.

"...back us up NOW!"

Not needing to be told twice his driver gunned the engine and the Challenger jerked backwards down the ramp and not a moment too soon. A SPIRAL, anti-tank guided missile fired from the Mi-24V, Hind-D passed six inches above the turret of the retreating Challenger and exploded against a tree a dozen feet behind the position.

Having missed the shot the attack helicopters gunner cursed in frustration and loosed of a barrage of 23mm rounds from the twin, nose mounted cannons. He was hoping for either a lucky hit or to startle the tank into seeking fresh cover, but receiving only an angry rebuke from his squadron commander whom he had not realised was watching. It really wasn't his day at all and if he hadn't been busy wasting ammunition he would possibly have noticed a Stinger being fired from elsewhere in the enemy lines.

Veneer watched the helicopter stagger as the missile struck the side of its port engine and explode. It wasn't a very big explosion, and although he knew the weapon had only a quite small warhead he was disappointed. He remembered once as a small boy in the run up to Bonfire night he had spent a week's pocket money on a biggish rocket with an impressive sounding name, but he had felt cruelly cheated at the feeble bang and lacklustre sparkles when he had let it off on the night. The Stinger seemed to have the same lack of punch as the 'Galactic

Zammer' because after the impact the pilot had steadied the aircraft and there it hovered, twelve feet above the ground and apparently undamaged.

The first derisive catcalls were sounding from the neighbours when a gout of black smoke issued from the port exhaust and the aircraft suddenly lost power. It dropped to the ground, bounced once and then toppled onto its side, its rotor blades shattering against the earth and the fragments flying off in every direction. The Hind-D didn't blow up and it didn't catch fire, but it definitely counted as a kill.

"Buggermesideways!" He allowed the launcher to be taken from him by Troper, muttering about sheer flukes and that it was his turn now.

"I thought that Stinger was a dud for a minute."

"Don't talk soft, do ya really think he would have carried on just sitting there if something hadn't got broke?"

They noticed that the 82nd men had fallen silent, and both Guardsmen began a soccer chant, pointing their fingers at the paratroopers as they taunted them.

"Oh it's all gone quiet, all gone quiet; it's all gone quiet over there!"

Any listening music lovers were spared the horrors of a second chorus by a 57mm rocket striking the hillside twenty feet below, and sending everyone in the vicinity headlong back into the shelter bays, where they rolled themselves into protective balls as the victim's squadron commander worked over the area of hillside that the Stinger had been fired from.

Once that Mi-24V had relocated, leaving in search of fresh targets for its remaining three pods and four SPIRALS' it carried, the Guardsmen re-emerged. Thirty-two rockets had added to the damage already inflicted by the artillery, but that damage was limited to the trees, hillside and defence works, but the downing of the helicopter had not endeared them to their neighbours. A rocket had caused a cave-in at the position occupied by the trio from the far side of the pond, and when the two Coldstreamers eventually reappeared, they paused in their frantic spadework to glare in a most hostile fashion.

Unable to think of anything else to say, Troper called across. "Nice morning for it!" He gave a half-hearted wave that was as sheepish as the awkward smile on his face, and ducked back out of sight.

Venables driver eased the big machine into their third firing position and the squadron commander cracked the hatch. Standing half inside the turret he studied the panorama before him, and nodded to himself in satisfaction before reporting on the battalion net that a half dozen Czech AFVs were retreating back the way they had come. The remainder were burning fiercely in the fields below, and none had come closer than a quarter of a mile.

All of 3 Troops vehicles were intact and ammunition expenditure had been light, so it was a pretty good start to the fight.

He took in the heavier than normal scent of pine, courtesy of all the freshly splintered trees, and smiled wistfully because he had always liked the smell of pine. Pine scented disinfectants, air fresheners and those tablet things that they put in urinals didn't count, they just weren't the same thing at all. He enjoyed the moment, even if the flavour was tainted with the stink of spent explosives, and then raised his binoculars to look off to where about three times the number of the last attackers was approaching the sunken lane.

The advancing battalion was coming on with two companies abreast, and those lead companies were fast approaching the sunken lane which the Major could only make out at that distance by the avenue of trees marking its passage. He studied the distant shapes, trying to fathom what calibre of soldier was manning these personnel carriers and tanks, and grudgingly allowed that they were probably veterans, judging by the combat spacing between the vehicles and general good order of the formation.

By his reckoning the left wing of this new attack would overlap 4 Company to encompass 3 Company's number 7 Platoon, and the right could well be driving on positions held by their neighbours 2LI, the 2nd Battalion Light Infantry.

Pat had visited the Wessex Regiment soldiers, those who were on loan to the Light Infantry, and he had no doubts about their courage and skill but the boundary between units was always the weak spot, the seam between two separate command and control organisations that could be widened and exploited by a determined enemy.

The Hussar's C Squadron, commanded by Jimmy McAddam an old acquaintance, was attached to 2LI and he was tempted to call them up, but there was nothing he could tell him that he wouldn't already be aware of and now was not really the time.

The sound of eight Fv-432s in low gear reverberated through the lines, working their way up the reverse slope to just shy of the crest, taking advantage of the tree clearance undertaken by the oppositions artillery which had given them another base plate position. On reaching the desired position the engine sounds quietened and the mortar crews 'Number Two's, with each weapons aiming post in hand, left the APCs as the two semi-circular hatches in the roofs of the vehicles were opened to reveal the medium mortars.

The business of laying-on, i.e., the placing of the individual aiming posts in such a fashion as to overlap exactly the vertical line on the mortars sight, was conducted between the Number One's and Number Two's. For a novice crew the laying-on could take minutes, but for the well-practiced it was but a matter of seconds.

"In Two!" had been shouted eight times in less than thirty seconds and the Number Two's were back with the vehicles. The mortars were ready for business.

The Hussars commander heard the distinctive 'ploop' of 81mm mortar rounds leaving the barrels, and they were leaving very rapidly indeed. Eighty mortar rounds were in the air before the first one had landed, and the Number Two's had retrieved the aiming posts at the run, clambering back into the vehicles, which were already moving off.

Peering through his binoculars at the oncoming Czech battalion, Major Venables was surprised to see not the geysers of earth and smoke that HE rounds would have caused, but thick white smoke. The ground immediately before the sunken lane took on the aspect of a dense fog bank, which drifted with the breeze towards the Czech formation, blotting out the lane and all visible clues as to its location. The drivers of the Czech armoured vehicles slowed down, not wanting to encounter the sunken lane whilst driving at full tilt. They knew that the obstacle was somewhere close by, but hitting it at forty miles per hour was courting serious if not fatal consequences.

The front rank slowed and almost instantly the combat spacing between vehicles was lost, the ranks of vehicles bunching up as result of the unannounced change of pace.

Venables looked up in response to a mournful droning overhead, and then having identified the sound he laughed aloud and thumped the rim of his hatch in appreciation of the cooperation between the mortars and the heavy artillery. "Beautiful, just beautiful."

Looking back in the direction of the approaching armour he raised once again the binocular's to his eyes, but could make out little.

Improved munitions were mixed in with the conventional shells, and these scattered Skeet above the clustered ranks of Czech armour. The thin top armour of fighting vehicles struck by the Skeet's were pierced and whatever lay beneath suffered accordingly. For the lucky ones this was an engine getting trashed, but for the unlucky ones their last moments were a burning purgatory from which only the sympathetic detonation of onboard ammunition brought a welcome release.

The Czech battalion commander, from his position in the rearmost rank of the formation, had no option but to urge his men to press on. The NATO artillery quite obviously had their range so to loiter was to invite total disaster. The leading vehicles pressed on, driving faster than they would have chosen to if given the choice and this resulted in a number of motorway style pile-ups. Some vehicles encountered the lane unexpectedly, plunged down into the defile at 30mph or faster, and came to a crashing halt against the far side, snapping axles and shearing drive sprockets. For the occupants of such vehicles never fitted with such niceties as safety harnesses, the result was in many cases fractured skulls and broken bones.

Vehicles following behind these found the way ahead blocked and were prevented from backing up and finding another way around by vehicles coming up behind.

A BTR-70s driver saw the hedgerow that bordered the lane at the last moment, and managed to brake to a halt, but before he could proceed to negotiate the steep bank at an appropriate speed his vehicle was rammed from behind by a T-72. Shunted forward with such momentum the APC pitched down the bank where it struck the unyielding tarmac, stood on its nose briefly before flopping onto its back. Only cutting torches could have opened the thoroughly mangled rear troop door, and the roof hatches were useless as a means of escape, so it was a blessing that all the occupants had been rendered unconscious.

A flight of German Alpha Jets took advantage of the confusion to stage a hit and run attack, dropping canisters of napalm along that section of the lane, which further blocked the lane and immolated those trapped within wrecked vehicles.

It was a moment that should have been capitalised on by either launching a counter attack, or by piling on the artillery fire, but they lacked the strength to capitalize on such a thrust, and only a second salvo arrived from the guns.

As the smoke screen began to dissipate Venables cursed the lack of available artillery but he knew that the Royal Artillery AS-90s were relocating because the Red Army's battlefield radar now knew within ten feet where those guns were.

In the fields beyond the avenue of trees he could see burning vehicles and other perfectly serviceable tanks and APCs milling about as a safe passage across the lane was sought. He could only guess at what was taking place in the lane and how many vehicles had come to grief there from the smoke and flames that were climbing skyward.

Calling up the CP he found himself talking to Pat Reed in person, and explained exactly how vulnerable the enemy force now was, but the CO had a bird's eye view thanks to Phoenix and was as equally as frustrated as the Hussar.

"Hello Tango One Nine, this is India Nine, we are trying for more air assets but we only got those Alpha's because I promised

them full and unbridled use of Mrs India Nine whenever they were next in town...over."

The levity of the CO's words could not disguise the underlying frustration he could hear in the voice, and he looked again at the armour stranded beyond the lane before replying resignedly.

"Tango One Nine roger, out."

He glowered into the binoculars as he saw the tracks and underside of a tank seemingly grow out of the lane as it climbed the steep bank, then the machine tipped over, crushing the hedgerow beneath it and accelerating into the field on this side of the obstacle, the T-90s long barrel traversing from side to side as it sought targets. The enemy had found one gap in the fire and wreckage and where there was one there was sure to be more.

His view was again obscured by smoke but this time the rounds were coming from the enemy, providing cover whilst they organised themselves.

In the absence of artillery, air strikes, or an armoured force of sufficient strength to sally forth and hit the enemy whilst it was off balance, another troop of tanks to support 4 Company was what was required. He had just the three troops worth of tanks and his own vehicle, there were no reserves and 2 Troops position was between 1 and 2 Company in accordance with Pat Reeds desire to have a strong second line, should the forward companies be rapidly overwhelmed. 3 Troop could not be moved left as they were crucial to the flank of the battalion's defence, which really said it all in regard to their circumstances. No matter how well they did now, they did not have the numbers to win.

Major Venables spat over the side of his turret as if to be rid of the taste of lost opportunities before ordering the driver to back them up and find an empty position nearer to 4 Company where they could lend a helping hand.

Whereas Pat Reed and Mark Venables were feeling merely frustrated, the commander of the 23rd was positively apoplexic with rage. His superior, the division's Romanian commander had treated him to an ear-blistering rebuke over the radio for his lack of foresight and planning, even before his first battalions attack had arrived. The divisional commander obviously expected it to fail so he had ordered the 23rd MRRs commander to prepare and launch a further attack using the rest of his regiment, or answer for the consequences.

First battalion was using smoke to cover its crossing of the sunken lane and shake out into formation once more, but despite already losing a quarter of its strength there was no reason its attack should not succeed.

However, Third battalion was forming up a klick to the rear of the farm and Second battalion, which had borne the brunt of the losses against the British marines and from whom had come the initial two-company attack from the lane, were now attached to the Third battalion.

The vehicle commanders of the two tanks and four APCs that had survived his regiment's first attack had been arrested and marched off into some trees nearby, their departure being witnessed by the battalion staff's from Third Battalion and their own.

The regimental commander had remained at the farm to observe, and from here he gave his orders to the staffs by radio, for an attack to be launched with the farm and sunken lane being to the right of the start line. The attack was to bear straight ahead until it reached the point where the lane curved away to run down the valley, and then the force would swing half right and drive for the NATO positions that had defeated the first assault.

As he handed the radio handset back to a signaller he chanced to see on the hills behind them the Romanian regiment that had trailed them was deploying in readiness for an assault. No doubt the remainder of the division was also deploying and he suddenly realised that the divisional commander thought he would fail.

A flurry of shots sounded from the trees where the vehicle commanders had been taken, the sound causing ominous echoes that lingered in his ears, and for the first time he felt the cold finger of fear.

Under the circumstances the First Battalion's commander did a good job of job of reorganisation on the hoof, but the formation was rather ragged and still trying to sort itself out when he gave the order to continue the advance. Under pressure himself to make progress he had pushed his subordinates to get across the obstacle and lost another two in the process, two precious plough tanks that ventured too far to the right in search of a safe crossing. Despite the suppressing fire being directed on their positions the French Foreign Legion paratroopers could not look such a pair of gift horse's in the mouth, they engaged both vehicles and destroyed them.

The 4 Company men had watched 3 Company's action and had been heartened by the result, but now as they watched the Czech's emerge from the ragged smoke screen, driving straight at them, it caused a few men to swallow hard.

The Soviet artillery which had slackened during the artillery duel now picked up once more, but it was concentrated on the fields and slopes before them, attempting weaken the mine fields which had to be there somewhere. There was heavier fire falling behind and to the sides of the Czechs intended victims, and they knew it was to isolate them, to divide and conquer. The Milan crews picked their targets and awaited the order to open fire, and the men in the fighting holes checked their spare magazines and grenades for the umpteenth time.

Major Venables and his crew were finding the going less than straightforward in their journey along the slope to support 4 Company. Vehicular movement between the two forward companies had been carried out by using an existing track half way up the hill, following the contours through the trees. By accident or by design this track had suffered particularly badly in the Soviet's preparatory bombardment. Fallen trees and shell craters had provided obstacles the tank could only seek to bypass, but having found their way around one obstacle and returned to the track they encountered further blockages within yards.

The radio transmission that warned of the renewed advance was not best received by the crew of a Challenger that had found itself in a cul-de-sac formed by fallen trunks.

"Arghfukit!"

Had the shelling not picked up then a crewman could have gone out on foot and found them a way through by now. The only area Mark Venables was sure had been spared this level of shelling was the reverse slope.

"Driver, we need to back up about thirty feet and then head straight uphill." There was no immediate response on the intercom and he was about to call again when the voice of Trooper Abbot, the driver, sounded in his earpiece.

"Er, no offence boss, but what makes you think we can find a route that way?"

"I don't know that we will, but I know we've tried every other direction except up." Shrapnel struck the turret, and the sound made them all feel strangely more vulnerable rather than snug behind armour plate. Mark Venables was trying not to let the feeling of exasperation get the better of him because they needed to be in a firing position already, not stuck in this maze.

"Just get this thing moving Abbot, there's a good chap."

He used the vision blocks to assist the driver as he first backed up and then pivoted the big machine. Major Venables brought the barrel of the 120mm gun to full elevation to prevent its digging into the hillside, and once that was accomplished he turned one of the radios to 1 Troop's net to inform them that the going was slow but they would assist just as soon as they could.

No matter how much money had gone into the research and development of the perfect seat, they hadn't cracked the problem yet. That was the considered opinion of Ann-Marie Chan as she tried to regain some feeling in her posterior. Her operators were used to these long hours, which was just as well because although they had been on-station for over fourteen hours, their day wasn't over yet.

On the ground the troops of both sides may be criticising their respective air forces for not being more visibly active on their behalf this day, but her screens gave a different story.

There was a lot of air activity behind the lines, with NATO interdicting strikes bound for the front or for autobahns carrying the US 4 Corps to the fight. She had four stacks of aircraft configured for air intercept that were employed in defending 4 Corps, and three wings of strike aircraft on the ground that she could not use because they were earmarked for close air support for 4 Corps when they eventually reached the front. It left her with an available, though somewhat ragtag force that had been attempting to thin out the Red armour before it got to Vormundberg. They were all desperately tired and in need of a rest that she was not empowered to allow.

The airborne operation had unquestionably dealt the enemy a severe blow, the Red Air Force was having to employ fields further from the fighting, and due to the losses in the tanker fleet most of the sorties coming from those bases had been unable to take off with full ordnance loads. She knew that would not continue, and indeed the Soviet's had been moving aircraft, including tankers, from other areas all morning, and sending them to the available fields. The Red AWAC fleet was another matter though, they had reactivated old Il-76s, the first type to properly fulfil that role, but they were being kept too far from the front to be effective. Ann-Marie could just about detect the weak pulse of one that had to be back over Berlin way, so unless that changed then her and her controllers were the kings.

Lt Col Chan could see there were signs of stacks building by the Soviet's, the stacking up of aircraft that experience told her had to be strike aircraft. A regiments worth of what she suspected were Sukhoi SU-25 variants had lifted off from Plzen-Line airbase and had tanked, the first time that had been seen to happen that day, before flying to Germany to RV with a trio of tankers and four flights of SU-27 Flankers. The second tanking had also been a first for strike aircraft that day, providing heavily laden aircraft with ample fuel reserves.

Lt Col Chan called up the AWAC's partner in crime, the JSTARS mirroring their racetrack circuit at 45,000 feet.

"Sabre Dance, Sabre Dance, this is Crystal Palace Zero Eight, over."

"Go, Crystal."

"It looks like the other guys are getting their act together, we have a regiment holding east of Dessau, loaded for bear and with nearby tanker support. What's happening on the ground right now?"

"First line at Vormundberg was breached and the first attacks against the second line are underway, but its localised at the moment...we are seeing divisions deploying in the rear though, and we are predicting that if no breakthrough is achieved within the next couple of hours the Reds will launch a general assault along the entire line."

Ann-Marie thought about that for a moment. It would take a couple of hours to get all the elements set for the divisional attacks and those regiments weren't going to carry on burning fuel for that length of time.

"Is there anything else you need or has that answered whatever question you had?"

"Just one more thing...how come you get to have the cooler callsign?"

Her opposite number laughed and then they both returned to the business at hand. She knew where the SU-25s were going to be used, and it wasn't against 4 Corps and it would be in the next few minutes, not two hours down the line.

She brought up a menu onscreen and cast her eye down the list of available units for those that had completed rearming and refuelling. There were three, one Greek, one French and one USAF, and she tagged two flights from each squadron for immediate take off, noting as she did that two regiments worth of fresh contacts were climbing toward tankers south of Plzen-Line, quite possibly prior to heading for 4 Corps, but it was the dozen radar contacts that were leaving the Dessau stack and making a beeline for Vormundberg which were of more immediate concern.

Abbot grunted in satisfaction as the Challenger crested the brow of the hill and halted.

"Please note boss, that I am not one to say 'I told you so'."

The hilltop had received serious attention, as logically it was a place dug in troops would be. It was pitted with shell craters and in places these overlapped, there was not a tree that still stood unharmed either.

No artillery was presently landing and Major Venables opened his hatch with caution, listening for the sound of incoming before heaving himself up and out, to stand atop the turret.

From the viewing blocks it had looked to be as much of a maze as the one they had recently given up on, and things didn't look that much more hopeful when viewed from outside at first, but then he saw it.

Jumping down off the Challenger he ran to a nearby pine tree that had been stripped of almost all its limbs so that it stood like a feature in a kids jungle gym, slashed and hacked at by shrapnel but nonetheless easy to climb thanks to the stumps of branches. He clambered up until he could see clear across the hilltop, and although it would be a something of a roller-coaster ride, climbing in and out of deep craters, it was do-able.

Mark Venables took the time to memorise the twists and turns they would need to take, and then he heard the crack of a main tank gun firing from the direction of 4 Company.

A signaller turned in his seat and raised an arm to catch Pat Reed's eye, the commanding officer of 1CG raised a questioning eyebrow.

"From Four Nine, *'Contact, Wait out...'* that's all sir."

Lt Col Reed nodded his acknowledgement to that signaller and took a message form from another. It was from brigade and the text of the message was unwelcome news.

JSTARS REPORTS FURTHER ASSAULT IMMINENT. ONE ARMOURED COLUMN, SIX COMPANYS DEEP, ALIGNED WITH YOUR RIGHT FLANK POSITIONS.

He wasn't sure that his two forward companies could deal with the simultaneous onslaught of over two battalions worth of armour without considerable help.

Pat crossed to the Royal Artillery reps position and noticing an unfamiliar face stood next to the RA lieutenant responsible for artillery support for the unit, and rightly assumed it was the heli-borne spotter who had been forced down. Being rather busy he gave a nod of welcome in passing and gripped his rep by the shoulder.

"Derek, I want MLRS, just a couple of rockets worth would be invaluable." He handed over the message form before returning to his former place.

"What's his name then, Derek?" asked the newcomer.

"Patrick Reed."

The newcomer's hissed response caused the rep to pause what he was doing.

"That's Reed?"

"Yes, why?"

"His son is with my unit."

"So how's he doing?" Derek enquired. "If he is anything like his Father then you've got a good one."

There was a long pause.

"He's dead Derek, killed this morning at Magdeburg."

"Oh shit...poor bastard." Derek thought for a second, and there was nothing in the Guards officers' manner than indicated he knew of the death of his son. Handing the appeal for MLRS support to the bearer of those sad tidings he then vacated his place.

"Can you take over with this request; I need to speak to the Adjutant."

The current combat air patrol covering Vormundberg was being found by two flights of three F/A-18 Falcons of the Spanish Air Force. Their own radars were on standby as they followed the steers from Lt Col Chan's controllers, guiding them on to the approaching targets and launched at long range all the AMRAAMs on their rails when instructed, but their targets did not contest the issue, rolling inverted and diving for the ground on burners the second the missiles were detected.

The AWAC had those twelve identified as SU-27s, not the type of aircraft a weenie straps to his back, and the controller providing the steers raised his eyebrows when they kept heading northeast, leaving the strike aircraft near Dessau with no cover.

The senior of the Spanish pilots could see on his datalink the aircraft abandoned by the interceptors, the SU-25s and tankers, and asked permission to engage with his own flight, the Caballero's, and the second flight, the Cuchillo's, which was granted by their controller who did not believe in looking gift horses in the mouth.

Lt Col Chan had cobbled together some help for the embattled troops at Vormundberg, French Jaguars for Wild Weasel flak suppression, USAF A-10s to stick it to some tanks, and Greek F-16s which when coupled with the Spanish F/A-18s should keep the Flankers busy whilst breaking up the inbound strike.

She was tired, and in organising the combined sorties her eyes hadn't left the screen in front of her, but they hadn't been seeing what was occurring either as her mind had been focussed on the task at hand.

It took a second for her to realised the Spanish CAP was off the reservation and making a beeline for the Dessau stack.

"What the hell..."

The F/A-18s were east of the Elbe and hustling to close the range so they could use their Sidewinders when powerful airborne radar illuminated them. Ann-Marie saw straight away what had happened and cut into the link, over riding her own controller.

"Caballero's and Cuchillo's, abortabortabort...Parase detenerse...Emboscada, it's an ambush...get the hell out of there, one of those 'tankers' is guiding SAMs."

At other times the rich Latin tones of the senior flight commanders voice would probably have made her toes curl, but this was not 'other times'. His voice was calm but he was not immediately complying with her instruction.

"Crystal Palace this is Caballero Zero One, their CAP ran away, we can take them."

Upon her screen the symbols for 'SAMs' have appeared; the software classified all fourteen as SA-10s.

"It's an ambush Caballero; the 'tanker' is guiding multiple SAMs!"

Her words were unnecessary; she saw the two flights split as they sought to break the radar locks on them.

To the northeast the 'fleeing' SU-27s reversed their course, hurrying back to their charges.

Ann-Marie watching helplessly as on her screen a pair of missile symbols closed with, and then merged with one of the Spanish Falcon's, the symbols disappeared from her screen. She darted a glance at her subordinate, the controller who had agreed to the Spanish pilots request, and despite the impassive features she could see from his eyes how desperately he wished he could turn back time.

Only two of the Falcons made it back to the relative safety of friendly lines and the senior of the two requested a steer to a tanker, having used up so much fuel on afterburner. It was not the same voice from before.

Had she not already had the Greek F-16s heading that way she would have been forced to weaken the line defending 4 Corps, diverting dwindling assets to cover the ground troops in contact.

It had come to that point, where the loss of just a few flights of aircraft could mean disaster. The Soviet plan had not worked, the regiments heading for 4 Corps would still be intercepted, but not those bound for the front.

The stack at Dessau broke up, the various elements making for their targets and Ann-Marie called up the Greek F-16s, and explained that the Vormundberg CAP was gone and it was now up to them.

"Timothy, is there a problem?"

The Adjutant had been talking intently with Derek for several minutes, and the C.O's words seemed to startle both men.

"Um, pardon?"

Pat hated it when officers of his seemed to be on a different page, but that had never before been the case with the young Captain.

"The MLRS request, is there a problem?"

The answer came from behind him though.

"Yes, sir." He turned to face the newcomer.

"All MLRS are about to carry out deep strikes on divisions beyond this one we are currently in contact with. Reloading of all launchers will take up to three hours."

All available anti-tank assets were tackling the Czech battalion moving on 4 Company and soon he was going to have to shift some of the Apache's and Lynx in preparation of meeting the even larger threat JSTARS had detected.

Whilst Pat Reed was mulling over these problems his Adjutant thanked Derek. He didn't know how or even when, he was going to have to break the news to the CO, but right this second was not the moment.

Pat came to a decision.

"Tim?"

His Adjutant sent the artilleryman back to his place before answering the CO.

"Yes, sir?"

"I want you to get onto the Argyll's, pass them the message from JSTARS and ask them if their kind offer of earlier is still open, plus I want you to inform Mark Venables that I am moving his 2 Troop up in support of the right flank, and tell him why."

On the reverse slope Major Venables Challenger had successfully traversed the side of the hill until it was directly behind the centre of 4 Company, but heavy shelling of that portion of the hilltop would have made their crossing back over a character building experience, but the shelling stopped abruptly.

Mark Venables acknowledged the adjutants transmission as he stood in the open turret with an AAC Gazelle guiding them across the hilltop, a door gunner leaning out to point the way around the jumbled trunks. The brow of the hill was in sight but they could not yet see the action taking place, but the sound of the defenders fire was rising and he was anxious to get into a position to support.

Gripping the GPMG mount for balance he braced himself as their course took them down into yet another shell crater, and up the other side. Cresting the edge of the crater he could now see their way was clear, and he waved his thanks to the Gazelle, which moved off.

"Steady there Abbot, one hundred metres until the ground drops off."

He ducked at the sound of an explosion to the right, glancing towards the source, seeing the wreckage of the helicopter hitting the ground, and then there was a roar as the Gazelle's killer passed overhead. It happened so fast that the Major had no time even to think of using the gimpy, and then he was ducking down again, inside the turret as spent cases rained down upon them.

Lt Col Chan had passed the air raid warning to the brigade headquarters for the troops at Vormundberg, but it had not been passed to the people that it mattered most to in time.

The Flanker that had destroyed the British Army Air Corps Gazelle splashed an Apache immediately after, both machines falling to its 30mm cannon. It turned its nose skywards and exploded, hit by all three of a Starstreaks projectile's. The Royal Artillery crew that had launched the high velocity missile died, their Stormer vehicle disintegrating under the 3000mph impact of a Kh-31P missile, the anti-radiation version of the Krypton anti-ship missile.

Venables fired the ten L-8 smoke grenades in the dischargers either side of the main gun. He now knew why the artillery barrage had ceased and he didn't know what good the smoke would do but they were very exposed on top of the hill, so it couldn't hurt.

"Hello all stations this is Zero, Air Red, Air Red, Air Red!"

The radios carried the very late air raid warning, which elicited a variety of retorts amongst the listeners but only one gave voice to his on the net

"No shit?"

A rather officious voice took exception to the tiny lapse in radio discipline.

"Hello unknown station this is Zero, say again callsign, over?"

Despite, or perhaps even because of the situation, the reply drew laughter.

"I'm sarcastic....." said 'Unknown Station'. *"Not stupid."*

The Challenger reached the brow of the hill and was beginning down the incline when a large hand plucked at it, lifting the rear of the main battle tank as if it were a toy.

Ann-Marie Chan's assumption that the type was a SU-25 would have been successfully challenged on technical grounds by an anorak speaking in a nasal monotone. It was in fact an SU-39, formerly a two-seat version of the SU-25 but with that rear seat removed to enable mid-air refuelling.

The 'Frogfoot' had its trial by fire during the Afghan War where it proved itself to be a reliable, close air support machine capable of absorbing a lot of punishment. Of a somewhat similar appearance to an Alpha Jet, it was the Red Air Force's best ground attack aircraft.

Colonel Ilya Morimsky had not had the best of days, flying once to Belgium and back at first light, once to France and back in the late morning, and each time with half the ordnance load his aircraft was capable of carrying. This mission however, held the promise of actually putting enough ordnance in the right place to *almost* justify the risks and the losses amongst his pilots.

The plan that had got them to the battlefield without loss had been his, thrashed out over a secure radio link to an army officer who had sounded almost intelligent. Leaving the same battlefield without loss was another thing entirely, however. Despite the best efforts of the aircraft designated to carry the AS-11 and Kh-31P anti-radiation missiles they were still seeing missile launches from the ground. Frighteningly fast Starstreak missiles blotted three of his aircraft from the sky on the first pass, and heat seeking Stingers that his AAA suppression aircraft could not detect had brought down another two of his regiment so far.

The regiment had divided into separate flights and endeavoured to attack the targets the ground troops wanted taking out once those assigned to AAA suppression had cleared the way. Morimsky himself leading a flight of four, two pairs of aircraft with one to identify the targets in question and then to highlight by laser designation whilst it was attacked with 500kg LGBs.

One of the targets the ground forces wanted neutralising was described by them as a Milan anti-tank crew beside a large tree on the hillside, but despite providing a ten figure map reference his laser partner could not identify it. It was a long hillside with a lot of trees on it and few features to get their bearings from. Eventually the voice on the ground had a tank fire a smoke round at the spot they wanted attacking and a laser was aimed at that point.

Not only the attacking armour had targets for them, artillery spotters and the crews of the Soviet helicopters had targets they believed were best dealt with by the SU-39s. Consequently it was not just 1CG that was to receive their best efforts, but 2REP, 2LI and the Argyll's also.

Once the lasing aircraft had identified the targets the flak suppression elements attacked and the strike aircraft waited a few moments before beginning their runs.

Morimsky had come straight across the valley, east to west and thirty seven seconds behind the AAA suppression sortie, and all he needed to do was follow a line projected onto his HUD until the automated weapon release system pickled off the ordnance. With his right hand he held the aircraft steady at 400 feet as the thumb of his left hand rose and fell on the counter-measures switches, discharging flares and chaff from the wingtip pods.

The first thing he'd noticed was the amount of smoke in the valley, and then he was passing above a trail of destruction as if some child had thrown a tantrum with his toys, smashing and scattering them. The trail ended at a line of stationary vehicles some eight hundred metres from the first visible NATO foxhole, rendered immobile by the mines that had blown off sections of track and then destroyed by tank rounds or missiles. The attack was stalling and unless a serious cull of the enemy anti-tank units took place it would never progress.

One of the AAA suppressors had already fallen; with its tail blown off it had crashed into the forested slopes of Vormundberg, whilst a second was limping home on one engine.

His aircraft rose as a bomb fell away and he banked hard right to follow the side of the hill, wincing as he saw an SU-27, one of their escorts, exploded by a missile.

The lasing aircraft reported the bomb he had released had detonated exactly on the illumination but there had been no secondary explosions, which led the Colonel to correctly assume they had attacked a remoted firing point and not the crew. He extended the air brakes by twelve degrees before reversing direction, having seen the whirling rotors of two British helicopters hovering just above the hilltop, and the turn brought down his speed even more.

Although he carried two AA8 Aphid missiles, one under each wing, he selected the belly mounted 30mm cannon and used the rudder pedals to line up on the first target. He fired a half second burst and saw fragments of perspex glint in the sun as the rounds struck home. He had kept the pipper of the gun sight on the engines above the cargo deck but the helicopter, a Lynx, was turning towards him and the cockpit bore the brunt. It immediately fell the short distance to the ground but he did not see it impact, he was already using the opposite rudder to bring the nose into line with an Apache gunship. His burst was high and he saw the cannon rounds hitting the ground beyond it, throwing clods of earth skywards and there was no time to adjust his aim.

Morimsky overshot and banked left, craning his neck as he did so to see if the Apache was still in sight but it wasn't. What he did see though were smoke grenades going off, drawing his eyes to a tank he had not noticed before.

He called his lasing partner but the man had kept his eye on the boss and already the British Challenger was being illuminated.

Selecting another 500kg laser guided bomb, Col Morimsky pulled back on the stick, gaining another 500 feet before turning back. The tank was moving towards the brow of the hill, half concealed by smoke but it was as good as dead. The Colonel had nothing against the men who were manning the vehicle but he had a job to do and as such he chose not to notice the figure stood in the commander's hatch, so to him the fighting vehicle was nothing more than some robot.

He heard the pilot of the aircraft illuminating the target shout, the airwaves carried a half formed word, which he could not recognise but the alarm in the voice was clear. The laser illumination ceased and Morimsky de-selected automatic release of the weapon, turning instead to manual at the precise moment something struck his aircraft hard. He cursed loudly because the impact startled him into inadvertently releasing the weapon.

He did not try to see how close the bomb had come to his target, the smell of fuel had seeped through into his mask and the needle of the engine temperature gauge for his starboard engine was climbing rapidly. He shut down the engine but found that something was causing a lot of drag on the right side of his aircraft; far more than a dead engine would cause, and only by keeping constant pressure on the left rudder was he able to correct the yaw the drag was inducing.

Things got markedly worse a second later when he was hit again as he overflew the French legionnaires, a wall of small arms fire rose to greet him but he heard only one audible impact. It was no louder than a loose chip flying up off a road makes when it hits the bodywork of a car, but his instrument panel and radio died, the needles sinking to zero and their illuminating lamps cutting out.

He made it past the NATO units to open countryside, heading back towards the Elbe but without a compass he was uncertain of the heading. Turning his head he tried to pick out a recognisable landmark but instead he saw the fins of a Stinger missile protruding from the starboard engine housing just behind where he was sat. After the initial shock of seeing the unexploded weapon he shook his head in wonder.

"How lucky can a guy get?"

He obviously could not tempt fate much longer and he was going to have to eject before the Stingers warhead decided to go off. Removing his feet from the rudder pedals and reached down for the ejector seat firing handle between his lower legs, but froze when he saw about two inches of fuel sloshing about in the foot well. The voids in the fuselage behind him were probably also awash with the highly inflammable liquid, and the rockets that would throw the seat clear would ignite the jet fuel which would set off the unexploded warhead.

Colonel Morimsky took back all he had said about being lucky and abandoned all ideas of leaving the aircraft in flight, looking instead for somewhere flat to put the machine down on.

He was still west of the Elbe but in territory the advancing ground forces had already passed through so every road would eventually be carrying logistical support convoys. He need not have to walk too far before finding a ride on an empty truck heading back towards the river. It was a mainly wooded area though and that was troublesome, because he had no way of knowing when his remaining engine was going to flame out for lack of fuel.

Just as he was starting to think he would never find somewhere to put down he saw a long clearing ahead, and he brought his damaged machine down lower, overflying it as he looked for obstacles. It looked clear as well as being a decent length so he circled around, jettisoning his remaining ordnance over the trees and spotting an east/west running road about two kilometres south. Easy walking distance provided he could get down in one piece.

Once he was lined up he jettisoned the cockpit canopy, tightened the straps holding him to his seat, and began the approach for a wheels up landing.

The SU-39 could glide, but without knowing the full extent of the damage to his aircraft he couldn't afford to shut down his remaining engine, in case it was the only system left that was providing power for the avionics. It would be ironic, he thought if in order to avoid burning he shut down the engine and crashed, because there was no electrical power to move the control surfaces.

The approach was straightforward and he cleared the treetops at the end of the clearing by a foot and throttled back, bringing the engine to idle without shutting it down. He flared, allowing the last of the flying speed to bleed off and then lowered the nose to avoid the tail catching and smashing the belly against the earth. Despite all that he was thrown violently forward against the seat straps when the aluminium belly met the earth, and the vibration, the bone shaking, jarring, seemed to go on forever.

The careering journey across the clearing ended as the crippled aircraft came to a halt, brought up against a bank of earth and a few moments later its pilot emerged without bothering to shut the remaining engine down, rolling out of the open cockpit and hurriedly regaining his feet before running a hundred or so metres and flinging himself to the ground behind an old fallen tree trunk near the edge of the clearing.

The sound of the aircrafts single operational engine carried beyond the clearing and through the trees, a noise as alien and invasive as the stinking fumes it gave off. Smoke leaked into the air from the battered fuselage but after a few minutes that had reduced to little more than whisp's. There was no fire, no explosion, and the pilot's still helmeted head emerged from behind a tuft of grass, peering at the noisy aircraft for long minutes. It did not seem fitting to leave the aircraft here with its jet engine still turning over, it had saved his life and it was only respectful that he showed his appreciation of that fact. He slowly regained his feet and after a few seconds hesitation he walked back to the aircraft, unaware that he was in the crosshairs of several gun sights.

"Are you going to shoot him, sergeant?" The question was whispered by a young Canadian subaltern to his platoon sergeants back.

Sergeant Blackmore of the Nova Scotia Highlanders rolled his eyes and carefully turned his head, ensuring no waving items of undergrowth gave away his position as he moved. 2Lt Ferguson was his fourth platoon commander in as many weeks. The first officer to hold that post was now the battalion 2 i/c, and his predecessor had lasted almost a fortnight before sticking his head up to see where some firing had come from instead of keeping it down even lower. Sergeant Blackmore could not remember the next ones name. On his third day, that particular young man had decided that consulting a map whilst out of cover had been a good idea. Mr Ferguson had joined the Highlanders recce platoon less than a day ago and already there was a book going. The smart money said young Mr F would not make it through the day, but it was Blackmore's to keep the man alive.

Plus of course, Blackmore had $100 riding on 48hrs!

"Sir, shooting him would be noisy." He whispered back. "And we are the recce platoon, not the anti-tank platoon. The anti-tanks are the battalion's loud buggers, and we are supposed to be the really quiet ones."

Ilya Morimsky was now stood upon the aircrafts wing, and leaning inside the cockpit, flicking switches, going through the proper shutdown sequence for the last time and the sound of the jet engine sank away to nothing. He patted the fuselage affectionately before walking south, taking a cigarette from a pocket in his flight suit and lighting up once he was clear of the stink of aviation fuel.

"And besides," Sergeant Blackmore explained. "It took balls to do that; I'll send Junot and Hicks to take him prisoner."

A pair of military policemen collected the Colonel from his captors, escorting him away through woods where men were taking down camouflage nets and stowing them away in their fighting vehicles in preparation to move.

Everywhere he looked Ilya saw enemy armour, the Highlanders LAV III Infantry Fighting Vehicles, the Coyote armoured recce vehicles of The Fort Garry Horse, and Leopard C2 MBTs from two different regiments, the Royal Canadian Dragoons and the Canadian VIII Hussars.

Morimsky told himself that his navigation had to be out and that he was further north than he had thought, because the alternative did not bear thinking of, a NATO armoured force on the loose amid his armies supply lines.

The time for concealment had passed, the crews mounted up and the armoured fighting vehicles of the 2nd Canadian Mechanised Brigade roared into life.

The close support from the air force hampered the efforts of the defenders long enough for a plough tank to get to within sixty metres of the first of the 4 Company trenches before it was destroyed by 94mm LAW's, fired point blank from the infantrymen's fighting holes, but the damage had been done, the minefield had been breached.

The sound of small arms fire and grenades almost drowned out the voice of a sergeant in the 82nd as he gave a sitrep to Pat Reed, communications had been lost with 4 Company command post and the platoon commander of 12 Platoon, the sub unit facing the breach in the minefield, was dead. The Czech's had taken four trenches after fierce fighting but they had been unable to increase that number, being repelled with heavy losses on their last attempt.

The cleared path through the mines had been blocked by good fire from 10 Platoons Milan team, firing across the front of 12 Platoon and knocking out a T-72 and a T-90, isolating a T-72, six BTRs and BMPs that had followed the mine plough through. Five armoured vehicles, including the T-72, were stopped and burning on top of 12 Platoons positions, but the infantry the APCs had carried were in and around the captured trenches and being supported by fire from their comrades beyond the minefield. The remaining two Soviet fighting vehicles had driven through the 12 Platoon position and further uphill to where the platoon in depth, 11 Platoon, had taken the pair under fire and destroyed both.

The American NCO wanted the enemy supporting fire suppressed in order for a counter attack to retake the holes.

After tasking the mortars to drop smoke in the way of the enemy support fire Pat called on 1 Troops commander and was alarmed to find that the troop commander had the only vehicle of the troop still in action. The other Challenger had been struck at the base of the turret, the shot had failed to penetrate but it succeeded in buckling the armour and fusing enough of it to the chassis that it could no longer traverse its gun. The Chieftain of the troop was undamaged but it was out of sabot and almost out of HESH. Pat told the man to 'wait out' and shifted to the battalion command net, but there was no response from Mark Venables on that means or by Ptarmigan. He called up 3 Company, but as they had not seen or heard from the Squadron Commanders tank he had to switch back to 1 Troop.

"Hello Tango One One, this is India Nine...where is your Sunray? Where is Tango One Nine, over?"

"Tango One One, I have heard nothing from my sunray for figs two zero."

It was almost a dilemma, not having sufficient tank killing power to enable the defeat of the enemy who were within 4 Company's positions, without diverting 2 Troop away from where they would soon be desperately needed. Fortunately the AS-90s of the Royal Artillery had completed their move to a new gun line and the Czech supporting fire dried up soon after the 155mm guns were turned on them.

The Czech battalion commander was on foot, having gotten as far as the mines where both tracks had been blown off, he and his crew abandoned the vehicle just prior to a Milan destroying it. He had neither the means nor the willpower to force his men to stand and fight, all the plough tanks had been knocked out and the defenders fire too accurate for the mines to be cleared by hand. He couldn't even get a ride, several tank and APC commanders saw their Colonel and his crew running from shell crater to shell crater, but possibly fearing he would order some futile action they ignored him, withdrawing back the way they had come.

With one crisis over the reports coming into 1CG's CP became more upbeat, a REME recovery vehicle reported it was with Major Venables callsign and had replaced a track blown off by a near miss during the air raid. With the track replaced the REME and Venables Challenger had left their very exposed position on the hillside, moving to 4 Company's CP before repairing the tanks communication's, damaged in the same air attack. They had found a scene of feverish activity there, the CP's roof had collapsed during the shelling but there had been no fatalities, the company headquarters staff had been released from their would-be tomb and were now frantically attempting to recover equipment, including communication's gear, which was still buried.

12 Platoon regained its lost fighting holes and took eight prisoners, but they had lost five dead and four wounded during the entire action, losses that Lt Col Reed felt obliged to make good from 1 and 2 Company.

A resupply was carried out for the men in the trenches; it was not so simple for the Hussar's though. Mark Venables and his crew traded vehicles with that of the damaged 1 Troop Challenger, transferring their ammunition to the Troop commanders vehicle before heading to the rear with 1 Troops Chieftain following. The Chieftain went for reloads and Mark Venables brought the damaged Challenger to the REME's makeshift workshop.

The Greek F-16s splashed one SU-27 Flanker and three of the SU-39s with AMRAAMs for the loss of one of their own, but it was more likely that the Soviet strike withdrew due to the escorting Flankers fuel states rather than prudence.

This time the AWAC's message was passed to all forces in good time and the Stinger and Starstreak crews stood down. The Jaguars of the Armee de l'Air realised almost as soon as they were above the contested hill that the Soviet AAA radars were still on standby, they had not been told their own aircraft were clear of the battlefield.

The first company of 23rd MRRs Third Battalion was cresting the rise to the left of the farms ruins when the Jaguars attacked with CBUs, they made a single pass down the length of the column, destroying three tanks and four APCs before disappearing to the southwest, but the AAA radars did not immediately light up, the operators hesitated still, allowing two flights of three A-10 Thunderbolts from the 103rd Fighter Wing to attack unchallenged. The seven barrelled 30mm cannons made a sound like tearing cloth as they fired, exploding eleven vehicles in a single pass before egressing to the west, scattering Gator mines from their underwing dispensers. One pilot found himself flying toward a half circle of stationary vehicles and a nearby cluster of men besides a ruined building. He had time for one long burst, walking it across a BTR-80, the T-80 beside it, and on across a pair of running figures.

23rd MRRs commander could feel the heat of the flames issuing from his burning command tank, even though the freezing muddy water had soaked his uniform. He heaved himself up onto his hands and knees in the puddle in which he had landed when he'd dived for cover, looked around for his 2 i/c and bawled angrily at him when he saw him listening earnestly on the signaller's second headset some thirty metres away, seemingly oblivious to the violence of just moments before. His Intelligence officer and an infantryman from his escort had been reduced to hamburger by the A-10s strafing run, but the regimental commander gave them not a second thought except to angrily kick loose a piece of intestine that had landed on his boot.

Two attacks had been defeated, two attacks by a total of six companies had failed to take and hold so much as a single NATO foxhole, and now those NATO bastards had tried to kill him without one of his AAA units firing a shot. He turned and looked at the ZSU-23-4 that was charged with his protection, it too had failed to take action in time, and surely that could not go unpunished, could it?

Radars started to come back up, an SA-9 was launched and a ZSU hit an A-10 in the port engine but then the Thunderbolts were clear. The French Jaguars were still in the vicinity though, knowing that at some point the AAA would react and they killed both the SA-9 launcher and the ZSU, causing the radars to shut down once again.

The regimental commander had witnessed the turret of the ZSU attached to his headquarters pivot, quite obviously under guidance from its radar and then shut down again after the French HARMs began arriving. Quite obviously an example was called for here, and who better to demonstrate what befell those who failed in their duty then he himself. He undid the flap of the holster on his hip before stepping off purposefully towards the vehicle in question. The sound of running feet caused him to glance over his shoulder, but it was just his 2 i/c so he carried on walking.

"Who was that on the radio?"

Obediently his 2 i/c took up station a couple of paces behind him.

"It was the divisional commander, sir."

23rd's commander began to demand as to why he had not been informed but the sentence was not completed. The men nearby turned and gawped at the sound of distant thunder, and flashes reflected by the cloud to the east. Some of the men recognised the sound and looked nervously at the skies above their heads. It was an infantryman from the escort who first looked away from the direction of the MLRS attack and noticed his regiments two most senior officers, the one lying face down in the mud and the one stood a little behind with his arm still extended, a wisp of blue/grey smoke dissipating around the muzzle of the pistol held in that hand.

23rd MRRs new commander holstered the pistol and gestured to the signaller who ran across.

"Halt the battalion and have the company commanders join me here, we have some quick changes to make and then they can resume."

The delay cost another twenty minutes, and when once more the armour headed west the regimental command group was included.

Pat Reed received word that the third and largest formation yet had entered the valley, and with it came a further air raid warning. He had expected it sooner but any delay could only be to the good in the long term.

He looked around the command post and up at its very substantial roof, deciding that Jim Popham could run the show for a while. He was a hands-on soldier and that was his excuse for leaving the main CP.

"Timothy?"

The adjutant raised a questioning eyebrow.

"Sir?"

"Call Sarn't Higgins, tell him to bring up a Warrior for me and Defence Platoons reserve section, and tell Jim Popham that until he hears otherwise, he has the battalion, understood?"

"Er, no sir, is that wise?"

Pat paused in the entrance to the CP, looking back at his Adjutant.

"Timothy, I just told you that until further notice Major Popham is the 'The Daddy', but that does not make *you* my Mother."

The Warriors had not yet arrived and random mortar rounds were landing over to the left so Pat ducked into the dugout cum briefing room to wait, and there found the two snipers, Stef and Bill sharing a mug of coffee.

"As you were, chaps." Both men had stood respectfully on recognising the CO, and now relaxed, sinking back onto their haunches. Pat squinted as if trying to see through the side of their metal mug, trying to discern the constituent parts that made up the hot beverage within.

"I don't suppose you have any sugar in there, do you?"

"If you want, I've got some artificial sweeteners somewhere, Boss?"

Pat pulled a face.

"I thought you two had been told to report to 1 Company?"

"With respect sir, the ground back there can be covered by a half blind clerk, the maximum range offered is only four hundred metres." He was looking for signs of anger or annoyance in his commanding officer, but none were apparent. "We were loitering here and looking for a lift on a battle taxi going forward, sir."

The sound of Rolls Royce Perkins, V8 engines reached them, winding their way around from hide positions in the rear.

The snipers thought their last orders did not befit their skills, and Pat was inclined to agree.

"Well you had better come along with me then."

The Warriors halted outside where all three mounted up, running to the vehicles in a half crouch as heavy artillery rounds moaned their mournful way westwards, seeking NATO gun line's.

Aboard 'Sabre Dance Two Four' the operators finished their post-MLRS strike estimate and passed on two sets of figures, the optimistic and the pessimistic, knowing the true figure lay somewhere between.

Elements of two divisions had been targeted, 9th and 13th Guards, both elite Russian units had been hit hard even if the lower figure were held to be true. It would be of little immediate assistance to the men and women blocking the juggernauts way to the autobahns though, the Hungarian division had finished its deployment into column of regiments and was moving now towards the units immediately in front, the Light Infantry, Coldstream Guards, Argyll & Sutherland Highlanders and the Wessex Regiment. All were British units of 3 (UK) Mechanised Brigade and the Guards were already in contact, but within an hour and a half the entire defence line from the Dutch 2nd Armoured Brigade on the left flank to the US 4th Armoured on the right were going to be fighting for their lives.

Down on the ground the anti-tank troop of the second Royal Marine unit, 44 Commando, hadn't waited for the Hungarians to begin their advance. The marines ducked around the Romanians left flank, taking the fight to the enemy and getting their punch in first. The sensors on Sabre Dance Two Four picked up thermal signatures consistent with explosions of armoured vehicles amid the Hungarian ranks.

The forward edge of the battle area was not the only scene of activity on the operator's screens, both the French 8th Armoured and Canadian 2nd Mechanised Brigades were now driving back towards the Elbe, and where they found enemy support units they destroyed them. Both brigades had detached small combat teams that headed west to provide a delaying force for the Soviet armour that would inevitably turn on them. A French company combat team had fallen on two batteries worth of Russian MSTA-S 152mm Self-Propelled howitzers and their ammunitions carriers being refuelled beside a road. The thick columns of black smoke and continuing secondary explosions punctuated the urgency of radio transmissions from Soviet troops under attack.

The route taken by Mark Venables Challenger had been picked up by the CO's driver who had followed the trail marked by the tanks caterpillar tracks over the hilltop. It was an unplanned by-product of the track plan enforced by the CO, no vehicles had been permitted to venture onto the hilltop where its thermal output would have glowed brightly for all to see for miles around, assuming of course that the 'all' had heat sensors in their recce vehicles/surveillance aircraft. With an air raid in the offing the Warriors hadn't hung around to admire the view, the rollercoaster ride had been endured by the vehicles occupants, terminating as it did a hundred and fifty metres from 3 Company's CP.

Pat Reed clambered from the lead vehicle and jumped down into a nearby shell crater, waiting for Guardsmen in the second vehicle to manhandle two boxes of Stingers that the company's CQMS had apparently requested. Sgt Higgins, Bill and Stef joined him, taking care to avoid the muddy water that was already starting to fill the hole.

Artillery had been falling on the forward slopes but suddenly it stopped.

Big Stef clambered up the side of the crater and looked for the next cover, it was another crater just a few yards away and he took advantage of the lull to jog towards it. A trio of jet aircraft screamed down the valley, flying parallel with the positions held by the Guards and 82nd men, Stef dropped to a crouch, taken unawares by their presence and feeling vulnerable above ground. He looked to see if they were friend or foe but the aircraft had gone, disappearing faster than his head could turn, and then the big Geordie was lifted bodily and thrown eight feet.

By chance Pat Reed had been looking in the direction the aircraft had appeared from and he had seen the large weapons carried either side of the aircrafts centre points. The aircraft, which he had identified as Mig-31 Fulcrums, were at less than a thousand feet and punching out flares and chaff. Two

Stingers chased the burning magnesium instead of the Soviet machines, which released the weapons one at a time, a small drogue parachute deploying from the base of each almost immediately.

The Guards Lieutenant Colonel hadn't been able to understand why they were dropping so far away from his defensive positions, and then noticed the first weapon to be released had disappeared from view in a rapidly expanding cloud of vapour that seemed to originate from within itself.

The vapour ignited.

The ground shook as though a giant had run a half dozen paces, the thunder of the detonations burst the eardrums of two men in the most forward positions, and the flash of the explosions left spots before the eyes.

Pat felt as though he'd run into a wall as over-pressure sent him tumbling into the craters mire-like bottom but immediately afterwards he was gasping for air like a landed fish. Dirt and light debris were sucked from the ground, drawn toward the growing, roiling balls of flame, following in the wake of the oxygen that they were feeding on.

Bill was the first to recover enough to crawl up the crumbling sides of the shell crater; the last of the fireballs was disappearing skywards, leaving behind smoke and confusion. Stef had landed in the churned mud at the side of the track, but he had regained his wits enough to give his mate a thumbs up that he was okay. Relieved, Bill looked towards the fields over which the fuel/air weapons had detonated; large burnt areas marked the spots below where the weapons had gone off.

A myriad of fires were burning in the fields, two hedgerows were aflame, and a grey haze of smoke polluted the air. In the middle distance more flames and smoke arose, though these were from one of the Fulcrums, brought down by a Starstreak before it could egress the area.

The weapons dropped by the Fulcrums had been far smaller than those used by NATO on the besieged towns, but their power had been frightening all the same. With all the dust and smoke in the air it took a moment for him to notice the damage that had been caused by the weapons incredible pressure waves.

"Sir, I think you had better look at this."

Pat Reed took a moment to respond, he was indulging in the resumption of an old habit, that of breathing.

Forcing his aching body into motion the half soaked officer disengaged himself from the almost freezing water and mud, dropping down beside the sniper and letting his eyes follow where Bill was pointing. At first he thought his attention was being called to the approaching enemy assault, but then his gaze fell closer to home.

"Ah." The CO took in the numerous small craters amidst the larger ones caused by the earlier questing artillery, using a single syllable to acknowledge recognition, and two to express a full understanding of the consequences.

"Bugger."

Rolling over he looked for the Defence Platoon sergeant and found him at the bottom of the crater, liberally daubed in mud from the same puddle that he himself had been deposited in "Sarn't Higgins."

"Sir?"

"Inform Zero that there are significant breaches in the minefields."

With the dawn that morning had come sniper fire but little else to concern Colonel Lužar or the men of the 43rd Motor Rifle Regiment. The sound of distant gunfire to the west had begun several hours before, reminding them that the war had passed them by for now, but then again no one was in any particular hurry to catch up with it. Only the youngest of the newly arrived recruits wanted to be in the thick of it, the remainder, especially the veterans, were content to remain at an ever increasing distance from the fighting.

In the late afternoon Lužar had been dozing, sitting at the commander's position whilst his gunner kept watch. He was woken by his gunner informing him that one of the infantry platoon commanders on the extreme left had reported hearing faint sounds of automatic fire from the southwest and possibly explosions, the sounds had stopped as quickly as they had begun and so the colonel instructed that the message be passed on up to division, where it was received without enthusiasm. The colonel returned to his slumbers only to awoken again a half hour later by Division ordering him to detach one infantry company to the divisional reserve for 'security duties'. Colonel Lužar was working out which company could be despatched and cause the least upheaval to the rest of the regiment as it filled in the gap, but division called again and requested a further company in addition to the first. It seemed to the colonel that he was the subject of a Candid Camera program when having decided on which companies would go, division changed their demand to that of a battalion. With a sigh he screwed up the notes he had made for the reshuffle of the rest of the regiments positions, and ordered his first battalion to prepare to move. His regiment had only three companies of tanks and only two of those were made up of main battle tanks. First battalions tank company were his PT-76 tanks, thinly armoured, under-gunned and getting long in the tooth, but he needed his heavier armour to deal with any counter attacks. He couldn't think that anything else would be needed by the division to guard its roads and bridges, or at least that is what he thought until he had a query about fuel re-supply from the CO of his Third Battalion. None of his regiment had been visited by a fuel truck to top off their tanks since before the river crossing, and even on idle the engines consumed diesel greedily.

He suddenly had a bad feeling that the no show by the fuel trucks and the requests for him to detach troops were linked somehow.

In just under an hour following the first order to detach troops his First Battalion moved out. A minimal screen from Second Battalion had occupied key points in First's positions, and an hour later the regiment's shift of positions was complete. Lužar informed division and requested an ETA on refuelling, but the reply was so lacking in real information as to be worthy of a politician.

Following the airstrike's the last remaining elements of 23rd Czech MRR had enjoyed a few kilometres of relatively trouble free motoring. Gator mines had halted a further five of their number but the aircraft had not returned and NATO artillery had left them alone, choosing to fire counter battery missions.

The ranks of armour were doing it differently this time; advancing in half companies whilst the remainder of that particular rank were in whatever cover was available, and ready to provide gunfire support.

2 Troop had the senior troop commander and he had been liaising with 3 Troop plus the surviving Apache and Lynx helicopters, dividing up the visible targets. When the leading enemy rank came within 3000m he depressed his radios send switch.

"Fire!"

The tank lurched as it sent a sabot round downrange and the extractors hummed, clearing the fumes of spent propellant that emitted from the breach as it reopen to accepted a fresh round and bag charges.

2 Troops commander had his eyes pressed against the rubber eyepiece of the commanders sight and when the gun smoke cleared from outside of his Chieftain he was gratified to see six clear victims, four tanks blowing themselves apart with the force of internal explosions, and two other tanks, a T-80 and a T-90 were stopped in their tracks with crewmen bailing out. The tank rounds had a far greater velocity than the helicopters TOW and Hellfire II missiles, so as he watched the glow of a missiles motor cut across his line of sight to strike a T-72, which vanished from view in the smoke and flame that accompanies a catastrophic kill.

By agreement they were only targeting the tanks, the enemy infantry fighting vehicles could be left for the time being, and it was only these lighter armoured vehicles of this half company that remained to go to ground and cover their comrades.

The second half company began leaving cover and many of its vehicles activated their smoke dischargers in an effort to remain hidden from the defenders.

2 Troops commander watched his own target disappear from view behind a smoke screen generated by white phosphorus. His eyes remained pressed to the sight as he switched to the thermal imaging facility and the T-72 reappeared in his sights, it's hot and warm surfaces picking out the main battle tanks shape.

The Chieftain lurched once more but he did not have to wait for the smoke outside to clear this time, the thermal sight showed the shape of the T-72s turret replaced by a bright shapeless flare of light. He looked for another target and indicated it to his gunner, so caught up in the excitement of the action was the young lieutenant that it took a call on the intercom from his driver to remind him it was time to relocate to another firing position. The intended target received a stay of execution as the Chieftain reversed out of its firing position and headed for the next.

This position was in sight of another firing position for armour, one that a 3 Troop Challenger was just entering. The 2 Troop Chieftain was moved into place with practiced ease by its driver and immediately acquired another target, but before they opened fire the Chieftains turret was struck by something on the left rear, where no enemy was supposed to be.

The troop commander looked through the viewing blocks and saw debris still falling to the earth but it did not originate from them. Smoke shrouded their neighbour; the Challenger was missing two drive wheels and the track on the right side was hanging off, so whatever had struck his Chieftain had been in all probability an integral part of the 3 Troop vehicle. As he watched he could see the turret moving, the main gun following the movements of a target so the crew were apparently fine. The Challenger fired and then a second later it simply blew up.

"Shit..."

"Are we hit sir?" The gunner had removed his eyes from the sight to make the enquiry.

He ignored the question for a second, puzzling over what had destroyed the Challenger and reasoning that as the enemy tanks were not yet in range then a missile had to have been responsible, but their current opposition were thought to have nothing more advanced than the AT-3 Sagger and AT-4 Spiggot, both of which had a range of only 2000m.

"Look for missile launches." He told his gunner. "Either on the ground or from a helicop..."

"Got it!" Cut off by his gunner he awaited the target indication, it followed a few heartbeats later once the laser rangefinder had locked down the distance to target.

"Target BMP-3, three thousand five hundred metres, extreme right hand burning tank..."

The troop commander saw the tank but not the BMP, so further indication must follow.

"Seen."

"Go One o'clock from burning tank, a small clump of trees..."

He increased the magnification on the sight, seeing only natural foliage at first but then he saw it close to the left hand edge, hull down and half in shadow so how his gunner had seen it simply amazed him. He stopped the gunners target I.D with a simple.

"Identified!"

A sabot already sat inside the 120mm main gun and he ordered a reload with HESH because the heavy tungsten steel round didn't have the range of the shaped charge round.

As he watched, the BMP launched a further AT-15 beam-riding missile at another NATO vehicle that its infrared laser was illuminating.

"Firing!" Again the jolt as the main gun fired.

The BMPs gunner had not had the benefit of any live firing practice and it had taken two of the precious missiles to destroy the first Challenger, he was now determinedly keeping the cross hairs on a second Challenger but the arrival of the HESH round ruined his aim.

"Shit...ineffective hit, reload HESH!" something had carried the round just slightly off target to strike the top of the BMP a glancing blow and ricochet off.

The AT-15 that was in flight continued to follow the guidance of the infrared beam, flying into the hillside where the cross hairs had ended up when the gunner flinched.

Angered at having missed, the BMPs commander did not do the sensible thing in bugging out, but looked instead for their attacker. The gun smoke was still apparent and the muzzle of the older Chieftain was a black hole that in his magnified sight seemed to be pointing right between his eyes, tendrils of smoke still leaching from it in the breeze.

It was a race and the Czech vehicle still had two missiles sat on turret-mounted rails before they had to reload.

"Hesh loaded!"

"Firing...!" The recoil threw the big guns breach back into the interior where it opened to accept another round.

2 Troops commander blinked to clear sweat that had run down his forehead and into his eyes, when they refocused he saw the Czech had already launched, the missiles exhaust fogged the sight picture.

"Driver, reverse!"

The Czech BMP commander cursed as he saw the British tank start to move backwards, but then the missile struck and the tank juddered to a halt. The Czech officer punched the air.

It was the last conscious act he ever made.

Through his binoculars 23rd MRRs commander saw the BMP being struck by the British tanks round and disintegrate in one catastrophic explosion. That particular BMP-3 had been with a Russian unit originally but had been knocked out during one of the abortive attempts to force a crossing of the Elbe. A sabot had gone through the front armour decapitating the driver and passing below the turret, where having then taken off the commander's legs it had travelled down the length of the troop compartment and exited by punching a hole in the rear troop door. A small electrical fire had been started in the driver's instrument panel through which it had passed; filling the vehicle with acrid smoke and the survivors had abandoned the vehicle fearing an explosion was imminent. The fire had petered out and for whatever reason the Russians had not recovered it, but a Czech armoured recovery vehicle had, towing it back to their own mobile repair shop where it had been patched up. The BMP-3s AT-15 Khrizantema missile system had been far in advance of anything on the Czech inventory, so the vehicles identifying numbers had been changed on the off chance someone may recognise it and ask for it back.

No more of the advanced and long range beam riding missile systems remained on 23rd MRRs strength, but the regimental commander allowed that in this attack they had at least trimmed the defending tanks numbers, something his recent predecessor had failed to do.

The British tanks had been concentrating on his own MBTs as they were the greater threat, but that had allowed the APCs and Infantry Fighting Vehicles to close to a range where they could use their wire guided anti-tank weapons to support the outclassed tanks. AT-3 Sagger and AT-4 Spiggot's were leaving their launch rails and forcing the defenders to change firing positions after each shot, this in turn was allowing the tanks to close to a point where the covering half companies had a sporting chance at actually hitting something. Greater artillery and close air support would not have gone amiss but both had become haphazard and he was getting the run around when he asked why.

Chobham armour had not been used in the protection of the Chieftain family of main battle tanks, and the AT-15 carried not just one shaped charge warhead, but two set in tandem. It was designed to defeat armour 1000mm thick even if plates of ERA, explosive reactive armour for deflecting the blast, covered the steel. The missile had struck the 56-ton vehicle in the last moment before the troop commanders Chieftain could have reversed from view. The impact and detonation lifted both gunner and commander from their seats, and only the loaders helmet saved him from a fractured skull when he was slammed upwards into the roof of the turret. A wave of stifling heat accompanied the darkness as all electrical power failed and thick smoke poured through a rent in the bulkhead between the drivers and main crew's compartments. The troop commander couldn't breathe in the choking atmosphere and it was terrifying how quickly hot gasses had replaced the oxygen.

He fought against panic as he used touch to find the hatch, groping his way upwards and forcing his jaws to remain closed unless his mouth fill with soot as his nose already had. He threw open his hatch and crawled out into the open, his exposed skin turned dark grey by just that short exposure to the smoke. That same smoke was pouring from the open hatch as if it was chimney, but allowing himself just one deep breath he leant back inside, reaching around until his hand found his gunner and locked onto a bicep, assisting him upwards. As he helped him out of the commander's hatch, the loaders hatch opened and the trooper who had fulfilled that function rolled from it and slid off the turret. The first sign of an interior fire announced itself as glowing embers within the smoke plumes issuing from both hatches. The driver's hatch had been blown out of its mountings by the missile and flames were already leaping from the opening. There was no chance at all that the driver could still be alive and so the survivors scrambled clear before the fire found the stacked bag charges in the storage bins.

Major Venables sat atop the turret of the damaged Challenger IIE, the radio jack plugged into his helmet so he could listen in on the battle. News of the loss of two of his tanks and five of his men were borne without a visible flicker, but a heavy hand had laid itself on his heart. War fighting was not war gaming, the dead were just dead and there had been little that was glorious in the manner of their passing, but they were his men and they had stood their ground when lesser men would have run, they deserved a better outcome.

A REME fitter with an acetylene torch and another with a pry bar were close to freeing the turret but once that was achieved they still had to take on a full load of ammunition before returning to the fray.

They weren't the only heavy armour unit using this workshop; Mark could see two other MBTs being worked on beneath camouflage netting. One was a Mk 10 Chieftain from the mothball facility, and the other was a Challenger but it too was a battlefield replacement. It lacked the boxy armoured barbette housing for the thermal imaging unit above the main gun, and the turret was lopsided, higher on the commander's side than the loaders which typed it as a Mk 1. Its original owners had been the 17th/21st Lancers; another proud regiment consigned to the history books.

Neither had battle damage, they were here because both had been subjected to minimal maintenance in the underground storage facility at Bicester, and machinery does not like being idle.

He looked around for crewmen to ask who they were for but failed to see any. The pry bar wielder provided the answer. "Replacements sir, for your regiments C Squadron. Transporters dropped them off this afternoon and we've been changing the engine packs, but the crews for them didn't turn up." The young soldier gave a shrug before carrying on.

"I heard they got taken out by an airstrike just down the road...shit happens, eh sir?"

Yes, Mark Venables had to agree with that one, but he had more immediate concerns that took priority over talking philosophy.

"Have they sent anyone else?"

"No sir, no spare crew left to send."

Venables had some men without tanks although not enough to make up a complete crew, but unfortunately that would probably change. A quick call had 2 Troops Sunray and his men heading back toward the REME workshop. He called up C Squadrons commander, they were not yet in action and he had no one to collect the two machines so he raised no objections. By the time that was complete, so were the repairs and the Challenger II headed off to reload.

As the Czech's closed to within 2000m the wire guided missiles criss-crossed the intervening distance. Artillery again fell on the NATO positions but it was light, lacking the weight of its opening barrages and 23rd MRRs commander was troubled, still he was being given evasive answers and the time had come to take his queries higher as to the pathetic artillery and air support. He had a pair of helicopters supporting him, a Mi-24 Hind-D and a Mi-28N Havoc, although being far from unwelcome, could not carry the same ordnance load of that of a regiment of ground attack aircraft.

"Get me division." He ordered his radio operator.

"Do you want to speak to the operations officer again, sir?"

"No, I want the divisional commander." His patience had run out.

"No one else, understand?"

The radio operator did understand and pestered his opposite number for several minutes before handing a headset and hand-mike across. 23rd's commander slipped the headset on and put the microphone to his mouth, pressing the send switch and dispensing with radio protocol and deference to rank, as he got straight to the point.

"Where's my artillery and air support?"

From the other end of the transmission he received a rebuke as to his lack of respect.

"Remember who it is you are talking to Colonel!" The Romanian snapped before continuing.

"You of all people should know how easy it is for someone of your current position to be removed." As threats went it could not have been clearer.

"If your advance becomes any slower that may quite swiftly come to pass!"

23rd's regimental commander was neither cowed nor apologetic.

"So have you checked your *own* six o-clock position lately, *sir?*"

There was a pause before a response was forthcoming, and he could imagine the Romanian peering anxiously back over his shoulder at his own second in command. It almost made him smile.

"112th MRR should be appearing on your right flank at any moment now, they at least advance as armoured troops should, with speed..........111th is coming up on your left and 93rd Tanks is coming up behind in support."

There was a further short pause and then the Romanian went on.

"They will have the same level of artillery and air support as your men, which is little for the time being because there has been a foul up, ammunition is not coming forwards and the gun

line's must conserve what they have until the problem is resolved."

It was a logical reason for why the fire had been so fitful, but it hardly explained the absence of the air forces fixed wing aircraft.

23rd MRRs rotary wing assets were working together, seeking out AAA vehicles. They had already destroyed two Royal Artillery vehicles; Stormer AFVs carrying Starstreak launchers in place of a 30mm Bushmaster cannon and turret. They were working a third, the smaller Havoc popping tantalisingly in and out of cover in an attempt to draw out the British vehicle into a position where the deadly Hind-D could engage and destroy it. This work was dangerous and demanding but helicopter crews were veterans. The greatest threat to their survival came from enemy fixed wing aircraft but the on-station A-50 Mainstay was sending a data feed showing that there were none within AMRAAM range of this portion of the battlefield at that specific time. The quality of early warning was not what the men at the front wished for, but losses in AWAC aircraft had made the Generals extremely cautious in risking those assets that still remained. The A-50s were so far to the rear that there would be less than a minutes warning of an inbound air raid, but that was sufficient for the men in the Hind-D and Havoc who kept a weather eye on the radar display as they hunted.

23rd's commander was still sat atop his own command vehicle observing the battlefield and trying to extract the reason for the conspicuous absence of the remainder of the air force, when the Mi-24 was transformed into a rapidly expanding ball of flame and shredded pieces of aircraft. A split second later the Havoc followed suit, the wreckage falling onto the bank of a small stream.

The Mainstays warning came a full minute later, and once that warning was given it shut down and dived to the east, away from the AIM-54 Phoenix missiles that had downed the attack helicopters.

Having launched on the helicopters at 180km, three flights of F-14D Tomcats of USS *Gerald Ford's* former air wing closed to 45km before following through with AGM-88C HARMs, and finally engaging the Soviet CAP with AIM-120 AMRAAMs.

Aboard Crystal Palace Zero Eight, Ann-Marie watched three pairs of US Navy F/A-18s pass below the dogfights and take out their primary target, the Romanian divisional headquarters that had spent too much time on the air and too little on the road, thereby allowing itself to be DF'd. The Tomcats HARMs had not been able to completely suppress the Soviet AAA, of the four surviving Hornets that went on to attack their secondary targets, the divisions gun and mortar lines, only two would return to friendly lines.

CHAPTER 7

North of Magdeburg: Same time.

The western bank of the river at the Soviet bridgehead rose quite steeply for sixty feet and flattened out for two hundred metres before rising again as a low hillside for a further two hundred. To prevent erosion the soil had been seeded with a hardy, long rooted variety of grass and conifers had also been planted five years before for extra binding of the earth.

Armies tend not to be particularly eco-friendly especially when on the move and this one had bulldozed its way up from the river's edge and away inland. The natural routes up the slopes to open country had been turned into quagmires by countless tracked armoured vehicles and in order to accommodate the wheeled logistical support transports, fresh routes were created by the engineers using chain saws on the young trees, before laying roadways of steel mesh matting across ground undamaged by the armour, up to the nearest metalled road. The result was one less of managed landscape and more of a construction site, with just the odd tree remaining here and there amid the morass of mud and metal.

When the Rzeszów Motor Rifle Division had crossed the Elbe it left a detachment of its engineers behind at the river, as had other divisions, where they could continue the building of further bridges and maintain the existing ones. Twenty-nine pontoon and ribbon bridges had been thrown across the Elbe irregularly spaced so that some were as close as thirty metres from their neighbour whilst others were several hundred metres apart. Speed rather than uniformity had been the prime force driving their construction the night before, to get men and vehicles across in sufficient numbers to establish a secure perimeter on the far bank before NATO could counter attack. The Soviet engineers working on the bridge furthest upstream, the autobahn bridge, had succeeded in spanning the gaps blown in the original roadway by British Royal Engineers, and the first tanks had crossed the bridge by the light of the dawn. That bridge had stood for all of an hour, Turkish F-4s had knocked down the temporary spans along with three pontoon bridges, at terrible cost to themselves especially as all the bridges had been repaired or replaced within two hours.

On each occasion that NATO aircraft had attacked, several bridges had been temporarily put out of action, but the attackers themselves had been hacked from the skies.

The company commander of 43rd MRRs engineer company had charge of four of the bridges, of which one was closed for repair and maintenance at any given time, but the weight of traffic had taken its toll on all of the temporary constructions. For twelve hours the bridges had been at maximum capacity as fifteen divisions had crossed onto the western bank of the Elbe. Once the bulk of the armour, headquarters echelons, and divisional logistic and combat support units had crossed, and convoys had moved the various divisions supply dumps over to the west of the river he had to take three of the bridges out of service for some emergency TLC. This remaining bridge was for east to west traffic and its approaches, as with every one of the river crossings, was marked at intervals showing it to be either an 'Up' or 'Down' route and field police checkpoints out of sight of the river were enforcing the correct flow of traffic.

On the eastern bank, close to the flowing waters, a temporary heliport had taken shape. Served by the helicopter regiments ground support vehicles it had managed a quick turnaround for aircraft requiring only reloads and fuel, but demand had outstripped available fuel stocks so a pair of Havocs and three Hind-Ds were on the ground there now, their engines shut down, the metal ticking as it cooled and contracted. The crews had gathered at a field kitchen were they sipped at scalding coffee and wolfed down hot food as they waited.

Security on the ground for the bridgehead was a fraction of that employed on air defence, the AAA sites were in evidence wherever anyone cared to look but less than a battalion of infantry and two companies of military police were forming the immediate perimeter. The land war had moved on and this area was now secure from ground attack, that was the official line, and no one had dared to ask why only fifteen divisions had crossed to the west of the Elbe, no one asked the nature of the business that was keeping three divisions tied up east of the river.

Outside of the General Staff and of course those units engaged in trying to unseat NATO Airborne forces from positions in their rear, it was not common knowledge that many of the most direct supply lines from the east had been cut, in fact for those in the know to be caught talking about it was to invite summary execution for the offence of defeatism.

There was a fairly steady flow of trucks going east to bring up more stores and war stocks, replenishment for the divisional depots, and ambulances were much in evidence too, but busy with a multitude of tasks the Major of Engineers did not notice that the traffic from east to west should have been heavier. His world was filled with the noise of metal on metal, tools being wielded in manual labour and the sound of his men exerting themselves in order to have the bridges fit to carry traffic once more and themselves back on dry land, close to the trenches for when NATO fighter bombers came visiting again.

A locking pin for one of the bridging sections had become bent and required changing before it sheared, the major and a sapper were employing muscle power to take the tension off the joint connecting both sections. They were using a manual winch attached to a length of steel hawser, anchored at one end to the other section, and it required their combined weight to take up the slack, working as they were against the rivers pull. Two other sappers were over the side of the bridge, suspended by safety lines over the water as they attempted to extract a banana shaped pin from a long straight hole. After fifteen minutes of sweat, the pounding by hammers and the grunting of obscenities aimed at the god of inanimate objects the offending item came free and was swiftly replaced. The major leant, panting and perspiring against the fender of the utility vehicle which carried much of the ancillary equipment, including the winch they had used. As the pin checkers pulled themselves back onto the road bed and moved along the bridge to the next section, he waved away an offered cigarette and looked toward the western horizon, judging that they had less than an hour's daylight remaining. Because he was looking in that direction he saw the vehicles at the top of the furthest rise, the sun was behind them and he had to use a hand to shade his eyes.

"What are those morons doing coming east on a westbound route?" He was speaking to himself but his companion stared in the direction his company commander was looking.

"Maybe the MP's are asleep, sir?"

Asleep or not he couldn't allow the vehicles onto the wrong bridge and he despatched the sapper to direct them in the right direction. The soldier jogged along the bridge towards the western bank and the major wiped the sweat from his eyes with a sleeve before fishing a water bottle from a pouch on his belt. He took only enough to rinse out his mouth, gargling briefly before spitting the fluid into the fast flowing waters of the river and replacing the bottle securely. A line of a dozen fuel trucks escorted by BTR-70s, was making its way slowly west across the bridge upstream of the one on which he was stood, he studied the way the bridge sections reacted to the load with a critical eye. It needed some serious work done on it before long or it was going to come apart, but that was a problem to be addressed by the Bulgarian engineers who owned it, not him.

Looking back towards the western bank he noticed that the vehicles on the skyline had not moved down towards the river, but some of them were moving left and right, away from the line of march so perhaps they had managed to work it out for themselves unassisted. By shading his eyes again he could now see that the traffic appeared to be tanks, so they had to be well and truly lost to have arrived back at the bridgehead.

His sapper had trudged halfway up the bank but had then stopped, turning and running back down the slope, losing his footing at one point and was now back on the bridge, waving his arms but the major could not hear what was being shouted. He looked back up at the crest at one of the tanks traversing the skyline, and saw that its main gun was pointing towards the bridge carrying the fuel convoy. Understanding came to him just before gun smoke spouted from its muzzle.

The 120mm HESH round screamed above the line of vehicles to strike the rearmost, the BTR at the convoy's tail end. A second round struck the lead vehicle, another BTR and left it burning, blocking the way for the trucks.

The Leclerc tanks of the French 8th Armoured Brigade on the high ground above the river started what would be a steady and systematic bombardment to destroy the bridgehead.

Machine gun fire cut down the running sapper and realising the position they were now in the major ran to the downstream side of the bridge, tearing off his belted equipment and steel helmet as he shouted a warning to his men. The unseen machine gunner switched fire to the running officer and the cracking sound of high velocity rounds passing close by spurred on the major who dived headlong into the frigid water. A tank round exploded the fuel truck at the head of the line now trapped by the wrecked and burning BTRs that had been the escort. Needing no further encouragement the sappers of the 43rd's engineer company followed their commanders lead, leaping off whichever bridge they happened to be on and swimming for it.

A short, vicious battle took place between the French and Soviet infantry backed up by the barrelled AAA sites the dug in Soviet's would have the advantage if they had time to recover from the surprise. ZSU-23-4 self-propelled AAA vehicles turned their quadruple cannon on the French and where they had no effect upon the main battle tanks, they were devastating against the lightly armoured French AMX-10P Infantry Fighting Vehicles and the infantry debussing from them. The French infantrymen used Milan, grenades, their vehicles 21mm cannon, and sheer guts to silence the ZSUs before fixing bayonets and beginning the business of trench clearing. Meanwhile on the far bank the crews of the attack helicopters had run to their machines once it was clear the bridgehead was under ground assault. Fingers flew over switches and the machines began to hum as batteries fed current to starter motors, the humming changed to a heightening whine that preceded the sight of rotor blades beginning to turn, but oh so slowly. The Hind-D nearest the field kitchen was not surprisingly the one most likely to take to the air first. The helicopters rotor blades had just begun to move with a blur when the French finally noticed them, and turrets began to swivel in the direction of the sound of the turbines.

A tank round exploded on the landing field and the first helicopter took to the air as if startled into flight by the detonation of high explosive. It's was the speedier of the trio of Hind's and it rose to ten feet, pivoted in the air to line up on a gap between two clumps of trees at the edge of the landing field and adopted a nose down attitude in order to gain airspeed more quickly. It was struck by a chance shell, the 120mm HESH round severed the tail and sent the aircraft cartwheeling into the ground where it caught fire. The French armour got the range of the machines still spooling up, wrecking them before they could get off the ground.

Satisfied that all the attack helicopters were taken care of the tanks moved on, seeking fresh targets and leaving a scene where black smoke boiled up from a field occupied by twisted and ruined airframes, exploding ammunition and burning fuel.

The major of engineers didn't fight the current; he allowed it to carry him along and struck out at an angle to the flow in a manner that would take him to the eastern shore but without draining all his limited strength. Tank rounds exploded on the sections of floating roadway where they connected to one another, or smashed into the pontoons that bore them. Any vehicles were engaged and able-bodied soldiers on the banks or upon the bridges were cut down without warning, but the only rounds landing near the men in the water were ricochet's or just poorly aimed.

The flow took him under several bridges which bore vehicles, their movement stalled by events and the reaction of the drivers and crews were mixed. Some officers were trying to get their packets of vehicles backed up, in the hope of regaining the eastern bank and saving the vehicles and the precious stores they carried, whilst in other places the BTR, BMP and BDRMs that had been the escorts were trying to make a fight of it. As more and more enemy armour began to appear, spreading out along the western bank, an air of panic began to settle on the bridgehead. Men were ignoring their officers and abandoning the vehicles, seeking the safety of the east bank. Willingly or unwillingly more men were finding themselves in the water, as a last resort in the quest for safety or as a matter of necessity, their retreat along the bridges being cut off by enemy fire. Many disappeared below the surface never to reappear; only the steadier men and the stronger swimmers prevailed where they had still been wearing all their equipment on entering the river. Those men were able to keep their heads as the weight of ironmongery dragged them below the surface, preventing panic turning fingers into uncoordinated rubber digits as they undid buckles and freed themselves from the ballast.

Obstructions in the water became more numerous, shattered sections of bridge drifting with the current, jagged edged and some slowly sinking were also amidst the floundering soldiers. Behind the major at the Bulgarians bridges the river was on fire, burning fuel had covered half the rivers width and was spreading downriver engulfing all before it. A drifting section of pontoon bridge carrying an ammunition truck was overtaken by the flames and minutes later the truck and bridge section disintegrated.

The river carried the major around a bend, and there in front of him was the last crossing of the Red Armies bridgehead across the Elbe. There were troops and vehicles on the bridge, all moving east and quite obviously the enemy.

Some hundred or so men were in the water along with the major, and he was still over a hundred metres from the shore. Eyeing the NATO troops worriedly he redoubled his efforts to reach the bank but that clearly was not about to happen before the current had carried him to the bridge. He wasn't alone in his fears and the tension was palpable as the first swimmer reached it. There was no gunfire from either the fighting vehicles or the men walking beside them, and the only action they took was with those men in the river who were clearly tiring and clung to the bridge when they reached it. Canadian infantrymen pulled those men from the water and left them sodden and gasping on the pontoons.

Several hundred yards further downriver the major pulled himself onto the riverbank and lay on the wet earth panting for breath. The crack of tank guns close-by announced that the Canadians had found what they had been seeking, the first of several depots of stockpiled bridging equipment that together would have kept the bridgehead in business even had twice the number of bridges been totally destroyed. Along two and a half miles of the river camouflaged dumps of bridging sections and pontoons had been established. The battalion of tanks and infantry crossed over to the eastern bank, and swung south with the intention of destroying as much of the Soviet's equipment as possible before recrossing at the Magdeburg autobahn bridge.

Looking back along the river smoke was darkening the sky prematurely, and floating wreckage, including bodies, was thick upon the water. He tried to remember if any bridging units had accompanied the divisions driving west, it was logical that there would be which was just as well, because he was pretty certain that there hadn't been time to move any of the spare bridging equipment to the western side of the Elbe.

The major couldn't believe that after all the blood and sweat that had been expended just getting a foothold across this damned river, NATO could take it back with so little effort.

Fighting off despair, the engineer officer stood on legs shaky with fatigue and went in search of his men.

Events on the ground were not only being followed with the greatest interest aboard Sabre Dance Two Four, the X-Band radar returns were being beamed via satellite to SACEUR's current locale and from there to over a dozen national headquarters. It was electronic, if not visual, confirmation of what the commanders of the various units on the ground were telling them, that the Red Army logistics train, already greatly hampered by the airborne drops, was at least for the time being severed.

For all the courage, skill at arms and élan displayed by the NATO troops, the contest of arms was not yet settled though. They had prevented the immediate reinforcement and resupply of the Soviet divisions in contact west of the Elbe, but to describe those fifteen divisions as being 'trapped' would be somewhat premature. Considerable fighting power existed, enough for the Soviet's to be able to continue the advance and still turn around enough units to clear a path back to the Elbe, thereby re-establishing the supply route once new bridging equipment could be brought forward.

Before midnight the operators aboard the E-8 would see the three divisions further east detach regiments from the hunt for the NATO airborne, and send them west with all three divisions bridging units.

To the west of the Elbe it was not Regimental sized formations that were ordered to turn about though. The Russian 77th Guards Tank Division began the business of changing its axis of advance by 180°, lumbering awkwardly around. Only by first allowing the support units to pass through the Tank and Motor Rifle Regiments on the narrow roads could the men and armoured fighting vehicles retrace their steps to the river and deal with the pitifully inadequate NATO units that had the audacity to try and trap a giant.

It was going to take time for that manoeuvre to happen, and in order to prevent the French and Canadians from preparing adequate defences, battalion sized units were receiving orders to leave positions guarding the flanks and attack the pair of NATO brigades on the Elbe.

There was nothing on the operators screens to suggest that the advance on the autobahns was hesitating, units identified by radio intercepts as being Romanian had come up on the flanks of the Czechs and were about to fall on the British and American trenches at Vormundberg. Behind those troops were two Russian divisions in the last throes of deploying and would soon be following on. They would overlap the Czech's and Romanians, encompassing the combined frontage of the

British, Dutch and US brigades. The French legionnaires of 2Rep and the Royal Marines of 44 Commando were already in receipt of artillery fire, and they were responding as the overrun 40 Commando had done, by sending out tank killing patrols rather than just hiding in their shelter bays and waiting.

Vormundberg: Same time.

Mark Venables Challenger left the small copse that hid the ammunition resupply point for his squadron, and motored back toward the ominous shape of Vormundberg. He had been listening with increasing anxiety to events on both the battalion and squadron nets, and even though it was only a five minute journey back to the reverse slopes he would have coaxed the machine into powered flight if he had been able.

His driver showed why he had been chosen to sit in the front seat of the squadron commander's callsigns, working the six forward gears to achieve 40kpm across open ground to the single, narrow metalled road that led back to the hill, and once upon that hard surface he got the sixty-two and a half tonne vehicle up to 55kph.

The trees cast long shadows, which closed over the MBT as it entered the pines that covered the feature, its passage shook the trees lining the road and continued to do so until the road sloped upwards and forced the driver to change down.

Mark Venables gripped the edge of the hatch and ducked to avoid a branch, but he did not order the speed slackened off.

The tarmac gave way to gravel and then the Challenger slowed, turning off onto the track that would lead it to the route over the top of Vormundberg.

Pat Reed had found himself in a purely spectator position, up upon the hillside and watching the Czech 23rd MRR coming on in contrast to the Romanians who were fast moving up on either flank. Although the 3 Company CP was close by he had not entered, it had not seemed appropriate to burden that company's commander with his presence, so he and his party stayed outside and observed.

Without the minefield the Czech vehicles advanced confidently, the direct fire support from their fellows in lieu of a standard heavy artillery barrage.

The tank fire from the hillside slackened as the troop attached to the Argyll's withdrew, repositioning themselves to best deal with the Romanians closing on the Scottish regiments positions. As the Czechs closed, the Hussars could no longer engage those in the fore, their barrels were at maximum depression. Those fighting vehicles their guns could still reach were engaged in the same way, a carefully aimed shot followed by a rapid relocation to another firing position. For every round fired by the Chieftains and Challengers they drew the fire of at least three enemy tanks and/or anti-tank launchers.

Tango One Two Charlie, 2 Troops problem child had started off by doing pretty well, its driver treated it with kid gloves and its kill rate had equalled that of the other Chieftain in the troop. When the troop commanders Chieftain was taken out it increased the pressure on the remaining pair of tanks in coping with the mass of targets within the troops arc of responsibility. Soon after that occurred the temperamental gearbox in One Two Charlie started again with the driver experiencing difficulty in changing from forward gears to reverse, and it was also inclined to jump out of gear at high revs.

The inevitable happened after they had destroyed yet another of the elderly T-72s, the rear gears refused to engage, leaving the vehicle exposed to retaliatory fire. The driver had done the only thing possible in the circumstances, with one track locked and the other churning forward he had the tank crabbing around through 180°, cursing the machine loudly for effect as he did so. A sabot round striking the side of the turret and careening away caused the Chieftains young loader to lose control of his bowels. The manoeuvre was nearing completion when they were hit again, this time in the engine compartment where the sabot defeated the armoured covering. The twelve-cylinder Rolls Royce engine absorbed the sabot round's remaining energy and the crew compartment was not breached, but the tank itself was dead, with diesel from severed lines gushing over metal turned white by the sabots impact. Flames were lapping around the turret, and its crew had bailed out, making good use of the smokes cover to gain the safety of the trees. They made their way to 3 Company's CP, on arrival they were unceremoniously bundled into the COs Warrior and sent back to the REME workshop to collect one of the replacement vehicles.

Heavy and medium shell and rocket artillery had been landing on the forward slopes for several minutes but it was not in the proportions that it had been when the battalion had been dug in at Magdeburg.

Pat Reed hated the banshee wail of the rockets; he could quite understand how grown men, trained and experienced soldiers at that, could soil themselves at the sound of one approaching.

He studied the approaching enemy, noting that despite the number of vehicles that were being destroyed there were still more than enough to go around.

Pat started at the sound of a single rifle shot close by and craned his neck to see who was wasting ammunition on armour, but what he saw was Bill and Big Stef lying within a bramble patch just downhill of his own position. The Coldstreamer was peering along the Swiftscope and spotting for the Staff Sergeant who was controlling his breathing as he took aim at his next victim. Pat unzipped his smock and fished out his self-focussing binoculars, which he raised to his eyes, looking in the direction the sniper appeared to be aiming. Several vehicles flitted across his view, all had their hatches firmly shut but then he saw a T-80 with additional antennae marking it as a command tank, and it had an open lid. The top of a head was just visible and he couldn't figure how Bill could consider such an impossible shot to be viable, but then the tank slowed slightly and the front end dipped down into a wide crater, exposing more of the cranium to view. The crack of the shot made him start again but his eyes were on the top of the

Soviet tankers head when the 7.62 round entered it, splashing the inside of the hatch cover with gore.

Pat took his eyes from the binoculars to look down at the snipers in amazement, such an incredible shot deserved some words at the very least, but Stef had already spotted another target and Bill, the last victim forgotten already, was moving his body around slightly, re-setting the placement of elbows and the line of his torso so that the weapon would point naturally at the fresh target.

Pat hunted for the snipers prey, but it was not a company or battalion commander this time.

Peering over the cover of a low bank, a young Czech infantry lieutenant looked for a firing position closer to NATO lines than the one they currently occupied. The BTR-60 he had been riding in had been knocked out but he had been lucky enough to escape along with three of his riflemen. A conscientious officer, he had gathered up other stray troops hiding in ditches amongst whom were numbered two AT-3 Sagger crews, and he had physically dragged these men from hiding places and put them to doing what they had been intended to, attacking the NATO armour. Crewmen and infantrymen who had escaped unscathed, or just a little bit singed in one or two cases from knocked out tanks and fighting vehicles, now became either the security for the Sagger crews, or the mules that carried the reloads. Neither of the anti-tank crews had scored hits yet, but they were contributing considerably to the British Hussars discomfort.

The lieutenant saw a likely spot but before he could indicate it to his men he was forced to roll to one side to avoid being crushed.

Through his sight Bill observed a BMP-3 almost run over the form he had already tagged as being a leader, if not an officer. He let the vehicle pass and lay quite relaxed, as the leader of the group Stef had directed him to send a rifle squad out of cover and across open ground. These men were not yet of any great importance to him and he let them go on unhindered, and it was only after they had dropped into fresh cover that he pulled the rifle butt into his shoulder just that little bit more firmly. The Sagger crews came next, although not both at once and he allowed the first trio to leave cover, burdened down with sights, launcher and a pair of missiles they moved much more slowly than the infantry squad had. Once they were twenty feet from the bank the second crew hauled themselves into view. The second crew was twelve feet from the bank before Bill fired; he worked the bolt, aimed, fired again and again worked the bolt. Six shots rang out with barely over two seconds between each as he first killed the rearmost man before working forwards. The first Sagger crew had still been on their feet, oblivious to the danger they were in and unaware that the second crew were lying sprawled in the mud behind them when Bill shot their gunner. A cry of alarm alerted the leading man who had looked back to see one of his mates face down and the other with a look of surprise on his face. That surprise was turned briefly to shock when Bill's fifth round made a small hole in his helmet, just level with his forehead. The leading man did not have time to begin the dive for the ground that his brain had told him was vital for survival, Bill's last round punched through his sternum and carried on through his chest to exit out the small of his back.

It was with horrified awe that 1CG's commanding officer regarded the sniper, but the staff sergeant was oblivious of the attention, focused as he was on his next target.

Aghast at the way his anti-tank crews had been killed to a man it took the lieutenant a moment to collect his thoughts and decide on his next course of action. His most effective weapons were lying in the mud between himself and the next position he had chosen, and clearly those weapons must be recovered. Acutely aware of the attention of an enemy sniper on this piece of the battlefield he raised his head above the level of the bank for one brief look. No shot rang out and he was able to judge that the wind had been in his face, so although he could not throw a smoke grenade as far as the first crews launcher, someone in the infantry squad across the way, could.

Spread out along the bank, lying on their stomachs, were the men he had designated the role of ammunition carriers, but even though the nearest was only four feet behind him, when he looked back at them he had to shout, loudly, to attract their attention as they seemed reluctant to make eye contact with him.

"Men, make sure you've a hand free because we are going to work in pairs."

Glances were exchanged amongst the men but the young officer continued unabated.

"We are going to have the cover of smoke, and as soon as it has reached this bank you all follow me. When we get to the first sight unit or launcher, the nearest two men grab it and carry on running. We will do the same for all the sights and launchers, ok?"

After a moment's hesitation one of the men spoke what was on all of their minds.

"Well actually sir, that sniper is a bit bloody deadly…is this really a good idea?"

The officer huffed in exasperation.

"I just said that we would have smoke cover, didn't I? He can't shoot what he can't see, so get set now because we go when the smoke arrives."

He gave quick instructions to the NCO in charge of the rifle squad by radio and then readied himself, his fingers dug into the soft earth for leverage and one knee drawn up as he stared fixedly up at the lip of the bank.

Bill had lain for long moments with his sights on the exact spot that he had last seen the leader/officer, his breathing was controlled as Stef told him a smoke grenade had gone off upwind of his aiming point. When the smoke appeared at the edge of his sight picture he took up the first pressure on the trigger and allowed his last breath to slowly escape. He was at the bottom of the breathing cycle as the man-made fog flowed across the bank, and he gentle squeezed, firing without seeing a target and absorbing the kick of the butt into his shoulder. Ejecting the spent case and jacking a fresh round into the chamber he then remained perfectly still, allowing the sights to settle back onto the same spot and waited.

It took over a minute for the grenades smoke to clear, drifting eastwards with the breeze it thinned first to reveal the first two crews with all their equipment, still lying in the mud where they had last been seen. As the smoke cleared downwind it revealed a single motionless figure slumped across the banks lip. Bill lay there for several minutes in the aim, but none of the ammunition bearers appeared.

Pat was not witness to the demise of the Czech officer, the first enemy vehicles had reached 3 Company's forward positions and were driving through 7 Platoon and 8 Platoon apparently unchallenged. The occupants of the trenches were out of sight, awaiting the enemy fighting vehicles presenting their most vulnerable side.

On the reverse slope a fire mission from 3 Companies CP was received by 2 Section, Mortar Platoon, and was quickly converted into a language the No. 1s understood.

"Charge three, elevation eleven zero zero, bearing seventeen thirty...two rounds smoke, normal fire!"

A T-90, Four BTR-60s, two BTR-70s and a pair of T-72 tanks penetrated the platoon positions, driving through toward the ground held by the in-depth platoon. From the firing ports along the sides of the BTRs the troops inside the vehicles kept up a sustained barrage of small arms fire, but there were no NATO troops visible.

Although Pat and the company commanders had covered this eventuality at the O Groups, he still felt uneasy watching enemy fighting vehicles traversing his lines uncontested.

The smoke began to land beyond the platoon positions; it was not a thick screen, not as thick as the screen used earlier to cause the pile-up at the sunken lane, but enough to provide some cover to 7 and 8 Platoons 94mm men.

Shrewd US Paratroopers and British Guardsmen threw smoke, adding a little more cover before they stood up in their firing bays, exposing their backs to the second line of Soviet vehicles.

Sixteen men stood and lifted the bulky weapons onto their shoulders, two were cut down almost immediately by automatic fire coming from firing ports in the BTRs rear troop doors, and one was decapitated by a 23mm cannon shell from the approaching second line.

It had proved difficult for the section and platoon commanders to coordinate and as such there was some duplication effort.

A single 94mm anti-tank round was quite able to destroy a BTR, as indeed the manufacturers claimed it was all that was required to kill any modern main battle tank, but experience had taught the men who used the weapons to fire in salvo's of at least two rockets be sure of knocking out even a T-72.

Both T-72s were hit several times and left stopped and burning, as were five of the BTRs, but the T-90 was hit only once by a hastily aimed shot that hit a track and brought it to a jerky halt without killing it. The surviving BTR-70 was completely overlooked, which gave its commander an insight into their predicament. The infantry section de-bussed, coming out fighting and taking cover in shell craters, of which there was no shortage.

For a few minutes there was an island of resistance within the battalion lines, formed by the BTR, its infantry section, and the crippled tank. Like a proud old bull surrounded by a pride of lions the Czech's kept the British and Americans at bay for a time, but it couldn't last.

Milan rounds fired from 9 Platoon positions, 3 Company's in-depth platoon, took out the both the BTR and the tank whilst 51mm light mortars and L79 grenade launchers pummelled the Czech infantrymen with HE. Shell craters do not offer the same protection as a well dug trench and when 9 Platoon men came forward they found no resistance, just three wounded men and seven very dead ones.

Mark Venables Challenger crested the hill in time to see the second line of Czech vehicles make the same error as the first line.

Keeping infantry inside vehicles only works if your enemy very obligingly present themselves to be shot at from the vehicles ports.

The 23rd MRRs commander watched his second line enter the NATO positions and then smoke obscured his view. On the radio he heard the same shouts of alarm as had come from his leading element, the hammer of automatic weapons drowning out the words and then they too went off the air.

They were under the guns of the NATO tanks now, the Chieftains and Challengers on the hillside above them no longer had any living targets to engage but his regiment now consisted of ten tanks, nineteen BTRs and a handful of AAA vehicles, and that included his own command group vehicles. Not enough to punch their way through the NATO troops holding the high ground between themselves and the autobahns but enough to perhaps establish a foothold, a crack in the NATO line that others could widen.

The NATO troops in the forward trenches were now firing directly at the approaching vehicles, the 94mm LAWs and Milan's killing a T-80 and a further three BTRs.

Taking up his radio handset again he ordered his infantry to debus at 100m from the trenches and fight through the first positions on foot, the tanks and BTRs would provide the gunfire support.

His own tank was travelling behind a T-90 and he ordered them to speed up and close the gap with the last of his regiment, and the T-90 duly accelerated but then came to a crashing halt amid a welter of smoke and flame. The commander's driver swerved to avoid it, and they themselves were hit on top of the engine deck by a TOW missile fired from a Lynx helicopter. The commander was thrown sideways, the force of the impact smashing his face into the RT set and he saw stars for a moment. His gunner brought him back to reality, shaking his shoulders and shouting that they had to get out. His face felt strange and he caught sight of his reflection in the glass covering the radios dials. His nose had a crooked look about it and the lower half of his face was scarlet and shiny with blood. He reached up and threw open the hatch, pulling himself half way out when they were hit again, this time on the turret. He screamed with the incredible pain as he was engulfed in a column of flame that propelled him out of the stricken tank and flinging him twelve feet from it, right in the path of his command groups fast moving ZSU-23-4.

Pat Reed watched the enemy vehicles brake to a halt and disgorge infantry, catching the defenders on the hop as they had again taken refuge in the shelter bays in the expectation of the next line of enemy following the same tactics as the previous ones. The Czech's grenaded three of the trenches, all which were sited to dominate an area of dead ground before the guardsmen and paratroopers realised their error. The Czech's thereby had a toehold to work from. By chance rather than by design the Czechs had their first success in 8 Platoons territory, which slightly overlooked the neighbouring positions in 7 Platoon.

Ownership of the dead ground allowed the Czechs to corral their remaining vehicles in relative safety, tucked out of sight away from 3 Company's anti-tank assets.

The platoon commander of 8 Platoon led a hastily put together counter attack to regain the three trenches, less than five minutes later, and shot through both legs, his platoon sergeant dragged him back to his trench, unceremoniously towing him over the muddy ground by the yoke of his webbing as high velocity rounds cracked past them.

From his viewing point Pat watched the action, his stomach knotting at the sight of the bodies left in the open, which highlighted the attacks failure.

3 Company's commander immediately ordered another counter attack, this time by 9 Platoon with 8 and 7 providing the fire support, but before it could get started the Czechs expanded on their success by attacking and taking a further four of the 8 Platoon fighting positions.

When the 3 Company counter attack did go in it got off to a bad start because the Czechs were now using the captured positions to fire down onto 7 Platoon, so in effect 9 Platoon had only a sections worth of fire support coming from what was left of 8 Platoon.

The Czechs brought forward two of their remaining tanks and a trio of BTRs firing at ranges of less than a hundred and fifty metres at the skirmishing 9 Platoon. The attack was defeated; worse, it had inflicted losses upon 3 Company that brought its ability to hold its remaining territory into serious doubt.

Sergeant Higgins crawled forward and tapped his commanding officer on the shoulder, pointing off to the left and right where the first of the Romanian regiments were now only 600m from the forward NATO positions on Vormundberg's lower slopes and just encountering the largely intact minefields before the Light Infantry and the Highlanders positions. The exhaust trails of anti-tank missiles crisscrossed the battlefield and balls of flame marked their terminus. The Soviet tanks fired on the move and Pat could see the glaring differences between the T-80 and T-90 tanks as opposed to the T-72 when they fired. The self-stabilising guns of the newer tanks pointing unwaveringly at targets despite the rollercoaster drive, and the more numerous, elderly T-72s who's fire had to be for effect only, anything to give the plough tanks a better chance at clearing paths through the minefields.

Lowering his binoculars he edged himself forward out of the shell crater and downhill a few yards in order to get a better look at the ground between 9 Platoon and the piece of hillside he was laying on. It was clear to him that any further attempt to retake the captured positions would be to reinforce defeat, the remnants of 8 Platoon had to pull back and merge with 9 Platoon, and with that done they must provide covering fire that 7 Platoon could withdraw under to then establish a fresh position just in front of 3 Company's CP. He did not have to offer advice though; the company commander gave Major Popham a sitrep before requesting artillery pound on the lost positions as additional cover for 7 and 8 Platoon's withdrawal. It took less than a minute for Zero to call up Three Nine with the result of his request; time of arrival of the first round would be eighteen seconds from the time of the present transmission.

When Pats ears picked up the drone of approaching shells he raised his binoculars, resting on his elbows and stared at the intended target area, but the drone changed to the nerve-jarring shriek that informed those that heard it that they were the target. The ground leapt beneath him, pummelling the air from his lungs again and again and he was aware that he was screaming out loud with fear. One shell, landing closer than the rest, lifted him and deposited in a heap further down the hillside. The world suddenly became silent and even the debris from the still falling shells was landing noiselessly all around him.

Strong hands grabbed him and pulled him under the cover of a slight overhang, Stef was looking into his face and he could see his mouth working but either no words were coming out or the shelling had deafened him. Eventually the ground stopped trembling and the silence was replaced by a high-pitched tone in his ears.

Pat pulled himself to his feet, his head still ringing, and with Bill and Stef assisting him he scrambled unsteadily up the slope to where he had been previously. He gaped at the damage and destruction that had been wrought in so short a time. Where 3 Company's command post had been was now just a hole in the ground, the logs that had helped support its sandbag roof were now splinted and charred, scattered about the immediate area along with shredded sandbags and remains that no longer resembled anything human. Back along the track the Defence Platoons Warrior was lying on its side and burning furiously but there was no sign of the men who had travelled here with him. The two shell craters in which they had been taking cover were now joined together into one elongated hole. All that remained was a Kevlar helmet hanging by a strap from the only remaining limb attached to a still standing but mortally wounded pine tree, a cloth name tape neatly sown to the DPM cover identified the owner simply as 'Higgins'.

The noise in his ears rose in pitch so as to be excruciatingly painful but then it faded, and he could hear the crackle of flames nearby and the crack of tank guns beyond. He flinched at the sound of shells passing overhead, and their detonations on the 8 Platoon positions, which were now in the hands of the enemy.

Turning to the two snipers he gestured at the tree-covered hillside.

"Perhaps we didn't get all of those infiltrators of theirs, I want you two to get up there and track them down..." his voiced petered out because both the snipers were shaking their heads.

"That wasn't Soviet artillery that did this sir, it was our own."

Pat looked confused; not quite grasping what was being said.

"Someone fucked up sir...we got through to the battalion CP and got the guns to adjust their fire, but it was our one five fives that did this."

There was nothing else really to say, except perhaps that sometimes shit happens in war, so the snipers left him then, finding a spot for themselves to the right of where the CP had been so that they could engage anyone attempting to hinder the 3 Company platoons withdrawal.

Pat looked over at the remains of the CP, thinking that whoever had been responsible had well and truly paid for that mistake, but he was now without a company commander or a headquarters staff for 3 Company. It was a cold and clinical way of regarding the death of six of his men in the CP and the ten from Defence Platoon, but grief was an indulgence that must wait.

4 Company were engaging the left flank of the Romanian 112th MRR, the enemy had approached boldly enough up to the point where the sunken lane cut across their axis of advance. The defile was now cluttered with the wreckage of Czech armoured vehicles, many still burning, and the Romanians found themselves in the same position as the 23rd MRR had been at that point. Only a handful of places allowed the vehicles to pass across to the fields on NATO's side of the lane, and the smoke from the Czech vehicles were proving a double-edged sword. It shielded the vehicles on the eastern side from view, but command and control went out of the window. In dribs and drabs the fighting vehicles negotiated the gaps in the lane and attempted to reform in their original unit formations on the far side, where there was no cover that would allow that to happen.

The Hussar's 1 Troop, the helicopter gunships and the Coldstreamers Milan crews selected, and then destroyed, targets with ease until the Romanians in desperation renewed their charge.

4 Company's lines weren't penetrated, the last vehicle of that particular wave was despatched at about the same time as half a dozen 152mm shells landed just west of the lane, delivering a smoke screen that was too thin and too late.

Jim Popham had control of the battalion well in hand and there were no problems on the left of the battalion, but command of 3 Company was another matter.

The young officers commanding the company's three platoons were unsuitable candidates for command of a company, two were too inexperienced and the third was badly wounded. Pat called the battalion CP and ordered his Adjutant to grab a competent radio operator and come forward in a Warrior to take command of the company before changing to the 3 Company net. According to 9 Platoons commander his sergeant was calling in adjustments to the artillery fire and eleven survivors of 8 Platoon, four of them wounded, had made it out and into his location. The seven able bodied had been amalgamated into his call sign and the wounded were being evacuated uphill to where Pat now was. That at least was good news, and he went on to report that although 7 Platoon had been pinned in their trenches, the properly adjusted fires had allowed them time to booby-trap their trenches before withdrawing, and they were now moving to the rear of 9 Platoon in preparation to dig in.

Pat made his way forward and met 7 Platoon; toiling under the burden of not just their own personal kit but boxes of link and extra grenades, 51mm rounds, spare Milan rounds and 94mm LAWs. It was the platoons cache of spare ammunition and all too precious to be abandoned or destroyed in place. The quarried obstacle was drawing curses and the heavy stores had to be passed up, hand over hand, before they could negotiate it, but the men worked together well as a team and it was soon accomplished.

A couple of months before Pat could never have conceived of fully functioning platoons made up of his guardsmen and American paratroopers, the mind sets for one thing were almost alien to one another, and the basic tactics that were second nature to these men of different army's had seemed at odds. Yet here he was looking at Yorkshiremen and Texans, Geordies and Californians who seemed joined at the hip.

Pat's orders were simply for them to dig in, tie in again with the Argyll's platoon on their right and have it all completed ten minutes ago, if not sooner. They got on with it, without undue questions and the very minimum of fuss, which allowed Pat to tag on behind the wounded as he made his way back up slope in the failing light to where Timothy had now arrived to assume command. Below him the artillery fires shifted from the overrun positions to further east, where the next formation of enemy vehicles had appeared. Pat paused for a moment, watching the enemy tanks spilling over the edge of the hill across the valley, driving hard for the valleys floor. There were just so damn many of them that it seemed for every Soviet vehicle they killed another ten appeared in its place. He thought briefly of the battalion his son was attached to, and thanked God that the Soviet's had forced their crossing to the south of the Light Infantry positions. He had enough concerns without having to worry about his son's safety too.

The ex-Adjutant, and now OC 3 Company, extended a hand and pulled Pat up the last couple of feet onto level ground.

"Thank you Timothy, and apology's for dragging you out here but I needed someone with more seasoning than the company subalterns."

Tim had taken stock of the situation and his radio operator was already ensconced in the remains of the CP.

"I'm using this sir." Timothy told his CO.

"It may have no top cover but it is at least below ground level, and of course one dearly hopes that lightning will not strike twice."

Pat nodded his acceptance.

"It's your company now so you do what you must?" The more junior officer shrugged and then after a moment he spoke.

"You realise sir that this is now the weak link in the line, the Hussars can only support us for so long before Soviet infantry start taking them out. I don't have the manpower left to defend them, and we cannot hope to hold out against anything larger than an APC company unsupported?"

"I know that Timothy, and I want you to consider pulling 9 Platoon back level with 7 when their position becomes untenable...it will mean abandoning everything except their personal weapons and fighting order, they couldn't possible pull out in time *and* haul all that stuff up here."

Timothy nodded his agreement and Pat indicated the little spur of ridge they were on.

"Whatever happens, you have to hold here...no more withdrawal beyond here or they will roll up 4 Company from the flank. I am going to pull a couple of men from each section in 1 and 2 Company and form a quick reaction force in Warriors. Jim Popham will command it and I will have him work his way into the trees next to the perimeter with the Argyll's, so shout when you are being most closely pressed and he will hit them in their flank, hopefully breaking their attack." The location in question was on the same contour as the CP and the flattish ground that connected the two places should make for a quick passage along the side of the hill by the vehicles.

There was just enough light for Pat to see his former adjutant grin.

"Don't worry sir, we'll play the anvil to Jim's hammer and kick the bastards back down the hill." With that he hurried down the slope to speak with his platoon commanders before the next enemy formation arrived, pausing only to give a cheerful wave before disappearing into the shadows.

Pat did not know it, but it was the last time he would ever see Timothy alive.

To the rear of Vormundberg, the 8 and 16 tonne Bedford's of the Hussar's logistical support packed up and left the copse, moving forward to the reverse slopes on the orders of Major Venables. In the past two hours the Hussar's squadron had lost a third of their number which made the time spent reloading, and therefore out of action, a critical factor in the defence.

Mark did not know what had happened to the Soviet artillery, he was just glad that it had, because he could now risk moving the pallet loads of main gun rounds into what had previously been one of the enemy gunners main target areas.

On arriving back on the forward slopes he had immediately amalgamated the remnants of No.2 and 3 Troop before sending One Three Bravo to reload.

There was no shortage of prepared firing positions but he preferred to stay as close as possible to the battalions centre, and so chose to sit behind cover and wait for the Romanian 93rd Tank Regiment to come within range. He sat on top of the turret where he could look across the valley, and he tried to ignore the stink of burnt rubber from the charred hulk of One Two Charlie, which sat off to his right with flames still feeding upon it.

Colonel Lužar had received radio orders to disengage all but two companies from the intermittent, yet ordnance-consuming contacts that had begun in the late afternoon. He was to turn around the greater part of his command, prepare to advance to contact back towards the bridgehead, and he had to have it done within an hour. It seemed unreal at first and he had felt the need to ask for clarification not once, but twice.

He had naturally requested an RV with his First Battalion in order to reunite his regiment, along with yet another request for fuel. The first request was rejected out of hand but the second was granted, so he asked for an ammunition replen too, and that was also granted.

He worried for the men he had to leave behind but as night had fallen and the regiment moved out he was consoled with the thought that he had done what he could. He had deliberately selected one of the best company's in the regiment for the least defensible area of the perimeter and had replaced the commander of the second company with his steadiest company commander. It was rough on the replaced man but Lužar wasn't running for the title of 'Most Popular'.

The location given for their rendezvous with the fuel and ammunition trucks was a firebreak in a forestry block, which happened to be half a kilometre from the regiment's current gun line. The commander of the regiment's battery of Akatsia 152mm howitzers was there to meet the regimental commanders' call sign when it arrived. Lužar clambered down to greet the officer but it had quickly become clear that it was not a social call. They strolled to a place out of earshot of the rest of the troops and his officer then gave the real reason for his presence.

"Colonel, my guns are down to their last forty rounds per barrel and the fuel situation has become worrisome. I wouldn't mind if I could get a straight answer from the logisticians as to what the problem is, but I either get bullshit or told it is none of my concern." It was too dark to see his officer's face but from his tone Colonel Lužar assumed that he had been having a frustrating time of it.

"How the hell can they say it is none of my concern? I'm telling you sir if I had the rounds to spare I'd lob a few in their direction!"

The shortage of both fuel and ammunition for the battery was a serious issue, as they were the primary source of artillery fire support for not just the battalion and a half that he had now, but also for the two companies attempting to cover a regimental sized frontage back on the perimeter.

Something serious had gone awry, he was certain of that now, but what he could not do was confide his opinions to his officers and men.

The colonel was able only to promise that he would speak with the commander of the supply unit that was serving them, and try to extract a few gallons for the battery's self-propelled guns and he took his leaving of the artilleryman. It occurred to him that these supply troops may well have information for him too, that they could indeed know the whereabouts of First

Battalion. They may be on detached duty but they were still his men and he could at least find where they were operating, and perhaps even the radio frequencies they were using in order to listen into their fortunes.

At the supply unit commander's vehicle he found the officer constrained by the presence of a colonel of field police who was there to thwart the unauthorised issue of fuel, ammunition or the answers Lužar wanted, but his driver had been more forthcoming. They had fuelled First Battalion after its detachment from the rest of the regiment and the battalion was supposed to have RV'd with them again two hours before, but had never shown up.

The driver confirmed that they had tried and failed to make radio contact and he supplied the frequencies to Colonel Lužar who'd uttered his thanks and left.

His own driver and his gunner were sat on top of the turret looking grim, and as he climbed up to join them he found out why.

"You two look like you are about to open a vein each…what is it now?"

The enlisted men exchanged glances and then his driver spoke

"Fuel sir…"

"Ammunition sir." his gunner interrupted, pausing only to shrug an apology to his crewmate.

"We haven't used that much in the way of main gun rounds but others have, and they didn't get full racks from the replen sir, just four rounds each."

Keeping his features neutral Lužar gestured to his driver to speak, although he knew he wouldn't like what he was about to be told.

"The fuel trucks aren't topping anyone's tanks off sir, they didn't fill us up they're just ensuring we have three quarters of a tank each. It's like the bastards are paying for the stuff out of their own pockets."

It was worse than he'd thought if they hadn't the wherewithal to fully replenish the force they were counting on to put right the wrongs. It had to be the logistics, he reasoned, somehow NATO had compromised the supply lines.

It took time for the ammunition and fuel trucks to visit every remaining vehicle in the regiment. In daylight it was a time consuming business, but at night under tactical conditions of absolutely no naked light to assist the process it was a drawn out process. Eventually of course the replenishment was completed and they moved out of the woods and into open countryside.

According to Colonel Lužar's reckoning they had eighteen miles to cover before reaching the bridgehead, and a tank could drink a lot of fuel covering that distance, so it came as something of a surprise to his battalion and company commanders when he did not choose to rely on a flank guard and forward screen to provide security for the bulk of the regiment so it could use the more fuel economical roads.

43rd MRR moved off the road and into arrowhead formation behind a screen of reconnaissance vehicles and before long everyone from Lieutenant Colonels to lowly private soldiers had caught on to their regimental commanders' mood. They moved in expectation of making contact with the enemy at any time, be it in the shape of a meeting engagement or a prepared defence.

The first indication of what they were up against came half an hour later, the recce screen called up with a sitrep and a map reference that Lužar ordered his driver to make for.

The dark shapes on fire damaged tarmac were all that remained of a convoy of over forty vehicles and Lužar dismounted in order to better investigate. There were no signs of the myriad cratering that would have accompanied an attack using cluster bomb units; a force had ambushed these vehicles on the ground he concluded.

He returned to his vehicle and they continued onwards until coming upon another convoy to have fallen to direct fire from the ground. The vehicles were all burnt out, carrying the scars of bullet and shell but not of the artillery or aerial variety. Shell craters were few. It was the first of many such scenes. More convoys, artillery gun lines, logistics dumps and AAA sites had also fallen victim and the 43rd MRR passed them all.

At ten miles back from the bridgehead they found the first signs of enemy casualties, a burnt out Leopard tank stood at the edge of a turnip field whilst extending away from it into the distance were its killers. They were also dead, killed by the Canadians heavier main gun that would have sent projectiles through their light armour with ease.

Weight of numbers had given the Soviet's a costly victory; accounting for that Leopard, one other and also a trio of TOW equipped vehicles.

It was difficult for Colonel Lužar to describe the emotions he was feeling as he regarded the corpses of BTRs, their crews, and the light tanks that were so easily recognisable due to their flat-topped turrets.

43rd Motor Rifle Regiment had found its missing battalion.

Regimental reconnaissance elements had crossed through the field several minutes before Colonel Lužar and his command group arrived. The armoured recce vehicles leapfrogged forward, moving quickly and efficiently to the next piece of cover, to await the command to resume the advance.

In perfect cover, the Canadian's of the 2nd Mechanised Brigade watched the specialist reconnaissance BTRs cautious movements, and in particular they noted where they disappeared into cover upon crossing the turnip field.

Several minutes went by without further movement. Five minutes became twenty.

"Hello Six Nine, this is Nine, radio check, over?"

2Lt Ferguson was peering down a Swiftscope, a scope previously sited by his platoon sergeant who had ensured the lens was in deep shadow before he had allowed the officer to use it.

The call was repeated twice before a slightly testy note appeared in the voice.

"Hello Six Nine, this is Nine*, radio check, over?"*

A lance corporal nudged the young officer.

"That means you, sir!" he hissed.

"Er, Six Nine okay thanks...over." 2Lt Ferguson saw the NCO shake his head in disbelief, and he cringed inwardly at having screwed up basic voice procedure, and to the commanding officer, of all people.

There was a pause at the other end as the CO wished down a plague of boils upon all 'subbies'.

"Nine okay, sitrep over?"

"Six Nine, no movement, no movement at all, over...oh hang on, I can see someone."

A single figure had appeared, striding across the field. He was wearing camouflage clothing just as soiled and muddy as the concealed Canadians wore, but his steel helmet and uniform was that of the enemy.

Young Ferguson could see him in quite sharp detail through the scope. He walked unconcernedly, empty handed, apparently unarmed, and also in need of a shave and a few square meals.

Six hundred metres distant from Ferguson, the enemy soldier stopped walking but did not take cover; he instead extracted cigarettes from a breast pocket and lit up, staring across at the woodland where the hidden Canadians waited.

With his attention on the lone soldier, Lt Ferguson all but missed the objects flying outwards from the same cover the BTRs had moved into. Smoke belched out, creating a dense screen that hid the enemy vehicles and the lone soldier. The Canadians heard the sound of the eight wheelers reversing.

A breeze carried away the smoke to reveal the enemy soldier once more, and behind him could be glimpsed one of the BTRs, still backing away.

Colonel Lužar finished his cigarette and sent it spinning away with a flick of a finger. He unzipped his smock, pulling out a soft, cloth, uniform cap bearing his regiments badge proudly, at which point he removed his helmet.

Ferguson watched the hatless soldier regard it for a moment, and then to his surprise toss it casually aside.

Pulling the old uniform cap into place, Leo Lužar turned his back on an enemy he knew was out there somewhere, and walked back the way he had come.

Arkansas Valley, Nebraska, USA.

Henry Shaw had become the sounding board for a fair percentage of those in the situation room, as the battle for Germany developed. He maintained a poker face as events across the Atlantic were depicted on the big screen, yet still there were those who would look from the screen to his face to try and divine from his expression how good or bad things were going. Surely they couldn't have thought everything was rosy, when air raids got through and dropped two of the main road bridges across the Rhine and the Weser that 4 Corps was reliant upon to get to the front?

It wasn't all bad news; the data stream from JSTARS was showing a comprehensively beaten Romanian battalion backing away from the British 2nd Battalion Light Infantry, thanks to damn good liaison and teamwork between all the Arms involved, not just that battalion of infantry.

Initially the artillery, tanks, and the attached Lynx and Apache helicopters had allowed the Romanians of the 112th Motor Rifle Regiments tank battalion to cross the valley floor unhindered by themselves, whilst the battered but still defiant parachute companies of the French 2REP, who were dug in to the front of the Brits, had held the enemy's attention. 112th MRR thought they were about to bulldozer the thin line of legionnaires that had been stinging them ever since they had crossed the crest of the east side of the valley. However, at 2000m the British had unleashed a textbook perfect TOT, with every weapon they possessed which had the range. The Romanians ran into a wall of fire from Milan, Hellfire, TOW, 120mm sabot and 155mm improved munitions.

The Legions parachute companies had successfully withdrawn through the Light Infantry and sixty percent of 112th's tank company had been destroyed, the remainder were fleeing and had become entangled with the battalion following on, spoiling the momentum of that units attack and providing the defenders with a target rich environment of armoured fighting vehicles milling about in confusion.

Further east the Canadian and French brigades had done well too, despite some of the critical comments coming from armchair warriors in this very room.

It was perfectly true that looking at the information currently available they could indeed have ranged further west towards the front and destroyed more artillery lines, fuel and ammunition dumps. However, the commanders of those two units did not have the benefit of digitally enhanced hindsight that their critics enjoyed. The commanders on the ground had to take a decision on how far their raiding parties could stretch their luck, before they ran into an armoured force and not just middle aged reservists doling out rations and rounds.

Henry's job today, when he wasn't answering questions from the President, was not to look concerned.

"General Shaw?"

Henry turned from the board and saw that the President was stood away from the main knot of onlookers and had a coffee mug in both hands. There was presently no sign of his physician.

He apparently wanted a word, and in comparative privacy too.

"Mr President?"

"It's looking better, don't you think?...I mean those divisions are totally cut off, boxed in on two sides and 4 Corps was been slowed but not stopped?"

"They can still win, sir."

The President was silent and in thought for a long moment, but he made no attempt to offer the spare mug to Henry.

"By this time tomorrow sir our airborne operation will have begun to degenerate into guerrilla warfare as the paratroops run short of ammunition and anti-tank weapons in particular."

The President winced and Henry was unsure whether it was his words as much as the heat of the coffee mugs burning the President's hand. He relieved the President of one mug and smiled when he saw the printing and logo on the side. However, after taking a sip he continued.

"The French and Canadians at the river have only a small ammunition and fuel reserve. The Soviet's won't have to get creative when they attack them either, there will be no elaborate pincer moves to pin them in place because there is no need, the Elbe is doing that for them anyway. So you see Mr President, it all comes down to Vormundberg and how long they can hold because the centre of that line is creaking under the strain."

The President looked at the plasma screen and the unit symbols where Henry had described.

The President raised his mug in salute; his was a high quality piece of pottery with the crest of the 82nd Airborne upon it.

Henry raised his own mug and clinked it against his commander-in-chiefs, but not too hard because his own was cracked and chipped, a cheap tourist souvenir that someone had probably bought on holiday in London. Henry drank from it proudly though, and looked again at the cheesy depiction on the side, of a soldier in a red tunic and wearing a bearskin complete with red plume.

London.

An energy saving journey, at sometimes painfully slow speeds, had turned a not unpleasant one hour and ten minute train ride from Colchester to London's Liverpool Street into one of purgatory, at three and a half hours duration.

Ray Tessler alighted carefully as he was far from 'mended' and had refused to take any of the offered seats on that overcrowded carriage his travel warrant permitted him to use. Being jostled, albeit it accidentally, had been character building in the extreme.

He was wearing new kit, and it gave off that slightly oniony odour of moth repellent that the MOD treats its uniforms with.

In addition to his aches and pains, Ray was feeling not a little pent up anger.

Held in military custody without charge, he had been questioned on whether or not he had overheard anything that would be of interest to a prosecution counsel in a war crimes trial.

Ray had answered all the questions truthfully. Sorry, but he had not help them. He had not heard anything about anti-personnel mines or prisoners being shot. However, if they would care to ask some questions that would be of interest to a defence counsel?

Ray was issued with new kit and a travel warrant before being sent on his way. He would not be returning to 1CG, he was now a member of 2CG. The 2nd Battalion was at full strength but he had four days leave before reporting for duty. There was a parting shot though, under no circumstances was he to contact anyone within 1CG and he was not to say a word about the questions he had been asked. To do so would tantamount to conspiracy, and grounds for immediate arrest. Did he understand?

Yes, Ray had assured them, he understood completely.

Ray found a pay phone and made a call.

"Hello, Mrs Reed? My name is Ray Tessler, Company Sergeant Major Tessler, and I need to speak to you urgently."

Gansu Province, China:

For the third time in an hour Richard Dewar's force slowly but carefully sank down into a firing positions as the sounds of other troops reached them on the wind.

During their infiltration of this most sensitive of regions of the People's Republic of China he had been concerned at the lack of activity on the ground, as if they had known the combined US/UK force was coming, and had a trap waiting.

What Major Dewar had not known was that the same inclement weather that had for a time grounded the helicopters the PRC were using, had also caught the ground troops without arctic clothing and equipment.

With the arrival of arctic standard lubricants for the aircraft there also came skis, equipment and clothing, bringing a resumption of foot patrolling.

By sheer good fortune the snowfall had resumed before the withdrawing M&AWC had reached the top of the avalanche site, heavy enough for them to be able hear and not see a helicopter land and take off at a spot further along the gully.

Richard had correctly deduced that something heavier than the light reconnaissance machines was putting troops on the ground, reducing the time it would take to resume normal coverage of the security forces area of responsibility because of the snow.

The problem of enemy troops coming across the tracks left in the snow by the American and British troops had been covered without successful resolution in the planning stages. One of the proposals had been for the combined force to wear boots that copied the tread of those issued to the People's Liberation Army, but all of the troops had vetoed that one. With two possible exceptions the British and US personnel all had feet much larger than the Asiatic norms, and besides which no one wanted to walk sixty-eight miles across mountains in brand new boots, the ones they had were broken in and fitted just fine, but thank you for asking anyway!

Richard lay in the snow now alerted by the sound of metal on rock, after which had followed fragmentary snippets of Cantonese, including laughter.

It was something of a relief to Richard, confirming the drop of troops in the area had nothing to do with them, they had not been compromised. A hunter force would hardly be talking, let alone joking around, if they were seeking an insurgent force or saboteurs.

Richard waited for ten minutes after the last sound of the enemy patrol had faded before resuming their march.

With Sergeant McCormack bringing up rear, Richard pushed on as quickly as he felt it safe to do, and hoped that that would be the last such hold up, because if their current rate of travel did not improve they could be for too close to the silos when the bomber force attacked.

Near Saratov, Russia:

Having arisen early Elena Torneski was looking for the first opportunity to leave the underground facility. It should not have been difficult she'd reasoned, because when she had left the Premier's side for her bed, he had been euphoric at the army having crossed the Elbe and establishing a large bridgehead, but so few hours later the cleaners had been summonsed again to mop up gore from the floor of the Premier's office.

Incandescent with rage was a fairly mild description of the Premier's mood, and he hadn't calmed down that much when she had been summoned to explain why the KGB had not foreseen the NATO airborne moves or detected the preparatory build-up. Had her agents in the various western governments been asleep at the switch?

Elena Torneski had left the command chamber with orders to find out why no warning had been received and she had no choice but to report back with answers when she had them.

Those politicians that could be contacted had all given her the same reply that SACEUR had cut them out of the loop so completely that not the vaguest hint had reached their ears.

Strangely, this had served in some ways to placate the Premier who reasoned that if a government no longer fully trusted it's military, and then they would keep a tighter grip on their nuclear weapons, wasting time in unnecessary debate, if and when their Generals asked for them.

The Premier had been toying with the idea of using battlefield nuclear weapons to stop 4 Corps, or smash any last lines of resistance west of the Elbe or possibly even both options. The spectre of a swift NATO reply in kind, which would negate any gains within hours, had of course always made those options too risky, up until now!

The Premier had sent his KGB Chief to wait in the ante room while he considered the possibilities and weighed up the odds, which he would do alone as he held his own General Staff in complete contempt. He did not hold Torneski in the same contempt but he did not ask her opinion on many matters either because she was after all, only a woman.

She knew that the Americans would not launch an ICBM against this facility because the moment a launch was detected the Premier would order a massive counter strike before even learning of where the enemy attack was directed. The Americans would use stealth bombers and for all their high tech wizardry they would still only come during the hours of darkness.

She had memorised when 'last light' would be, and for her own safety she should ideally be at least forty miles upwind of this place by then.

Sat in anteroom for hours, the wall clocks audible *tick-tock* had grown louder as the day had worn on, or so it seemed to her.

Ironically, where it had been General Allain's plan that had thwarted her escape from the Premier's secure hideaway in the morning, it was another part of SACEUR's plan that facilitated her leaving it in the very late afternoon.

The destruction of the ribbon bridges was the deciding factor for the Premier. It wasn't that he was bored of shooting his own military men, he would just rather kill tens of thousands of NATO's men and women instead, and he now believed he could do it with impunity. However, Torneski had been summonsed when reports of the French and Canadian action along the river had been received, and she had thought for a moment that it was her turn for a bullet in the spine.

Although the military held the means to deliver the nuclear weapons, it was State Security, the KGB, who retained the warheads. It was to prevent the military using them to overthrow the government, a sensible precaution really, and the head of that state security left the facility in order to supervise the hand-over of six 5-kiloton air launch SS-N-26 warheads for immediate use.

Seven hundred and fifty-nine kilometres north northwest of the bunker, the last of the camouflage was being cleared from the runway and secured, lest any should be sucked into the F-117Xs air intakes.

Patricia had run diagnostics on the aeroplanes systems hours before, and also on their ordnance, getting a red light on an AMRAAM self-guidance board, meaning that it may fail to guide onto the target without the Nighthawk illuminating its target for it, but otherwise finding they were good to go.

With her job done there she had managed to catch a few hours of sleep, waking in the failing light.

Not finding either Caroline or Svetlana in the command bunker she had been about to make her way through the dark woods, back to the Nighthawk, when she had been stopped by one of the Green Berets and given both the password and a warning to stick to the established paths with an ear open for a challenge by sentries.

She had returned to the command post where an update had been received on the progress of the bomber forces roundabout route. The attacks, although the targets were over four thousand kilometres apart, had to be simultaneous. No one involved at the sharp end of the operations had been told of the mission at sea, but as intelligent, reasoning individuals it would not have surprised any of them that the mission had a briny side to it. Take-off time was advanced by twenty minutes due to a tail wind the bombers were experiencing.

They had time for a leisurely meal of MREs and then a last check was made of the runways surface by troops wearing PNGs before Patricia and Caroline climbed aboard the Nighthawk.

The take-off went without technical hitches of any kind; the aircraft easily cleared the trees at the runways end before turning onto the heading for their first leg, unaware that they had compromised the presence of the landing field for all time.

In order to move more quickly from one area of the cordon to the other the deputy commander of Militia Sub-District 178 had decided to cut the corners, using the tracks through the forest.

The map he was using had not been updated for thirty years so he had taken it cautiously; leaving the mass of metal he was travelling in to frequently check his compass.

He had approached the airstrip from almost the opposite direction to that of painfully shambolic advance his superior was leading, and the engine sounds from the Nighthawk prevented the nearest Green Beret listening post from hearing the fighting vehicle draw close.

The deputy commander was checking his compass when he recognised the sound of a jet aircraft running its engines up prior to its take-off run, and then two minutes later the aircraft passed just a hundred feet above his head, a shadow that briefly eclipsed the backdrop of stars in its passing.

41" 29' N, 171" 17' E.

There was a definite sense of tension growing within the confines of the pressure hull that had nothing to do with the barometric scale, thought HMS *Hood*'s captain. Each of the allied hunter-killer's had in turn dropped back to a distance where they could safely creep toward the surface unheard by their prey, and deploy floating antennae's before returning to station, fully briefed in what was required.

The captain had briefed the department heads and they in turn had informed each member of the crew that the long days tiptoeing along ended today, but only a successful conclusion to the stalk could influence the direction of the war in their favour.

The captain had done the rounds, looking into the faces and eyes of teenage ratings that had reached maturity in outlook in the space of weeks rather than years. It was not that long ago that he would have witnessed a disgruntled crew had he announced then that despite their hard work and skill in locating the enemy boomer, another vessel would be carrying out the attack.

The war was not one of point scoring for these young men, they didn't care who fired the final shot, they just wanted it over with and their homes and loved ones safe again.

The time of the attack had not been widely announced, and yet within a very short space of time it had been common knowledge. The closer the hour drew near, the more palpable the feeling in the air.

The captain had dealt with the pressure in a manner he had discovered years before, and it had never failed. The monotony of clearing the administrative back-log, writing annual personnel assessments and a report on this vessel, which had been launched less than a year before wiped away all tension, drowning it in the necessity of creative and analytical thought. Did he think the standard of her construction met Royal Navy requirements? *Absolutely!* He had typed.

So engrossed was the Captain with his department chiefs reports into the their subordinates abilities and how these could be improved upon even more, that it took a call from the control room to bring him back to the here and now.

It was fifteen minutes before the ordered time of attack when he entered the control room and he noticed straightaway that there were several off watch personnel present.

"Gent's." he said in a low voice.

"This is the control room of one of Her Majesty's warships, not the terraces of a football stadium and as we are now going to quietly assume action stations you need to be elsewhere, clear?"

He first checked the time, ten minutes to go, and then the plot, which showed the Chinese boomer still half encircled by themselves and the three US submarines. His Number One had the watch and all was as it should be.

"Captain, sir?" he turned in the direction of the voice, towards the sonar department where one of the operators was sat with a slight frown.

"Yes, what is it?"

The operator had apparently heard something because he did not immediately reply, he was still facing his captain but his eyes were focussed elsewhere. After a moment the blank expression disappeared and the young man spoke about what had occurred, and why that concerned him.

"Sir, mechanical noises roughly on a bearing of Two Nine Nine." The captain knew without looking back at the plot that the USS *Santa Fe*, the designated shooter for the imminent attack lay in that direction, but the operator was not finished. "They are very faint but...but a little louder than I would expec......." Some further faint noise interrupted him momentarily but he had no difficulty in identifying it.

"Bow doors opening, sir"

There was still six minutes to go, and the captain was about to query what he had just been told but a look of alarm appeared on the sonar operator's face and was then voiced in his report.

"*TorpedoTorpedoTorpedo*....two...three, now four torpedoes in the water *astern of the Santa Fe, captain!*"

Another operator spoke up.

"*Santa Fe* launching noisemakers and increasing speed sir.........the boomers heard it, she's spooling up too, captain!"

Of course she damn well heard it, the captain though bitterly, they'd have to be under sedation to miss it.

"Captain?" his First Lieutenant had an expression on his face that clearly read 'What the *fuck* just happened?'

"It's the mysteriously absent *Chuntian*, Number One, she is missing no longer."

If the captain had to theorise then it would be that she had been off station on some mission of importance and on her way back she must have rumbled the NATO vessels, flooded her tubes out of earshot and then crept back in to make her attack. There was no way that she could know what the flotilla of western submarines had intended on doing in just a few scant minutes, but as a spoiling attack the Chinese captain couldn't have chosen a better moment even if he'd planned it.

The sonar operators were feeding information to the control room, tracking the torpedoes and the other vessels, "Captain, the first two torpedoes are closing rapidly on the *Santa Fe* and the other two have acquired the USS *Columbia*."

"The first weapons have begun rapid pinging and are accelerating for the *Santa Fe*...two more weapons launched captain, these have just turned to the north, they're steering for the *Tucson* sir, they knew where she was too."

The *Chuntian* had to have made her approach from the northwest, the captain mused to himself, because she must surely have heard *Hood* from any other direction. *Columbia* had been between the British and Chinese attack submarines, masking them from one another.

Tucson turned away from the approaching weapons and her blade count rose considerably whilst closer to home the *Santa Fe* released another noisemaker and began a radical turn to starboard but only one of the Chinese torpedoes went for it. The other ignored the newly activated counter measure and although it was travelling too fast to match the US submarines turn it did not matter. The weapons proximity fuse triggered at twelve feet from the vessels stern casing, plates buckled inwards and the seams between them parted, flooding the submarines engine compartment in just seven seconds. Her captain ordered crash surface but before air could be pumped into the ballast tanks the second weapon having swept through the bubble cloud and reacquired, struck the base of the sail and exploded.

Hood's captain looked at the control room clock and noted bitterly that the second hand was only just sweeping around in its first full circle since his sonar department had alerted him. Just sixty-one seconds ago the one hundred forty strong crew of *Santa Fe* had been alive and as blissfully oblivious to their peril as everyone else on the western vessels.

The board told him that *Columbia* was between themselves and the *Chuntian*, so the *Hood* could not fire without the risk of hitting the American Los Angeles class vessel unless one of two things happened, they manoeuvred into a position where a shot would not endanger the friendly vessel, or...

The second option occurred even as the captain was thinking it.

"Control Room, sonar...explosion on the *Columbia's* bearing...sound of bulkheads buckling and general breaking up noises."

The captain felt a void open in the pit of his stomach. Another vessel and her crew gone, just like that!

"Sonar...what is the *Xia* doing? I want you to keep on her because if you lose her we are up the proverbial without a paddle, clear?"

"Aye aye, sir!"

"Weapons...do you have a solution on the *Xia*?"

His weapons officer had been working on a firing solution on the newly arrived PLAN attack submarine and the captain's question took him unawares. The captain read that on his face. "As soon as you have a solution on *Chuntian* launch two Spearfish at five second intervals. That should keep those Chinese on their toes and buy the *Tucson* a little breathing space but cut the wires once number two is away." He explained.

"Our friends are on their own for the time being but that boomer cannot be allowed to slip away...we may have a slim advantage in that neither PLAN vessel is apparently aware we are here, that of course will change once we launch though."

"Captain, sonar...aspect change on Xia, sir?"

The weapons officer got busy and the captain turned his attention back to the sonar department, looking at his watch as he did so, barely a minute had passed since the *Chuntian* had appeared so the only surprising thing about the *Xia*'s reaction was that it hadn't happened several vital seconds before.

"Go, sonar?"

*"*Xia *still increasing turns, now at twelve knots and rising...vessel coming around to starboard...now heading zero seven seven, sir."*

The Chinese ballistic missile submarine was turning across the *Hood*'s bow, a clear confirmation that the Boomer was unaware of them but then the hull rang as the *Xia*'s sonar went active, sending out several pounding beats of sound to check who else was in the neighbourhood.

"That's torn it." muttered his Number One.

"It helps with our solution though."

The *Xia*'s helm went back over as soon as she detected the *Hood*. She came around to a course leading directly away from the Royal Navy submarine.

"Captain, we have solutions on both vessels."

He nodded, pausing for a moment to question his own tactics before deciding that they were indeed correct.

"Bring us up to fifteen knots on a heading of zero one eight, assign one and two to the *Chuntian*, three and four to the *Xia* but do not cut the wires on three and four, we'll guide as long as we can, however, reload one and two with Spearfish straight away." In the background his orders were repeated aloud and he stood calmly, allowing the vessel to respond as ordered.

The deck tilted beneath his feet before levelling as the required heading was achieved.

"Captain, heading is now zero one eight at fifteen knots."

"Very good, flood one through four, open outer doors and shoot."

As soon as the weapons were away he turned his attention towards the engagement between the *Chuntian* and the *Tucson*, the US vessel was defensive and had launched two weapons at the Chinese vessel whilst running from the torpedoes that were homing on them. The *Tucson*'s weapons were not under guidance from the weapons operators, she had cut the wires and reloaded straight away so the weapons were pinging and therefore visible to the enemy vessel. It is far easier to avoid a threat you can see than one you cannot, as the case would have been had operators been guiding the weapon.

HMS *Hood* would guide her weapons in using the information available to the Royal Navy weapons operators, and although her captain doubted they could steer them all the way unseen it was the best he could do for the American vessel at present.

Ahead of them the *Xia* was still building speed when she released a whole series of noisemakers, the sound of her screw disappeared as the *Hood*'s sonar's were drenched with the counter measures masking sound.

As the information on the boomers movements tailed off to nothingness the captain moved from the weapons operator's positions to that of the sonar department.

"What's she doing?"

Several minutes had now elapsed since the *Xia* had launched the first noisemaker and that device had just ceased to produce gas bubbles, it was now sinking silently toward the distant ocean floor.

"Sorry sir, too much racket." The operator made some fine adjustments but then gave a half shake of the head.

"Nothing at all, she's kept the noisemakers between us to hide, sir."

That wasn't too smart thought the captain, carrying on in a straight line wasn't hiding because they knew her heading, unless...

"Come right to One Three Zero...standby countermeasures!"

The weapons officers turned in his seat to pose a question. "A hard turn might cut the wires captain, shall I do that anyway?"

"No, not at present Gavin, I am actually trying to prevent that from becoming necessary."

His weapons officer did not understand, but then a sonar operator enlightened everyone except the captain who had already guessed correctly.

"*TorpedoTorpedoTorpedo*...high speed screws bearing zero one two. Two torpedoes just emerging from the bubble cloud!"

"Launch counter measures...bring us up to two hundred feet but keep this heading." The captain looked over at his weapons officer who was wondering just how his captain had known the Chinese had launched weapons directly back the way they had come.

"It's what I would have done in his shoes, Gavin."

With *Hood* heading towards the noisy surface of the ocean the Chinese torpedoes went for the *Hood*'s noisemakers.

Hood's own torpedoes stayed under their operators control as they entered the bubble cloud created by the *Xia*'s counter measure, the operators used the torpedoes as an extension of their hydrophones although the Spearfish systems were nowhere as sensitive as the submarines sensors. They waited in anticipation of regaining contact with the Chinese ballistic missile submarine but as the torpedoes emerged out of the bubbles into clear water once more they only detected another cloud of bubbles ahead.

"What speed was the *Xia* making when contact was lost?" the captain enquired.

"Twenty four knots, sir." His Number One stated. "There was no indication that she was slowing or had finished accelerating."

"Humph!" The captain exclaimed disparagingly.

"Our intelligence sources stated her top speed was only twenty two knots."

The *Hood* was still making fifteen knots, a long way from her best speed but any faster would certainly ensure the control wires to the Spearfish would break.

"She's drawing away captain, do we increase speed?"

With a shake of the head the captain dismissed the idea.

"I think perhaps that is what he wants." Turning to the helmsmen he gave brief instructions.

"Come left again to Zero One Eight but maintain this depth and speed." He was trying to put himself in the opposing captain's head, trying to predict where the boomer would be in five minutes time but he couldn't allow himself to get tunnel vision. "Sonar?"

"Yes, captain?"

"What's going on with the *Tucson* and *Chuntian*?"

"Captain the Chuntian *is bearing three one one, heading two eight four at twenty four knots, range six thousand three hundred metres, depth two four five, ...the* Tucson *bearing three five zero, heading zero at thirty one knots, range twelve thousand, depth four zero zero sir."*

That was good, the Chinese attack submarine was running from the Spearfish but she would now know that her charge was in peril from the *Hood*.

The commanding officer of Her Majesty's Submarine *Hood* had an easier job of putting himself in the place of the *Chuntian*'s captain, he'd be getting out of the way of the

Spearfish and then coming after the Royal Navy submarine with all guns blazing.

"Are one and two reloaded?"

His weapons officer nodded and replied. "Yes sir, thirty seconds ago."

It was another minute before their torpedoes entered the bubble cloud created by the last series of noisemakers the *Xia* had dumped in its wake, but this time on passing through to the other side the operators could hear distinct propeller noises, as blades churned away at the ocean at the same depth and heading as previously detected.

"Contact re-established captain, she's making turns for twenty seven knots, bearing zero one eight, heading same, range four thousand two hundred!"

The captain felt a flush of relief; an awful doubt had existed in his gut that the big missile boat would simply have vanished. He glanced at the board, the range to the target that had been given was from torpedo number one and he added the distance from *Hood* to that weapon, six thousand nine hundred metres.

"Weapons, go active on both torpedoes, accelerate them and cut the wires."

"Aye aye sir, going active on weapons one and two...accelerating and cutting the wires...closing bow doors for reload of tubes three and four captain."

"Very good...keep this heading and give me thirty four knots for two minutes."

"Aye sir, maintaining heading of zero one eight and making turns for thirty four knots for two minutes."

The captain paused to allow his orders to be carried out, feeling a vibration in the deck as the *Hood*'s single screw began thrusting the vessel through the water at its maximum speed.

As the submarines speed increased the sonar reception deteriorated and with nothing to listen for in real time a leading sonarman took the opportunity to rewind the recent recording of the *Xia* and analyse it with a practiced ear. He knew the intelligence assessment on its speed and as that was clearly in error he sought for some clue to the secret of its true performance. A discovery came swiftly, but not to the question he had set.

Filtering out the sound of the pounding screws he listened keenly to the sound of the vessels reactor pump and then to an earlier recording.

"Captain, sonar!"

The captain approached the leading sonarman's station where a set of headphones was offered.

"Yes, Kentleigh?" the captain placed one headphone against his right ear and enquired. "Exactly what am I listening to?"

"That's a recording taken four days ago of the *Xia* with all but the sound of her reactors high pressure pump filtered out."

The captain listened to a slow and faint noise that sounded rather like asthmatic wheezing. He nodded to the sonarman who pressed a key on the workstation in front of him. He heard a metallic click in the earpiece as the soundtracks were switched and then the same rhythmic wheeze; he listened hard and concluded that it was the same.

"Okay I'll bite, what's your point?"

"Sir, the second recording is only five minutes old."

The self-discipline that the captain exercised at all times in front of the crew almost, *almost*, snapped. The sound of the high-pressure pump operating on a vessel travelling at only three knots could never ever sound the same as one working flat out.

"Come left to zero degrees and make your speed three knots." He ordered before patting Kentleigh on the shoulder. "It seems that the Peoples Republic have themselves quite an effective submarine decoy which we knew nothing of before, well done."

As *Hood*'s speed dropped off the sonar department sought to re-establish contact, the operators listening for some give-away noise amid the natural hubbub of the Pacific that could only be man-made.

Of the *Tucson* there was no trace, the US attack submarine had defeated the weapons sent against it and gone quiet, shrouding itself in silence as it began a stalk of the killer of its sister ships but she was now miles away and of no immediate assistance to HMS *Hood*.

They knew the *Xia* could not be far away, and in fact she had stopped running and launched a torpedo shaped Ghost Lamp, a pre-programmed decoy that was designed to emit sound waves that exactly mimicked its parent. The *Xia* had as a sensible precaution a Ghost Lamp programmed to run at their own top speed and loaded at all times in a torpedo tube where it required only the tube to be flooded and the bows doors opened. This Ghost Lamp had promptly failed, leaving a trail of bubbles behind as it sank into the stygian darkness below the boomer.

A second Ghost Lamp had been hurriedly prepared and launched, emitting an *almost* identical acoustic signature to that of the *Xia*. The Chinese weapons officer, working furiously at his console, had only moments to load the necessary sound files into the decoys memory, and he had patched and pasted quite literally the first available 'pump noise' file in the *Xia*'s sonar history library.

Xia herself had gone deep behind the cover of her noisy countermeasures and reduced her speed to a slow walk, listening with satisfaction to the western attack submarine thundering past in pursuit.

HMS *Hood*'s sonar department listened to the mournful pinging from west, northwest of two of their torpedoes as they swam zigzag courses in an effort to reacquire the *Chuntian*. They noted grimly an explosion to the north, northeast as a Spearfish silenced the Ghost Lamp that had suckered them in for a while, and they recognised the *Chuntian* as she headed their way at ten knots, too slow to be waking the neighbourhood but not slow enough to avoid detection by a western sonar suite. *Chuntian*'s solid fix on Hood's position had faded as the British submarine lost way and her captain was desperate to re-establish contact. Coming in at ten knots would allow his own sonar operators to work whilst hopefully prompting a reaction from the *Hood*.

The British captain ordered another course change once three knots had been achieved, bringing the vessel right around to a heading of Two Seven Zero because he was certain that they had overshot the Chinese missile boat, but that was the only factor he was certain of.

"If you were the boomer then where would you be, Kentleigh?"

The operator took a moment to answer, consulting the details he brought up on the screen before responding.

"There's a thermal layer another two hundred feet below us, I'd be under that by a good margin, sir."

The captain considered it.

"Okay, and on what heading?"

"In the opposite direction to the one we were on." Kentleigh replied.

"I'd want to get as much distance as possible between us."

The Leading Sonarman had answered with a calm confidence and the captain decided to run with it.

"Come left again to One Nine Eight...make your depth seven hundred feet and take us there *slowly*."

The Hood turned onto the ordered heading even as she sank away from the light of the surface above her. She had not reached the required depth when the sonar department reported again.

"Captain, sonar...aspect change on the *Chuntian*, now making turns for twenty eight knots."

"Range, bearing, course and depth?" he asked.

"Sorry sir we are in the layer now so there's nothing consistent on the panel." The captain understood, the thermal layer made accurate sonar readings impossible on anything on the opposite side.

His Number One stepped close, speaking in a low voice so as not to distract the crewmen's concentration.

"What do you think sir, she can't have heard us?"

"No I don't think so, although I think her sonar suite is an *awful lot better* than intelligence gave it credit for I reckon she is dangling herself as bait to try and tempt us into launching on her, thereby giving away a position that she and the *Xia* can both launch on."

"And if we don't fire on her..." his Number One mused. "....they get to close the engagement range, considerably."

The captain nodded in agreement and spent a second longer in thought before reaching a decision and clapping his second in command on the back.

"There is another course of action we can take that they don't seem to have considered though."

"Sir?"

"We are resigning from the *Silent Service*, forthwith." He laughed at his Number Ones expression and then turned to address the control room.

"In a few seconds we will be below the thermal layer, I want the Spearfish in tubes one and two readied for shots at the *Chuntian* and three for a snap shot at the *Xia*...the Spearfish in tube four will also be for the *Xia* once a proper solution is worked out...so let us take advantage of the layer while we have it and open bow doors."

Behind him the Weapons Officer instructed the Torpedo Room to flood tubes one, two and three and open the outer doors. All eyes were on the captain, whose own were directed at the sonar operator he was stood beside.

Anticipation has a way of stretching time, and like the track runner in the blocks who knows the seconds between the words "Get set." and the starters gun, can seem as long as minutes, so the officers and ratings felt time slow down.

At last Kentleigh nodded emphatically

"Clear of the layer sir."

"Thank you." The captain raised his voice.

"Go active on the sonar, three pulses only and standby torpedoes."

Had the *Chuntian* been moving at a stealthy three knots she could have locked down the Royal Navy submarines position to within two feet when the waves of active sonar pounded out, but she was at flank speed and was therefore aware of the sources approximate direction only, and she would not even know for certain she had been launched on until she slowed, so her captain ordered his vessel to come back to ten knots, finishing the sprint well short of where he had originally planned.

The *Xia* on the other hand did the opposite, she was like a burglar tiptoeing towards a house over the back garden in the dead of night when suddenly the security lights come on, she froze for a heartbeat and then bolted, but at 7000 tons submerged that description was in rather relative terms.

"Contact bearing one eight zero, range seven four zero zero, depth eight zero zero."

The operator had only reported a sonar echo reported the position of something large enough to reflect sound waves back at them, something large like a whale, a large school of fish or a submarine. There were no allied submarines in the area apart from the Tucson and she was too far north at the moment.

"Tube Three, match bearings and shoot."

A slight tremble through the deck plates evidenced the launch and lights on the Weapons Officers panel confirmed the fact.

"Weapon running correctly, sir."

"Thank you...sonar?"

"Sir?"

"Tell me about the *Chuntian*?"

"Sir, bearing two nine eight, heading one seven zero, range nine thousand, speed twenty four knots and slowing, depth four nine zero...five zero five, she's joining us below the layer sir."

"Tubes One and Two then please, while she's still too fast to hear the launch...shoot!"

Again, the vibrations in the deck plate, and confirmation of the weapons status a moment later.

"Captain, we have a solution on the *Xia.* Bearing one eight zero on a heading of one seven nine, range seven three nine zero, depth eight zero zero, speed nine knots and rising?"

He nodded in acknowledgement.

"Very good...runtime on weapon number three please?"

"Fifty five seconds, sir."

Looking at his wristwatch the captain allowed the second hand to progress another twenty seconds, he knew the *Xia* would launch counter measures and he was hoping the interval would be sufficient to ensure that both weapons were not foxed by the same noisemaker.

"Tube four, match bearings and shoot."

For the fourth time in less than a minute and a half the vessel vibrated slightly as compressed air boosted a torpedo out into the open water. The Spearfish torpedo accelerated into the blackness of the Pacific's depths steered toward its target by impulses travelling along the wafer thin cable that unravelled behind it. Its own sensor package was in standby mode as a weapons operator aboard the *Hood* sent guidance instructions that placed the weapon in a tail chase with the fleeing ballistic missile submarine. The Spearfish from tube four was kilometres behind the *Xia* but like tubes three's weapon ahead of it; it was outpacing the big submarine. *Hood*'s captain was quite happy for the *Xia* to keep going as it was in a straight line as fast as it could, his operators had steered both Spearfish into her six o'clock, every submarines blind spot.

There was little for him do now except wait for something happen.

He took a look around the control room at his officers and ratings, all of whom were hard at their own particular trades. He wondered if any of them knew that the outcome of the war could quite possibly rest in their hands? They were all far too busy to stop and think of the consequences of failure.

"Captain, sonar..." it was time to get back to work. *"....aspect change on Xia, course change fifteen degrees to port, now heading one six four."*

So the *Xia*'s captain had turned to allow his sonar to look behind. They would run now to their best speed and begin chucking out countermeasures.

"Very good...come left to one seven zero, maintain this depth and speed, please."

"Aye aye, coming left to one seven zero, maintaining depth and speed, sir."

"Captain, weapons?"

"Go ahead 'Weps'?"

"Sorry captain, weapon three is now showing a red light."

At fifteen knots he would not have been surprised if at least one wire had snapped due to the additional stresses, but that was not what the weapons operator was reporting.

"What is the nature of the fault?" he demanded, wanting further information before he would order another weapon launched.

"Sir, the system is telling me it is a non-specified error...sir, I now have a green light once more."

The captain did not immediately respond as he considered cutting the weapon loose anyway. There was a lot riding on this attack and it was not something he could allow to pass without considering the odds. Had the *Hood* been built with six tubes he would indeed have ordered a further weapon launched at the *Xia*, but it only had four and they were all in use.

"Thank you weapons, if the error repeats itself on that Spearfish cut the wire and reload immediately, understood?"

"Aye aye, captain."

No sooner had that operator finished then a sonar operator was calling for his attention. Weapon four had eaten up the distance now and the PLAN crew was reacting.

*"Captain, sonar...*Xia *launching countermeasures and coming right to two one three."*

"Thank you sonar...Weapons, status of weapon four please?"

"Sir, weapon four running correctly and now twelve hundred metres from the *Xia*."

It was time to accelerate the spearfish. "Increase speed on both weapons please but retain control."

Ahead of them the Chinese boomer as if hearing his words launched two torpedoes of its own before ejecting more countermeasures and making a radical turn to port.

The weapons operator controlling number four steered the Spearfish around to follow the turn whilst number threes operator used the opportunity to make up distance by cutting the corner, steering straight toward the vessel.

The *Xia* reversed its turn and number fours operator cursed under his breath.

"Sir, the wire to number four has broken, but the weapon is guiding independently."

"Very good..." Any relief he felt on the assurance that weapon four was guiding began to wilt with the next report.

"Control room, sonar...Xia has launched another decoy."

The captain just knew what was coming next.

"Captain, weapon four is rapid pinging...weapon four is accelerating and *tracking the decoy,* sir."

The plot showed the *Xia* continuing its starboard turn whilst the decoy continued straight ahead, with the Spearfish from tube four completely fooled and closing rapidly.

"Status on weapon three, please?"

"Weapon three is still under control and closing on the *Xia*, captain."

"Control room, sonar...explosion bearing one nine seven, weapon four has destroyed the decoy...captain please be advised the weapons from the Xia *appear to be steering independently on a heading of zero three zero, and we are currently outside of their detection sphere."*

That at least was some good news; they would not have to risk losing contact in manoeuvring to avoid the *Xia*'s torpedoes.

"TorpedoTorpedoTorpedo...two weapons in the water bearing three one zero, range seven five zero zero, heading one six five, speed forty five knots...*Chuntian* has opened fire on us captain."

The captain acknowledged the last report before commenting.

"If he was trying to put us off our stroke he's left it a bit late, and travelling at that speed they will have precious little fuel left when they get close." There was no way that the Chinese attack submarines weapons could influence the outcome now he thought, but they would eat up the intervening distance so he would have to keep a close eye on them.

"Captain, permission to accelerate weapon three and cut the wire?"

"Granted."

The *Xia* began to reverse its turn once more but feinted, turning even harder to starboard and pumping out noisemakers as fast as it could but the Spearfish was too close for them to have generated enough sound in time to register on the weapon.

The Hood's captain watched the plot, the tight turn the boomer was performing and the Spearfish closing at fifty knots, closing until both tracks merged…and then diverged.

"*What the…*"

"Captain, weapon three has failed, sir."

That damn red light earlier the captain thought, cursing himself for not cutting the wire at the time and launching another weapon instead, but it was too late now to waste effort in self-recrimination. The Spearfish continued unwaveringly onwards without any attempt to reacquire its target.

Had the captain been alone he would without doubt have lashed out at some inanimate object, but now was not the time or place.

"Aspect change on the *Xia*, target is now making turns for ten knots, bearing two zero zero, range four nine five zero on a heading of one eight three, depth six eight zero…six seven zero, she's heading up captain."

"Captain, *Chuntian*'s torpedoes have acquired us…impact in two minutes, sir?"

He took a deep breath and dismissed the feeling of unfairness that had briefly invaded his thoughts.

"Thank you…reload tubes three and four with Spearfish, come left to one eight eight and give me turns for twenty knots…standby countermeasures."

"Aye sir, reloading three and four with Spearfish…heading is now one eight eight…making turns for two zero knots…countermeasures loaded and ready, sir."

"Captain, wires have broken on one and two…sonar reports weapon two has acquired the *Chuntian*…Chuntian launching countermeasures and accelerating but maintaining her course and depth."

The captain felt a tinge of respect for the Chuntian's captain, his job was to protect the boomer and he was obviously intent on just that. Heading towards a weapon in the vain hope that noisemakers launched into his vessels wake would distract that weapon was a plan doomed to failure. The attack submarine moving at full speed was far noisier than any gas-generating countermeasure could ever be, but despite this the Chinese commander was trying because there were no other options open to him.

The captain looked towards the weapons board, seeing red lights still shining on the status boards for tubes three and four but he made no comment, knowing that the forward torpedo room troops were the best there was and nobody could do it any faster right now.

"Sonar, status on *Xia* please?"

"Sir, her forward speed is down to five knots but she's going up fast. Depth now two six zero, course same."

"Weapons, reload One and Two with Spearfish as soon as you can, and do you still have a solution on the *Xia*?"

"Yes sir, constantly updating it captain." His weapons officer looked slightly puzzled.

"Is she trying to hide in the surface noise clutter or something, sir?"

The captain gave him a tight smile but one that was totally devoid of humour as he answered with a question of his own. "Think about it a moment Gavin, what would a boomer's launch profile be?"

"Er, probably maintaining an even keel, making no headway at a depth of between sixty and one hundred feet, captain...he's going to launch his missiles, isn't he sir?"

The captain did not answer because just then the red lights on the board turned to green. "Flood Three and Four, open outer doors, match bearings with the *Xia* and shoot."

The torpedoes were launched, and even as they left the tubes every member of the crew heard the first solid *Ping* from one of the *Chuntian*'s fast approaching weapons.

"Launch countermeasures, come left to one five zero at thirty knots, make your depth two zero zero!"

"Control room, sonar...explosion at bearing three one eight...very faint breaking up noises."

On the plot the tracks of the *Chuntian* and *Hood*'s Spearfish had met head on. No one cheered.

The *Chuntian*'s crew may have lost the battle but the *Xia* could still win the war for them.

Hood's captain took hold of the back of the coxswain's seat for support as the deck canted to one side and tilted as the *Hood* headed up to the surface, turning out of the Chinese torpedoes path as she went.

The *Xia* reached one hundred feet below the surface and came to a dead stop. Her bow doors opened and she launched three torpedoes towards the *Hood*, which could plainly be heard now.

In her current stationary state discharging noisemakers would be a futile act, and as she carried no more of the Ghost Lamp decoys it was a race against the Spearfish she could also hear in order to launch her ICBMs.

On a count of three, he and the ships political officer's keys turned in their respective secure weapons panels and initiated a fully automated launch routine. He knew exactly which target each missile was allotted to and what their place was in the launch sequence. If only one missile was launched before the torpedoes struck, the second attack in history on Pearl Harbour would be a thousand times more devastating than the first.

The vibrations resounded through the big Chinese submarine as the outer doors of the launch tubes opened two by two and seawater began to fill the voids around the missile launch canisters sat within.

Aboard the USS *Tucson* they listened to the sound of the battle in full knowledge of what it would mean should HMS *Hood* fail to kill the *Xia* before she launched. They had tracked every torpedo from each vessel from the time they themselves had outrun the weapons *Chuntian* had sent after them. Every twist, turn and feint of the combatants had been recorded and plotted. And never before had the crew of the US submarine felt so totally impotent as when the *Xia* came to a dead stop and opened her launch tube doors.

They heard the distant, double ping of torpedoes own sensors as they acquired and the sound of the weapons propellers become shrill as they drove them at their targets at maximum acceleration. Finally the hammer blows as warheads detonated, followed by the gut churning sound of bulkheads buckling and the sea rushing in.

CHAPTER 8

Gansu Province: Same time.

Colonel Chandler could see sparkles of light ahead of his own force, they seemed to be anything but randomly targeted as there were concentrations at whichever level the aircraft of the Wild Weasel sweep under Dark Light flight were. Each short-lived flash of light represented an exploding shell dispensing expanding clouds of shrapnel.

It was shocking to behold and the colonel who had flown across Baghdad on the first raid of the Gulf War could honestly say that what he now beheld had to be four, maybe even five times heavier than what had been thrown at them on that night.

Searchlights probed the heavens and he could almost pinch himself in order to check he was really here and not watching a WW2 newsreel.

Twenty-eight miles to the east he could see a similar scene in the direction of the airbase and the space centre, but only at the airfield was the attack being pressed without casualties. It was ironic that at the one target where aircraft had passed so close to the gunners that they could make out markings with the naked eye, they were unsuccessful in downing a single one.

The airbase attack opened with B1-Bs dispensing runway cratering weapons and mines along the tarmac, this was carried out at an altitude of just sixty feet.

The Tower, tank farm, and hangars were attacked even as the runway was still being cratered by the B1-Bs submunitions. Laser-guided weapons struck every hanger and this destroyed all but two of the Flankers based on the airfield. Owing to the inclement weather all had been brought in from the dispersal shelters that were open on three sides to the elements and kept in the hangars free of snow and ice. No CAP had been in place due to the extreme remoteness of the location and its distance from the nearest known enemy forces, but instead a pair was kept on permanent runway readiness.

The airbase attack ended with the SAM radars being taken out as they hurriedly came up, and the pair of Flankers stranded at the runways end disappeared in the single explosion caused by a Maverick landing between them.

All the targets on the revised list for the space centre were in hardened shelters that required high altitude attacks with BLU-116s, and these attacks cost them two of the precious B2s to massed 90mm AAA that found the aircraft despite radar having never acquired a solid lock.

Chandler had heard rumours about the Chinese air defence zones, both the fixed and mobile ones. He always figured they were just story's, kind of like the everlasting light bulb and the salt-water combustion engine.

According to the stories that Chandler had heard the Chinese never threw anything away, they had vast warehouses filled with weapons that were maintained religiously, despite their age. From horse drawn Japanese anti-aircraft guns to modern self-propelled, high altitude pieces and latest generation SAMs, they were stored together awaiting a time when they may be needed.

The thing that had convinced Chandler that the stories were nothing more than popular legend had been the claims that the secondary targeting systems were not laser or radar based, but audio. The altitude of the approaching enemy aircraft would be calculated by the sound of their engines, pre-cathode ray style. Pinpoint accuracy would be unnecessary or so the story went, a thousand guns throwing a wall of fire up into the general direction of an aeroplane would more than compensate for the lack of high technology.

Looking at the sky ahead he now knew the tales had not been bar room banter.

The stealth forces trillion dollars' worth of state-of-the-art airframes no longer had the advantage; the playing field had been levelled by weight of numbers and all were being targeted upon the American aircraft using technology from the era of the crew's grandparents.

Ahead of Chandler and the main force there was a flash of light that was larger than all the rest and a moment later a trail of fire was streaming back from a point in the night sky ahead. After a few seconds it angled downwards, gaining in length and girth as the angle increased and the fire spread.

Chandler switched to the Black Light frequency but he did not transmit, he just listened

"...Black Light Zero Four eject...Zero Four eject, eject, eject...come on Jeanette, punch out, get the hell out of there!"

There was no response on the radio and Zero Four's plunge ended abruptly, a ball of flame rising up to mark the crash site.

"Black Lighters from Zero One, did any of you guys see a chute?"

"Zero Two, Negative."

"Zero Three, Negative."

"Black Light Zero One from Spear Gun One, that's a negative from my Lancers too."

There were other fires on the ground that Chandler could see; no doubt some belonged to the other pair of F-117As and the two B1-B Lancers from Spear Gun that had already fallen to AAA.

It was clear that without any further radar sites to take out, his Wild Weasel force was providing nothing more than target practice for the Chinese gunners.

"Ring Master, Ring Master, Black Light One...we're getting murdered here!"

"Black Light this is Ring Master, get your people out of there and standby to hammer any radars that come back up."

He waited for the acknowledging *"Roger"* before ordering the main force into a holding orbit while they were still clear of the silos air defence zone.

Chandler wanted to see what the gunners would do once they realised that there were no more aircraft overhead, he was hoping the fire would slacken.

As Chandler's B2 circled he could see the flames leaping high from over in the east and guessed that the tank farm beside the airbase was the main source. The flames eclipsed any sign of damage that may otherwise have been visible from the space facility. He wished he knew why they had been ordered to attack pointless targets there, the intelligence reports clearly indicated the old vehicle assembly building had become an MT maintenance facility six months before once work on the new and larger assembly building had been completed. The 'solid fuel booster store' they had attacked had been a dummy; they knew that and had seen the photographs of its empty interior during the initial planning stage back on Mindanao. The real storage facility was sited three miles away from the nearest building, where any accident would not cause any damage to the rest of the facility. It said a great deal for his crews that they had pressed home their attacks even though all had known they wouldn't halt the PRC putting satellites up, and wouldn't even delay them beyond the time it would take to clean up.

The AAA protecting the silos did not appear to have slackened off in the slightest and the clock was running, he couldn't afford to delay any further.

He would lay money that a pair of fighters had already scrambled out of Lanzhou with more to follow, but he was far more concerned with the time it would take to launch the ICBMs in the silos which were there primary targets.

The highly corrosive and unstable liquid fuel could only be pumped into the missiles tanks immediately before launch, and the best available intelligence put the time needed for this operation to be anywhere between twenty minutes and two hours.

If Colonel Chandler allowed a minimum of ten minutes for the Chinese Premier to be informed the region was under air attack and to make a decision to launch, then Chandler had only eleven minutes remaining before the ICBMs were launched at their targets, if the lower fuelling figure were to be proved correct.

"Spectre One, Two and Three I want you to gain angels forty, send your activation signals to the RERs and standby…… Spectre Four and Five form on me and follow me up to thirty thousand…….Javelin One, take your aircraft north and standby to make a dummy pass on my word......Fire Arrow Zero Two hook east at twenty thousand and standby also.... " In a very short time he had a plan in place to divide up the massed guns protecting the silos, he had no doubt that it would work because the defenders could not afford *not* to react to approaching aircraft, but would it work enough? He could not afford to unduly risk his own aircraft or Spectre Four and Five because they were the back-up's for the attack, they would break once they had succeeded in drawing fire but the remainder would continue on into the cauldron.

Chandler's aircraft was levelling out when Spectre One reported the successful activation of all six RERs and green lights on all six weapons.

"Roger Spectre One, this will be a simultaneous drop on all six targets just as planned, but I want twice the spacing between aircraft plus a thousand feet of vertical clearance. The rest of us will turn in toward the target to draw some guns our way in thirty seconds time, so you wait twenty seconds longer and begin your runs."

He received three acknowledgements and had time left for a deep breath before banking hard right, bringing the nose around to point toward the silos and opening the throttles all the way.

The sky ahead was receiving a fairly equal share of attention but pretty soon he noticed that change. The bursting shells seemed to home in on his flight level and he pushed the nose down in response, losing five thousand feet before levelling out.

Fire Arrow Zero Two was caught almost immediately by a searchlight, a second later two more locked on, trapping it in a cone of light for all to see and all to shoot at. The F-117As pilot twisted and turned the aircraft in a vain attempt to throw off the searchlights, before rolling and diving for the valley floor. Chandler watched the manoeuvres with trepidation, the Nighthawk isn't built for high-speed aerobatics, and it is not terribly keen on the medium speed variety either. It relies upon stealth rather than the classic fighter aircraft qualities to achieve its mission goals. Pilots who have unwisely tried to throw the aircraft around the sky like some stunt machine have found the F-117A flying away without them, in several different directions at once. The colonel was unable to follow the Nighthawk with his eyes so he did not then know how its pilot fared, but to the west he saw fire in the sky as yet another of his B1-B Lancers fell.

A near miss shook the B2 he was flying and he decided that his flight of three had done all it safely could for now so he ordered them to break off and reform to the south once more.

A SAM radar came up, sweeping the skies with radar energy until a Dark Lighters HARM obliterated the transmitter vehicle. A searchlight passed across Chandler's B2, the glare robbing him of his night vision but then the man-made turbulence ended and they were back in the clear.

Chandler couldn't see Spectre aircraft carrying out the attack but he banked around and peered out into the night sky at where he thought they would be.

"Come on guys and gals" he muttered to himself. "One good run and we can all go ho....."

A 90mm shell pierced the composite belly of Spectre Three and detonated as the rotating dispenser was in the process of cycling the second BLU-116 out of the weapons bay. The B2 disintegrated a bright flare of light in the night sky and then it was gone.

In the central command bunker a quarter of a mile from the line of silos they could neither hear nor feel anything that was going on around them, such was the depth below ground and thickness of the walls, and yet the screech of audible alarms shook the staff there more than the actual sight of five of the silos being destroyed would have done.

The five weapons successfully released had flown true, homing on the splashes of light of a wavelength no human could see unassisted, to penetrate the silo caps and explode inside where the volatile fuel was being pumped into the ICBMs added to the destruction.

The subterranean fuel tanks ruptured and the contents flash ignited causing an over-pressure that wrecked the integrity of the underground structures. The ground buckled, bulged and burst open with a roar, the valley was momentarily lit up like day as the fireballs expended themselves. Slabs of reinforced concrete flew hundreds of yards to smash into the frozen earth whilst the tremors caused by the explosions ventured even further from the sources, radiating outwards like the ripples on the surface of a pond to shake the very walls of the valley.

High above the valley floor on the ridge top the accumulation of snow about Site Six shifted. Its grip with the rock and ice loosened, the mass began to move slowly at first but it was unstoppable now, it gained momentum and swept down towards the edge. The laser designator in its niche was swamped before the weight of snow tore the securing ice screws free and the designator joined just one of many avalanches and rock falls triggered around the valley.

"Was that all six, was that all the silos?"

Colonel Chandler didn't catch the callsign of the person asking the question, the one who asked what they all wanted to know.

"Ringmaster, Spectre One?"

"Go ahead, Spectre Four?"

"I don't know if Three released on silo six, I was looking real hard but I only saw five clear strikes."

"Roger.......Spectre Four this is Ringmaster?"

"Ringmaster, Spectre Four, we just dialled in designator six's freeq, and it's no tone, I say again, negative tone on target six at this time.....resending activation codes......Ringmaster, *negative tone, negative tone,* over."

Chandler was still for a moment, allowing his brain to absorb what must follow. Switching to intercom he spoke, an edge of determination in his voice.

"Send it."

Arkansas Valley, Nebraska, USA

Wild cheering erupted before the message had been completely read out and Henry Shaw shouted for silence. Those giving voice were almost exclusively civilians.

"I will have silence in this room." He growled, glaring at the slower to respond.

"This is a *War Room*, not the bleachers...this thing is not over yet."

The President took the message slip from the signaller and read in silence.

"How many were aboard *Santa Fe* and *Columbia*, Henry?"

A flicker of surprise passed over General Shaw's features, he too was ignorant of the messages entire content.

"I am not entirely sure, perhaps as many as three hundred in total Mr President."

He handed across the message.

"They were ambushed by the missing attack submarine; HMS *Hood* collected both her and the *Xia.*"

Henry read the message himself, trying to recall who, if anyone, he or his son and daughter may have known on the vessels, or perhaps parents whose pride and joy whom they had raised and had such hopes and dreams for were soon to be destroyed by a stranger at the door in uniform.

His thoughts were interrupted by another signaller. A folded message slip held outstretched.

He took it with a nod, opened out the single sheet and read the two words printed upon it.

"Mr President, we have a message from 'Circus' sir"

Circus was the codename for the airstrike on the ICBM silos and the President could tell from his tone, kept professionally neutral, that it was not necessarily one of cheer and victory.

Damn stupid name for a military mission he thought, and not for the first time. He raised an eyebrow and his heart thudded at the response.

"It reads, *Crescent Moon.*"

The crescent, the incomplete circle, a thing not finished.

"Thank you Henry, please send back *Cauldron*......" he paused, remembering something and embarrassed that he may just have sounded callous.

"General, our troops on the ground.....have they had time to withdraw?"

Henry could see that this was important to his commander-in-chief. Tens of thousands were fighting and dying, a global nuclear war could be just minutes away, but he needed this, this gesture, an assurance that his humanity was still intact.

It was unfortunately irrelevant whether or not they were out of danger, because they were just plain out of time. But he did not say that.

"Mr President, Dick Dewar and his men are free and clear, they are miles from the valley by now."

Gansu Province, China: Same time.

The snow fell heavily, creating a visage that would not be out of place in a 'White Christmas' setting if not for the thunder of the massed guns defending the silos echoed throughout the mountains. It masked the sound of heavily laden men whose steps compressed the snow with what would be an easily audible crunching sound, at any other time.

The site of the avalanche was well behind the Royal Marines but they were only midway across the narrow, slanting valley. Only another twenty minutes at their current pace would bring them to the foot of the northern rock wall.

The white thermal facemask worn by Rory Alladay absorbed the moisture he exhaled, preventing the tell-tale fogging that would otherwise result in the cold, frigid conditions.

He was totally exposed on a patch of ground as flat as a billiard table; there was no cover for a hundred paces in any direction. Nothing quite catches the eye like movement and he had been able only to slowly lower himself into a crouch when he had first caught a whiff of tobacco smoke before he recognised the outline of the Chinese soldier in white camouflage gear set against the starkly blank background of the valley floor.

He was close, close enough to hit with a snowball had they been engaged in any less lethal activity and the only thing that had saved Alladay from detection was the Chinese soldier was looking up toward the sound of an aircraft passing unseen overhead.

Rory was scout, or 'walking point' as the Americans would have it, and the remainder of his callsign were moments behind.

"Enemy."

The single word quietly spoken into the boom mike was all that was required to have the M&AWC troops freeze in place before slowly turning to cover their assigned arcs and take up prone firing positions.

The Chinese soldiers head turned as he attempted to discern the aircraft. He was relaxed, his gloved left hand gripped the stock of his compact QBZ-97 assault rifle but the right held a reversed cigarette, its red end masked by the palm of his hand.

He took a long pull, enjoying the nicotine before exhaling and as the sound faded his head turned back.

He started as he caught movement in his peripheral vision, which was followed almost instantly by a momentary difficulty in catching a breath, but the sensation, along with all senses, thought and feeling ended as if a switch had been flicked.

Rory lowered the dead soldier carefully into the snow to ensure silence. The cigarette which had fallen from lifeless fingers sizzled for a half second in the snow and its glow was quenched.

The dark handle of a fighting knife protruded from the juncture of the throat and underside of the mouth. Once the body was laid down Rory braced the dead man's chin with the palm of one hand and withdrew the blade, feeling it scrape on vertebrae as it came free and cleaning it quickly yet thoroughly on the Chinese soldiers clothing. The blade, which he returned to its scabbard, would not be frozen in place by his victim's blood or brain matter when he next needed it.

The question of what the soldier had been doing there, and where the rest of his patrol was, remained. It was obvious he had not come alone to this place, so was he just lost or were his mates nearby?

Richard Dewar's interrupted his thoughts, whispering a question, a requirement for an update.

"Sitrep, over?"

Rory gave the situation report in low tones, without embellishment and included his thoughts. Once complete he collected his bergan from where he had dropped it and took up a prone position beside it, covering the way ahead as Major Dewar brought up the remainder of the M&AWC.

The unnatural light reflected off the clouds distorted the green hues of Rory's night sight as it had his PNG's. His range of vision was increased however and he could make out the end of the flat area as the shapes of a low cluster of snow covered rocks and boulders were now visible.

Looking over his shoulder he could now make out Major Dewar at the head of the well-spaced line of men; it was time for him to move again.

Rising to the kneeling position he heaved the bergan onto his back and put his weapon into his shoulder, swinging the weapon through a 180° arc, staring intently into the sight before standing and stepping off toward the rock in the centre of the cluster.

A bright light shone from beyond the ridges, not a strobe-like explosion but one of sustained duration. It lit the far rock wall and spread downwards to encompass the snow covered floor as the source climbed higher in the sky. After several seconds the sound reached them. Harsh light and noise from boosters providing three hundred thousand pounds of thrust now filled the valley, seemingly little diminished by their distance from the silo.

The rock Rory was walking toward shot him.

Arkansas Valley, Nebraska, USA

A single line of script originating from 'Circus' flashed up on the screen.

'ICBM LAUNCH'

The blinking of a half dozen call lights on telephones began just a heartbeat later.

Henry lifted the telephone receiver before him, depressing the button above urgent light above the button marked 'MDA', Missile Defence Agency.

"This is General Shaw."

Gansu Province, China: Same time.

Richard had been looking off to his left arc when he, and his callsign, had been caught like deer in the proverbial headlights.

The established drill for such a predicament, had they been in Europe, the African bush or even a rain forest would have been to freeze in place and literally 'make like a tree', but here in this narrow, bare valley there were no such items to be mistaken for. To move or to drop into cover was to draw unwanted eyes.

The top of the far valley wall had suddenly lit up and that light increased to encompass them all.

The line of Royal Marine Commandos closed one eye, their sighting eye to preserve night vision, and with the other they made best use of the illumination to study their surrounds without turning their heads, remaining motionless as the roar of rocket motors reached them, a roar that almost but not quite drowned out the single shot that cracked out.

Rory Alladay dropped as if his legs had been cut from beneath him, and none but Rory had seen the firing position. Richard stifled the urge to go immediately to aid a comrade of many years, as quite obviously the rest of the cadre was undiscovered.

The flaming light rose into the night sky and faded. Richard felt gutted that after all they had endured the mission had ultimately failed, an ICBM was in the air, and to make matters even worse a comrade was down.

Slowly the Marines began to edge into an arrowhead formation, one best suited to such situations, allowing the flanks to remain covered but permitting maximum firepower to the front without someone shooting his mate in the backside.

A bang announced the flight of a parachute flare rising from their front and its journey into the heavens was marked by a trail of smoke. With a sharp popping sound the flare came to life above and behind them, silhouetting the marines in its chemical light.

The enemy knew that the one man they had accounted for, Rory Alladay, would not be alone and the view of the canyon floor now differed markedly from less than a minute ago.

From the Chinese point of view the threat was too close in for them to call in mortar, artillery or air support, so the Chinese commander elected a reconnaissance by fire instead.

A wiser commander would have ordered just one of his men to fire at suspicious shapes though, not the whole section.

Muzzle flashes emitted from each of the 'rocks' ahead of them.

Richard was in the process of dropping prone, his ears ringing painfully from the loud cracks of high velocity rounds passing close by, when he was struck a fierce blow on the right side of the chest. He landed hard, the breath driven from him and his right arm numb from shoulder to fingertips.

The weight of his bergan pressed him face first into the snow, smothering him in his suddenly disabled state its sheer weight preventing his lungs from fully inflating. Spots danced before his eyes and he realised the vulnerability of his position. Adrenaline assisted him to roll onto his right side where his left hand could reach the quick release buckle of his bergan. Free of its burden he rolled prone once more with incoming small arms kicking up the snow about him and striking the bulky pack.

Richard's job was to control the fight, not squirm about attracting the incoming but he had to first get himself into a position where he could do that job. The bergan was being used as an aiming point so groping for the pistol grip of his M4 he rolled clear of the bergan and awkwardly brought the weapon up one handed with the intention of putting some rounds down, inaccurate or not, in the general direction of their attackers but he sensed, rather than saw, that something was amiss with the weapon. The weight and balance were all wrong.

Behind him the M&AWC had reacted automatically, beginning the business of winning the fire fight.

The single aimed shots from the professionals, the marines, proving far more effective than what appeared to be 'point and blat' by the opposition.

Richard Dewar used the light from the flare to quickly examine himself, his weapon, and to also see what he could of his enemy.

There was no blood but there were several tears in his arctic whites. The M4 had been wrecked by a round that had struck the body of the weapon but had been deflected off the working parts and exited via the butt. Just a length of decapitated buffer spring was left protruding from where the telescopic butt assembly should have been.

He removed the full magazine and laid the weapon aside, it was useless now, so Richard studied the opposition instead.

Five muzzle flashes were apparent from ahead of them, which he assumed made the Chinese troops of section strength.

An entrenching tool stood upright, visible in the muzzle flash of their squad's automatic weapon which explained what the lone soldier had been doing, supposedly on sentry whilst the rest of his section dug in.

When Richard Dewar had gone down, Sergeant McCormack had immediately taken over, directing the marine's fire. They ganged up on the enemy's squad automatic weapon first before pairing up on the riflemen.

The parachute flare flickered, approaching burnout and a second took its place, but the fading light was good enough to reveal the smoky launch position for Sergeant McCormack to loft a 40mm grenade from his M4s underslung launcher, mortally wounding the Chinese section commander.

Someone threw smoke and someone else unwisely broke for the rear before the smoke had established itself as a temporary cover from view. A flurry of rounds from the marines cut the man down.

Light filled the valley again, a hundred times brighter than the tail flame of the ICBM, and when it faded in intensity it was to take on the reds and gold's normally associated with the beauty of sunsets, reflecting off the side of the valley from its source on the other side of the mountain.

The ground bucked violently, triggering rock falls and avalanches.

Richard knew without looking what the cause was.
With night vision totally shot he shouted a warning, telling his men to brace themselves, and then he gasped in shock and not a little fear.

As if the door of a giant blast furnace had been suddenly opened behind him the snow began to melt and the ice beneath it started to thaw. Richard could hear the sounds of the opposing force bugging out, slipping on the incredibly slick melting surface, crawling backwards, one or two firing random shots into the smoke cover until they judged they were far enough away to try to get up and try to run. Those who made it upright were struck by flying rocky debris, and knocked flat by a blast wave that triggered further rock falls.

Sound accompanied the shock wave, the most terrible blast of noise Richard had ever heard. It fractured the soul in its awful intensity, reducing brave men to trembling shades.

After the blast wave had swept over them and beyond Richard lay for a long, long moments, his thermal clothing soaked in melt water, listening to the clap of doom echoing off the mountain peaks.

"The peaks!" he though in alarm, rolling on his side in a puddle of melt water to look.

"Get up!" he shouted to his men, all prone upon the melting ice, some on their sides, curled into balls hugging their knees with eyes wide with fear.

"Leave the bergens, leave everything but personal weapons, ropes and climbing gear...move!"

Men stirred at his words but two did not, remaining in foetal positions.

Sergeant McCormack rose up onto his knees and looked to his left, up the rising valley towards the centre of the mountain range, at mountains that no longer wore a cap of white.

"Get up and follow the boss if you want to live...get up and *RUN*!" he shouted, reinforcing Major Dewar's words.

Richard crawled forward to where Rory lay.

The reddish glow was diminishing as the fireball dissipated but its light still reflected off Corporal Alladay's left eye, the bullet which killed him having entered the right. Richard removed the ID disks from around the fallen man's neck.

"Sorry Rory."

Atop Rory's Bergen was a coiled 60m rope, held in place with webbing straps and secured with a quick release buckle. Richard took it and also snatched up the M4 that lay beside the body. He stood carefully, and then slipped and slithered as fast as possible towards the rock wall.

The only enemy he could see were laying still or moving feebly.

The closer to the wall he got the more traction he found beneath his feet, the rock dust and debris from above acting like grit on an icy road.

Turning about he saw all of his men up and moving but strung out, although Sergeant McCormack had taken up the tail-end-Charlie position, assisting a limping marine and chivvying along the remainder in that gruff and aggressive Glasgow accent of his.

At the wall of the narrow valley Richard slung the weapon across his shoulders and began to climb rapidly, using the remaining glow by which to see hand and footholds until he came to a rock shelf after thirty metres or so. He just hoped it was high enough.

Lifting his smock to reach his hammer and pitons he furiously drove two into the rock face, grunting with the effort of each blow and quickly attaching himself to them by his harness, clipping a carabiner through the eye of each before hammering a further piton into the rock. He attached one end of Rory's rope through the eye, tied it off and threaded the other end of the rope through a chemical light sticks eye and knotted it. Snapping the light stick, Richard activated it and dropping the rope into the returning darkness. He had no schermoulies to hand; it was Sod's Law of course, just when he could have used the light to provide illumination for his men to climb by, there were two in the left side pocket of his bullet perforated bergen, somewhere out there on the canyon floor and lost to him now.

He braced himself and set the rope about his shoulders, belayed on.

"Make for the light, use the rope as a guide...for fucks sake *CLIMB!*"

The fireball was fading rapidly now, and the fullness of night returned.

With a 'whoosh' a schermoulie climbed into the night, trailing amber sparks behind it and lit with an audible pop. It had been launched from above, from the top of this rock face.

Below him three of his men were climbing, two more had reached its foot whilst Sergeant McCormack and the limping marine were thirty metres away.

He could hear a rumbling from higher up the valley.

Two Chinese soldiers appeared in the light of the para-illum, standing upright with weapons held loosely in their hands. They were looking away from the marines; heads turned towards the noise behind them. They suddenly discarded their weapons, tearing off webbing equipment and scrambling across the ice towards the dangling rope.

The first of Richards men reached him, breathing heavily and perspiring, he did not pause but instead he too pounded a piton into the rock face and belayed himself on, dropping his own rope to assist his mates.

Vibration joined the sound now, and Richard was shouting louder in order to be heard, shouting encouragement, directing his men's hands and feet to holds that he could see but they could not.

Another schermoulie arose into the darkness, illuminating the valley for several hundred yards until it bent around out of sight and up sharply in the direction of the centre of the mountain range.

"Holy mother of God!" the marine next to Richard uttered in horror.

To those men climbing, the sight spurred on tired limbs to greater effort.

It was a truly terrifying view to behold, the melt water of a glacier bursting around the bend, a great wave breaking upon the rock wall with a thunderous boom, water dashing higher than their belay point.

A Chinese soldier slipped and fell on the melting ice floor, looked behind at the approaching wave and froze. He may have screamed but if he did so that cry was lost forever. In an instant he was gone, and a moment later his companion too was engulfed.

"Climb, CLIMB!"

The wave reached them, spray showering over Richard as the once parched and arid mountain valley of only a few weeks before, became the host to a maelstrom.

It was two hours later that the surviving Royal Marines of the Mountain & Arctic Warfare Cadre reached the top of the valley, climbing in deathly silence, and not a little shock. Four Green Berets left behind as guides by Garfield Brooks solemnly shook hands with Major Dewar and three men, the remaining marines having been swept away by the flash flood.

Arkansas Valley, Nebraska, USA

"This is General Shaw". Henry had no noisy interruptions now; a shocked silence had taken a hold.

"Thank you, stay on the line." Still holding the receiver to one ear he spoke calmly.

"Mr President we have a confirmed missile launch from the remaining silo and we are tracking it on a roughly south easterly heading..." he was relating in a steady voice the information arriving from satellites and ground tracking stations that still functioned.

"...sir the weapon has 'mirved', we now have nine re-entry vehicles in three groups on diverging courses...central Pacific...western seaboard."

The President felt a cold hand close over his heart.

"...Pearl...San Diego...the third group has a slightly higher orbit...too high for the US." Henry continued.

"Thank God for small mercies, but where are they aiming for if not the United States?" asked the President.

The third target was in actual fact geographically the closest target to the silo from which the ICBM had been launched, but much further south and therefore its trajectory would require an orbit of the lower half of the southern hemisphere in order to reach it.

At the other end of the line the intended target had just been deduced, along with the times before which the warheads re-entered the atmosphere.

"Roughly two more minutes to Pearl, three to San Diego... and seven minutes ten seconds to Sydney, Australia, Mr President..." Henry had to force his voice to remain steady.

"Air defences are being alerted." He continued. "....of the three re-entry vehicles being tracked in each group, two are likely to be decoys...there are two Patriot sites and three ballistic missile defence capable Aegis warships on picket at both Pearl and San Diego..."

"And Sydney, Henry?" the President asked urgently. "What does Sydney have?"

Henry did not look at the President, he couldn't.

"Just Natalie's ship." said Henry Shaw quietly. "Just the *Orange County."*

"Mr President!" called a navy captain. "On speaker's sir...the O.O.Ds of the USS *Chosin, Mobile Bay* and the *Nimitz."*

"Mr President, Lieutenant Commander Fortnum, Chosin is launching Standard 3 missiles as we speak...AN/SPY2 is tracking three targets entering the atmosphere above the Hawaiian Islands."

"Lieutenant Commander Hastings here... USS Mobile Bay's *SPY2 has three targets approaching San Die...we have launched Mr President,* Bunker Hill *is also launching...we are continuing to launch..."*

"This is Commander Willis, USS Nimitz...*the* USS Orange County *is tracking a trio of low orbit inbounds crossing above Christmas Island, Mr President..."*

"All missiles expended by Chosin, Lake Erie *and* Port Royal, *but the Patriot batteries at Hickam are still launching...we have two...we have...we... we have three confirmed kills...we have three ...all three targets destroyed, Mr President..."*

*"Shore batteries firing Patriots...*Princeton *has launched her last Standard 3...*Mobile Bay *has expended all Standard 3 missiles...*Bunker Hill *has expended all missiles..."*

*"Mr President...*Orange County *has the three low orbit inbounds over central Australia..."*

"Three...I can confirm three targets destroyed!"

"What..?" the President was frowning. "Three targets where, Dago or Sydney?"

"San Diego, Mr President...this is Lieutenant Commander Hastings, O.O.D of the USS Mobile Bay, *I can confirm three targets destroyed, SPY2 is clear, there are no further targets!"*

"How many?" the President asked urgently. "How many missiles did you launch in order to destroy all three targets?"

"Over a hundred at Pearl, Mr President...perhaps more."

"Two hundred and four SM3s and thirty Patriots were launched here at San Diego...I don't know at what point we killed all three..."

Commander Willis interrupted at that point.

"I am stepping out on the bridge wing Mr President...there is no longer light pollution here since the blackouts were imposed...beautiful night...okay, the air raid sirens have just begun to sound in the city...police car sirens too...ships in the harbor are sounding 'collision'..."

Over the speaker they could hear the wailing of the sirens on shore, it sounded reminiscent of old news reels of London's Blitz, but the combined ships sirens input seemed celebratory rather than a warning of approaching danger.

"Orange County is launching!"

Only several hundred yards distant the air defence picket for the aircraft carrier began launching her entire inventory of sixty eight Standard 3 missiles, ripple firing continuously. The noise was horrendous, drowning out the words even though Commander Willis was shouting in order to be heard.

It was midnight in Sydney, the ships sirens and the missiles launching vertically created the impression for some residents that perhaps the war was over?

"That's it..." shouted Commander Willis's voice over the speakers. The sirens on shore and in the harbor were again audible. *"'Rounds complete' as my father would have sai..."*

The shriek that emitted from the speaker at that point was electronic, not human; it tore at the senses while it lasted, only as long as it took for an electro-magnetic pulse to burn out the microphone and transmitter at the other end.

All eyes were on the now silent speaker, willing the voice of Commander Willis to resume.

A small tiny voice broke the silence, issuing from a telephone receiver hanging by its cord.

Terry lifted the receiver and listened before speaking.

"I'm sorry, he is not available right now but please repeat what it was that you were just saying?"

General Shaw was walking with a straight back to the conference room's door. Only the marine sentry could see his expression and the look on the young man's face spoke volumes.

"Mister President, the Missile Defence Agency confirms a nuclear detonation in the ten megaton range, one minute ago above Sydney, Australia."

Little Rock: Montana: Same time.

In a hardened shelter in Colorado code named 'Church', a plasma screen displayed icons for two helicopters lifting off the carrier *Mao*, both machines were designated for an anti-submarine sortie, and both headed unerringly toward a small submarine icon bearing an Australian flag...

To be continued in 'The Longest Night'

I will be posting updates on the series page on Facebook: https://www.facebook.com/ArmageddonsSong
and my Blog at http://andyfarmansnovels.blogspot.co.uk/

UNIT SYMBOL	UNIT TYPE
	ANTI - TANK
	ARMOUR
	ARTILLERY
	HELICOPTER
	BRIDGE/BRIDGING UNIT
CSS	COMBAT SERVICE SUPPORT
	ENGINEERS
	FUEL
	HEADQUARTERS
	INFANTRY
	WORKSHOP
	MORTARS
MP	MILITARY POLICE
	RECONNAISSANCE 'RECCE' 'RECON'
SF	SPECIAL FORCES
	SUPPLY
	TRANSPORT
	PARATROOPER AIRBORNE INFANTRY
	MECHANISED INFANTRY
	AMPHIBIOUS MECHANISED INFANTRY
	WHEELED IFV
	AMPHIBIOUS TANK
	SELF PROPELLED ARTILLERY
	SELF PROPELLED MORTAR
	SELF PROPELLED AAA
	ARMOURED RECONNAISSANCE VEHICLE
III	'O.P' OBSERVATION POST
	SNIPER'S HIDE

■	SECTION OR SINGLE VEHICLE
■■	TWO SECTIONS ETC
■■■	PLATOON TROOP
I	COMPANY BATTERY SQUADRON
II	BATTALION
III	REGIMENT
X	BRIGADE OR MRR
XX	DIVISION
XXX	CORPS

DIFFERENTIATING BETWEEN 'FRIEND' AND 'FOE'

ENEMY FORCES ARE ALWAYS COLOURED **RED**, HOWEVER, ON BLACK AND WHITE MAPS THIS WILL OBVIOUS NOT BE APPARENT THEREFORE ENEMY SYMBOLS ARE ALWAYS 'DOUBLE BOXED'

=

AND FRIENDLY FORCES 'SINGLE BOXED'

=

UNIT IDENTIFIERS

B [armour] 2 RTR	'B' SQUADRON 2 ROYAL TANK REGIMENT
A/C [artillery] 30	'A' TROOP 'C' SQUADRON 30 FIELD REGIMENT ROYAL ARTILLERY
D [engineers] 19	'D' SQUADRON 19 REGIMENT ROYAL ENGINEERS
1/1/1 [infantry] 2CG	1 SECTION, 1 PLATOON 1 COMPANY 2ND BN COLDSTREAM GUARDS
A [HQ armoured recce] Blues & Royals	SQUADRON HQ 'A' SQUADRON THE BLUES & ROYALS

Characters (In no particular order...)

I was asked whom the characters in Armageddon's Song were based upon, and to be honest there are a few who are amalgams of people I have met throughout my life.

'The President' is an easy one as I tend to picture a situation and hear dialogue form before I write. I found that the 'ideal' of a President was not a real person but rather one created by Aaron Sorkin. At least so far as speech and mannerisms, in my mind's eye anyway, President Josiah Bartlet, as portrayed by that brilliant American actor Martin Sheen, pretty closely fits the bill. Mine of course is a little more complex as will be discovered. A good person by nature who may have trouble sleeping some nights, owing to his being forced to work in dirty political waters.

'Regimental Sergeant Major Barry Stone, 1st Battalion Coldstream Guards' is a combination of three terrifying individuals (to be a young soldier in the British Army in the early 1970's)

RSM Torrance, Scots Guards, who reigned over the Infantry Junior Leaders Battalion at Park Hall, Oswestry in Shropshire.

Garrison Sergeant Major 'Black Alec' Dumon, The Guards Depot, Pirbright, Surrey and later Garrison Sergeant Major London District. And finally Regimental Sergeant Major Barry Smith, 2nd Battalion Coldstream Guards.

Sergeant Major Torrance was outwardly fierce but inwardly fair, and an ideal individual to be dealing with a couple of thousand 15 years old schoolboys who had to be turned into the next NCO Corps of the British infantry.

'Black Alec' is of course a legend. Those dark, sunken eyes and unblinking, cold stare. 'Captain Black & The Mysterons' except for that voice, the gruff Yorkshire accent that barked a command out on one side of a parade square and flowers in their beds outside Battalion Headquarters a quarter mile away would wilt and die.

RSM Smith was a pretty decent actor I think. The act was to make everyone, including young subalterns, believe he was perpetually angry and a heartbeat removed from downright furious.
I was on barrack guard one night when one of the old soldiers, an 'old sweat' with a few campaigns under his belt, and as it turned out at least one demon, went berserk. He had a rifle and bayonet attached to it in a barrack room he was trashing. The Picquet Officer voiced the possibility of arming the Picquet Sergeant, with obvious consequences, should the soldier in question make a fight of it, which he would have. The RSM intervened, whatever past trauma was troubling the soldier, he knew about it. He sent everyone away except for a couple of us and he waited out the storm. The RSM entered on his own an hour later, and spoke in a normal voice for long minutes before exiting and handing me the rifle before leading the soldier to the medical centre, speaking quietly to him all the time.
Next day, RSM Smith was of course once more a heartbeat removed from outright furious.

General Henry Shaw USMC, another easy one, but also oddly out of time. It was back in 2004 when I added General Henry Shaw, and in my mind Henry is Tom Selleck as 'Frank Reagan' except that 'Blue Bloods' was not yet screened. Possibly Mr Selleck played another role around that time which was solid, professional and reliable-to- the-end in character. If I say so myself I do like General Henry Shaw, I could serve under a leader like that.

Sir James Tennant, the Commissioner of the Metropolitan Police is to me 'Foyle's War' Michael Kitchen an exceptionally talented British actor of the finest type.

WO2 Colin Probert, Coldstream Guards.

When we first encounter Colin he is out in the 'Oulu' shadowing a patrol on Sennybridge training area. He is a bit senior to be 'Dee Essing' as a man of his rank should be running the office, keeping on top of the admin and as the company level disciplinarian; he should be ensuring no one is slacking off. Officers are not going to do that. However, Colin is a soldier, not an administrator and not a 'Drill Pig', so getting out with the students is something he would contrive somehow.

Colin is a Geordie from Newcastle who did not fancy shipbuilding, when there were still ships to be built of course, and made his way to the Army Recruiting Office armed with his O level certificates.

Brookwood station is where he arrived at 'The Depot' he may even have visited the gents before the 4 Tonner arrived, and seen 'Flush twice…it's a long way to the cookhouse!' graffiti on the wall of trap one.

'Cat Company' aka Caterham Company, is where Colin would have been introduced to the first mysteries of the British Army in general, and The Guards specifically.

A Platoon Sergeant and a buckshee Guardsman/Household Cavalry Trooper (the B.R.I, Barrack Room Instructor) would teach them how to iron, polish, bumper and buff, plus who and who not to salute.

I can see him sat on the end of his bed, sporting the haircut to end all haircuts as he polishes his boots for the first time, wondering what the hell he has let himself in for.

Colin is 6' 2"tall, so initially he would have been posted to 4 Company on arrival at Victoria Barracks, Windsor.

Selection takes place on height alone when you are a lowly and buckshee Guardsman. The tallest go into 1 Company; the next go to 4 Company. The short arses, 5'10" dwarves in comparison, find themselves in 3 Company. 2 (Support) was a mixed bag which could reduce a Drill Pig to drink as they were the specialists, the Mortarmen, Recce Platoon, Anti-Tanks and Assault Pioneers. They came in all shapes and sizes.

With promotion and courses such as Section Commanders, Platoon Commanders, and the All Arms Drill Wing, Guardsman Probert has become a Warrant Officer.

Sergeant Osgood.

Nobody knows his first name, and even Mrs Osgood calls him 'Oz', but he joined the army from the coal mines, tired of strike pay and bleak prospects.

Oz is already married when he joined the army, and Sarah had a baby on the way back then.

The Osgood's and Colin will have quickly to become friends. When Janet and Colin eventually marry, Sarah would take the newly wed under her wing and show her the ropes, guiding her away from pitfalls such as those purveyors' of innuendo, and assassins of character, the pad-hags.

With Colin and OZ away on exercise or deployed on operations the wives support each other.

Christina Carlisle/Svetlana Vorsoff.

I recall once seeing Anna Chapman, before she was notorious, and being struck by the way she stood out in a room, at complete odds with spooks such as Terry Jones in the book, but I fancy Svetlana would have that same effect.

At 5'10" tall, with curly chestnut hair to the backs of her legs and a dancers physique, Christina/Svetlana, is too strikingly beautiful to be a spy.

Having been robbed of a normal life and set to bedding whichever men and women the state required Caroline/Svetlana still had greater expectations. She does not object to the bedroom gymnastics it is just that it is not on her terms.

The Seventh Chief Directorate, into which she had been recruited, dealt with visiting foreign diplomats, politicians and businessmen. Her mind and high IQ are of little importance to her employer, it is her talent as a seductress and her talents between the sheets that are the only assets they value.

Somehow, Christina/Svetlana winds up in London with a flat in Knightsbridge and a legitimate six figure salary job at a leading merchant bank in the City.

She is living the life, or is she?

Major Constantine Bedonavich.

Constantine was an able and courageous pilot. He drove the SU27 Flanker until younger pilots were on the verge of making the old man of the regiment look precisely that.

His wife, Yulia, until recently the Prima Ballerina at the Moscow State Ballet, had friends in high places and instead of Constantine leaving the service he instead moved to London to take up the post of Deputy Military Attaché at the embassy of the Russian Federation.

The good major did of course need to undertake a course in fieldcraft and trade craft for 'new agent and asset handlers' at the embassies.

Yulia's involvement with a billionaire entrepreneur and the divorce which followed, served to drive Constantine into his work rather than into a bottle, and the major developed into a highly capable spy handler.

Sir Richard Tennant.

Sir Richard wears two royal jubilee medals, his 'undetected crimes' medal aka Long Service and Good Conduct medal, along with the Queens Police Medal, but two other ribbons occupy the first two spaces. The General Service Medal with Northern

Ireland clasp, and the South Atlantic medal. The Commissioner had not always been a copper; he had spent six years in the Blues and Royals, serving in the Falklands War as well as a couple of tours in Ulster.

Rather than sign on for another three years Corporal of Horse Tennant became Constable Tennant and attended the Metropolitan Police Training School at Hendon.

Theodore Kirkland (The President).

I have not given Mr Kirkland a political party affiliation. It does not really have any bearing on the story whether he is a Republican or a Democrat, he represents America in this story.

At the start of the tale the President has no affection, nor enmity either, for the military as he is just an academic who found himself in politics without actually encountering the military along the way.

I have left him as a good man but with a few flaws, because he is only human, and one who happens to be in the chair when a war starts.

Vadim Letacev (The Russian Premier).

My apology for coming up with a wholly unoriginal villain. He is Charles Dance (with his bad head on) and Vlad the Impalers more sadistic brother.

A man with no redeeming features, megalomania, a serious case of psychosis and probably halitosis too!

Lieutenant of Paratroops, Nikoli Bordenko.

"Ey, kak dela?" ("How are *you* doin'?")

I had a platoon commander once who was pretty much the suave and dashing Nikoli. The Joey Tribbiani of British

Airborne Forces, until injury forced a change of pace, and he came to us. I was never quite sure whether the injury was caused by landing badly after jumping out of an aircraft, or a bedroom window?

Good officer and a good soldier.

Flight Lieutenant Gerry Rich, RAAF.

Flt Lt Rich is very similar to a former double glazing salesman from Melbourne who joined my team in the 80's. He spoke about Australian celebrities as if they were friends and neighbours. He had the gift of the gab and Paul Hogan should have charged him royalties for all the lines Neil stole. He developed into a pretty good copper too.

Anthony Carmichael.

The only Russian spook I have ever met, knowingly, wore a pinstripe suit, the regimental tie of the Hampshire Regiment and spoke English with an accent a 1950's BBC newsreader would have been proud of.

The Cast

The Americans

Theodore Kirkland	The President
Gen Henry Shaw USMC	Chairman of the Joint Chiefs
Terry Jones	Director CIA
Joseph Levi	CSA, Chief Science Advisor
Art Petrucci	CIA Chief of Station, London
Max Reynolds	CIA Langley
Scott Tafler	CIA Langley
Alicia O'Connor	Computer game programmer
Ben Dupre	Director FBI
Dr David Bowman	USS *Commanche*
Admiral C Dalton	USS *John F Kennedy*
Admiral Conrad Mann	USS *Gerald Ford*
Admiral Lucas Bagshaw	USS *Nimitz*
Captain Joe Hart	USS *Commanche*

Captain Rick Pitt	USS *Twin Towers*
Commander Kenny Willis	USS *Nimitz*
Lt Cmdr. Natalie Shaw	USS *Orange County*
Lt Col Matthew Shaw	USS *Bonhomme Richard*
Lt Nikki Pelham USN	USS *John F Kennedy* & USS *Nimitz*
Lt (jg) Candice LaRue	USS *Nimitz*
Col Omar Chandler	USAF
Major Caroline Nunro	USAF
Captain Patricia Dudley	USAF
Major Glenn Morton	USAF
Lt Col 'Jaz' Redruff	USAF, AC Air Force One
Major Sara Pebanet	USAF, Co-pilot Air Force One
Sgt Nancy Palo	USAF Air Force One
Major Jim Popham	82nd Airborne
Lt Col Arndeker	USAF
Captain Garfield Brooks	Green Berets
Senator Walt Rickham	US Senate
General 'Duke' Thackery	5th US Mechanised

	Bde
RSM Arnie Moore	82nd Airborne
Captain Daniel King	Black Horse Cavalry
Master Sergeant Bart Kopak	Black Horse Cavalry
The French	
Admiral Maurice Bernard	*Charles De Gaulle*
Admiral Albert Venesioux	*Jeanne d'Arc*, ASW Group
Lt Arnoud Bertille	21e Régiment d'Infanterie de Marine
The Filipinos	
Colonel Villiarin	Cebu guerrilla forces
Sergeant 'Bat' Ramos	Philippines National Police
The Russians	
Vadim Letacev	Premier
Admiral Pyotr Petorim	Red Fleet
Marshal Gorgy Ortan	Army Group West
General of Aviation Arkity Sudukov	Air Force

General Tomokovsky	Army Group West
Svetlana Vorsoff	KGB 'Sleeper'
Anatoly Peridenko	1st Chairmen of reformed KGB
Elena Torneski	2nd Chairman of KGB
Alexandra Berria	KGB stringer
Col Gen Serge Alontov	6th Guards Airborne
Lt Nikoli Bordenko	6th Guards Airborne
Major Constantine Bedonavich	Deputy Military Attaché, London
Vice Admiral Karl Putchev	*Mao*

The Australians

Perry Letteridge	Prime Minister
Gen Norris Monroe	1st Brigade
Cmdr. Reg Hollis	HMAS *Hooper*
LS Craig Devonshire	HMAS *Hooper*
AB Philip Daly	HMAS *Hooper*
AB Stephanie Priestly	HMAS *Hooper*
Flt Lt Gerry Rich	15 Squadron RAAF

Flt Lt Ian 'Macca' McKerrow	15 Squadron RAAF
Sergeant Gary Burley	1st Armoured Regiment
Tpr Che Tan	1st Armoured Regiment
Tpr Chuck Waldek	1st Armoured Regiment
Tpr 'Bingo' McCoy	1st Armoured Regiment

The New Zealanders

Barry Forsyth	Prime Minister
Sergeant Rangi Hoana	1st Bn Royal New Zealand Infantry Regiment

The Chinese

Guozhi Chan	Chairman
Tenh Pong	Defence Minister
Marshal Lo Chang	Peoples Liberation Army
Admiral Li	PLAN *Mao* Task Force

Captain Hong Li	PLAN *Mao*
Captain Jie Huaiqing	PLAN Special Forces
Captain Aiguo Li	PLAN *Dai*

The Brits (Second to None and therefore on the right of the line!)	
The Rt Hon Tony Loude MP	PM
The Rt Hon Peter Dawnosh MP	PM
The Rt Hon Victor Compton-Bent MP	PM
The Rt Hon Matthew St Reevers	Defence Minister
The Rt Hon Danyella Foxten-Billings	Defence Minister
Marjorie Willet-Haugh	'M' Head of SIS
Sir Richard Tennant Commissioner	Metropolitan Police Commissioner
Lt Col Hupperd-Lowe	1CG

Lt Col Pat Reed	1CG
Major Simon Manson	1CG& 2CG (pre Australia)
Captain Timothy Gilchrist	1CG
RSM Barry Stone	1CG
CSM Ray Tessler	1CG & 2CG (pre Australia)
WO2 Colin Probert	1CG
Sgt 'Oz' Osgood	1CG
Guardsman Paul Aldridge	1CG
Guardsman Larry Robertson	1CG
L/Cpl Steve Veneer	1CG AA Section
Guardsman Andy Troper	1CG AA Section
Guardsman Stephanski 'Big Stef'	1CG Sniper Section
L/Sgt 'Freddie' Laker	1CG Sniper Section
S/Sgt Bill Gaddom	RMP attached to 1CG Sniper Section
Major Stuart Darcy	Kings Royal Hussars
Major Mark Venables	Kings Royal Hussars

2Lt Julian Reed	Royal Artillery
Sergeant Rebecca Hemmings	REME LAD attached to 1RTR
Major Richard Dewar	Royal Marines, Mountain & Arctic Warfare Cadre (M&AWC)
Corporal Rory Alladay	Royal Marines M&AWC
Lance Corporal Micky Field	Royal Marines M&AWC
Sergeant Bob McCormack	Royal Marines M&AWC
Sergeant Chris Ramsey	Royal Marines, SBS
Major Guy Thompson	G Squadron 22 SAS
Guardsman Dick French	G Squadron 22 SAS
L/Sgt Pete 'Sav' Savage	G Squadron 22 SAS
Lt Shippey-Romhead	Mountain Troop 22 SAS
Flt Lt Michelle Braithwaite	47 Squadron, RAF
Sqdn Ldr Stewart Dunn	47 Squadron, RAF
Rr Admiral Sidney Brewer	HMS *Ark Royal* ASW Group

Rr Admiral Hugo Wright	HMS *Illustrious* ASW Group
Captain Roger Morrisey	HMS *Hood*
Sub Lt Sandy Cummings	HMS *Prince of Wales*, Fleet Air Arm
Lt 'Donny' Osmond	HMS *Prince of Wales*, Fleet Air Arm
Lt Tony McMarn	3RGJ
Captain Hector Sinclair Obediah Wantage-Ferdoux	1RTR
Anthony Carmichael	KGB 'Stringer'
Janet Probert	Army wife
Annabelle Reed	Army wife
Sarah Osgood	Army wife
June Stone	Army wife
Jubi Asejoke	South London teenage criminal
Paul Fitzhugh	IRA 'Safe House' provider
PS Alan Harrison	Metropolitan Police
PC Dave Carter	Metropolitan Police
PC Sarah Hughes	Metropolitan Police

PC John Wainwright	Metropolitan Police
PC Phil McEllroy	Metropolitan Police
PC Tony Stammer	Metropolitan Police SFO SCO19
PC Annabel Perry	Metropolitan Police SFO SCO19
Cpl 'Baz' Cotter	Wessex Regiment 'Four One Bravo'
L/Cpl 'Dopey' Hemp	Wessex Regiment 'Four One Bravo'
Pte 'Spider' Webber	Wessex Regiment 'Four One Bravo'
Pte Adrian Mackenzie	Wessex Regiment 'Four One Bravo'
Pte 'Juanita' Thomas	Wessex Regiment 'Four One Bravo'
Pte George Noble	Wessex Regiment 'Four One Bravo'
Pte Mark Barnes	Wessex Regiment 'Four One Bravo'
Pte Shaun Silva	Wessex Regiment 'Four One Bravo'

Terminology & Acronyms

Terminology &	Acronyms
Numeric	
1CG:	First Battalion Coldstream Guards
1RTR:	First Royal Tank Regiment
2CG:	Second Battalion Coldstream Guards
2LI:	Second Battalion the Light Infantry
3RGJ:	Third Battalion Royal Green Jackets
'5':	Slang term for MI5
'6':	USN carrier borne strike aircraft (Intruder)
'A'	
A-6:	USN carrier borne strike aircraft (Intruder)
A-10:	US built single seat, close air support, tank killing aircraft (Warthog)
A-50:	Russian built AWAC version of the heavy Il-76 transport aircraft (Mainstay)
AA:	Air-to-Air
AAA:	Anti-Aircraft Artillery
AAC:	British Army's Army Air Corps
AEW:	Airborne Early Warning
AFB:	Air Force Base
AFV:	Armoured Fighting Vehicle
AGM:	Air-to-ground missile
AIM:	Aerial Intercept Missile
AK-47:	Updated derivative of the

	Kalashnikov assault rifle
AKM-74:	Romanian derivative of the AK-74
ALASAT:	Air Launched Anti Satellite missile
AMIP:	Area Major Inquiry Pool (Metropolitan Police)
AMRAAM:	Advanced Medium Range Air to Air Missile (Slammer)
AN-72:	Russian built transport
Apache:	US built helicopter gunship in service with US and Allied forces
APC:	Armoured Personnel Carrier
Army:	3 x Corps + combat and logistical support
Army Group:	3 x Armies
AP:	Anti-Personnel
ASW:	Anti-Submarine Warfare
AT:	Anti-Tank
ATC:	Air Traffic Control
ATF:	Bureau of Alcohol, Tobacco, Firearms
ATO:	Ammunition Technical Officer (Military bomb disposal officer)
AV-8B:	US developed version of the Harrier II.
AWACS:	Airborne Warning And Control System
AWE:	Atomic Weapons Agency (Aldermaston)
'B'	
B1-B:	US built supersonic swing wing early stealth bomber (Lancer)
B-2:	US built stealth bomber (Spirit)
B-52:	Heavy USAF bomber (The Buff aka Big Ugly F***er)
Backfire:	Russian built supersonic swing wing bomber (TU-22M)

BAOR:	British Army Of the Rhine
Battalion:	3-4 Rifle Coy's + combat and logistical support (Bn)
BBC:	British Broadcasting Corporation
Bde:	Brigade (3 Bn's + combat and logistical support)
Binos:	Binoculars
Blackjack:	Russian built supersonic swing wing bomber (TU-160)
Blinder:	Russian built supersonic bomber (TU-22)
BMP:	Tracked AFV
Bn:	3-4 Rifle Coy's + combat and logistical support (Battalion)
Boomer:	Ballistic Missile Submarine (SSBN)
Box:	Slang term for MI5 (Post Office Box 500)
Bradley:	US AFV
BRDM:	Russian built four wheeled Reconnaissance vehicle
Brew:	Tea
BTR:	Russian built eight wheeled APC
Buckshee:	Free item
Buckshee:	New and inexperienced
Buff:	B-52 Heavy USAF bomber (Buff aka Big Ugly F***er)
'C'	
CAD:	Computer Aided Dispatch
CAG:	Commander Air Group
CAP:	Combat Air Patrol
Carl Gustav:	84mm medium anti-tank weapon
CBU:	Cluster Bomb Unit
CCCIR:	Police Information Room Senior Controller
CCCP:	Cyrillic alphabet for 'Union of Soviet Socialist Republics'
CG:	Coldstream Guards

Challenger: Current series of British MBTs
Charlie Gee: 84mm medium anti-tank weapon
CHARM: 120mm self stabilising main tank gun with rifled barrel
Chieftain: Former series of British MBTs
CIA: Central Intelligence Agency
CIC: Combat Information Centre
CIC: Commander In Chief
Civvy: Civilian
CNN: Cable News Network
CO: Commanding Officer
CO: The Commissioner's Office (NSY: New Scotland Yard)
Colly: Her Majesty's Military Correction and Training Centre (HMCC)
Company: 3 x Pl's + logistical support (Coy)
COMSUBPAC: Commander Submarines Pacific
Corps: 3 x Div's + combat and logistical support
Coy: 3 x Pl's + logistical support (Company)
CP: Command Post
Cpl: Corporal
CQMS: Company Quarter Master Sergeant (Colour Sergeant rank)
CSA: Chief Scientific Advisor
CSM: Company Sergeant Major (WO2 rank)
CTR: Close Target Reconnaissance
CVR(T): Combat Vehicle Reconnaissance (Tracked)
CVR(W): Combat Vehicle Reconnaissance (Wheeled)

'D'

DEEP STRIKE: Air and SF attacks on logistical targets 100k + behind the lines
DefCon5: Peacetime
DefCon4: Peacetime; Increased

	intelligence; Strengthened security
DefCon3:	Increased force readiness
DefCon2:	Increased force readiness – Less than maximum
DefCon1:	Maximum force readiness
DF:	Defensive Fire
DF:	Direction Find
Div:	3 x Bde's + combat and logistical support (Division)
DPM:	Disruptive Pattern Material (Camouflage)
DZ:	Drop Zone
'E'	
E-2C:	US built Carrier borne early warning aircraft (Hawkeye)
E-3:	US built AWACS based on Boeing 707 (Sentry)
Eagle:	USAF swing wing, twin engine, single seat, all weather, fighter (F-15)
ECM:	Electronic Counter Measure
ELINT:	Electronically gathered Intelligence
EMCON:	Electronic Emission Control (Radio and Radar silence)
EMP:	Electro Magnet Pulse
ESM:	Electronic Surveillance Measures
Expo:	Explosives Officer (Police bomb disposal officer)
Extender:	Aerial Tanker derived from Boeing 707 (KC-135)
'F'	
F-14:	USN swing wing, twin engine, two seat, strike fighter (Tomcat)
F-15:	USAF swing wing, twin engine, single seat, tactical fighter (Eagle)
F-15E:	USAF swing wing, twin engine,

	single seat, all weather, strike fighter (Strike Eagle)
F-16:	US built multi-role fighter (Falcon)
F-117A:	USAF stealth fighter bomber (Nighthawk)
F-117X:	Northrop experimental stealth fighter bomber testbed in service with USAF
FAC:	Forward Air Controller
Falcon:	US built multi-role fighter (F-16)
FAO:	Forward Artillery Observer
FBI:	Federal Bureau of Investigation
FEBA:	Forward Edge of the Battle Area
Fencer:	Russian built two seat interdiction and attack aircraft (SU-24)
Flanker:	Russian built single seat, twin engined fighter (SU-27)
FLIR:	Forward Looking Infra-Red
Flogger:	Russian built single seat, single engine fighter (MIG-23)
FLOT:	Forward Line Of Troops
Fox One:	Radio call from a pilot announcing his firing an AIM-9M Sidewinder missile
Foxbat:	Russian built high speed interceptor (MIG-25)
Foxhound:	Russian built high speed interceptor (MIG-31)
Foxhound:	Infantryman
FPF:	Final Protective Fire
Frogfoot:	Russian built close air support, ground attack aircraft (SU-25)
FRV:	Final Rendezvous Point
Fulcrum:	Russian built single seat, twin engined fighter (MIG-29)
Fullback:	Russian built advanced two seat

	fighter bomber (SU-32)
FUP:	Forming Up Point
'G'	
Gdsm:	Guardsman
Gimpy:	General Purpose Machine Gun
GPMG:	General Purpose Machine Gun
GPS:	Global Positioning System
Green Beret:	US Army special forces unit
Green Maggot:	Sleeping bag
GRI:	General Research Institute (Chinese espionage service)
Grumble:	Russian built anti-aircraft missile system
'H'	
HARM:	High speed anti-radiation missile
Harpoon:	Anti-shipping missile
Harrier:	British designed VTOL Strike fighter
Hawkeye:	US built Carrier borne early warning aircraft (E-2C)
HE:	High Explosive
HESH:	High Explosive Squash Head (shaped charge warhead)
Hind-D:	Heavily armoured helicopter gunship
Hornet:	US built all weather strike fighter (F/A-18)
HUD:	Heads Up Display
HUMINT:	Intelligence gathered by humans
'I'	
ICBM:	Inter-Continental Ballistic Missile
IFF:	Identification Friend or Foe
IL-76:	Russian built heavy transport aircraft
Intruder:	USN carrier borne strike aircraft (A-6)
IR:	Information Room (Metropolitan

	Police)
IR:	Infra-Red
IRST:	Infra-Red Search and Tracking
'J'	
Jaguar:	British/French ground attack aircraft
JNAIRT	Joint Nuclear Accident and Incident Response Team
JSTARS:	Joint Surveillance and Target Attack Radar System (air to ground surveillance)
'K'	
KC-135:	Aerial Tanker derived from Boeing 707 (Extender)
Kevlar:	Carbon fibre armour
Klick:	Kilometre / a thousand metres
'L'	
L/Cpl:	Lance Corporal
L/Sgt:	Lance Sergeant
Lancer:	US built supersonic swing wing early stealth bomber (B1-B)
LAW:	Light Anti-Tank Weapon
LSW:	Light Support Weapon
Lynx:	British, fast, tank hunting helicopter
LZ:	Landing Zone
'M'	
M&AWC:	Mountain & Arctic Warfare Cadre (RM Specialists)
MAC:	Military Airlift Command
Mach:	Speed of sound (at sea level = 1,225 KPH / 761.2 MPH)
Maggot:	Sleeping bag
Mainstay:	Russian built AWAC version of the heavy Il-76 transport aircraft (A-50)
MAW:	Medium Anti-Tank Weapon
MBT:	Main Battle Tank

Mess:	Sleeping quarters/Dining area/Bar/social organisation
Met:	Metropolitan Police
MFC:	Mortar Fire Controller
MIG-23:	Russian built single seat, single engine fighter (Flogger)
MIG-25:	Russian built high speed interceptor (Foxbat)
MIG-29:	Russian built single seat, twin engined fighter (Fulcrum)
MIG-31:	Russian built high speed interceptor (Foxhound)
Mirage:	French air superiority fighter
MLRS:	Multi Launch Rocket System
MP:	Member of Parliament
MP:	Military Police
MP5:	Heckler & Koch MP5 9mm SMG and carbine
MRCA:	Multi Role Combat Vehicle
MRR:	Motor Rifle Regiment
MSTAR:	Battlefield radar system

'N'

NAAFI:	Navy Army Air Force Institute (shop and bar facilities for British forces)
NAS:	Naval Air Station
NATO:	North Atlantic Treaty Organisation
NAVSAT:	Navigation Satellite
NBC:	Nuclear Biological Chemical
NBC:	National Broadcasting Company
NCIS:	National Crime Intelligence Service
NCO:	Non Commissioned Officer
Nighthawk:	USAF stealth fighter bomber (F-117A)
NSA:	National Security Agency
NSY:	New Scotland Yard

NVG	Night Vision Goggles
'O'	
O Group:	Orders Group (Briefing)
OP:	Observation Post
Oppo:	Buddy
Oulou	In the countryside. In the middle of nowhere.
'P'	
PC:	Police Constable
Peewits:	Possession With Intent to Supply (The Misuse of Drugs Act 1971. S 5 (3)
Pickle:	Release bombs
Pl:	Platoon: (3 x Sections)
PLA:	Peoples Liberation Army
PLAAF:	Peoples Liberation Army Air Force
PLAN:	Peoples Liberation Army Navy
Platoon:	3 x Sections (Pl)
PLCE:	Personal Load Carrying Equipment (Webbing)
PM:	Prime Minister
PNG:	Passive Night Goggle
PRC:	Peoples Republic of China
PS:	Police Sergeant
Ptarmigan:	British, secure battlefield communications system
Pte:	Private
'Q'	
Q Bloke:	Quartermaster
QM (T):	Quartermaster (Technical) - (W01 rank)
QRF:	Quick Reaction Force
QRH:	Queens Royal Hussars
'R'	
RA:	Royal Artillery
RAC:	Royal Armoured Corps
RAF:	Royal Air Force

Rapier:	British AAA missile system
RE:	Royal Engineers
REME:	Royal Electrical and Mechanical Engineers
Replen:	Replenish
Rfn:	Rifleman
RIO:	Radar Intercept Officer
RM:	Royal Marines
RMP:	Royal Military Police
RN:	Royal Navy
ROC:	Republic Of China (Taiwan)
ROC:	Generic term for the Taiwanese military
ROE:	Rules Of Engagement
RORSAT:	Radar Ocean Reconnaissance Satellite
RQMS:	Regimental Quarter Master Sergeant (W01 rank)
RSM:	Regimental Sergeant Major (W01 rank)
RV:	Rendezvous Point
RVP:	Rendezvous Point
'S'	
SA:	Surface-to-Air
SA80:	British 5.56mm calibre individual weapon
Sabre:	British tracked reconnaissance vehicle
SACEUR:	Supreme Allied Commander Europe
SAM:	Surface to Air Missile
Samaritan:	British tracked armoured ambulance
Samson:	British tracked armoured recovery vehicle
SAR:	Search-And-Rescue
SAR:	Synthetic Aperture Radar
SARH:	Surface to Air Radar Homing

SAS:	Special Air Service (recruits from British Army)
SASR:	Special Air Service Regiment (recruits from Australian Army)
Saxon:	British, wheeled APC
SBS:	Special Boat Service (recruits from Royal Marines)
Scimitar:	British tracked reconnaissance vehicle
Sea Harrier:	RN V/STOL Fleet defense aircraft
Sentry:	US built AWACS based on Boeing 707 (E-3)
SFO:	Specialist Firearms Officer (Police)
SIS:	Secret Intelligence Service
Sitrep:	Situation report
Six:	Directly behind (Six o'clock position)
SLBM:	Nuclear powered ballistic missile submarine
SLR:	Self-Loading Rifle
SMG:	Sub Machine Gun
SO12:	Special Branch (Metropolitan Police)
SO13:	Anti-Terrorist Squad (Metropolitan Police)
SO14:	Royalty Protection (Metropolitan Police)
SO16:	Diplomatic Protection Group (Metropolitan Police)
SCO19:	Specialist Firearms Unit (Metropolitan Police)
Spartan:	British tracked vehicle for AAA, MFC, Engineer or Recce
SP HVM:	Self-Propelled High Velocity Missile
Spearfish:	British advanced, high speed, wire guided torpedo

Spirit:	US built stealth bomber (B-2)
SRAM:	Short Range Attack Missile
SS:	Surface to Surface
SSBN:	Ballistic Missile Submarine (Boomer)
SSG:	Diesel powered guided missile submarine
SSGN:	Nuclear powered guided missile submarine
SSK:	Diesel powered attack submarine
SSN:	Nuclear powered attack submarine
Starstreak:	British advanced, high speed anti-aircraft missile
Striker:	British tracked AT vehicle
STOL:	Short Take Off and Landing
SU-24:	Russian built two seat interdiction and attack aircraft (Fencer)
SU-25:	Russian built close air support, ground attack aircraft (Frogfoot)
SU-27:	Russian built single seat, twin engined fighter (Flanker)
SU-32:	Russian built advanced two seat fighter bomber (Fullback)
Sultan:	British tracked, armoured command vehicle
SWAT:	Special Weapons and Tactics
'T'	
T-64:	Russian designed MBT
T-72:	Russian designed MBT
T-80:	Russian designed MBT
T-90:	Russian designed MBT
TAO:	Tactical Action Officer
TAVR:	Territorial Army Volunteer Reserve
TEL:	Transporter Erector Launcher
Thunderbolt:	US built single seat, close air

support, tank killing aircraft (A10 / Warthog)

Tomcat: USN swing wing, twin engine, two seat, strike fighter (F-14)

Tornado F3: British/German twin seat, swing wing fighter

Tornado GR: British/German ground attack aircraft

Tpr: Trooper

Triple A: AAA (Anti-Aircraft Artillery)

TU-22: Russian built supersonic swing wing bomber (Blinder)

TU-22M: Russian built supersonic swing wing bomber (Backfire)

TU-160: Russian built supersonic swing wing bomber (Blackjack)

'U'-'V'-'W'-'Z'

UGM: Un-Guided Missile

USAF: United States Air Force

USMC: United States Marine Corps

USN: United States Navy

USSR: Union of Soviet Socialist Republics

VTOL: Vertical Take Off and Landing

Warrior: British AFV

Warthog: A-10: US built single seat, close air support, tank killing aircraft

Wild Weasel: Dedicated, specialized, AAA suppression mission

Willy Pete: WP: White Phosphorus

WO: Warrant Officer

WP: White Phosphorus

ZSU: Russian designed series of Self – Propelled AAA vehicles

Trivia

Volume Three and Four side tracked me with the details of commercial and military satellite operation. There are a fair few dead satellites up there but as it would cost more to refuel them than to replace them. Their technology has been superseded anyway and therefore there are two disposal options, up or down. Down requires vastly more fuel to accomplish safely than boosting to a higher orbit but there are two places that spacecraft go to die. A graveyard orbit of about 403km above the Earth and a cemetery, of sorts, 3900 km South-East of Wellington, New Zealand at the following coordinates 43°34'48"S 142°43'12"W. Even if you could dive that deep it would not be advisable to visit. Aside from the exposed nuclear reactors of military satellites that were guided to splashdowns there, it is a toxic dumpsite for chemical weapons and old Soviet nuclear reactors.

I found the potential for new stories lying about everywhere I happened to research. For instance, there was a tiny coral atoll in the Pacific, six hundred miles from anywhere, but a hundred feet deep in inedible crabs, bad tempered sea birds and nitrogen rich Guano. (Bird poo.)

That atoll became at various times, a pirate base, a significant fertilizer resource, a retreat, a military base, the scene of several shipwrecks, and also of serial rape and murder.

The atoll's sole financial asset is long gone, but the crabs remain. (Isn't that just like life?)

Île de la Passion

French Guiana was a place I knew virtually nothing of until an attack upon the ESA facility by either China or Russia seemed to be a necessity. It is a place that was much fought over by the old European empires.

When Wolfe brought an end to the French rule in North America, France was in a quandary as to where to relocate those colonists who wanted to leave. Return to France was not an option for a bunch of losers, but they were good Catholics in the clutches of the heathen Protestant British, they had to have their souls protected if nothing else. French Guiana was the eventual site for those who had lost 'New France' to end their days.

Has anyone seen 'Papillon'?

Henri Charrière, 'Papillon', was a prisoner in the colony but not on Devils Island, that was a fabrication. Only people convicted of treason went to Devils Island.(Good movie though!)

There are whole websites dedicated to fans of Henri Charrière, and discussion groups debating the type of crimes the fans would consider committing in order for them to be incarcerated and live out their fantasy of being a Henri Charrière, and escaping from somewhere on coconuts. Suggestions that, *1/* The book was intended as a novel, and not a memoir, *2/* That Henri is dead (Born in 1904 so he'd be pushing 110 at the time of writing), or *3/* That he really was a murderer and deserved to be a convict, can lead to expulsion from the various groups.

Papillon makes life imprisonment *Cool!*

The odd case of the destroyed tooling.

The F14 Tomcat was without doubt a phenomenal war bird and one that arguably still had a decade or so left of useful life. Aircraft, like champion boxers, one day meet the young hungry wannabe who hands them their ass. No one stays at the top indefinitely. The mystery is however, why did Dick Cheyney order the F14D production halted when it was still on top of its game, and why was it so important to have the tooling destroyed so none could ever be built again, without a huge cost implication?

The ignominious end of the Aussie 'Pig'.

The F111D of the Royal Australian Air Force was quite iconic but getting a little long in the tooth. Of the forty three aircraft in the fleet, eight have crashed since 1973, twelve have been sold to museums or put on static display, but twenty three were chopped up and buried.

Now that wasn't very polite!

(Since the publication of edition 1 I have since learned that the original purchase agreement specifically prohibited resale of the aircraft by Australia and consequently the sale of the aircraft to a major arms dealer was cancelled after the US Government intervened. Apparently the aircraft could only be returned to the USA or rendered permanently unusable. Those they could not give away to museums and airbases as gate features were stripped and buried.)

ABOUT THE AUTHOR

Andy Farman was born in Cheshire, England in 1956 into a close family of servicemen and servicewomen who at that time were serving or who had served in the Royal Air Force, Royal Navy and British Army. As a 'Pad brat' he was brought up on whichever RAF base his Father was posted to.

Andy joined the British Army as an Infantry Junior Leader in 1972 at the tender age of 15, serving in the Coldstream Guards on ceremonial duties at the Royal Palaces, flying the flag in Africa, and on operations in both Ulster and on the UK mainland.
In 1981 Andy swapped his green suit for a blue one with the Metropolitan Police.
With volunteer reservist service in both the Wessex Regiment and 253 Provost Company, Royal Military Police (V) he spent twenty four years in front line policing, both in uniform and plain clothes. The final six years as a police officer were served in a London inner city borough and wearing two hats, those of an operation planner, and liaison officer with the television and film industry.

His first literary work to be published was that of a poem about life as a soldier in Ulster, sold with all rights to a now defunct writers monthly in Dublin for the princely sum of £11 (less the price of the stamp on the envelope that the cheque arrived in.)

The 'Armageddon's Song' trilogy began as a mental exercise to pass the mornings whilst engaged on a surveillance operation on a drug dealer who never got out of bed until the mid-afternoon.

On retirement, he emigrated with his wife to the Philippines.

Lightning Source UK Ltd.
Milton Keynes UK
UKOW02n0750161216
290105UK00002B/34/P

9 781326 184209